an air of treason

Books by P. F. Chisholm

The Sir Robert Carey Mysteries
A Famine of Horses
A Season of Knives
A Surfeit of Guns
A Plague of Angels
A Murder of Crows
An Air of Treason

Writing as Patricia Finney

Lady Grace Mysteries
Assassin
Betrayal
Conspiracy
Feud

Children's Books
I, Jack
Jack and Rebel the Police Dog
Jack and the Ghosts

Other Novels
A Shadow of Gulls
The Crow Goddess
Gloriana's Torch
Unicorn's Blood
Firedrake's Eye

an air of treason

a sir robert carey mystery

P. F. Chisholm

Poisoned Pen Press

Copyright © 2014 by P. F. Chisholm

First Edition 2014

10 9 8 7 6 5 4 3 2 1

Library of Congress Catalog Card Number: 2013941236

ISBN: 9781464202209   Hardcover
      9781464202223   Trade Paperback

Poisoned Pen Press
6962 E. First Ave., Ste. 103
Scottsdale, AZ 85251
www.poisonedpenpress.com
info@poisonedpenpress.com

Printed in the United States of America

This book is dedicated to my wonderful band of beta-readers who save me from making even more mistakes than I actually do and in particular to:
Kendall Britt and
Sallie Blumenauer
who tell it as they see it and immeasurably improve every book they read for me.

Many many thanks.

saturday 16th september 1592, morning

It was the devil's own job, it truly was, thought Hughie Tyndale. How the hell had he agreed to it? Why had he agreed to it?

The internal voice that never missed a chance to jeer at him was quick with an answer. So ye wouldna hang, it said, why else?

"I'll hang if I manage it," Hugh said back to the jeering voice.

The jeering voice said nothing because this was plainly true. If you got caught killing someone, you generally hanged. All the more if they found out why you were killing him, which they probably would if they used the boot or the pinniwinks or whatever it was the English authorities used when they urgently wanted to find out something. And killing a cousin of the Queen would most certainly draw their attention.

He'd tried before to get close to the man he was to kill and failed miserably. Several times. That time in St. Paul's Walk by Duke Humfrey's tomb. The place had been crowded despite the plague running through London. It was full of ugly men in worn jacks, while Carey the Courtier, the man he was supposed to kill, had wandered by dressed in many farms' worth of velvet and pearls, deep in conversation only a yard away.

Of course he hadn't been intending to do the killing out in public. The first part of the plan was to go to work for the man, find out everything about him and pass it on to Scotland. How? He didn't know, but someone would tell him, apparently. Then he would do the killing and if he could get away in time, he'd be free as a bird. That was according to the mysterious man who said he worked for the Earl of Bothwell. When the funeral had been held, Hughie could visit a certain goldsmith in London town and receive a pile of gold. Allegedly.

Hughie shifted his weight and consciously straightened his back. He'd do it, of course he would. He wouldn't hang; he'd be rich. So now he wondered how he could be sure he stood out among all the mob of unemployed servingmen under the Cornmarket roof—without being so obvious about it that he tipped off the Courtier. Bothwell's man had warned him, the Courtier is a lot cleverer than he looks or sounds.

Oxford Cornmarket, with its smart lead roof held up on round pillars down the centre of the street, was packed with men and quite a few women, people having come to the hiring fair from villages and towns for miles around. The Queen and all her Court and baggage and hangers-on were at last only seven days away. The city fathers and the university were in the last contentious stages of setting up the elaborate expensive pageantry of welcome. No doubt most of them were in meetings, speechifying at each other.

The whole of Oxford seemed to be armoured with scaffolding. The streets were clean for the first time in twenty-four years, and some of them were being newly paved, some boarded over.

A college steward was standing on a box, shouting aloud from a list.

"I want eight carpenters, four plumbers, five limners, eight labourers for college of Trinity," he bellowed. "Thruppence a day until the Queen leaves, a bonus from my Lord Chamberlain if all work is done before the Queen arrives, another bonus if nothing is amiss when she leaves."

Those were good terms. Some of the men standing around Hughie shifted toward the steward, even though several of them didn't look like skilled men but like simple bruisers.

A few of the girls were surrounding a stout woman on another box, roaring her needs—laundresses, sempstresses, confectioners, cleaners. An entire new city was foisting itself awkwardly on the scholarly city of Oxford, like an eagle on a blackbird's nest.

Hughie backed a little to the wooden pillars of the smart merchant's house next to the church. Most of the men there were quite a bit smaller than him and a few looked at him sideways.

His quarry would come, of course he would. The Courtier needed at least one henchman and Hughie would be perfect for him. Where else was he going to find so cheap a servingman with Hughie's abilities?

Hughie scanned the better-dressed men walking around amongst the people for hire. Most were stewards and college bursars, narrow-eyed, tight-pursed. A few were clearly harbingers for the Queen or the greater lords.

Hughie knew the Courtier was in town for sure, and would probably leave again on Sunday afternoon. Possibly earlier. He had arrived late on Friday night, dressed in hunting green with one spare mount and a lathered pony heavy-laden with packs. That was quite impressive, Hughie had to admit. It was more than forty miles from London to Oxford and he hadn't really been expected so early—Hughie had been carefully buttering up Lord Chamberlain's steward and making himself pleasant to the minor officials of his household on the assumption the quarry would travel with his father.

No, according to the horseboy Hughie had been paying on retainer at the main carter's inn near Christ Church, the man had arrived Friday night, both horses and the pony exhausted, at around seven o'clock. Forty miles in a day—despite the heavy cart and pack horse traffic on the Oxford Road—meant he must have been using the higher causeway reserved for the Queen's messengers, and galloping at least half the time. The man himself was tired but quite alert enough to make sure Hughie's helper carried the heavy packs up to his room and then was tipped a sixpence to guard the door. The Courtier saw the host, paid for the room, and ate the ordinary for his dinner.

He had no henchmen with him, not one. Not even the surly-looking borderer who had been shadowing him in London. So it stood to reason that he would be in need of at least one follower. At least one.

Hughie peered through the shadowed forest of humanity again. He had to be there, where else would he find a serving-man? He had to come.

"What's your name?" came a snappy voice beside him.

It wasn't the Courtier. Hughie looked as nervous and as thick as he could. "Oh ah, Hughie, an' it please yer honour, Ah'm a…"

The steward tutted and passed on immediately. It was Hughie's accent, he knew that. Not only was it a harsh voice, like a corncrake, but you could easily hear in it that his first language was Scotch not English. And although cheap, the Scotch were notoriously dangerous employees.

Someone who had been leisurely buying a pie from a nicely shaped girl under the portico opposite, spun round to look at him.

God above, it was him! Hughie did his best not to stare, modestly looking at the ground. The man was well-built, tall, chestnut hair under his hat and a goatee beard that needed trimming, extremely bright blue eyes and beaky nose, and a breezy manner that breathed of what he was and what he thought of himself.

Carey the Courtier was first cousin to the Queen in two different directions, one of them firmly on the wrong side of the blanket, according to Bothwell's man's clerk. His father's coat of arms said so proudly, boasted of it in fact, blazoned with three Tudor roses. You couldn't hardly put it plainer, the clerk had sneered, and the English heralds had allowed it, the scandalous Papistic perverts.

This was the man he had to kill: Sir Robert Carey, youngest son of the Lord Chamberlain, Baron Hunsdon, connected by blood and marriage with half the Court as well as the Queen. Carey was currently a controversial deputy warden on the English West March, where he was interfering in things that didn't concern him.

Mind, he hadn't looked quite so full of himself the time he'd been pointed out to Hughie at the Scottish Court, but that had been in the summer and he'd had a stressful few days there.

Carey did seem a little worried and he hadn't seen a barber for a couple of days either. Would he remember the disastrous last time Hughie had made a play to work for him? That was the point. God, those musicians had been angry.

Carey had come over and was standing in front of Hughie, looking him up and down.

"Quhair are ye fra?" he asked in passable Scotch.

That shouldn't have been a surprise to Hughie, yet it was. He stuttered.

"Ay…ah…Edinburgh."

"Quhat are ye at sae far fra yer ain country?"

"Ah'm trying to get maself home, sir," said Hughie, getting ahold of himself, switching to English and straightening his spine.

"Oh?" One of the man's eyebrows had gone straight up his forehead.

"Ah come south on a ship wi' a merchant, but we had a falling out and Ah'm heading north now."

Carey came closer and looked Hughie up and down again, carefully. He stood still for it, feeling a blush coming up his neck.

"What's yer trade?"

"Ma dad wis a tailor, sir, I prenticed tae him but it didna suit me well…." That had been his uncle Jemmy, not his dad but no matter, near enough.

The other eyebrow went up and Carey crossed his arms and started stroking his goatee thoughtfully. "Did you grow too tall to sit sewing all day?"

Och thank God, thought Hughie, excitement rising in him. Is it working? Is it really working?

"Ay, sir." It was quite true he had got too tall. Sitting cross-legged all day had cramped him something dreadful, though not as much as frowsting about indoors all the time. "Once Ah grew and got my size, I couldnae stick the tailoring, so I prenticed wi' a barber for a while and then after I got…ah…intae a wee spot of bother…I hired on as a merchant's henchman to come south, sir."

Carey beckoned Hughie to turn his head and lift his hair. Ah, yes, looking for a ragged ear from having it nailed to the Edinburgh pillory for thieving. No, Hughie's ears were still the shape God had given them.

"What was the spot of bother?"

This was the lie absolute, the only one completely adrift from the truth.

"It wis a riot, sir, in Edinburgh, after a football match. Ah killed a man and the procurator banished me from Edinburgh for a year and a day."

"Hmm. How did you kill the man?"

Hughie improvised. "Ah hit him on the head with an inn table, sir."

Carey nodded, looking cynical. It struck Hughie that lying about it was actually fine, so long as he could come up with a more believably serious killing-method when he needed it. Only not as serious as it had actually been, of course. Carey wouldn't hire him if he boasted about killing his uncle.

Hughie knew he was too saturnine and large to be able to look innocent and so he settled for looking hopeful. Come on, man, Hughie begged silently, thinking of the pile of gold that would be his when he'd done the job. I'm what you need. Come on.

The man had his head on one side, appraising Hughie with his eyes narrowed. "Do you know who I am?" he asked.

"Ah, no, sir. Sorry, sir."

"What's your name?"

"Hughie Tyndale."

"Like the translator of the Bible in King Henry's reign?"

"Ah…maybe, sir?"

Who the hell was that? Hughie thought. He used the name Tyndale because he wasn't inclined to tell them his right sur-name and that was where his family came from originally. "Ah dinna ken…"

"No matter. So you're looking for a master who might take you north?"

"Ay, sir." He risked it. "And disnae mind ma voice."

Carey nodded absently. He seemed to be thinking, appraising Hughie again. There was a faint frown on his face. "Have I ever met you before? I was in Edinburgh as a young man."

"Ah..." Oh God, oh God, he'd remembered. "Ah...when was it, sir?"

"Oh, about ten years ago now."

"Och, Ah wisnae mair than a lad..."

"Yes, of course. Or perhaps one of your family?"

"Perhaps, sir."

Hughie's stomach was getting tighter and tighter. This might work. The Courtier hadn't turned away. It might work. Please God, let it work.

The man in front of him in the mud-splashed hunting green and long boots, laughed and slapped his fine gloves on the palm of his hand.

"So you know how to tailor and barber and you can fight?"

"Ay, sir. That I can."

"Fourpence a day, all lodging and food found. Will that do you?"

"Ay, sir?" Hughie heard his voice tremble. It wasn't riches, but it wasn't bad, a whole penny a day better than labouring, which he'd done before and didn't like. "Ah, sir, that'd be fourpence a day English?"

Carey laughed again. "Oh, yes. I might even be able to get you some livery if my father's feeling generous."

"Ay, sir?" It was working. "Ay, that's verra...ah...very good, sir."

Carey stripped off his right glove and his right hand came down on Hughie's right shoulder and gripped. Hughie looked down at it, with the bright golden ring on it and a couple of nails almost regrown.

"Excellent! Do you, Hughie Tyndale of Edinburgh town, swear to serve me faithfully according to my commands within Her Majesty's law and your right honour, so help you God?"

"Ay, sir, I do."

"Then I, Robert Carey, knight and deputy warden of Carlisle, swear to be your good lord as long as you serve me well, so help me God."

They spat on their palms and shook hands. It was the old-fashioned way, the way of Hughie's grandfather, when the duties had gone in both directions from man to master and back again. Hughie felt a vast golden bubble of relief escaping from his lungs. No matter that he'd sworn fealty to the man he was to spy on and, in due course, kill. He'd sort it out with God later. God would surely understand that he had no choice.

saturday 16th september 1592, noon

The first thing that Hughie Tyndale found after becoming Sir Robert's henchman was that he hadn't been walking fast enough. He kept getting left behind as Carey forged through the crowds of the hiring fair to the desk at the centre where the master of the fair kept his register. Carey signed his name and paid the tax, Hughie made his mark. He could in fact write but he had decided long ago not to make too much of that.

"Can you read?" Carey asked him when he saw the mark.

"Ay, sir," Hughie said. "Ma dad put me tae the Dominie to learn ma letters."

"Good, read that," said Carey pointing at the words of the indenture the clerk was writing up three times. Hughie struggled through the easier words despite some of it being in some kind of foreign.

"Hmm, creditable," said Carey as the clerk tore the indenture in three, gave Carey one part, Hughie himself the other part, and kept the third. It was for a year and a day from the hiring fair, plenty long enough to do what Hughie had to. On the other hand, making it official in the modern way as well meant that killing Carey would be petty treason and he might burn for it. If he got caught, of course, which he wouldn't.

Gulping slightly he half-trotted after Carey's long stride, out from under the roof and into the alehouse on Carfax opposite the tower, where Carey bought ale for both of them and they toasted each other, sitting in the window.

"Whit will ye have me do, sir?" Hughie asked, then stopped himself because you should really wait for the master to speak first.

Carey didn't seem to mind. "I lost my body servant to… well, to a flux in London," he said, drinking deep and looking surprisingly sad. "That's why I hired you, so I hope you really did prentice with a tailor for a while. I urgently need someone to make sure my Court suit fits me properly."

"Och," Hughie frowned, "Ah dinna ken much about English Court fashion, sir."

"You don't need to, I know plenty. You only need to be able to sew."

"Ay."

"If you can't do it, I'll have to find a tailor for the work, but I hope you can as there's a dreadful dearth of tailors in the town at the moment."

"Ay, sir. I hear the Queen's coming."

"Indeed she is and I want to make sure she likes me well enough to pay me my fee and confirm my warrant as deputy warden," said Carey. "Meantime, where are you staying?"

The money he'd been given by Bothwell's man to take him south had run through his fingers with dreadful speed. Hughie had slept under a haystack the night before. He'd had nightmares that the stone mushrooms holding the base of the huge stack of hay off the ground were shortening so he'd be crushed and he kept waking, covered in sweat to find rats using him as a convenient ladder to get up into the hay. He'd scrambled out into the grey dawn feeling horrible.

"Ehm..."

"No matter. There'll be a truckle bed or a pallet for you somewhere. Can you ride?"

"Ay, sir, well enough." He'd ridden before he could walk of course, but he'd also been in Edinburgh learning to sew at the time when most lads got their mastery on horseback.

"You've used a pike, I expect. Sword and buckler work?"

"Ay, sir, a little. Wi' the Edinburgh trained band."

He'd loved the trained band as a lad, rushing off to the musters like an arrow from the bow to work off his pent-up energy, while his uncle complained at the loss of time. His uncle had been a hard man....Too bad he'd—well, no reason to think about that. It hadn't been his fault.

"Of course. We'll play a veney or two when we get to Rycote," said Carey. "Come along. You can have my spare horse and we'll be going. They should have recovered enough from getting here and we'll take an easy pace now."

They had been heading all the while to the stables of the inn where two smart-looking horses stood ready, saddled and bridled, and the pack pony dozed stoically with one broad hoof tipped, the packs very badly stowed.

Carey saw this, narrowed his eyes, and checked them. "Nothing stolen," he said, opening a very fine leather pistol case. Hughie glimpsed two matched dags inside and his mouth almost watered at them. Were they snaphaunce locks? Wheel-locks? Would Carey let him fire one?

Hughie and Carey between them took all the packs off and re-stowed them with a better balance. Naturally, Hughie got the smaller mount, but he was used to his legs dangling a bit. Carey was a tall man, too; Hughie wasn't used to looking straight at anyone.

Carey mounted in a way Hughie hadn't seen since his child-hood—hands on the saddlebow and leaping straight up, not touching the stirrups until he was seated. He looked pleased with himself at the trick. "Hmf," he said, as he found the stir-rups. "Come on Hughie, up you get."

Hughie tightened the girth a little to allow for his weight and climbed into the saddle the less showy way. Lack of prac-tice made heavy weather of getting his leg over the beast's back. He'd learnt the other way, but hadn't done it for a long time and wasn't about to risk landing on his back in the straw and dung of the inn stable.

Carey nodded and clicked to his horse, took the pack pony's leading rein and led the way forward into the High Street and eastward, over Magdalen Bridge and into the countryside.

Carey put his heels in. "We're going to Rycote, which is where the herald I talked to says she is at the moment. It belongs to Lord Norris, poor chap. I want to talk to my own lord, the Earl of Essex, very urgently so if you see anyone in tangerine-and-white livery, shout out to me. Same if you see anyone in black and yellow."

They went up to a canter as soon as they were clear of the large herd of pigs being brought into the city as components of porkpies, sausages, and spit roasts for the arrival of the Court. The smell was acrid, catching at the back of Hughie's throat, and several of the pigs seemed up for a fight.

Past them they were still heading upstream into a steady current of farm carts laden with fodder and wheat and apples and late raspberries and chickens in cages and, on one occasion, a cart laden with barrels of water that smelled horrible, probably containing crayfish for the Queen's table. It was a flood tide of food, drawn in by the whirlpool of the Queen's promised arrival.

saturday 16th september 1592, noon

As he crested the brow of the hill, Sergeant Henry Dodd of Gilsland and Carlisle Castle, blinked and yawned. He had been up and very busy all the night before, getting even with Sir Thomas Heneage, and now he had been in the saddle since dawn. He thought he'd made good progress though the Oxford Road was terrible in some parts, great potholes where the winter rains had tunnelled between the rough stones laid by monks, laying bare the orderly even-sized cobbles that were the hallmark of the ancient giants that built the border wall as well. Or were they faeries? There were different tales that gave both possibilities and it stood to reason it couldn't be both of them.

The Courtier had insisted it was all done by ordinary men called Romans who spoke Latin like the Papists, and had come over with Brutus thousands of years ago. That made some sense of the slabs of stone you sometimes found with well-carved letters in foreign, though Dodd doubted that grinding them up and drinking them in wine would cure you of gout.

He knew he had to stop because he urgently needed to find a bush. Unfortunately the road was very straight and the brush had been recently cleared back from the verges. He also had to water his horses at some stage. Straight roads were giants' work as well, or Romans'. He wondered how they had done it so far across country.

Bushes had been rare among the great broad fields northwest of London, though he was coming into enclosed land now. At last he'd spotted a handy-looking small copse well back from the road a little way ahead.

Dodd shifted in the saddle and hoped he hadn't caught a flux in London. He was riding the soft-mouthed mare and leading the horse he had decided to name Whitesock, on the grounds that he had the one white sock on him. The mare had a nice gentle pace to her but something made him prefer Whitesock for his sturdy determined canter and lack of nonsense. You didn't often meet a sensible horse, especially here in the South where so many of them had been ruined by overbreeding. Dodd clicked his tongue and moved the horses closer to the bushes. The mare pulled a little and her trot got choppy while Whitesock blew out his nostrils.

Hmm. Dodd peered between the leaves to see if anyone was waiting there, sniffed hard, couldn't smell anything except previous travellers' leavings. And he couldn't wait much longer, damn it.

So he loosened his sword, pushed into the bushes, which were luckily not entirely composed of thorns, saw nothing too worrying, and hitched the horses to the sturdiest branch. Then he found a bare patch, dug a hole with his boot heel, and started undoing the stupid multiple points of his stupid gentleman's doublet so he could get his stupid gentleman's fine woollen breeks down to do his business.

Just as he was about to drop them, he heard a stealthy movement behind him and turned around with his hand on his sword.

A bony creature was standing there in rags, holding out a rusty knife.

"Giss yer money!" hissed the creature that didn't seem to have many teeth.

Dodd blinked at him in puzzlement for a moment.

"Whit?" he asked.

"Giss yer money."

"Whit?" Dodd genuinely couldn't work out what the creature was saying because the idea that something so pathetic might want to rob him was simply too unbelievable.

The creature came closer with his dull knife high. "Money!"

"Och," said Dodd, pulling the breeks down, hoicking his shirt up and squatting anyway because he couldn't wait any longer. "Whit d'ye want tae do that for?"

"I don't want yer 'osses, just yer money."

Dodd looked down and shook his head.

"Yer interfering with me opening ma bowels," he growled. "Could ye no' ha' the decency tae wait?"

"What?" asked the creature, frowning with puzzlement and lowering the knife.

"Wait!" snarled Dodd as the little grove of bushes filled with London's fumes. The creature stepped back and lowered the knife a little more.

"Now," said Dodd, looking about for non-nettle leaves or even a stone so long as it was smooth, "Ah'll gi' ye a chance. If ye go now and pit yer silly dull blade awa' Ah'll no' kill ye. Right? D'ye hear me?"

"Money, I want yer money!" insisted the creature.

"Och no, awa' wi' ye, Ah've better uses for it. I'm givin' ye a chance, see ye?" Dodd was trying to be peaceful and gentlemanly, and it just wasn't working.

The creature was clearly deranged because he suddenly lunged closer.

"I'll cut yer then!" he shouted, "Giss yer money or…"

"Och," sighed Dodd as he shifted his body slightly, straightened his knees, and punched the creature in the face with a nice smooth stone he'd just picked up.

The poor creature was clearly a Southern weakling, for he folded up at once. Dodd picked up the rusty blade and threw it in the bushes, finished his business, covered up his leavings and went through the stupidly complicated fuss of the retying of points that gentlemen had to suffer every single time.

Then he left a penny beside the man bleeding gently from the mouth, on the grounds it was gentlemanly and, in any case, Carey's money not his. He shoved back out of the ill-starred bushes to find the horses watching gravely and chewing on some leaves. He mounted Whitesock for the next stage, took up the mare's reins and put his heels in.

Whitesock changed smoothly and started pounding stolidly along, followed in a scramble by the mare. Dodd laughed for a moment, a rare indulgence as no one was looking.

It seemed all the terrible tales you heard about southern footpads and sturdy beggars were just those—tall tales to frighten southron weans. The rest of the journey would be easy, even though his head had that oddly fixed metallic feeling in it of not having slept.

He could be in Oxford by the evening if he pushed it, he thought, but what was the point of that? He could use some more of Carey's money to stay at a proper inn, get some sleep, and then come into Oxford city nice and leisurely on Sunday morning. That would get him out of having to go to church with the Courtier and listening to some boring sermon about turning the other cheek. That thought made him laugh again.

He slowed down to a walk and looked about him, taking in the sunshine and berries in the hedges and the peaceful fields being cropped by fat cows before the autumn ploughing for winter wheat or barley. There was no hurry. He was enjoying himself.

saturday 16th september 1592, noon

As Carey the Courtier and his new servant Hughie Tryndale trotted along the rutted road that led to Rycote, he was keeping his eyes open for the unmistakeable signs of the Queen's progress.

He saw some on the other side of a hill where men were busy mending the disgraceful road, trundling wheelbarrows full of rocks to fill in the potholes and hammering down a corduroy of logs into the slopes to give the Queen's carts somewhere to grip in the soft earth they would soon turn to slurry.

He took a turn off the main road that led in that direction and rose in the stirrups to peer over the hedges—not a lot of stock in the fields, where a boy was leading the cows in.

As they came alongside the road menders, he found the master who was sitting on a rock, criticising.

"Which way is the Queen's Court?" He got a laconic thumb pointing further along the road.

He shifted the pack pony to the middle, so Hughie was behind and he was in front. You could think of the Queen's Court as a kind of army or a very large and disorderly herd of sheep with some sheepdogs in the centre and a few wolves around the outside. Generally, as with armies, the further out you were, the more disorderly it got.

There had clearly been some riders crossing hillsides, presumably the Queen's regular messengers taking shortcuts to avoid the no doubt thoroughly overwhelmed village of Rycote. Lord Norris was entertaining Her Majesty for a few days while she prepared to descend on the university city itself.

They followed the muddy track across pasture covered in molehills until they crested a hill and looked down into the valley of Rycote.

Carey could see at once that not all of the Court was there. He supposed some of them must still be packing up at Sudley or unpacking at Woodstock and a lot of them would have gone straight on to Oxford to grab the best camping and sleeping places. That suited him.

Carey was sure that his father's household would be setting up in one of the colleges. He could probably have found out where if he'd bothered to ask, but he didn't want to have to explain to anyone why he had bolted from London on Friday morning. Firstly he had to find his own lord, Robert Devereaux, Earl of Essex, who would certainly be in Rycote Manor and as close to the Queen's majesty as he could get. Therefore, to find his lord, all he had to do was find the Queen.

Carey stared down at the swollen village, frowning with worry. He had deliberately escaped from his parents, particularly his mother, leaving the best of his men, Sergeant Henry Dodd, behind him in a very ticklish situation. On Friday morning he had faked a large hawking expedition after redeeming his Court suit from pawn at Snr Gomes' shop. The plan had worked brilliantly and he had been away from the falconers and beaters and dogs by an hour after dawn on Friday, thundering along at a messenger's pace as he had done so often before, changing horses regularly. He enjoyed doing that, loved the sense of distance destroyed by his horse's legs. Even having to keep to a slower pace because of the pack pony, he'd made good enough time to get to Oxford by evening.

However he had, no doubt, severely annoyed his father and infuriated his mother, quite apart from leaving Dodd in the lurch. He had done it because he had put together in his mind what had really been going on with the sale of Cornish lands and the Jesuit priest. And it had made a picture that appalled him.

The clue that had given him the whole plot had been that code name "Icarus." If he was right about who Icarus really was...if...That was why he was here.

Unfortunately, he didn't think the Earl would want to hear what he had to say, and if he did listen would probably be extremely angry as well. Carey sighed. And that would mean the Queen would be angry with him and so he'd have very little chance of coming away with his warrant or his fee. Particularly not the fee.

Carey scowled at his horse's ears and pulled again at his regrown goatee as they carried on down the winding road to the village.

There had been a whole host of excellent reasons why he had grabbed at the chance to become deputy warden of the West March under his brother-in-law, Lord Scrope. One reason could be summed up as the *problem* of the Earl of Essex.

Robert Devereux, Earl of Essex, was his second cousin via the scandalous and outrageous Lettice Knollys, the earl's mother and his Aunt Katherine's daughter. Carey was related to an awful lot of the Queen's Court where the ties of blood were both useful and dangerous. With Robert Devereux it wasn't just about family.

He had liked and admired the man. He still did. There was something about him. But what was it? Time and again the Earl had done something, said something so outrageously stupid or hotheaded that Carey had been on the verge of turning his back on his cousin. Always in the past he had kept faith with the man. But it was becoming more and more difficult.

Take the summer of 1591 for instance. The Earl of Essex had insisted on taking men to France to help the King of Navarre win the throne of France. Carey, up to his eyes in debt again, had gone with him, the first time since the Armada that he had gone to war.

There in the pinched, muddy, and ugly campaign with Henri of Navarre, he had found out many things about himself. One of them was that he was actually good at war. He had found that he was a good commander and could keep his men both alive and at his side. His desertion rate was half anybody else's. He had hit it off well with Navarre, who was a very canny fighter indeed and had offered him a permanent place at his side.

Robert Devereux looked every inch the perfect leader—large, loud, magnificent, very good at hand-to-hand combat, chivalrous, honourable…

He was useless. He was sloppy. He didn't send out scouts. He didn't understand anything about artillery. He didn't pay attention to the lie of the land. He didn't see the lie of the man either—how the King of Navarre never really committed himself to the alliance. Sure enough, in the end, Navarre left Essex and the English to hold Sluys and then went off and raided fat countryside while they guarded his back.

Carey didn't blame the man; he was doing what princes do, but why hadn't Essex seen what was going to happen when Carey could so easily? They had all missed out on good plunder and got bogged down in the damp flux-ridden misery of a siege.

He shook his head and glanced back past the pack pony to young Hughie. The man must have been gangling a few years ago but had now filled out and probably didn't realise how dangerous he looked with his broad shoulders, big limbs, and saturnine face. Like most Scots he always looked as if he was nursing a grievance until you spoke to him and then his face opened out with a smile and was almost pleasant. It remained to be seen if he knew one end of a needle from the other and Carey would wait a while before he trusted his face to the man's razor.

Hughie was looking up the road past Carey. "Whit's that?" He pointed, then blushed and added, "sir?"

It was a mummer's cart, brightly decorated and full of costumes and scenery with a tent on top. At first Carey thought it was stuck, but then he caught sight of a very small personage in bright gold-and-black brocade with farthingale sleeves, sitting on a white pony looking very annoyed. Her tiny size and childish face made her anger funny. However, Carey knew that it would be most unwise to laugh at the Queen's Senior Fool and muliercula, Thomasina de Paris. She had two women with her and two men in the livery of the Master of the Revels. They were all some way back from the cart.

There was a boy driving the cart, looking very hangdog.

"If you don't know who I am," shouted the tiny creature, "then I've got no further use for you. And in any case I heard you left one of your company behind in London, sick with plague."

Carey reined in at once. An old man was climbing up clumsily from the depths of the cart, sweating heavily in the sudden sunlight, his face pale. He had a rash on the middle of his forehead, spreading down his nose.

Thomasina instantly backed her pony away from the cart. "Stay there!" she shouted. "No nearer."

Carey opened his pistol case.

The old man got down unsteadily from the cart and stood there, holding onto it with one hand. He coughed.

"How long since you left London?"

"A few days…" started the hangdog boy.

"Last spring," shouted the man hoarsely. "We've not been in London since…April."

"And where's your Fool?"

The boy started to cry. "Left us!" shouted the man. "Went his own way."

"How dare you!" shrieked Thomasina. "How dare you bring plague near the Queen's Court? Get away! Go back to London at once and stay there until you've got better or died." The high voice was tinged with the London stews and the mummer stepped back at her fury.

The old mummer swayed by his cart, his mouth opening and shutting, bright blood on his lips.

Carey began loading his pistol. Sometimes men went crazy in the first onset of plague, as their fever rose and they became delirious. That's why they had to be shut up in their houses, cruel though it was, because if you came within ten feet of them you could catch it and die and all your family with you. Half the purpose of the Queen's summer progresses was to get her out of London and away from the plague.

"We've got no money," sniffled the boy. "He said we had to come because we haven't got no money what with the theatres all shut and Mr. Byrd wanted singers."

Thomasina pulled a small purse from her saddlebag and threw it to the boy. "Get yourselves back to London," she said to him more gently. "Keep away from people. If any of you are alive in six weeks' time, you may apply to the Master of the Revels again."

The old man was shouting hoarsely again, making no sense at all, about how he was owed money and he had a new play and the rest would catch up with them. The boy started crying again. Neither of the Master of the Revels' men had firearms and were standing there looking as if they were about to bolt.

Carey rode up beside Thomasina and aimed his pistol at the man. It was a long shot and he hadn't wound his other dag, so he rested the gun's barrel on his left wrist and breathed out to steady his pounding heart. With those death-tokens on him, shooting the old man would be doing him a kindness.

Another lad, with bandages round his neck, climbed trembling out of the cart and persuaded the old man back into it.

Thomasina had acknowledged Carey's backing with a quick glance and a lift of her shoulder. He saw she had a throwing knife in her right hand, from the sheaf she kept under her wide sleeves. Although she was only three-and-a-half-foot tall, her childlike round face had a few lines on it. She could still pass as a child if she wanted to, and perhaps she did. She had begun as a tumbler at Paris Garden and was as good with throwing knives as Carey's previous servant, Barnabus.

They took their mounts widely around the stricken cart, Carey keeping his pistol pointed at the mummers all the way. One of the Master of the Revels' men stayed on the road to be sure the mummers didn't try coming into Rycote again. No doubt all of them would die out there in the field.

Thomasina was shaking her head and puffing out her breath as she slipped her knife back under her brocade sleeve. Once they had put some distance between themselves and the plague, Carey bowed to Thomasina from the saddle. "Mistress Thomasina," he said to her, "what an unexpected pleasure!"

"Ha! You're not sickening for anyfing yourself, are you?" she snapped at him, "I heard your servant got plague and died of it."

"Mistress," said Carey reproachfully, "do you think I would be coming to Court if I had knowingly been near the plague? That wasn't what he died of." And how the devil did she know that?

"What about *him*? Is that Sergeant Henry Dodd that I hear so much about?"

Hughie's mount pecked suddenly. "Er…no, that's Hughie Tyndale, my new manservant."

Hughie's mouth was half-open and he looked shocked. Perhaps he was recovering from his new master treating someone who looked like an overdressed little girl with such respect. Or maybe he was frightened by the plague.

"Oh, 'e got plague then?" asked Thomasina.

"Not as far as I know, mistress. There hasn't been plague at Court, surely?"

She shook her head. "We've been on progress since before it started to spread in London. If I had my way, I'd let nobody come near the Queen what hadn't been in quarantine at least forty days and scrubbed with vinegar as well."

"Surely with the Court around her…"

"It's the idiot players and musicians all coming up from London to make their fortunes. As if there weren't enough of them in Oxford already." Her voice was changing back to the way courtiers spoke but she turned and fixed him with gimlet eyes. "So what are you doing here?"

Carey almost coughed but stopped himself. "Really I'm on my way north for the raiding season after my father very inconveniently ordered me south," he said. "I want to speak to my lord Earl of Essex urgently. After that I'll be on my…"

Thomasina snorted. "So you won't want to talk to the Queen?"

"Of course," Carey continued smoothly, "I would be utterly delighted if you could arrange an audience for me, Mistress Thomasina, but I know what it's like on progress and…"

Thomasina's brown eyes were narrowed. "Hmm. Well, there might be something you could do for me. I can't promise, but…"

Heart hammering again with the hope that he might actually be able to talk to the Queen directly and even (please God!) get his wardenry fee and warrant, Carey took off his hat, held it against his heart and bowed low in the saddle.

"Mistress, if you can bring me to the Queen, I will forever be in your debt…"

"Yes, yes, Sir Robert, I know all about you and your debts, no need to add to them. You can do me a small service first and then we'll see, eh?"

"Whatever you want, mistress."

He couldn't leave his dag shotted and wound when he put it back in the case and he didn't like the thought of trying to unload it while riding—always a ticklish business which could take your hand off if the powder exploded at the wrong moment. He aimed at a crow sitting on a branch ahead and pulled the trigger.

He missed. The crow flew off the branch in a puff of feathers and the other crows rose up into the sky cawing and diving. Thomasina's pony skittered, the pack pony came to a dead stop, and Hughie's horse pirouetted for a moment before he got it under control again. Carey's own horse was a hunter and not at all concerned. Thomasina's two women were walking and one of them jumped and clutched the other, while the Master of the Revels man looked near fainting. He smiled at the thought of what Dodd would likely think of such jumpiness at gunfire.

"Where are you planning to stay?" Thomasina wanted to know. "With your elder brother? Your father's already in Oxford, I think."

"Er...no."

"Suing him, are you?"

"No, that's my brother Henry who stole my legacy. But George thinks he can still order me around."

"You won't find space with his grace the Earl of Essex. He's just sent most of his men ahead to find a good place for his pavilions at Oxford, so he's in the manor house with the Queen and Lord Norris."

"I would very much like to see him..."

"Don't push it, Sir Robert. I have no pull at all with Essex." Her face was wry with distaste. "How's your reverend father?"

"Very well, mistress, thank you...in good health."

She smiled then. "Now he's a good lord, keeps the old-fashioned ways." Once upon a time, Thomasina had been one of his creatures on display at Paris Garden stews, bought from Gypsies. She had learned her tumbling there and Lord Hunsdon had been the person who showed her to the Queen at a masque.

"In trouble with him again, are you?" she asked, seeing through him as usual.

"Er...possibly."

"Well, try the Master of the Revels then." She tapped the white palfrey onward with a whip decorated with crystal beads that flashed in the sun. "You could make yourself useful there."

"How? My tumbling is middling to poor and my acting..."

She sniffed at his sarcasm. "You can sing, Sir Robert, and he now has a desperate need for good tenors 'cos one of 'em's dead of plague and the other's dying on that cart. I'll find you later."

She gestured for Carey to go past her and so he went to a canter up the path.

saturday 16th september 1592, afternoon

They had to rein in well before they got to the church, the place was such a bedlam of tents, carts, fashionable carriages bogged in the mud, servingmen, people generally. You could hardly move at all. No women under the age of thirty were visible, but boys were running about everywhere because this was the Queen's Court, not the King of Scotland's, and propriety was usually observed.

All the main barns were guarded by the Queen's Gentlemen Pensioners in the red-and-black livery from her father's Court that they wore on ordinary days, no doubt because the harbingers and heralds would have stockpiled food in them for the progress, bought on treasury tickets in advance. They were oases of order.

The rest of the village was essentially a fair. At the back of the church some large makeshift clay ovens stood surrounded by faggots of wood with more being brought in on the backs of trudging peasants.

Carey took one look at the only alehouse in the place, where a skinny middle-aged woman with a hectic look in her eyes was raking in cash. He didn't fancy his chances with the queue.

Still the smell of pies was making his mouth water. He'd eaten the pie he was buying when he heard Hughie's Scotch accent; he'd had bread and ale as usual when he got up but that was all. Now he was starving. So he did what he often did on progress, and come to think of it, at war. He turned his horse to the left and rode slowly around the mass of humanity.

At last he saw what he was looking for—the Earl of Cumberland's blue-and-yellow-chequered flags around a small cottage surround by a mushroom ring of tents.

Carey immediately rode toward the cluster, followed by Hughie, who was looking nervous, and by the pony which was busily taking mouthfuls of everything green and poisonous it could find in its path.

A large henchman in a Clifford jack barred his way.

"What's yer name and what's yer business?" he demanded, his voice from the Clifford lands in Chester.

"Sir Robert Carey, come to see my lord, one follower, two horses, and a pack pony," said Carey, looking around for the Earl. There was a table set up in a muddy orchard behind the cottage and sitting there was definitely none other than Sir George Clifford, third Earl of Cumberland, known as the Pirate Earl. Only now he was standing up and playing a veney with his opponent, a man in the buff coat of a master at arms.

A yell announced a hit by the earl on his opponent. They saluted each other, then dropped their veney sticks and sat down at the table again. Carey wasn't sure what was on the table, but it didn't look like playing cards.

The henchman had sent a lad to talk to the earl. Carey watched with a smile.

Next moment, Cumberland had bounced to his feet and was striding across what remained of the vegetable garden to where Carey was waiting. He slid down from the saddle, prodded Hughie to do the same, and bowed as Cumberland came up to them, wreathed in smiles.

"My Lord Earl," Carey said formally.

"By God, Sir Robert," laughed Cumberland, "where the devil have you been? How's Carell Castle treating you? What's this I hear about the Grahams and the King of Scotland and…?"

Cumberland pumped his hand and clapped him round the shoulders.

"My new servingman, Hughie Tyndale," Carey said. Hughie managed a reasonable bow, then reconsidered and went on one knee to the Earl.

"Tyndale? Are you from there?" the Earl asked with interest, waving him up again.

"Ah…ma family…is…was…m'lord," Hughie stuttered, "I think…"

"Ran away to Edinburgh, did they?" asked Cumberland. "What's your trade then?"

"Ay sir, Ah wis prenticed tae a tailor sir but it didnae suit and…"

Cumberland bellowed with laughter.

"Don't tell me you've got yourself the perfect combination at last?" he shouted. "I thought that was your little thief Barnabus. Where's he gone?"

"I'm afraid he died of the flux in London." No point in going into details.

"Not plague?"

"What do you take me for, my lord?"

"Well, I'm sorry to hear it. I was hoping he could teach me knife-throwing one of these days. Speaking of which, come and look at this."

Carey told Hughie to find somewhere to put the horses and fetch some food for them, and to make sure the baggage stayed with them and not to unload the pony until they were under cover. Then he went over to the orchard with Cumberland.

"Now then. D'ye see what we're doing here?"

The master at arms was standing four square by the table, arms folded. Carey looked down at the very nicely carved ivory and ebony chess set on a gold and silver board that Cumberland had robbed out of a Spanish ship a season before. It looked as if Cumberland was losing as usual, but Carey thought he could see some useful opportunities for the queen, possibly.

"Now then…" said Cumberland, his dark face beaming. He was sporting a gold earring in his right earlobe like the Spanish grandee he took it from, and Carey thought it looked better on him than on Sir Walter Raleigh. None of his portraits showed that he had a piratical crooked smile with a tooth missing that somehow caused devastation among the ladies of the Queen's bedchamber and worse than that amongst the Maids of Honour. However, like Carey himself, Cumberland had the sense to leave the maids strictly alone, for all their sighing and fluttering. He wouldn't risk joining Sir Walter in the Tower for marrying a Maid of Honour in a hurry. Anyway, he was already married to the formidable Margaret Clifford.

"Mr. Simmonds, would you mind if we went back a move?"

The master at arms nodded and Cumberland replaced two pawns, which were in position to take.

"Now then, see here. Chess is a dreadfully dull game, in my opinion, but this makes it fun. Normally with two pieces of equal power we'd throw a die or a coin to decide which wins the fight."

"Yes," said Carey who actually preferred the newfangled way of doing it where the first that was in place took, regardless of power. That removed chance from the game and made it a matter of pure skill which suited him better. "And you're fighting a veney instead?"

"Exactly! First hit wins the piece."

Carey laughed. Cumberland was a very good fighter. "What an excellent martial exercise."

"Of course. I think I'm doing better with this game than the last one, Mr. Simmonds."

"Yes, my lord," said Simmonds tactfully and Carey smiled knowingly at him because it was obvious to him from the board that in the long term, the Earl would lose no matter how good his veneys.

"Are you playing a puissant queen?" Carey asked.

"Oh yes, compliment to Her Majesty and all that. Makes it a better game anyway. We should play a game, Sir Robert."

"I'd be delighted, my lord," said Carey, quite truthfully with a little tickle of excitement under his ribs at the idea he suddenly had for some side bets on himself to win.

"So, what are you doing here anyway?" asked Cumberland later as they sat on a couple of stools and Carey munched the heel of a game pie from the Earl's table. "Lowther already kicked you out of Carell?"

"Not yet, though it's a tricky situation," Carey explained as much as he was willing of the tricky situation, then changed the subject. "I'm really here to talk to the Queen about my warrant and get my fee…"

"Hah! Good luck. She's in a terrible mood at the moment."

"Why? She's usually happy on progress."

"No idea. Everything was fine until just after we got to Rycote and then suddenly…clouds! Thunder! Kaboom! Zap! Poor Devereux didn't know what had hit him…."

"How much trouble is he in?"

Cumberland smiled. "On Friday Devereux was driven from the presence in a hail of shoes, muffs, and one surprised lapdog, and today is out hunting to recover his spirits and bring Her Majesty some suitable trophy to calm her down…ideally venison."

"So what did he do?"

The elegant tawny shoulders shrugged. "Nothing. For once he's been angelic. He's starting to get the benefit of the customs farm of sweet wines though he hasn't found anyone to manage it for him yet. He's recovered financially from his forays into France, more or less, though there are the usual rumours that he's done something stupid with his money again."

Carey said nothing to this despite Cumberland's expectant look. He also didn't mention that the Earl of Cumberland himself was famous as the man who was taking good fertile land and pouring it into the sea as he fitted out one privateer after another in hopes of taking a big enough prize to recoup himself. The Royal Spanish treasure fleet probably wouldn't be enough by now.

"So you don't know the reason for Her Majesty's ill humour?"

"No, it's probably just the wind changing in her internal weather, that's all. What do you expect if you call her Astraea?"

"Do you know where my lord of Essex is hunting?"

"No idea. He's ignoring me at the moment. It's all Cromwell and Mountjoy and his other cronies. Maybe tonight at my ball—poor Norris asked me to arrange it so the Queen won't be bored."

They look around at the destroyed hedges, foraged apple trees, dung heaps, and escaped dogs that made a ragged new perimeter to the village. Every landowner dreaded the arrival of the Queen and all her Court on progress, and many had been known to fake absence so as to avoid the honour.

"My Lord Norris was saying he'll have to remit all the rents for the next five years until the place recovers," Cumberland commented as he went back to his chess-veney game. "Thank God I live too far north for her to turn up at my place."

Carey laughed. "Your wife would love it."

"She wouldn't. She's not a fool. What about you? My Lord Hunsdon found you a juicy little heiress yet?" Carey shook his head. Cumberland looked comically appalled. "Oh, for God's sake, Carey, you're not still mooning after Lady Widdrington?"

Carey's expression chilled and he cocked his head as his hand dropped to his sword hilt. The Earl put his hands up, palms out placatingly.

"All right, all right, let's not fight about it, I completely agree that your cousin Elizabeth is a wonderful, sagacious, virtuous, and beautiful woman and a perfect match for you, but for pity's sake…"

"Yes?" growled Carey.

"She's poor!"

"So what?"

"And she's married. I heard something about your last run-in with her husband. But even once he's dead, how can you ever afford to marry her? It's just not practical."

Carey's expression was mulish. "I love her," he said.

Cumberland shook his head at his friend's lunacy. "What does your father say?"

"He married for love, too."

"Maniacs, the lot of you. I blame the Royal blood. Come on then, which way should I go here?"

Carey blinked down at the board. Simmonds' face was carefully neutral so Carey looked for a trap. There were two obvious moves that would lead to a very nice ambush, but there was one move that wasn't obvious at all. Carey was willing to bet that Cumberland hadn't noticed it. Damn it, what his friend said was perfectly true and only what all his friends had been telling him for the last five years, but…

He didn't care. He was a landless younger son and common sense dictated he must marry money or land. But he had to have Elizabeth. There was simply no alternative.

"You could move your puissant queen from here to here," he said. Simmonds' granite face shifted infinitesimally to sadness. "Sorry, Mr. Simmonds," Carey added, because he had just destroyed a very nice march on the king.

Cumberland stared, frowned, stared again. "By God, Carey, how do you see these things? Amazing! Right." He moved the carved ivory queen. "Check, I think."

Carey was sitting down, playing Mr. Simmonds at the new style of chess with no veneys, dice, or coins plus the puissant queen who shook everything up so well, when he heard a caressingly familiar voice beside him.

"*Alors, M. le Deputé,*" came the Italianate French. "*Je suis vraiment enchanté de vous voir autrefois.*"

Carey shot to his feet. There was a tiny pause during which he checked to make sure that it was indeed none other than Signora Emilia Bonnetti, looking amused. Cumberland had a very unattractive smirk on his handsome face.

"Emilia!" he said, bowing to hide the fact that his memory was in an uproar. "Signora Bonnetti, I, too, am utterly delighted to find you here in such an unworthy setting." He said it in English because that was a dig at Cumberland who was clearly playing his very own puissant queen. Anyway, it would be rude to speak French in front of the earl who was no linguist.

Emilia smiled again, with her head tilted perkily. This time instead of a feathered mask and crimson silk gown and dancing slippers, Signora Bonnetti was modestly dressed in a black *devoré* velvet slashed with grey satin in a Parisian style and was wearing small but determined hobnail boots. Her black hair was modestly tucked under a white linen cap, but she wore a crazily tilted little black hat with a feather in it, making every other woman in the world look unforgivably dowdy.

"Hey, less of the unworthy, Sir Robert," boomed Cumberland, putting his arm around Emilia's waist. "Signor Bonnetti is helping me find good wines from Italy for my household and his delightful wife has been…advising me."

Carey nodded, cynically wondering how far the advice had gone. He found himself looking at the place just below the modest neckline of her bodice where, a month or two ago, he had bitten her very gently on a summer night in a rose garden. She brushed the place with her hand, which made him smile.

Signora Bonnetti wound her arm into Cumberland's elbow and looked up at him, smiled back.

"So you do know each other?" Cumberland asked, very smug.

It wouldn't be the first time he and Cumberland had collided over a woman, but he thought the Earl was making a point here about his romantic notions. And, uncomfortably for him, it was a good one. He wondered exactly how much the fascinating Signora might have told her new lover about Carey's disastrous plottings at the King of Scotland's Court. Emilia was watching him carefully, her black eyes full of amusement and something else—he wasn't sure what.

"Yes," he said, deciding to push his luck a little, "we met at the King's Court in Dumfries."

"Ah," said Cumberland, "so that was before your unfortunate journey to Ireland and your problems there, my dear."

Emilia Bonnetti, who must know by now exactly who had caused those potentially lethal problems, laughed a little. "Oh, yes," she said, "but my lovely Lord of Cumberland save my life, Sir Robert, after my poor husband was forced to leave Ormonde's Court in such a hurry. My lord gave us passage from Dublin in his ship…"

"The *Elizabeth Bonaventure*," Cumberland put in. "You remember her, Carey, we faced the armada in her and I've had a new mast fitted…"

"Thank heavens!" said Carey with complete insincerity. Oh God, this complicated everything horribly. Was she looking to get back at him? What had she told Cumberland? What had she told everyone else? The Court was a nest of gossip that made a ladies' flower-water party look like a collection of Trappist monks. Had any of what she must have been saying got as far as the Queen? Not directly, of course; the Queen was very unlikely to receive an Italian adventuress into her presence, despite the sweet wines….

Sweet wine. Essex had the farm of sweet wines and he would be looking for a suitable agent to run it for him. What would Essex make of Emilia, Carey wondered.

"How is your husband, Signora?" Carey asked, still sticking to English.

"Well," she said with a little pout of her lips, "the Irish…'ow you say?…zey drink like ducks but not appreciate good wine and when zey promise to pay, zey lie."

"Tut," said Carey.

"So, we are here now. At least ze English like to drink well… And perrrhaps…zey will pay?"

The opening was there, so he took it, simply on general principles, with no idea of where it might lead. And he did owe her something for the trick with the guns. "I wonder if you've spoken to my lord of Essex yet, Signora?"

The faintest shadow crossed Emilia's face, followed by another diamond smile. "Not yet…'e has been very…*occupé* with the Queen who is verry cross.…To be a *mignon* is 'ard, no? 'Oo would do such a thing?"

And she tilted her head in a way which Carey suddenly found annoying. "Mignon" had several loaded meanings on top of the simple translation of "King's favourite." In the context of the Scottish Court it meant the King's catamite. In the context of the English Court and the Queen…

"Indeed," he agreed blandly.

"You could put in a good word for the Signora, Sir Robert, couldn't you?" said the ever-helpful Cumberland. "My lord of Essex often speaks of how you saved his bacon with the Queen a year ago in France."

"If I could get to see him, yes, perhaps," Carey said. "As he doesn't know I'm here…"

"You are friends wiz milord Essex?"

Emilia was looking intent, the way she had when they bargained in the summer. Carey couldn't help himself, he smiled cagily and spread his hands. "He gave me my knighthood in France, Signora, and was my commander when we fought for the King of Navarre. He's also my second cousin."

Her lips compressed. For some reason she was furious and Carey wondered why. It's all right, he wanted to tell her, if you're not trying to buy guns to sell to the Irish to be used against the Queen's soldiers, I won't cheat you. Of course, she might not be after just the farm of sweet wines from Essex; she was likely to be here for quite other reasons as well as the obvious one of espionage.

"*M. le deputé*," she said to him with a nice curtsey. "We must speak about this when my 'usband is 'ere, as I am only a poor little woman oo knows nossing of money or farms."

Cumberland laughed, caught her shoulders and gave her a smacking kiss on the cheek.

"I love it when she talks English," he said to Carey. "It sounds so funny."

Emilia's tinkling laugh told Carey a lot more than it seemingly did George Clifford. He didn't give the Earl of Cumberland much chance against the Earl of Essex if Emilia met the noble lord. From her sideways look at him under her remarkably long lashes, it seemed that she and her complaisant, well-horned husband might be willing to negotiate a fee for the all-important introduction to Essex. Possibly some of that fee could be in-kind...

No, came the sternly righteous part of him. That's enough. You have to find a way to pay the men for the autumn if the Queen is too ill-humoured to give you your fee. And after what Elizabeth did for you in Scotland!

Could he take the risk of dealing with the Italian spies again? If he could find a way of spreading the responsibility a little as he had not been able to do before, perhaps? If he had some kind of authorisation? Perhaps he could talk to Thomasina again? There would be dancing that evening, another less cautious part of him thought, and perhaps I will dance with Signora Bonnetti again? Perhaps. No more than that, of course, but...

At least Elizabeth won't be watching, that part of him explained to the stern-faced puritan who came from Walsingham; she'd never find out....But that was another unexpectedly bleak thought. And she probably would, somehow.

Cumberland had started rubbing noses with Emilia. She laughed again and nipped his nose between her knuckles and he squawked.

"Be'ave, milord," she said severely. "What will Sir Robert think?"

"I know exactly what he's thinking, my little darling," said Cumberland, piratical grin at full force. "Aren't you, Carey?"

So she's told him, or he's guessed, Carey decided philosophically, so probably no chance of even a polite pavane with the Signora. Maybe for the best.

"Indeed, I am, my lord," he said with diplomatic ruefulness. "So I'd better go and see if my new servingman has made off with my Court suit. My lord...Signora..."

He bowed elaborately to both of them and plodded back through the mud to the horse-crammed kitchen yard of the little cottage that Cumberland had taken over.

There he found that Hughie Tyndale had done quite creditably. All three of the horses were munching away at nosebags, had been untacked and rubbed down and were tied up at the corner of the yard, next to Cumberland's carthorses and a string of pack ponies.

The packs with Carey's Court suit and jewels in it had been piled next to the wall and Hughie was squatting watchfully next to them, munching a pennyloaf with some cheese and drinking ale from a jack.

"We'll stay with my lord Cumberland tonight, Hughie," Carey said as he pushed between the horses, "Not sure where exactly, but we can hope to be in the dry."

"Ay, sir."

"Have you looked at my suit?"

"I had a quick look but Ah couldnae unpack it out here in case o' the wet, sir."

"Quite right. Let's see if Clifford will loan me a dressing room or similar."

The Earl of Cumberland was busy, said Mr. Simmonds stolidly, but had given orders that Sir Robert should have anything he wanted—except the delightful Signora, since, as his friend, the Earl wanted to make sure he did nothing rash to upset his headlong pursuit of romantical ruin.

Ha ha, George, very funny, thought Carey, oddly relieved. Simmonds showed him to a shed that was being used as a tiring room as it was dry and reasonably well-lit with a stone-flagged floor and bars on the window—no doubt a dry-goods store since it didn't even smell of salt fish or cheese.

He and Hughie carefully unwrapped the pearl-encrusted velvet doublet and hose from the hessian protecting it and hung it all up on a bracket on the wall. With Hughie's help he tried on the doublet and knew at once from the way Hughie went about it that the man had indeed worked for a tailor. No, the costly doublet was far too tight on the shoulders—he might even split a seam if he danced a volta and needed to lift the woman. Before they had finished deciding what to do about letting it out, a boy knocked and squeaked, "Message for Sir Robert."

"Eh? Who from?"

"I'm not to say, sir, I'm just to take you there."

"Should I…er…shift my shirt to meet this person?" Carey asked hopefully, but the child shook his head vigorously.

"No, sir, just come straight along…she's in a hurry, she said."

Perhaps it was the Signora wanting to cheapen over his commission for putting the Bonnettis in touch with the Earl of Essex? Perhaps she was bored with Cumberland? Perhaps she had fond memories of their dalliance in Dumfries? He certainly did.

"Just take the padding out of the armholes and wings," Carey told Hughie cheerfully. "It'll do the job and look fine. You know how to do it, don't you?"

"Ay, sir," said Hughie, ducking his head, "Ah'll come in fra the lining and reseam after though."

Carey shifted the doublet up and down again, tight across the back too and flatteringly looser around the waist. Carlisle and the incessant riding and training was improving his figure even more than war in France had, but it was annoying that all the improvements were in places difficult to alter. No doubt about it, ten years of Court life had softened him badly despite jousting and tennis and swordplay. Now he was back in form again. That was pleasing and might please the Queen, too.

Carey smiled complacently at the half mirror nailed on the wall. He hadn't tried on his cannions and would have to hope they were all right; altering them would be even more complicated. He would have to use his riding boots as well or find and borrow some dancing slippers—it didn't really matter so much on progress, but still…Mind, his hose were in a poor state, having been darned several times by Barnabus. So boots were the better choice.

"You're sure I shouldn't change?" Carey asked, glaring at the boy severely. Whose child was he, anyway? Carey thought back fondly to his days as a page at the young Queen's Court, with his father, just before the Revolt of the Northern Earls.

"No, sir," said the boy, luckily bright enough to understand what he was worrying about. "Oh no, sir, it isn't Her Majesty, I'd make sure and tell you if it was and check for musk-scented boots too."

"So I should hope," said Carey, disappointed. He unbuttoned the heavy pearl-embroidered doublet and Hughie helped it from his shoulders, unlaced the sleeves, and turned it inside out before hanging it up.

Still buttoning up his old hunting doublet, Carey followed the page boy out of the cottage, along the rutted lane and down another lane to a small tithe barn. There he came upon another scene of chaos because clearly the place had been commandeered by all the mummers and musicians of the Court. On the ground floor, already eaten bare by the Court, bad-tempered choristers of the chapel in their livery coats were practising polyphony very poorly. In another corner, by some feed bins, were acrobats and tumblers, practising a complicated sequence of somersaults and jumps to build a pyramid. The master of the tumblers, a slightly built handsome Moor in a black brocade doublet and hose, was supervising with iron patience. The pyramid wobbled and collapsed.

"Try again," he said, "this time Master Skeggs as second rank base, and Will the Tun as first rank."

The page boy was climbing a ladder in front of them that led to a half-loft still full of hay that made your nose twitch. When Carey followed him, he took a narrow path through the sweetly smelling piles of fodder to a nook at the back which had been laid over with rugs. There none other than Mistress Thomasina de Paris was sitting neatly with her knees folded under her in her white damask and gold tissue gown, with her costume trunks behind her.

Carey flourished a bow to her. "Mistress," he said, "I have to say I was hoping to meet another Queen, but I would like to ask your advice on..."

She skewered him with a look. "Tom," she said to the page boy, "go sit at the top of the ladder and...no, in fact, pull it up and sit next to it. Understand?"

"Yes, missus," said the boy and forged a path back through the hay, looking determined.

Carey shut his mouth and looked quizzically at the Queen's Fool. She gestured for him to sit down and he decided against trying to sit on a rug as the points of his doublet were too tight to his hose to allow it. He perched on one of the boxes.

They sat in silence for a moment.

Just as Carey was about to open proceedings by asking conventionally after the Queen her mistress' good health, Thomasina took a sealed letter from the rug beside her and handed it to him without a word. She was looking immensely disapproving.

Carey held it in his fingers, looked at it. That was the Queen's personal seal, the small one. The one she never gave to anyone else.

Fingers a little unsteady, he opened it. The letter was in fact a warrant from the Queen, stating that Sir Robert Carey was her trusty and well-beloved cousin and acting in her behalf and requiring any who read it to assist him in any way he asked.

It wasn't the warrant for his deputyship; it was very much better than that. But it didn't say anything about what his office was nor why exactly he might need assistance.

Heart pounding, Carey refolded the letter carefully and put it in his inside doublet pocket.

"I have been asked to ask you…" began Thomasina judiciously.

"Mistress Thomasina, I know how Her Majesty's mind works insofar as any mere man can. Bear with me, please. If you are speaking on behalf of anyone other than our dread sovereign Queen Elizabeth, would you please say so now?"

Thomasina nodded her head once and then folded her lips. Carey counted twenty of his heartbeats because they were going faster than normal. "Thank you, mistress. You were saying?"

"I have been asked to ask you to investigate a…a death that happened some thirty-two years ago."

What? Carey didn't say that. He tried to think whose death, then asked, "Before or after I was born?"

"Do you know the month?"

"The Queen was godmother at my baptism, I know that, but it was a little late for some reason. My mother always said I was a summer baby and bound to be lucky."

"In which case the death happened after your birth. It was on the 8th September in the year of Our Lord 1560."

There was something about the date, but he wasn't sure what. Something important to be sure, family stories from when he was very little, family gossip, something about his Aunt Katherine's gown being ruined on the hunting field. Something that had caused arguments between his father and mother. Carey closed his eyes for a moment. He had been such a little boy, still in skirts, riding experienced barrel-shaped ponies, youngest of a string of seven boys and two girls that lived. Only Philadelphia was younger than him, and he was hardly ever noticed except by his wet nurse, which suited both him and Philly very well indeed. What was it?

He opened his eyes and smiled. "I deny it," he said. "The bill is clean, I was nowhere near. I have an excellent alibi from my wet nurse, as well as being hampered by my swaddling bands."

Mistress Thomasina looked unamused.

"This…death changed many lives," she said, obviously expecting him to have heard of it nonetheless. "It happened only a few miles from Oxford, at Cumnor Place."

"Cumnor?" Damn it, what was it about that name?

Thomasina rolled her eyes. "I suppose most of our generation were never concerned by it and your parents wouldn't speak of it," she said, pouring wine from a flask into a small coral cup for herself and twice as much for Carey into a silver goblet. From a sandalwood box, she offered sweet wafers which Carey refused. "I had no idea myself who Her Ma…who was being spoken of. I didn't even recognise the name of the victim."

Carey said nothing, watching carefully. Who the devil had died thirty-two years ago; why all the mystery?

"I say death," Thomasina was being judicious again, "but at the time the word being whispered was *murder*."

Well of course it was; that wasn't surprising. After all, why bother to investigate a death if you didn't think it was murder?

"Was there an inquest?"

"Oh yes," said Thomasina, "though it took a year to decide on death by misadventure."

That and her tone of voice did send Carey's eyebrows upwards. "A year?" Most inquests had decided within a week.

"Yes. It didn't matter, though. The suspicion was enough."

Would the bloody midget give him the name? Why was he supposed to guess? He felt doltish at all these riddles, actually sighed for the brutal simplicity of Carlisle where people tended to tell you to your face that they hated you and had put a price on your head. He was quite proud of the fact that his own head was rumoured to be worth at least £10 in gold to the Graham surname.

Thomasina wasn't even looking at him anymore but into a corner where there was nothing but a particularly fine Turkish rug, woven with strange squared-off houses and birds.

"I told her to let it be, that the trail was thirty-two years cold and that no one really cared anymore....And she snapped at me that she cares and that as her goddamned nephew is so clever at ferreting out the truth of things that don't concern him, he may as well make himself useful in her behalf for a change."

He grinned. That had the authentic ring of the Queen's voice. Thomasina was an excellent mimic. Carey could almost see his cousin's high-bridged nose and snapping brown eyes under her red wig, the red lead giving bright colour to her white-leaded cheeks.

Nephew. That was an important message to him in itself. He was also her cousin through his grandmother, Mary Boleyn, sister to the beheaded Ann. But he was the Queen's nephew through his father, bastard son of Henry VIII, and her half-brother. That meant that this was Tudor family business.

"Mistress," he began as tactfully as he could, "I'm afraid I'm too young and ignorant to…"

"This death is that of Amy Dudley, née Robsart."

All his breath puffed out of his chest. Carey knew that name.

"The Earl of Leicester's first wife…" he asked, just to be sure, "who fell down the stairs at Cumnor Place and…?"

"And died," said Thomasina. "Sir Robert, something happened two days ago that upset Her Majesty and put her clean out of countenance. She has been in a rage ever since and was even let blood out of season for it. When she had news that you were coming, she told me to…I was told to tell you to look into it."

"Look into the death of Robert Dudley's first wife?"

"Or her goddamned murder, as the Queen calls it," added Thomasina quietly.

"She knows it was murder?"

Thomasina nodded. "But…but…" Carey was horrified. The Queen was telling him to look into it, a direct order. Usually she allowed at least the polite semblance of choice. Of all things the Queen could have ordered him to do, this was surely the most perverse, the most ridiculous, the most—well, for God's sake, the most dangerous. To him. He was being ordered to go and stir up a thirty-two-year-old nest of vipers. There had indeed been family gossip about it when Carey was a boy and worse than that. Carey knew that his father had quietly bought up and burned a number of inflammatory pamphlets published secretly by the English Jesuits until the presses could be found and destroyed. Those pamphlets accused the Queen and her then-favourite, Robert Dudley of murdering Dudley's innocent wife between them. Other suspects in the case were, of course, Sir William Cecil; later Lord Treasurer Burghley; Christopher Hatton, the attorney general who danced his way into the Queen's favour and never married; even Lettice Knollys, the Earl of Leicester's eventual second wife and the Earl of Essex's scandalous mother. There had been something going on that his father dealt with when he was fourteen, something about a man called Appleyard, Amy Robsart's brother.

Quite possibly every single member of the 1560 Privy Council could be a suspect for the killing.

"But why?" he burst out. "The woman has been in the ground for thirty-two years and…"

"In Gloucester Hall chapel in Oxford, in fact," Thomasina corrected him.

"In Oxford and…Why now?"

"The last time she came to Oxford was in 1566," said Thomasina, seemingly at random.

"Yes?"

"She's very clear, Sir Robert. She wants the death investigated and she wants you to do it, but she will not tell you why. She shouted at me when I pressed her about it."

"But, mistress," said Carey carefully, "the Queen must know she is by far the most…er…the one most likely to be suspected as the murderer now as well as then. What were the words she used to you exactly?"

"You do it as you see fit, and you report to her through me—directly to her if necessary."

"She knows that this is a very ugly swamp and she may not like the smells that come up if I stir the mud?"

Thomasina smiled shortly. "She wants it done and she will have you do it."

"And if I find irrefutable proof that she was the murderer?"

The midget's eyes were cold. "She didn't tell me, but no doubt she would expect you to keep it quiet."

He could do that, of course, he wasn't a fool, but God, he hoped he wouldn't have to. "And what if it is simply that the evidence I find points to her?"

Thomasina shrugged which made her look both worldly wise and girlish. "She didn't say. But how could it have been her, Sir Robert? Surely she would simply have married Leicester anyway once the wife was dead and gone, no matter what the scandal? If she'd done it? Once she had damned her soul that way, where was the problem damning herself again? You can only hang once."

Clearly Thomasina had been worrying about it, too. She sounded reasonable, but…the Queen was a woman and therefore by nature unreasonable.

"I'll need to see the report by the coroner and the inquest jury's verdict and any witness statements," he said, hoping to play for time while the documents were searched for and copied.

Thomasina reached into a box beside her and brought out a sheaf of papers which she handed to him. They were all certified copies, written in the cramped secretary script of one of the older Exchequer clerks.

"I have to say what I'm investigating when I ask questions. I can't possibly keep it secret." Thomasina shrugged again. This was an impossible task, Carey thought with a sigh. "Does Her Majesty know I haven't yet been paid my wardenry fee?"

Thomasina looked blank. "You had two chests of coin from her…"

"They were free loans. This is my fee of £400 which I was also promised. Separate and different." Nothing. "Mention it to my loving aunt, will you, Mrs. Thomasina? Try and get it into her head that soldiers need to be paid or they won't fight, that's all I ask. And by the way…I wanted to ask your…advice on the Bonnettis."

"The Italian spies?"

"Especially Signora Bonnetti." He looked carefully into space. "I am hoping to introduce her to my lord of Essex to help him with his farm of sweet wines. I want to be sure that the Queen has no objection." Yes, by God. He'd learned a lesson in Dumfries.

Thomasina tilted her head. "I will send you a message if there is a problem, Sir Robert. In the meantime…you'll do it?"

"I shall think about it," said Carey, "and then I shall give her an answer."

This was the Queen's invariable answer to anyone who wanted her to do anything at all, in particular marry. Thomasina knew that, too, and smiled briefly. He was joking. He had absolutely no choice in the matter.

He stood and bowed to the Queen's Fool.

When he and the page boy had put back the ladder and climbed carefully down, he was nearly knocked over by two swordsmen hacking at each other with theatrical gusto. He circled the fight, saw it was simply the first veney against the second veney, and slipped out of the tithe barn where he found Hughie waiting for him.

They walked back to Cumberland's camp. On the way, Carey spotted an elderly laundress with a big basket of shirts and bought a new shirt for Hughie from her on the spot, had him change into it, and gave her the old one to try and clean. It cost the same as fine linen would in London but was clearly some kind of hemp. Hughie seemed pleased. They walked on, Hughie admiring the whiteness of the shirtsleeves.

"Is it true," he asked, "that the Queen canna stand a man wi' a dirty shirt in her presence?"

"Very true," said Carey. "She's notorious for it." Hughie was chuckling. "What?"

"Ah wis just wondering if she'd ever met the King of Scotland?" Hughie sniggered and Carey had to laugh as well. In the unlikely event of Her Majesty the Queen ever being in the same room as the young King, who rarely even wiped his face, let alone washed his body or shifted his shirt, a hail of slippers and fans would be the least His Majesty of Scotland could expect. For certain his subsidy from the English Treasury would suddenly dry up.

Hughie carried on, shaking his head, to the tiring room while Carey went in search of somewhere relatively peaceful with good light so he could read the inquest papers.

saturday 16th september 1592, late afternoon

Carey was impressed when he looked at the work young Hughie had done on his doublet shoulders. The young man had unpicked the lining, taken out just enough of the padding and rearranged the rest to make room for Carey's extra sword muscles and then sewn it all up again as neat as you like. It seemed to be true he had been prenticed to a tailor.

"Well done, Hughie." He put the watch candle down and felt for his purse. There was still a bit of money in it so he gave Hughie sixpence for the job. The amount of money he had seemed to be going down with its usual alarming speed. He wasn't yet ready to encase himself in Court armour of velvet and pearls so he wandered out into the crowded afternoon.

The Earl of Cumberland's men had finished enclosing the whole orchard in a large marquee, laying boards between the trees. Some of the later-fruiting trees still had apples, pears, and golden quinces hanging on them which scented the whole tent. The ones that had already been picked were being decorated with hanging pomanders and little silk bags of comfits. The banquet tables were against the further wall of the tent and the more open part of the orchard had been completely boarded over, with the raspberry and blackcurrant canes taken out, to make a dance floor. Her Majesty would dance that evening in the light of the banks of candles being carefully set up in readiness, but only a couple of them were lit so far.

Meanwhile in the other corner the musicians were tuning up and arguing over the playlist while the men of the chapel were still practising. Carey stopped and listened—Thomasina was right, there were only two tenors and one of them clearly had a bad sore throat and a head cold.

He was just thinking he should go back to the cottage tiring room and shift his shirt and change to his Court suit, when Thomasina swept in, followed by her two women who towered over her.

She stood on a stool and bade the choirmaster have his men sing an air for her, a piece of music which was ruined by the tenors any time they had a line to sing above *doh*. Carey was shaking his head at his cousin's likely reaction to the singing and wondering why the chapel master didn't simply change the air for something in a lower key, when suddenly Thomasina skewered him with a look.

"Could you sing that line, Sir Robert?" she snapped.

Carey remembered too late that she'd said something about his voice, bowed and smiled. "I'm no great musician, mistress, and I'm sure the chapel master could find a much better…"

"He could if we were in Oxford or London, but not here where nobody can read music even if they can sing and we daren't let in any of the musicians from London. You can read pricksong, can't you?"

"Well, yes, but I…"

The brown button eyes glared again and Carey realised that there was probably some purpose to all this. He bowed again.

"I'll do my poor best, mistress."

He got some very haughty looks from the chapel men who were understandably nervous at the idea of a courtier singing with them. That nettled him. He knew he could sing and in fact music had been one of only a few childhood lessons that could compete with football.

He stepped up to the candle and took the handwritten sheet of paper, squinted at it. A little tricky, but not impossibly difficult.

Mr. Byrd had him sight-sing the entire piece solo to a lute, then grunted and took him through it with the chapel men several times. The result was much better, he knew. With the spine of the music held for them by his voice, they could manage the complex interweavings required of them.

"Hmm," said Mr. Byrd, "well done, Sir Robert, very accurate."

"This is new, isn't it? I feel sure I've never heard it before."

Mr. Byrd and Thomasina exchanged looks and Byrd bowed. "Thank you, sir, I have only just finished it."

Could it have anything to do with the death of Amy Robsart, then? Surely not. It was only a piece of music, an air in the Spanish style, magically worked by William Byrd, an excellent chapel master, perhaps even as good as his predecessor Mr. Tallis. True, he was a Catholic, but he had miraculously survived a brush with Walsingham's pursuivants in the early eighties and had amply repaid the Queen for her backing of him.

Carey hummed through the whole thing again while he went to try on his dancing clothes. It turned out that the trunkhose and cannions of the suit were also a little tight but would do for now. Hughie had done wonders with his hard-used boots— stuffed rosemary and rue into them, polished them with beeswax and tallow, made them verging on respectable.

He had a little time before he needed to be in the transformed orchard. The inquest report and coroner's report were, of course, written in Latin which had been a subject that had never once won a battle with football. He knew French very well, which gave him the Norman French you needed for legal documents, but he could only struggle and guess with Latin.

So he walked over to the small stone village church where the Queen's secretaries would set up their office. He spoke to the Queen's chief clerk, Mr. Hughes, asking for someone who knew Latin but wasn't too busy. Hughes gestured at the row of men standing at high folding desks, busy writing. Carey walked past them intending to ask one of the greybeards who were experienced and fast, but then he spotted the second-to-last man, a gawky spotty young creature whose worn grey wool doublet was older than he was from its fashion. The boy looked up and blinked at him short-sightedly. On impulse, he stopped.

"What's your name?"

"John Tovey, sir." He had a strong Oxford town accent.

"Can you translate this for me?"

The boy took the paper and blinked at it. "This is quite simple. Are you *sure* you need it translated, sir?"

Carey smiled. "You don't normally work for the Queen's clerks, do you?"

The boy blushed. "I'm...I'm the priest's son here," he stuttered, "I...I came to help to...to..."

The boy's fingers were inky and had a scholar's callus on the right index finger, so he probably was a genuine clerk.

Carey fished out another groat, a little less than a screever in London would have charged. "Go on," he said, "English it as quick as you can. I'm due at the dancing."

John Tovey nodded, gulped his large Adam's apple against his falling band, took the documents from Carey and spread them out on his desk in the pool of light made by his couple of candles. The light in the church was poor. What followed was remarkable enough that Carey blinked his eyes at it. The boy simply laid down a fresh piece of paper, picked up and dipped his pen and started scribbling, with his finger tracing along the lines of Latin. No muttering aloud, no scratching out, he just wrote down the English for the fiendish Latin.

Carey looked around at the whitewashed walls and carvings. It had been badly damaged at some time in the past, no doubt at the time of the stripping of the altars. There were headless statues and the windows were boarded up.

"Carey!" boomed a voice behind him and Carey spun to see a large boyish man with a curly red-blond beard and wearing an eye-watering combination of tawny slashed with white. His doublet was crusted with amber and topaz, the white damask sprinkled with diamond sparks.

Carey's left knee hit the tiles as he genuflected. "My lord Earl of Essex," he said formally, genuinely pleased to see his lord.

Robert Devereux, Earl of Essex, favourite of the Queen, bustled across the aisle to Carey, gesturing for him to stand and slung an arm across his shoulders. Essex was a couple of inches taller and at least a hand's breadth wider than Carey, who was neither short nor narrow. Essex was a man designed by God for the tourney and he loomed and laughed loudly.

"Sir Robert, how splendid! I thought you were still in Berwick chasing cattle raiders…"

"My noble father ordered me south, my lord," Carey said and on that thought, he remembered why he had been so anxious to see Essex. His stomach tightened. He had important information for the Earl about some investments of his and what Carey thought had really been going on. Unfortunately the news was very bad and Carey had been the Queen's messenger of bad news often enough that he was nervous about it.

"I heard about you being in some scandalous brawl in the Fleet Prison," said Essex. "What the devil have you been up to? Is it true you gave Mr. Vice Chamberlain Heneage a bloody nose?"

"It is, my lord," Carey said and told him an edited version of the last few weeks of activity. Some of it made Essex tip his head back and shake the church rafters with his bellow of laughter. John Tovey jumped like a startled cat at the noise.

"But it was the matter that happened later which brought me here, my lord," he added. "I wanted to talk to you about some lands you've bought in Cornwall…"

Essex's face suddenly shut down, switching from a handsome boy's face to something quite masklike.

"I don't own any lands in Cornwall."

"You don't?" Carey was shocked. He had been so certain that the code word Icarus meant the Earl of Essex.

"No. There was a man called Jackson hawking them about a few months ago—recusant lands with gold in 'em, he said—but I don't own any."

"That's wonderful news, my lord," Carey said, smiling with relief. "You were absolutely right not to buy. I was very concerned because the whole thing was a lay to coney-catch…people at Court." He had been on the verge of explaining his theory as to who had set the lay and why, but something stopped him. Essex wasn't looking at him and his arm was not heavy across his shoulders anymore.

"Hmm, shocking," said Essex vaguely. "Well, I didn't."

Alternatively, Essex had indeed bought the lands but had heard rumours already about their worthlessness and was lying about it in hopes of selling them on. Carey studied his face. Most courtiers, like Carey, shaved or trimmed their beards short to a goatee or a Spanish-style spade-shape. Essex, blessed with a luxuriant bush of red curls, grew it as nature wished and combed and oiled it every day. It left less of his face to read. For all his easy manner, Essex was a true courtier. Carey couldn't be certain if he was lying or not.

"I'm sure plenty of men at Court have been caught by Jackson's Papist lay, but not me," Essex added.

He had to do it. He had to warn Essex of the real source of the trouble, if only because his own fortunes were still bound up with Essex's.

"Perhaps Sir Robert Cecil will be disappointed," Carey said very quietly, in case any of the other clerks working away at the desks by candlelight as the light faded had been paid to listen.

Essex's blue gaze felt like a blow on the head, but then he looked at the boarded higher windows of the church.

"Yes, he always is, poor crookback."

Carey said nothing. Essex had been Burghley's ward as a boy and had grown up with Burghley's second son, Robert, who had suffered from rickets as a child. It had never been very likely that they would be friends.

"So," boomed Essex, "what are you here for, Sir Robert?"

Carey paused before he answered because he wanted Essex to help with the Queen's impossible order. "I'm hoping for my fee for the deputy wardenship," he explained, "but Her Majesty wants me to do something else first."

Essex grunted sympathetically enough and allowed himself to be drawn outside the church walls and into the watery dregs of afternoon. Clouds were marching up from the west in great armies which didn't bode well for the dancing later.

He explained the whole circumstance and Essex shook his head. "Jesu, rather you than me," he said. "That's a nasty matter."

"Did your stepfather ever tell you anything about it?"

Essex shook his head vigorously. "No, nothing. Wouldn't even let his first wife be named in his presence."

"Your lady mother?" Carey asked cautiously. "Did she… er…?"

"You'd think she'd have been jealous of Amy Robsart, as my stepfather's first love, but she wasn't. She was jealous, exceedingly. But not of Amy Robsart."

Carey said nothing. They both knew the woman Lettice Knollys had real cause to hate.

"I'll be seeing my lady mother later," Essex said. "I'll mention it to her if you like."

"That would be very kind, my lord. I need all the help you can give. But surely the Dowager Lady won't be coming to Court?"

"No, no, of course not, the Queen won't have her. But she's staying in Oxford at the moment so I'll see what I can do…"

That was hopeful—if the Earl remembered his promise and if he actually kept it. Carey thought of mentioning Emilia's suit, but then decided not to. After all, she hadn't yet even offered him a proper fee for the introduction to Essex. There was a nervous cough behind him. Carey turned back to see John Tovey standing there in his worn grey doublet, holding a close-written piece of paper and looking scared.

"Mr. Tovey," said Carey affably, "Have you finished?"

"Y…y…yes," stuttered the boy."D…did you want me to sign the copy?"

Carey shook his head, took the translation and read it carefully; a little to his surprise, some of the Latin had meant what he had guessed it did. As the Earl was still standing there, avid with curiosity, Carey passed it to him and he read it, too.

"It all seems in order, Sir Robert. The jury found it was an accidental death."

Carey was so surprised to hear Essex say this that he looked carefully to see if the Earl was joking. No, there was no twinkle in the blue eyes, no smile, but no puzzled frown either. Essex saw nothing wrong with the accounts at all.

"Yes, my lord," he said after a moment's thought and didn't say any of the things that had struck him forcibly even while he had been struggling with the Latin. He caught John Tovey's eye and saw from the terror there that the boy knew who Amy Robsart was and had spotted what he had in the dry legal phrases. So he had better deal with that.

"I must go and meet the Queen," said Essex. "I'll do what I can for you, Sir Robert. I'll arrange for you to talk to my lady mother—I'm sure she'll be very happy to do it. But best not to mention the...er...the property business to her. She won't be interested and might take it into her fluffy head to buy some, eh?"

There was an unfilial wink and a laugh and then the Earl turned and strode out of the churchyard, letting the gate bang behind him. Carey bowed to him as he went, honestly impressed at how well the Earl could fake genuine amusement. So that was who had bought up the Cornish recusant lands, was it? Of course Lettice Knollys' son would have done the business for his lady mother. It made a lot of sense. Carey wondered if Sir Robert Cecil yet knew that detail—he would undoubtedly find out. Perhaps it would be a good idea for Carey to be the first to tell him? Or perhaps not. He would likely be annoyed, and Carey didn't want Cecil to know how much he knew about the Jackson affair. Though he probably did.

Carey sighed at the weary complexity of Court life and turned to John Tovey, who was still standing there like a post, mouth open, Adam's apple working every so often. His spots were more visible in the dull daylight, but he had done a creditable and more importantly fast job on the Latin. Carey sat down on the stone bench looking over the churchyard, the only part of the village not being camped on or grazed by the Court or its animals.

"Mr. Tovey, how old are you?"

"T…twenty, I think, sir."

"Are you looking for a place as a clerk?"

The boy flushed—he was almost certainly not twenty but a couple of years younger at least.

"Er…yes. Yes, I am, sir."

That was why rootless, penniless, but educated young men would come and clerk for the Queen on progress—in hopes of a cushy office job with perks. Some of them weren't disappointed.

"What can you do?"

"I…I…can read and translate Greek, Latin, Italian, French, and write good secretary hand and italic as well. I can cast up accounts in Arabic figures and I…I know something of medicine and herbs."

"Your father?"

"Is…the priest here. He taught me first and then, after I was prenticed to an Oxford 'pothecary, I went as a servitor at Magdalen, though at first they wouldn't have me."

"Why not?" There was a pause while the boy blushed ruby red and stuttered.

"I'm a b…b…bastard, sir."

"Is that all? So's my father. Did yours acknowledge you?"

"Yes, sir, but he never married my mother for fear of the Queen. She…er…she d…d…doesn't like priests to marry."

"Your mother?"

"Is dead, sir. A few years ago."

"And you want to leave Rycote, seek your fortune?" He must, look at the place!

The boy flushed dark, gulped, and nodded convulsively once.

"Excellent. Would you like to work for me, Mr. Tovey, as my clerk? It would involve coming with me to Carlisle, I'm afraid."

"Where's that, sir?"

"A long way north. Next door to Scotland."

"Oh." A pause. Then another convulsive nod. Carey stepped closer, put his hand on the boy's shoulder and gripped. "Well then, if your father gives permission, I will be your good lord if you agree to be my man."

The boy nodded and said "Yes, sir," firmly enough. They shook hands on it. As it wasn't a hiring fair there was no need to go and pay fees or sign indentures, though for form's sake Carey intended to talk to the lad's father. He hadn't at all meant to recruit a clerk as well as a henchman, despite his hatred of paperwork. However he had to do something about what Tovey had read and unexpectedly understood. Bribing him sufficiently would cost a lot more than simply paying him wages every so often. And, anyway, if the boy was telling the truth about his accomplishments, he'd be getting a very good University clerk out of it.

"We'll go and see your father, shall we? Get his permission? Do you know where he might be?"

"In the alehouse," shrugged the boy. "He won't care."

They passed the place on the way back to the orchard and young Tovey was correct: his reverend father was drunk, playing quoits with the blacksmith, the miller, and the butcher. Once he understood what his base-born son was telling him, he was blurrily delighted that Carey was employing the boy without his even having to pay a shilling for the office. Tovey knelt for his father's blessing and got a wave of the hand and a few mumbles for it.

The boy asked if he could go back to the church to finish some work for Mr. Hughes and be paid for it. This was entirely reasonable and saved Carey from having to find somewhere for the boy to sleep since the clerks always dossed down where they worked. The dusk was coming down fast and the air crisping as he strode to the orchard.

Carey didn't really want to go and dance, even if there had been any chance of dancing with Emilia again. But he had to, if only to kneel to the Queen as part of the crowd and make sure she saw him. Mistress Thomasina had kindly given him an excellent way of being conspicuous without importunity. But his head was buzzing with the implications of the inquest findings into the thirty-two-year-old death of Amy Robsart. No wonder the jury had taken a full year to report, and had done so in such a way as to satisfy both conscience and, no doubt, covert influence from the Queen, Dudley, and who knew where else? The whole pile of papers must have been quietly buried in the Oxford town muniment room. It was lucky Thomasina had been able to find it and give him a copy. He was a little surprised they hadn't been burned in a mysterious fire. Did she know what was in them? Maybe not; she wouldn't understand Latin.

Back in the little tiring room, Carey waited until Mr. Simmonds had come out, clad in a smartly brushed buffcoat with his cloak over his arm, ready to attend Cumberland at the dance. His Court suit was hanging up ready, smelling of rose petal powder with the clean shirt he had managed to pack in his hunting satchel when he left Somerset House the day before. He had kept it carefully for exactly this chance. He sniffed his armpits and frowned. Could he wash anywhere? Riding forty miles in a day was a sweaty business and he'd ridden in from Oxford in the morning as well.

There would be stews in Oxford for the naughty students, but none here in the little village. There would be hip baths in Norris' manor house which the Queen and her ladies would use. No doubt Essex was stepping into something organised for him right now. Where was Cumberland? A small pack of boys ran past him downhill, shouting in excitement about something going on in the duck pond.

He shucked his hunting doublet and hose, left them hanging on another peg. Scratching fleabites from the last night at the inn, Carey ambled barefoot in his shirt down toward the village duck pond, singing the tune he'd just learnt.

A grey-bearded man in a sober black doublet and gown suddenly turned and stared at him as if he had spoken, then hurried after him.

"Sir," he said, "that tune. Did Heron Nimmo teach it to you?"

"Eh?" said Carey, irritated at being interrupted in his thoughts, "No, the Queen's chapel master. Why?"

The man flushed and bowed. "My apologies, sir, I mistook you for a friend."

"I don't know anybody called Heron Nimmo. You should enquire of Mr. Byrd, perhaps. The Lord Chamberlain, my father, might know him if he's a musician?"

The man bowed again, muttered to himself, hurried away. Carey sauntered on down to the duck pond. He found Cumberland and half the Court there, busily wading into the pond and the stream feeding it and washing as best they could.

Villagers were lining the banks and watching with gaping mouths. Some of them were women, peeking round hedges and clutching each other and giggling. Grinning at the sight of the richest and most powerful men in the country splashing about naked in cold water for fear of a fussy woman of fifty-nine, Carey stripped off his own shirt, hung it on a post, and waded in.

The water made him gasp but it was quite refreshing. You had to be careful because the stones on the bottom were covered in weed and very slippery. Cumberland saw him and whistled.

"Christ, Sir Robert, who tried to slit your ribs?"

Carey looked down at the purple scar he had collected in the summer and completely forgotten about.

"A Scotsman with a knife. Cost me £20 to get my black velvet doublet mended afterward."

Cumberland laughed. "Where is he now?"

"In Hell, my lord, where do you think?" Carey answered coolly, since he had in fact killed his man to the great approval of the assembled Carlislers. The inquest on that death had taken twenty minutes and found it lawful killing in self-defence.

Cumberland slapped him on the back and offered him soap, which Carey took. Just in that moment, as he bent to wash his armpits in the water, he half-heard a familiar sound and his body instinctively clenched and ducked, well before his mind could tell him what it was.

His foot caught on a slippery stone and he went over sideways with a splash, swamping Cumberland and two other Court sprigs, one of whom had been silly enough to put his clean shirt back on before he was well away from the water. Pure reflex made him grab the nearest thing from underwater, which unfortunately happened to be the Earl of Cumberland's leg. That took the Earl over as well.

Cumberland came up again, blowing water with weeds on his head, the light of battle in his eyes. Carey had to dive sideways to avoid a very accomplished wrestling grab by the Earl, which meant his shoulder went into the legs of somebody else and took him down as well.

The whole scene degenerated into a wrestling free-for-all. Carey climbed out of the shouting, splashing, yelling clump of nobility as soon as he could, quickly soaped his armpits and then was well-rinsed by the Earl of Cumberland pulling him back into the pond and dunking him. It took a very nice break-free taught him by Dodd to get out of the Earl's expert grip so he could use a willow branch to haul himself up and cough water.

The entire village was now gathered to watch the fun, including the quoits players, vigorous betting going on and the boys cheering on their favourites while the village dogs barked their heads off. The noise was amazing which meant Carey could speak quietly to get under the sound and penetrate to the Earl of Cumberland before he could be thrown again.

"Look there," he said, pointing.

Cumberland stopped laughing suddenly, frowned. They waded across, shoving wrestlers out of their way to a willow root on the far side where some highly offended ducks were hiding as far up the tree as they could get in their webbed feet.

A crossbow bolt was buried deep in the wood, the notch bright and new.

That was the sound he'd heard. The snick of a crossbow trigger being released. He and Cumberland looked at each other. The bolt was an ordinary one from a hunting bow. Not one for small game, but for deer. The bolt was a good six inches long, heavy and sharp. If it had hit him it would probably have killed him.

"I was wondering what you thought you were doing," said Cumberland thoughtfully. "Thank you, Sir Robert."

True, it could have been aimed at the Earl and not at him; they had been close enough together. And Cumberland too had enemies, notably the Spanish and the French and probably some inherited Border feuds as well. But when Carey felt which way the bolt's tail was pointing and traced the line of its flight across the stream, he thought it was at chest height where he had been standing in the moment he heard the trigger. Behind him had been a low wall and some bushes. Carey waded back across the pond as the wrestlers calmed themselves and started climbing out and drying themselves. Bets were being settled. He peered over the wall. The ground was soft but well printed with many feet and no way of telling among them.

"Or do you think it was you he was after?" The Earl was already on the bank, rubbing himself down with a linen towel. Carey shrugged and followed him, hoping to use the towel as well since he hadn't brought one.

"I don't know, my lord," he said, blinking at the tree where the crossbow bolt was buried.

"Well, it wasn't an accident, that's sure," Cumberland said, handing him the dank towel. "With a bolt that size, whoever shot it wasn't after duck."

Carey shivered suddenly but only because he was wet and the sun was setting. He rubbed himself briskly, finished, and pulled his shirt back on. Typically the Earl was now chuckling and shaking his head so his earring flashed.

"By God, Carell's done ye some good. That was fast. Do you find a lot people trying to kill you at the moment, eh?"

"Well yes, my lord, I understand the Grahams have my head priced at £10 in Dumfries."

Cumberland hooted. "Not nearly enough, the skinflints. I'll tell 'em to put it up to £50 at least."

"Your lordship is too kind," Carey said smiling, although he still felt cold. That was far away on the Borders where he rarely went anywhere without a padded jack reinforced with steel plates on his back, and Dodd behind him. For God's sake, this was Oxfordshire in fat, soft southern England. It wasn't supposed to happen, whoever the assassin had been aiming at. And who the hell had tried it?

Emilia Bonnetti was dousing herself in expensive rosewater to clean herself as there were no such things as proper baths in this peasant bog. She knew how persnickety the old English Queen was and had an intricately smocked fresh shift to wear under her stays. Her beautiful crimson silk gown had been left in Ireland, alas, that goddamned hellhole of a country. No doubt some uncouth chieftain's wife was wearing it now. Dante Aligheri was completely wrong: Hell was a green boggy place where the air was constantly damp from the equally constant rain and the people were charming, intelligent, sometimes remarkably good-looking but lethally unpredictable. Only God knew how near a thing it had been for herself and her husband; only she knew how nearly they had died.

She had borrowed a dancing gown from the wife of one of the musicians who probably made a very good thing out of it, seeing what the woman charged. The gown was tawny, which did not suit her colouring at all but would have to do as there was no choice. Her slippers were also borrowed, a different shade of tawny, and didn't fit properly.

She was in a peasant's main room, getting dressed with the few other women at Court who were neither ladies-in-waiting nor maids of honour; they were wives of lesser courtiers mainly. Maids of honour, pfui. Dishonour, more like. Emilia had heard of Raleigh's proceedings with Bess Throckmorton and was shocked. She had been a virgin when she married and it had taken some work to stay intact when her cousins came calling. However, once you were legally married and had given your man an heir, it didn't matter in the least what you did, in her view. Bonnetti himself was well aware of what she did and they often planned one of her campaigns together over a jug of their wine. On her part, she ignored his activities with chambermaids. They were excellent business partners. The wine made good profits when everything went well and the customers actually paid up; much more profitable was the trade in information. The barrels of goods and gold that went back to the Hague to pay for the wine would often have secret compartments with coded news in them from Signor Bonnetti to keep the stupid English Customs and Excise men and the pursuivants happy. Her own methods were better.

Tonight she had two quarries: one she had taken before, the tall chestnut-headed, disgracefully handsome cousin of the Queen, with his piercing blue eyes and his (she had to admit) quite polished manners. The other…well, she would have to be very careful not to actually catch that one or the whole plan would be ruined. She had only to wing him slightly, as it were.

Once that had happened…She pulled the corner of her eyes and carefully brushed on kohl to make them seem even darker. She never used belladonna for that purpose as she liked to be able to see what she was doing.

A lady's tiring maid was sewing in place the unfashionable square neck and small lawn ruff that stood up awkwardly behind her head. Even the woman's small attendance had cost her tuppence, for God's sake.

Emilia's hair was in an artful chignon—that had taken her hours to achieve—partly covered by a lacy little cap and her jaunty hat with a pheasant feather in it.

She had no pattens to protect her slippers from the mud, but Oxford's men had laid old rush mats on the path to the large tent that covered the orchard. The English were good at that kind of artifice because of their miserable climate. That whole part of the village was already filling with brightly dressed people, though the candles weren't lit yet. The banquet wasn't set either but you could hear the musicians tuning up.

It certainly wasn't time to arrive, so she retreated again and watched from the open horn window as the activity gradually built to a crescendo. She was watching for one man in particular, that chestnut-headed son of a king's bastard, an espionage plum she meant to pluck.

Emilia bit her bottom lip and frowned. Every time she thought of him, her stomach fizzed like a firework with anger and…well, yes, with desire. She was far too old and experienced to imagine that she was feeling love, but Jesu, her brain stopped working properly every time she looked at him.

No. She must concentrate. She had two aims. One was to be introduced to the Earl of Essex and begin the delicate process of impressing, attracting, and befriending him. She didn't know how much M. le deputé would want for that valuable connection—of course he hadn't mentioned a price, was himself far too wily.

She had had to leave her best pearl necklace with the musician's wife as a deposit and most of her bracelets and rings had been hocked either in Dublin or Oxford. At least she had her new gold and garnet necklace from George around her neck. Could she find something else Carey wanted? Perhaps? She hoped so.

Her fingers fumbled a little as she drew on her small kid gloves and pick up her fan. She had put extra red lead on her cheeks, knowing she would appear sallow in this goddamned tawny velvet that the pink and insipid Englishwomen liked so well. She had artless black ringlets escaping down her neck and a stylish hat…and she had herself.

And she would have Carey that night.

saturday 16th september 1592, afternoon

Henry Dodd rode Whitesock and the mare into the main inn-yard at Bicester on Saturday afternoon and hired the luxury of a whole room to himself. He saw to his animals, ate steak and kidney pudding in the common room, and had a mug of aqua vitae to settle him for bed.

Then the barman looked sideways at him and asked, "Where's your warrant, then what gets you half-price for booze?"

"Ah…" said Dodd, this being the first he'd heard of a warrant.

"Your horse has the Queen's brand on him," said the barman, frowning. "Stands to reason you've got a warrant unless you've prinked the pony."

That sounded like something that meant "steal." Dodd frowned back. "No, I haven't." And in his view, he hadn't. He'd received the horse quite rightfully in the course of settling a dispute with the horse's previous owner, but they might not look at things sensibly down here in the mysterious South where nobody spoke properly or seemed to care what surname a man bore.

"Ay," said Dodd, drinking his brandy, "Ah'm riding wi' a message from ma Lady Hunsdon to her husband the Lord Chamberlain."

Later he would remember the man sitting by the fire with a gaunt hawklike face and a wide-brimmed hat who looked up at that. At the time he didn't properly notice.

"Hmm. Where are you from anyway?"

"Berwick," lied Dodd on general principles. None of the soft Southrons had heard of Carlisle and there was nothing wrong with a little misdirection. Especially as he didn't of course have any kind of warrant with him at all. For good measure he added, "I serve the Lord Chamberlain's son, Sir Robert Carey."

The barman was wiping the bar now, still not looking at him. Dodd smiled and lifted his mug to him, paid for his board and went upstairs. He was still dressed as a gentleman in a smart grey wool suit of Sir Robert Carey's and he carried a sword, but nobody knew better than him that he was in fact, thank God, no kind of gentleman at all and never would be. He was a tenant farmer and Sergeant of Gilsland, in charge of one troop of the Carlisle guard, that was all.

By the South's ridiculous way of looking at things, he had in fact stolen one of the Queen's horses from the Queen's vice chamberlain and he had no intention of explaining the circumstances to anyone at all until he had caught up with that bloody man Carey. He got into a bed that didn't smell too bad and fell asleep instantly.

He woke in the darkest part of the night with the thought "Time to go," ringing through his head.

He dressed quietly, getting better at putting on his complicated suit. Moonlight shone through the luxurious Southern panes of glass. Holding his boots, he went to the door, unbarred it, and found it had been locked on the outside.

"Och," he said disgustedly and sat on the bed. No doubt there was someone sleeping on the other side of that door, waiting for him. Perhaps it was something to do with the damned warrant the barman had asked about. He went to the small glass window that opened onto the courtyard, which he knew had a gate that would also be locked at this time. The stables were directly below on this side of it, the kitchens on the other side. He needed at least one horse.

No help for it. Perhaps it was a pity to mess up the comfortable little room but there was really no help for it. From the moon's position he thought he had a couple of hours until dawn so best to get started.

Softly he tapped the floorboards—too solid. Then he tapped the wall between him and the next room. Withies, lightly plastered. He hadn't an axe but he did have a broadsword which he would now have to sharpen.

It took some strength and sweat to do it quietly, but he broke through the plaster low down behind the bed, smelling of where the bedbugs had their hiding places and then through the withies on his side, pulled them outward to a panicked exodus of creepy crawlies. The filling was only rubbish and then there were the withies for the wall on the other side. Working as quietly as he could, a giant rat up to no good, he weakened them with his sword and broke them, brought kindling over from beside the luxurious fireplace and built it up against them. Then he lit the tallow dip from the watchlight and lit the small bonfire. He had some aqua vitae left so he sprinkled it about around the fire to catch when it got hot enough.

He sat back on his haunches and watched the flames catch, enjoying the sight as always, the feeling of power as fire flowered where it shouldn't, then caught himself and pulled on his boots, buckled his sadly blunted sword on his hip and picked up his hat.

The flames were climbing the wall and had gone partly through. He took the jack of ale left on the table and kicked through the wall bellowing "Fire! Fire!"

A fat man in his shirt and two boys sharing the trundle bed in the next room started up, all shouting with fright. Somebody further away took up the shout.

Dodd slung ale all around the fire, but not on it, kicked some more of the wall, put his hat on his head and ducked through the flaming hole he'd made into the next room where the fat man was desperately scrabbling on his breeches and trying to move his strong box. The two boys had already opened the door and run. Dodd went through onto the landing, found a big man lying across his door just waking up and kicked him twice in the cods.

Then he went back to the merchant. "Shall I help ye carry that, sir?" he asked politely, speaking as Southern as possible.

"Yes, yes..."

So he and the fat man in his breeks and shirt carefully carried the interestingly heavy locked box onto the landing, down the stairs crowded with other frightened customers, some of them in very fine velvets half put on.

He took the lead, elbowed through the throng, and helped carry the box out into the courtyard where there was a fine mizzle. It must have been dry recently for the thatch over his room was well alight now, billows of smoke going up and the rats coming out of the roof squeaking. The innkeeper was straining to open the big gates to let his neighbours in to help.

"Thank you, sir," puffed the merchant, "If I may give you..."

"Nay sir, glad tae help, I must see after my horse now."

Dodd slipped away from the man and went into the stables where a brave but stupid boy was trying to lead the horses out without blindfolding them first.

Dodd went to his own nag and put his hat across the beast's eyes and put the bridle on. "See ye," he said to the frightened boy struggling in the next stall with a rearing kicking mare, "Dinna let them see and they'll let ye help them."

The boy put his statute cap across the mare's eyes and she started to calm down. Dodd got another bridle from the wall and put it over her head. He couldn't bring himself to grab a different horse, seeing as how none of them was a patch on Whitesock. The boy had followed his advice and managed to bridle two more horses.

"Ah'll take them out," he said to the boy who was coughing hard and disappearing as the smoke filled the stable. "Just unhitch the others and drive 'em before ye, then stay out of the stables."

The hayloft above was likely to catch soon and Dodd didn't want the lad on his conscience as well. Then, slowly and gently, Dodd took four snorting horses through the door and out into the courtyard where he let all but Whitesock get away from him. They helpfully caused much more confusion there along with two hysterical dogs and an escaped pig, and disrupted the bucket chain. Bless the mare for her common sense; she headed straight for the open gate and he swung himself up on Whitesock shouting, "I'll fetch her back!" and galloped straight out of the gate and up the road, leaving the other horses for dust and catching the mare's reins as he passed her.

Two miles up the road in the darkness he could still see the glow of the fire and could hear no hooves behind him. He started to laugh then. Well, it was funny. Here in the South nobody seemed to have the least idea about anything. Imagine thinking that locking the door on him would stop him?

saturday 16th september 1592, evening

Hughie's ears were burning as Carey praised him for the work he'd done on that Court doublet. It had been a pleasure really; it was a lovely piece of work by a fine London tailor. It would be a pity to put a knife through it, and quite difficult as well because of the quadruple thickness, the heavy embroidery and pearls, the padding. So he wouldn't do that.

Carey changed his shirt and left the other on the floor as he hopped about putting on his hose. Hughie helped him into the canions and trunkhose, held up by a waistcoat of damask. The doublet weighed many pounds, Carey went "ooff" and made a wry face as his shoulders took the weight, though he must be used to wearing a jack that weighed much more at about fifty pounds. Hughie then had to tie and retie the points at Carey's back three or four times to get them at exactly the right length so that they held the doublet and trunkhose together but allowed him to dance. Carey took his long jewelled poinard, having left his workmanlike broadsword in the Cumberland armoury.

Hughie coughed. "Will Ah be attendin' ye at the dancing, sir?" he asked. He had brushed his woollen doublet and cannions, just in case. Carey's answer was a swift critical glance, sweeping Hughie head to toe and somehow making him blush again. There was a curt nod. It seemed Hughie passed muster.

They walked with a herd of other gallantly overdressed young men to the orchard which was now a glowing palace, the fruit still left on the trees making a sweet fresh scent to battle with the rose-scented candles and the raucous smell of men and wine.

The musicians sat and stood in a corner on the new boards of the dance floor. They were playing loudly—it would be a noisy night as the boards creaked and thundered under the boots and slippers of the Court.

Of course all the local gentlefolk were there with their unmarried daughters and sisters—the women tricked out in as much costly splendour as the men or indeed more, wearing tokens of their dowries. They gathered in shy drifts near the banquet tables and the high stands of candles.

The Queen wasn't there yet, nor were the great lords of her Court—the Earls of Essex, Oxford, Cumberland. Carey hesitated as he looked at the groups of henchmen and courtiers and then made some kind of decision, took up a place near the Earl of Essex's men. He started talking to a man with a sharp Welsh face.

Hughie stood behind him near the canvas wall, watching carefully, wishing his Edinburgh doublet was better fashion since all the other servingmen were very fine in good wool or even velvets with brocade trim.

Many of Essex's henchmen were in tangerine and white which suited nobody except the ones who were rosily ginger, and not really even them, Hughie thought critically.

They all waited, talking quietly while the music tinkled in the background, conducted by a short round man. Every so often he would pick up and play a different instrument.

Hughie jumped. Trumpets had sounded, the short man stood up and waved his arms, there was a rustle of tension, the sound of boots on boards. Hughie craned to see the red and gold livery of the Gentlemen Pensioners of Her Majesty's Guard. They fanned out and stood by the entrances and by the carved wooden seat with an awning of brocade lions set at the end of the dance floor.

Hughie was expecting the Queen next, but it was a herd of women, to the sound of pipes and viols. They were arm in arm, some of them older, eight of them juicy and pert in their teens and all wearing the Queen's black and white colours, designed to their taste. It was a fine sight and interesting for the mixture of French and Spanish fashion, with the big wheel farthingales coming in now even in Scotland.

The music stopped. More trumpeting. Men were shouting "The Queen! The Queen!"

Hughie blinked. A broad long man in dazzling white with red hair and an impressive beard paced in slowly, leaning down to someone much shorter in black velvet and white damask blazing with jewels and pearls, who had her heavily ringed white hand tucked in the crook of his arm.

In a smooth sweeping motion, the whole mob of people in the tent went to both their knees. Nearly falling over, Hughie did the same, squinting to see the cause of it clearly.

Through the lanes of cramoisie, green, black, tawny, rose, and even daring sky blue, all the men with their hats off, went…

A smallish elderly woman entered wearing a bright red wig sparkled with diamonds and a small gold and pearl crown, different-coloured ribbons all over her black velvet gown with a huge Spanish farthingale under it. Her face was white with red cheekbones and her eyes snapping and sparkling black as they looked about around her people. Hughie's blood went cold as he realised he still had his hat on and scrabbled it off before she could see, leaving his hair standing up on end. The penetrating gaze swept past and didn't seem to have spotted him.

There was a loud shout of "God save the Queen!" and all the people shouted it three times.

The Queen walked to the chair under her cloth of estate, turned about as she let go of the big man's arm, smiled down at her kneeling courtiers.

"My lords, ladies, gentlemen, and goodmen," she said in a penetrating contralto voice. "We thank you for your loving greeting and attendance upon us and hereby order you all to your feet in our presence, so we may enjoy the dancing arranged for our entertainment by our well-loved Lord Norris and Earl of Cumberland." A round-faced man with a worried look stood up and bowed low to her. The Queen clapped her hands.

"Up, up, on your feet, all of you, never mind your knees," she said with a magical smile. "What shall we have first, Mr. Byrd? A coranto?"

The short fat man bowed and pointed two fingers. The musicians started up the dance-measure as the lines of courtiers quickly sorted themselves.

Hughie had no idea how to dance Court dances, though he could give a good account of himself at the Edinburgh fair day, which put him in mind of something he had done for Lord Spynie once at a Court dance and that had worked very nicely. Everybody had thought that the fat burgher, whose daughter Spynie had taken a fancy to, had gone outside for air and then died suddenly of a fit sent by God in punishment for his avarice.

Hughie watched as Carey joined the lines of dancers, smiling and talking to the small dark Welshman on his left. Hughie sidled along the wall to be nearer the musicians. He wanted a metal harp or lute string, that was all. You never knew when you might get the opportunity to earn your gold.

saturday 16th september 1592, evening

Emilia watched Sir Robert Carey and calculated where she stood among the other women so she would be his partner for the measures halfway through the country dance that was next. Oddly enough, her prey seemed not to have noticed her yet. Perhaps he was being coy.

She fluttered her fan across her face, the last crimson remnant of what had worked for him in Scotland and smiled to him under her lashes. He acknowledged her with a polite tilt of his head but that was all. Had he been gelded by the Scots then?

She took hands with the provincial English girls on either side of her in their ugly provincial English gowns, stepped forward, stepped back, her borrowed velvet rocking around her hips with the other women's careful farthingales, stepped sideways, stepped back, such a boring dance, thank God she had a mind that learned such things easily, stepped forward, take hands with a spotty boy that had used far too much white lead on the spots, spin, dance a measure with him, spin again and back to the women's line, and so along by two partners.

At the far end she knew the Queen was in the line of women and at the other end was the ginger man, Essex, her mignon and no doubt her paramour, the wicked old bitch.

And step forward and back and sideways again. That bad man Cumberland was giving one of the prettier provincial girls the kind of smile he had given her across a hall in Dublin, and that was unfair, the use of a culverin to sink a rowing boat, for the girl was stricken by it like a rabbit at a fox. Perhaps she would be well-guarded by her menfolk.

Emilia sighed, spun, danced, stepped forward and back and then, quite unexpectedly, there was M. le deputé who had so helpfully and expensively sold her guns for Ireland. Well, he had sold them to her stupid husband who had been too excited at the thought of blackmailing the Queen's nephew to check them properly and so nearly brought about not just their deaths, which Emilia could perhaps have forgiven from Purgatory, but much worse, their ruin.

She smiled at him and wished for a feathered mask. He looked down at her gravely, spun her, danced, spun her again and all with the most depressing propriety.

Damn, damn, damn him, he was playing hard to get because there was a clear admission of guilt in his humorously raised eyebrow and the sparkle in his so-blue eyes.

Jesu, what an annoying man. Her stomach was fizzing again; she was lusting after him like one of the stupid provincial girls. That was not at all the way to do it. He was supposed to be hot for her, not the other way around. However there was no question that she wanted more of what he had so scandalously and lustily given her in Scotland. She definitely wanted him. When they danced, her whole body had risen to him, trout to a lure. Goddamn him.

She smiled again with particular lasciviousness at the next man to spin her round, a willowy youth in pearl-grey satin. And then she quite consciously stopped herself. She had to bank her fires so they could work where they were really needed. But she still needed that valuable introduction to the Earl of Essex. Her satisfaction for the guns would have to wait. It was lucky she had a secret contact here.

She paced forward and back and sideways again and found herself dancing with the Earl of Essex himself, now in white satin and white velvet, sparked with diamonds, trimmed in gold. He blanked her completely. Should she dare to ask? No, the music was too loud and the Queen would see. She had to take the normal route, through Carey or another follower of the Earl. Damn. Of course, that was why Carey was playing hard to get, he had been ten years a courtier. He knew his worth.

She let the moment pass. At the last measure, cleverly timed, the Queen and Essex danced together. The Queen was a good dancer, light and brisk on her feet. Then Essex expertly played the part of a man in love and leaned solicitously over a woman at least thirty years senior to him, who giggled and flirted and Holy Madonna, had her stays scandalously low and her hair uncovered by a cap, as if a maid of fourteen. Disgusting!

The two bowed and curtseyed to each other—the Queen not very much and the Earl a great deal from his great height and the other dancers all clapped.

Emilia's feet were already sore and pinched in their borrowed dancing slippers and much-darned silk stockings. What could she bribe the Deputy with if not herself? She had only received one good necklace so far from Cumberland and it looked as if she would have to say goodbye to it now.

Hmm. She moved toward the broad-shouldered lad whom Carey had had at his back when he came in, instead of the lanky dour-faced man he had in Scotland. This one had a square raw-boned face and seemed only quarter-witted, but was wearing an Edinburgh cut doublet. He had been hanging around near the musicians, who weren't bad at all, considering. Now the youth was at the back, near the bowls of wine and mead, watching for the signal from his master.

It came—Carey caught his eye and made a move with his hand. The youth bowed slightly, turned and poured wine into a plain silver goblet he was holding. He took a quick mouthful, surprisingly well-trained to Court ways, then brought it over to his master, a small towel on his arm and offered it with a bow. Carey drank it off.

Then he turned to bow to the Queen, who said something to him that made him tense. Emilia was getting used to English after becoming quite proficient at the barbaric tongue of Scotch—the two languages were brothers after all. She was sure the Queen had said something about singing. Carey bowed again and moved through the crowds to the musicians where the men of the chapel were lining up to sing. Carey stood at the end of the row, took a sheet of music and squinted at it. He looked very odd there, gaudy in his pearls next to the plain chapel men with their black robes and white collars.

The fat music master was explaining the music, Emilia thought, saying something about writing it that very afternoon and would Her Majesty care to hear his poor rough first attempt sung for the very first time? The Queen inclined her head, said something which caused sycophantic titters of laughter among the courtiers.

Carey smiled like a man accepting a challenge to duel, opened his mouth, waited for the beat, and sang the opening, perfectly on the note. The boy-sopranos speared their way into his line and the bassos, other tenors, and altos came in. It was a Spanish air, newly set in the modern Italian way, but she hadn't heard it before. It was somehow both sprightly and wistful.

The words were English and didn't quite fit...she didn't understand them. Emilia closed her eyes. It had such a sound of the South, of the Mediterranean, you could almost smell the olive trees and dust in it, the hot dry sun in it. Ah, the sun.

Something made her look at one of the musicians at the back of the group. He seemed transfixed, a handsome greybeard, he had stopped playing his viol. A tear was tracking its way down his creased cheek.

Emilia turned away at once as the music casually knotted her throat. She had to catch a tear out of the corner of her eye with the corner of her handkerchief before it caused her kohl to smear. What had she seen there in that old man's face? Shocked surprise, then something raw, something full of longing. Did the air remind him, too, of olive trees and sunlight like a golden knife? Or perhaps of something else, a lover? Her tear had come from her longing for her children, not any stupid man, of course. They were lost to her, locked in their convent, unless she could bring off the coup she needed. Bonnetti didn't care because he was a man, he could get more. She would not.

Someone was singing solo now. The tune was complex but he had support from the pipes. Someone with a very fine strong voice, a clear tenor that allowed the notes to flow like water.

It was M. le député again. There he stood, sight-singing the complex tenor line and the bassos coming in again now to wind about the stem of his voice like dark green snakes.

There was another damned tear in her eye. Again! Because his voice did bring the blue blue sky of the South with it, somehow, the vivid intense lapis lazuli that you never saw in the grey North and she missed it and she missed her children....

She could not even cough. She had to stop breathing. She caught that tear, too, no more please, M. le deputé, my heart will not stand it and in any case it's all your fault that I'm still here in the Northern wastes.

Thank God the boys were singing now, one of them sharp from nerves, the men, too, weaving and parting and finally coming in sequence to an end against Carey's sustained note.

Just a little silence afterward, that heartbeat of silence the people needed to bring themselves back from the land of music, the highest compliment any audience could give. Then ordinary applause, the Queen smiling and clapping her embroidered gloves as well.

The adult musicians were grudgingly approving, the boys staring up at the Courtier. The senior chapel man shook Carey's hand. The Queen said something that sounded complimentary about her cousin at which Carey promptly stepped forward and went down on two knees to her, his lips moving although Emilia couldn't hear what he said.

The Queen laughed and gave him her hand to kiss which he did and stayed on his knees. Again his lips moved and the Queen tapped his nose playfully—but possibly quite painfully—with her new Chinese fan. He rose, bowed, stepped back, bowed again as the Queen too turned aside to speak to another person on his knees, looked wry and rubbed his nose, sneezed.

The Queen was now talking to Essex again and the chapel men started singing once more to the chapel master's nod, a song that only needed one tenor and was easy. Emilia started manoeuvring toward Carey through the crowds now sweating in the heat from the candles. Such a very fine piece of manflesh, she thought coldly, what a pity to kill him. But still, it had to be done. First Essex, though.

She barged neatly past two dowdy women making for the banquet table with jellies and creams. She got in front of Carey as he reached to take his goblet from his servingman. She made sure she was turned away from him so he would suspect nothing and he trod on the back of her gown as he was supposed to.

"Oh!" she squeaked as she heard the pop of one of her points. She turned and was surprised to see him, of course. "Monsieur le député," she trilled, "May I speak to you?"

She said it in Scotch, on the grounds that she spoke that language better and it might give them a little privacy while not excluding the young servingman whom she had suddenly, just that moment, recognised as her contact. More of the English Court would speak French than Scotch, that was sure. Also she wanted Carey to remember their affair and even feel guilty, if possible.

He bowed slightly, his eyes hooded. "I'm so sorry, have I torn your gown, Signora?" he asked. "You know how clumsy I am." Like most men who called themselves clumsy, he wasn't at all. And he had apologised for his clumsiness before, in Scotland. Ai, her stupid heart had started beating hard again.

"No, no," she told him. "It was me, I was pushing in front of you because I want one of the rose almond creams that I love so much."

He smiled, reached a long arm over the scrum of women and brought out a pretty little sugar paste bowl full of rose cream. Emilia took it quickly. It had a little carved sugar paste spoon sticking out of it and she started eating it immediately, very quickly and carefully. Actually it was wonderful, smooth and sweet and creamy with the scent of roses. The English were very good at this sort of delicacy thanks to their miserable cold climate.

She scraped up the last smears of cream and laughed. "Delicious! And quite unobtainable in Italy, where you would need to freeze it first with snow or it would go off in the heat." This time she was speaking French which was so much easier.

Carey's eyebrows went up; politely he responded in French.

"What a good idea, Signora," he said, "frozen creams—perhaps the Queen would enjoy them?"

Emilia shook her head, making the feather bob and the ringlets fly. "Impossible, Monsieur, you must have high mountains that have snow in summer within one day's running distance and very clever cooks."

"The cooks we have, and the runners," smiled Carey, his eyes intent and patient. "Alas, the snowy mountains, no."

"Also to eat it you need good teeth or the cold makes them twinge."

"Ah," said Carey. "In that case, perhaps not a good idea for the Queen."

Emilia giggled. Of course, the Queen, like most of the sugar-loving English, had terrible teeth. Now then. How could she find out his price? Well, she could ask him. That might even be the best way to go.

She twined her arm into his confidingly and put the sugar plate bowl and spoon down on the banquet table. Her own teeth would certainly no longer stand up to crunching sugar plate.

"Monsieur, let me be frank with you," she said. "My husband and I have contacts and knowledge of sweet wines." They were still speaking French because she wanted to be understood by any embassy listeners. "You are the Earl of Essex's man, who has the farm for sweet wines?"

"More than that. He knighted me, Signora."

Even Emilia knew how important that was, how difficult it was for a man to be knighted at this Queen's Court, where the Queen was so stingy with honours and didn't even sell them like a civilized person.

"I can help him with his farm of sweet wines," said Emilia. "All I need is for you to introduce me to the Earl so I can introduce my husband to him. "

"Now? Tonight?" Like all courtiers he wanted to spin the negotiation out to get more than one bribe.

"Yes, or someone else will get it." Suddenly there was sweat trickling down under her smock, it was hard to pretend indifference in this life-or-death matter.

"Do you want to buy the farm of sweet wines from him?"

Jesu, if only! "No," Emilia admitted, "we want to manage it for him so he makes the most profit possible. We also want to import many very fine sweet wines from my country and sell them." She left unmentioned how immensely valuable to many people might be information straight from the Queen's favourite, just in case he hadn't thought of that angle. "If milord Essex does sell the farm to someone else, we can still work with him because he will still need to import sweet wines to drink."

"Hmm…"

"I know we can find good wines at such low prices everyone will still make so much money," Emilia added, "perhaps a small commission for you…"

She let the sentence hang in the air and Carey didn't so much as blink at it floating past. He wasn't going to be fobbed off that way, it seemed.

"Fifty pounds cash," said Carey, "or the equivalent in jewellery. Now."

"Now? Jesu Maria…"

He shrugged, a very French gesture Englished. "You may be able to find someone else to make the introduction," he said still in French. "They might even cost less. But this is your last chance until the Queen is back at Whitehall because after this, the Court will go to Woodstock and then to Oxford where there will be no women at the University entertainments. The Earl will be closeted with the Queen or attending on her and no one who isn't already one of his own or the Queen's will be able to meet with him."

Oh God, he was right and he knew it. She bit her lip. He was right. How could she pay him if he was insisting on payment in cash down not in-kind? Which he was; she could see it in the cool set of his face.

She fumbled at her neck where gleamed the gold and ruby necklace Cumberland had given her—rightful plunder, he'd called it, from a Portuguese trader snapped up in the Bay of Biscay. She had a little velvet purse in her petticoat pocket, she took it out, put the gold necklace into it and waited. Carey must know exactly what the necklace was worth because that was the amount he had asked for, the greedy bastard.

She held the purse tightly, cocked her head a little against the uncomfortable standing ruff behind her head. In Ireland she had learned not to hand over the bribe before the paid-for favour had been done. Carey smiled, half bowed to her and headed across the dance floor, through a violent volta that was spinning and thundering on the boards. The musicians were sweating in the heat from the candles and the bodies as they played, but Emilia noticed that one of them was missing—the viol player who had wept at the Spanish air.

Mr. Byrd was looking very annoyed, speaking with the Earl of Essex. "…you can't trust any of these yokels," he was complaining. "He was only one of the Oxford waits but good enough to play for the Queen and this is how he repays me for the chance I gave him? Damn it, I was hoping to take him to London with us.…Ah yes, Sir Robert, thank you for singing with us earlier."

"Yes, indeed," added the Earl of Essex. "Her Majesty was very pleased with it, she told me so. Also she asked if your nose is better now?"

"It will be, my lord," murmured Carey. "When she has given me my warrant as Deputy Warden and, of course, my fee."

Essex laughed. "Good luck!" he shouted. "You'd do better to sing with the travelling gleemen and save up your fees.…"

Shut up about his goddamn voice, you stupid lout, Emilia thought, and smiled brilliantly at Carey.

"You nearly caused terrible damage to me, Sir Rrrobert," she purred at him in English.

"I did?" said Carey, "How, Signora Bonnetti?"

"Why you made me cry, rremembering the South, and that would have made my face all swollen and ugly."

"Impossible," boomed Essex gallantly in French, accented but fluent, "No amount of tears could do that." And, yes, he had swung from a stare at her cleavage to looking at Carey questioningly. Right. She had done all she could. Now he had to earn the necklace.

"Of course, my lord," said Carey smoothly, already ahead of her. "May I present the brilliant and extraordinary Signora

Emilia Bonnetti, wife to the merchant Giovanni Bonnetti, who was arranging the wholesale import of excellent sweet wines to the Scottish Court, last time I met them?"

Essex smiled and held out his hand. Emilia took it and curtsied low, her lashes modestly lowered and, she hoped, a fetching blush on her cheek.

"And where is your husband, Signora?"

Where was the little man now? Oh yes. "He is in Oxford, talking to the butlers of the colleges, I think." They were all speaking French now. Most of the English were good linguists because who could possibly want to learn their awful ugly uncouth bastard tongue, the spawn of Dutch and French?

"He has reliable suppliers?"

"Of course, directly from Italy with no interference from the London vintners at all." That interested the Earl—fewer middlemen meant cheaper wholesale prices, of course. And the London vintners were notoriously greedy in a land full of greedy men. "He is very experienced with all kinds of wine and importing and exporting all kinds of things....You must talk to him, milord, because I am only a poor foolish woman...."

"But you are interested in the farm of sweet wines?" Essex asked with typical English unsubtlety. "Which I hold?"

Emilia managed not to sigh. When in England..."Yes, milord," she said, "of course. We are not wealthy enough to farm it directly for you, but we can manage the farm and bring in the very best wines from Italy."

The price the Earl named was breathtaking and impossible. "Plus one barrel in every ten as a gift to me, directly," he added.

Outrageous! God, how greedy the English were. But in fact, it could be done, because the English couldn't grow drinkable wine in their horrible damp country but did drink wine, and in astonishing quantities. And there were things they made that you could send south—dull boring things like finished wool and iron guns and coal, that you could exchange for a lot of wine which the English wouldn't know was cheap.

"Milorrd," she giggled, curtsied again. "I would be honoured if I can speak to my husband about this matter and my husband, too, will be honoured but…"

They bargained carefully until the number of barrels they had to give the Earl was one in twenty. No matter. She had made the connection. Now she needed to strengthen it.

She offered her hand to the Earl, who gripped it with surprising strength, then turned it over and kissed the palm like a lover. He stood between her and the Queen so she couldn't see, but the meaning was plain. She tingled all over, caught Carey's cynical smile, also found herself smiling with pure delight. Hooked, by God, she could still hook them. She gave a little tremble as she curtseyed once more—ay, her poor knees and her pinched toes—fluttered her eyelids as she looked up at the towering gold and white of the favourite.

"Milord, I must not trouble you anymore with my foolishness," she whispered.

He leaned in, gingery and pink under the white lead paste on his face. "Will you join us for the card game afterward, Signora?" he breathed.

"I am a terrible card-player," she lied. "My poor woman's brain cannot even remember the points."

"Perhaps I can teach you," smiled the Earl.

"That would be such an honour, milorrd," she said in English. "Then yes, if you will 'elp me not lose too much and make my 'usband angrry. Thank you, thank you, milorrd."

She stepped neatly away, retrieving her hand from the Earl's grip, and dived into the group of women trying to get a drink of spiced wine from one of the silver mixing bowls. Emilia's teeth were creaking with thirst in the heat, and as soon as she tasted the stuff they were drinking she knew she could make the sweet wine farm work for her, Signor Bonnetti, and even the Earl.

Carey stood behind her, blocking her escape from the group of women, so she finished the deal by handing him the black velvet bag with the necklace in it. His fingers explored it expertly to be sure she hadn't coney-catched him, then he smiled down at her as she curtseyed to him with her best modest smile.

"Are you happy, Signora?" asked the chestnut-headed reiver. She had to curtsey again while she sorted her thoughts. Would he be jealous? That would be nice.

"Oh very happy, M. le deputé, it is easy to see why the Queen loves milord of Essex. And you? Are you happy?"

He shook his head and put the bag containing fifty pounds' worth of gold and garnets that might be rubies into his inside doublet pocket. "What is it that makes me fear we may never meet again?" he said with a creditable attempt at an abandoned lover's face, so Emilia had to laugh at him. He was quite right. He had cheated her, sold her bad guns, caused a nightmare in horrible Ireland, made the Spanish keep her two surviving children in the Flemish convent and forget their Italian, become prim, prosy, boring little Flemings.... But still there was that thread of lust between them. Clearly they would not meet again—now that she had hooked the Queen's favourite—no matter what her stupid body felt about it. And she would try and find a way for him to die because he clearly knew too much about her and her husband. She might even be able to get her necklace back.

saturday 16th september 1592, night

Carey went outside the hot tent to blow his nose properly and rub it. The Queen had practically broken it with the end of her fan and meant to as well. He had naturally taken the opportunity when he knelt to her of reminding her of the warrant for his office at Carlisle and his fee. She had told him he already had a very good warrant and should use it.

"Without any money to pay my men…?" he had begun pathetically and that was when her fan clipped the end of his nose so painfully his eyes had watered.

"Do as I bid you," she had said, steely-eyed.

At least I've made sure that it's really the Queen who wants me to investigate the Amy Robsart death, he thought, trumpeting into his handkerchief again. And then along had come Emilia

Bonnetti insisting on her introduction and even paying his fee with her necklace. He knew where she must have got it—perhaps Cumberland would be willing to buy it back? Perhaps not.

And Emilia had done it all very nicely, from the "accidental" bump at the banquet table to her conversation with the Earl who was, as always, clearly in desperate need of ready cash. Carey just hoped the Bonnettis could find a good financier to buy the farm and actually do what Emilia said they could. The fact that they were obviously spies mattered not at all, so long as Essex used them carefully, the way Walsingham would. It was Walsingham who had taught Carey that the way to deal with spies and informers was to know who they were and keep them close so you controlled what they found out and what they told their handlers. Spies were only dangerous if you didn't know their identities and whereabouts. It was notorious that Essex was trying to take over Walsingham's networks and the Bonnettis would probably lead him to some very juicy information. Perhaps Giovanni could be turned, the way his brother the sword master had been. He hoped in a detached way that they would survive somehow, for Emilia's sake. What a woman!

When he went back in, he saw Hughie hanging around looking nervous and smiled at him. "Thank you," he said. Hughie blushed and looked surprised.

"Ehm…?"

"I like a henchman who sticks at my back despite opportunities to dance with pretty girls," Carey explained, pointing to the girls whirling between the trees. Some of the servingmen were partnering them since this was a jig, a dance for the common people. The Queen was fanning herself and talking to Essex again as she watched, her face alight with laughter.

"Ay, sir?"

"Nobody's trying to kill me around here," Carey said, watching his face carefully. Had Hughie shot that crossbow? "In Carlisle, though, it might be a serious matter if you weren't near me."

Hughie looked distasteful. "Ay, sir, Carlisle's all fu' wi' English Borderers."

"Yes, true."

Carey was very thirsty and knew the wine was too strong to do any good. What he needed was at least a quart of mild ale to wet his throat, but where could he find some?

"Hughie, go fetch me a flagon of spiced wine." Hughie nodded and plunged toward the scrum around the wine and brandy barrels at the corner of the tent.

Carey left the marquee again and picked his way around the hedges to the musicians' entrance, where he found Mr. Byrd drinking tobacco smoke from a clay pipe and looking very disgruntled.

"I don't suppose you play the viol, too, Sir Robert?" he asked.

"No, Mr. Byrd, not at all. I was taught the lute but can't say I learnt it, since my playing is painfully poor."

"And yet your voice is excellent, sir."

"Thank you, but I can't take any credit for it. Simply a gift from God, for reasons that He no doubt understands."

Byrd proffered the pipe, lifting his eyebrows, and Carey took it and drank some smoke. The tobacco was good although it had no Moroccan incense in it and it didn't make him cough, just smoothed some of the edges. Byrd smiled in the darkness.

"Yes, indeed, there's music for you. Who knows where it comes from or where it goes or why." He sniffed and scowled heavily. "Or musicians either."

"Oh?"

"I'm one viol down in any case because the players from London had plague and have been forbidden the Court. So I hired me a replacement and now he's gone off somewhere, I don't know where."

"I'm sorry I can't help you, Mr. Byrd."

"His face is annoying me now, I'm sure I've seen him before. So what did you want, sir?"

"Er…would you have any spare mild ale anywhere about you to wet my poor dry throat?"

Byrd smiled again. "We've got a proper Court ration, half a gallon apiece. You can have that damned viol player's pottle, if you like." The chapel master even ducked back into the tent to fetch it for him and Carey took the large heavy leather mug, toasted Byrd, and gulped a quarter of it in one. That was better. It was very good, the manor's brewer had obviously taken care with it as the Queen herself was notorious for mainly drinking only mild ale. It was weak, refreshing, and slightly nutty.

"Did you know that Spanish air before you sang it?" Byrd asked. Carey shook his head.

"It was a pleasure to sing."

Byrd bowed a little, looking thoughtful. "Funny thing that," he said in an awkwardly casual voice. "The Queen asked for it particularly, but I didn't make the tune. She played it for me herself."

"Oh?" Carey didn't say anything more, waited. Had Byrd been told to give him information?

"Yes, she picked it out on one of the lutes this afternoon and told me to set it at once so we could sing it this evening and then later in Oxford."

"You did that in a couple of hours? I'm impressed, Mr. Chapel Master."

Byrd smiled. "It wasn't any trouble at all, just unrolled as easy as you like. Perhaps it could do with a little trimming, or perhaps more embellishment."

"I wouldn't touch it…I thought it was perfect as it was."

Byrd wagged a finger at Carey. The pipe of tobacco was finished; he had knocked out the dottle and put it in his belt pouch, but was showing no sign of going into the tent again. "Only God is perfect, sir, that's what the Moors say, isn't it?"

Byrd was doing his best to look guileless so Carey resigned himself to having to probe. "So what made an old Spanish air so important to the Queen, I wonder?" he asked and then added on impulse, "She has asked me to look into an important but difficult matter for her and perhaps you can help me."

Byrd nodded. "Sir Robert, I have a few moments before we must play again for the tumblers." They drew aside, away from the tent and also clear of the hedge. "The air you sang was written on a piece of parchment, wrapped around something that looked like a piece of leather or a stick. I think it was found in the Queen's privy baggage when we arrived here and it put Her Majesty out of countenance. It seems there was music written on it and that is what she had us sing."

"What else was written on the parchment?"

Byrd shrugged. "I didn't see that, Sir Robert, only the Queen saw it. I glimpsed the staves when she opened it out to pluck it on her lute for me to transcribe." Byrd patted Carey's arm. "I know Her Majesty ordered Mrs. de Paris to find you and set you on the scent. She said she had heard you were as fine a sleuth dog as Walsingham and thanked God you were here. But that's all. She said nothing else about it, except that she has kept the parchment and bit of leather in a purse close under her stays."

Carey nodded, bowed shallowly. "Thank you, Mr. Byrd. If you find out anything else, please will you tell me?"

Byrd bowed back. "Of course, sir." He turned to the tent opening.

Carey had circled round and re-entered when the musicians struck up a bouncy martial tune with drums for the tumblers. The grave Moor with his walking stick was standing at the back, watching narrow-eyed as the boys and men danced and somersaulted and swallowed swords and threw themselves at each other across the dance floor, and the boys climbed the trees and jumped off onto pyramids of men. Then Thomasina bounced from her place by the Queen's skirts to shouts and cheers from the courtiers and threw herself into the air, bouncing, turning, and then at last leaping high onto the top of the pyramid of men and boys where she stood on the shoulders of the topmost boy and breathlessly sang a lewd song of triumph.

He looked around at the bright crowd. Hughie was by the banquet with the other men-at-arms and servingmen like Mr. Simmonds, staring at the tumblers' show, the flagon still dangling empty in his left hand. He had clearly forgotten all about fetching spiced wine. Emilia was across the other side of the room, amongst Essex's followers, talking to a Welshman, Essex's current favourite. Thomasina was mimicking a different great man of the Court in each verse of her song and was doing a particularly good imitation of the haughty Sir Walter Raleigh who wasn't there on account of still languishing in the Tower for sowing his seed in a maid of honour. Idiot. Serve him right. The soft Devon accent and haughty head were unmistakeable, even when a midget only three and a half foot high did them. Carey had thoroughly disliked the man, had got into a fistfight with him over a tennis court back in the eighties, which had been smoothed over by his father. The progress following that had been remarkable in that Carey was consistently billeted with Raleigh, who was not yet at all important, and had had to share a bed with him a couple of times. They had come to an understanding eventually over card games, but still…What an arrogant fool.

The rest of his mind was turning over the Amy Robsart problem, the one the inquest report pointed to with such shocking honesty. Surely the Queen hadn't actually read that report? She was sitting under her cloth of estate now, laughing at Thomasina who was currently guying the hunchbacked Sir Robert Cecil. Mind you, there was no way of telling what the Queen was thinking; she had been at Court all her life and knew a thing or two about keeping her counsel.

Why the devil did she want the thing brought up again? Why now? Did it have something to do with the scrap of parchment written with music? Why?

The Queen was standing and holding out her arms to her people. All the Court went to their knees again, Carey included, just missing a lurking patch of mud with one of his knees and nearly staining his last remaining good pair of hose. He really hoped Hughie knew how to darn. Maybe when he met his father at Oxford, he could snaffle a few new pairs?

Her Majesty said a loving goodnight to her people and then paced out to the sound of trumpets, leaning on the arm of the Earl of Essex, who was looking pleased with himself. The Gentlemen of the Queen's Guard went ahead and behind, making red and gold borders around the maids of honour and the ladies-in-waiting, who were following the Queen, the younger ones rolling their eyes sulkily at having to leave the dancing so early.

Carey could see Emilia amongst the Earl's followers at the end of the procession, the tilt of her feathered hat unmistakeable. Ah well. Perhaps another time. (A lucky escape, you idiot, said the puritanical part of him.)

Carey caught Hughie's eye and beckoned him to bring over the flagon and pour for him. The lad started and looked guilty, dived into the scrum of servingmen by the large silver spiced wine bowl and disappeared. Finally he emerged, wading upstream against the flood of other servingmen, dodged a couple of whirling dancers, and came over. Carey lifted his silver cup and Hughie served him quite well, pouring carefully and using a linen napkin on his arm to wipe any drips.

When Carey sipped the wine, he nearly gagged—it was a spiced wine water, very sweet, mixed with brandy and spices and a hint of bitterness from the cloves. The attempt to hide its dreadful quality hadn't worked. Still it was wine, so he drank it.

As soon as the Queen had gone, the musicians had struck up an alemain and the roar of voices went up another notch. He watched the peasant dance for a while, wondering if he wanted to dance anymore.

God, it was hot. Carey changed his mind about dancing, moved out again into the darkness, feeling for rain first because he did not want to damage his (still only half paid-for) Court doublet and hose. There were torches on some of the trees so you could see something in the flickering shadows.

Carey was still thirsty, so he followed the sound of water back to the stream, tipped out half of the syrupy wine in his goblet and refilled it with water caught carefully from a small rapid over a mossy stone. You never knew with water, but he'd found in France that wine generally cleaned it well.

Sipping cautiously, Carey decided it was much better and even the bitterness of cloves in it was refreshing, like well-hopped beer. Away from the torches and candle-lit tent, the evening was still and some stars were coming out, powdering the velvet cloak of the sky with diamond dust. The evening must be much warmer than you'd expect at this time of year, despite the clearing sky. Carey was burning up in his Court suit.

He spotted the dim outline of the church spire and went toward it. The clerks would no doubt be bundled up asleep inside, along with other courtiers' servants, since there, at least, they wouldn't be rained on despite the hardness of the floor.

Once in the churchyard he wondered what he was there for, since he wasn't about to go and roust out John Tovey from his sleep just for the sake of it, after all. Still the church pulled him as he gulped the watered wine. Perhaps it would be cooler in there. He opened the door carefully, shut it behind him carefully and paced with great caution down the aisle. On either side were dozens of bundled figures, quite tightly packed, wrapped in their cloaks. Some had managed to beg, borrow, or steal straw pallets to ease the stone flags under them.

It wasn't cooler in here, damn it. He went up toward the altar, still too hot and still dry-mouthed with thirst. All the Papistic nonsense had been cleared away years ago, the altar had been moved so that it was a proper communion table, the saints of the altar screen had lost their heads and been whitewashed, the Lady chapel had no figure of the Madonna on the plinth at all, though there was a puzzling carved frieze of deer around the walls. They looked oddly alive, even seemed to move.

The soft snoring from behind him was forming itself into a strange rhythmic music. He looked up at the boarded windows, one or two left intact with the old style full of scriptural pictures for the illiterate. Those were their only way of learning the gospels as they were denied hearing the Word of the Lord by the Vulgate Latin of the old Mass. That you couldn't see the sky though the silvery light told him that the moon had risen. What were the reiving surnames up to on the Border? It was a church. Perhaps he should pray?

He drank again, took his hat off belatedly and thought about Amy Dudley née Robsart, poor lady. She had died on the 8th

September 1560, the year of his own birth, perhaps not very long after he was born, a summer baby. He smiled, thinking vaguely of his wet nurse and how he had loved her when he was tiny, when his mother sometimes frightened him on her visits back from Court with his quite terrifying father. They had become better friends when once he was breeched and he had realised how kind they were, compared to the parents of most of his friends.

He knocked back most of the rest of his wine, wondering why nothing seemed to ease his dry mouth, and sat on one of the benches against the wall. Nobody was sleeping there, perhaps because the stones were broken. There was more old destruction in the Lady chapel than the rest of the church. The plinth the statue had stood on still had a crescent moon, stars, and a snake carved on it.

Why was he so hot and thirsty after drinking so much ale earlier and then a whole flagon of watered wine? And another peculiar thing was that he didn't need a piss at all. His insides seemed to have turned suddenly into a strange desert.

And now something really odd was happening. The white-washed stone of the church was seeming to billow around him slowly, as if it were only painted curtains at a play. The white-washed walls thinned and thinned and swayed in and out and back and forth like the dancers, to the rhythm of the snore-music around him.

He couldn't stand the heat anymore and his head was hurting, his mouth glued with drought. He had to cool down. He fumbled for the buttons of his doublet, undid them with hands full of thumbs, then had to feel around the back where his poinard hung for the points and then he thought of taking his belts off, which he did, and then he broke a couple of laces and the doublet came away at last. He took the thing off his shoulders, wondering why it had got so much lighter and hung it on a headless woman saint holding a wheel.

He was still too hot and his eyes weren't working right. Everything was blurring and billowing in front of him, and the moon must be shining through a window somewhere because he could see well in the darkness, make out the outlines of snoring clerks and Court servants on the floor. The vest that held up his paned trunk hose and canions was making him hot now so he set about undoing the buttons and laces for that. It was a nightmare of inextricable buttons and laces so he broke the damned things and wobbled as he pulled those off as well and hung them on a saint holding a castle next to the pearl-covered doublet and stood there in his shirt with his hose dropping down and his boots still on. He burped.

Blinking, rubbing his eyes which were getting worse and worse, licking lips like leather with a tongue of horsehide and panting with heat, a small part of him finally thought to wonder, "Am I ill?"

The last time he had felt so bad was on the *Elizabeth Bonaventure*, Cumberland's ship, chasing the Armada north through the storms of the North Sea. He had been hot, dry, dizzy, blinding headache…

Well, said the sensible part of him, it couldn't be a jail fever because that was what nearly killed me in 1588 and you never get it twice.

Was it plague? Christ Jesus, had he caught plague in London and brought it to the Queen?

His distant hands trembled as Carey felt himself for buboes, as his head started to swell to twice its size and then four times. No lumps, nothing. He wasn't bleeding anywhere either, but the furnace of his heart was pounding louder and louder like the drum for the acrobats and the church itself was dissolving around him into gauzy billowing curtains.

He had to get out. But he couldn't. He was standing still, his legs too far away to command. He was panting like a hound. He needed help. Was there anyone? The clerk? What was his name?

"Mr. Tovey," he croaked, "Mr. Tovey…"

He tried again, he couldn't shout, the voice that had flowed so well earlier was now a cracked whisper. He had to lie down or fall down. So he carefully put his goblet on the bench again and sat cross-legged on the flagstones as if he was in camp in

France. His whole body had turned into an oven and at least the stones were cool. In fact they looked very inviting and as the stone church had somehow turned to a tapestried tent and billowing fine linen, so the broken stones of the Lady chapel were becoming pillows and bolsters specially for him.

He lay down full length on them, liking the cool and softness on his burning face.

There was quiet movement behind him. Somebody was lighting a candle end at the watchlight by the altar.

He moaned in protest, the light was far too bright as it came too close, it hurt his eyes. He tried to push it away, punch whoever was trying to hurt him with a spear made of light. Through tears he saw Tovey's bony anxious face, shape-shifting to a skull amongst the soft billowing stones and the saints singing headless.

"Sir Robert!" Tovey's voice cracked through his headache. "Are you sick, sir?"

"Ah'm not drunk," Carey told him. "Don't think s'plague…"

Tovey flinched back for a moment but to his credit, didn't run. Carey felt a bony hand on his forehead, saw the frown, the candle brought close to his face, Tovey feeling his armpits and groin, oh God, do I have the tokens on my face? Carey wondered, because he felt as if there was a bonfire on each cheek.

Tovey frowned suddenly, one of his fingers brushed Carey's leather lips, then the damned candle came near again.

"Sir, please look at the candle flame," Tovey said. The boy suddenly had some authority in his voice. Carey frowned at the yellow-white blaze in his eyes but did his best to look straight at it. Splots of light danced in his vision, strangely coloured, and the stone saints sang the Spanish air from earlier, rather well in chorus in a different setting.

Maybe it was plague after all? "Don't…come…near…" he whispered. "Get everyone out…Might be plague…"

The boy felt his forehead again as if he was a mother. He shook his head.

"Sir Robert, what have you drunk?"

"'M not drunk…" He knew that. It took more than a couple of quarts of mild ale and a goblet of not very good spiced wine to make him drunk.

"I know." The boy looked about, spotted the goblet, took it from the bench, sniffed the remnants in it, stuck a finger in them and licked it. There was recognition on his face, "Mother of God," he said, papistically. Then something in his expression hardened. "Sir Robert, you've been poisoned."

Had he? Good Lord, why? Or was it an accident when the poisoner was after bigger game? Fear swooped through him and the saints started singing a nasty discord. He reached up and grabbed the boy's woollen doublet front. "Tell the Earl… of…" Damnit, who? Wossname? "Essex, tell Essex. Don't le' the Queen…"

"I have to make you purge, Sir Robert," he said. "Get the poison out of your stomach…"

Rage gave him more strength than he realised, and he swiped the boy away, got to his feet. "Tell…Essex first!" he shouted. "Queen! Lord Norris! Don' le' 'er drink spiced wine…."

Burning with rage at whoever had done this, he started for the door, heard shouts, found more people around him, holding him back. Lots of them. He knocked a couple of them down, found his arms held, damn it, somebody swept his legs from under him and he landed on the stones, half a dozen people were sitting on him. He was fighting and roaring incoherently at them to stop the Queen drinking spiced wine and then Tovey's face with a fat lip and a bruised chin was close to him again and the mouth moving and making words and he finally heard the boy.

"Coleman and Hughes have already run to the manor house, s…sir," said Tovey. "We've warned her. If she hasn't already drunk it, she won't."

It penetrated. Tovey was shakily holding a wooden cup and the other clerks were cautiously letting him sit up enough to drink. He was even more thirsty than before, dry as dust, dry as death. Interesting, who could have done it? Emilia? Hughie? One of the musicians or chapel men? Somebody else? Please God, the

Queen was all right. She had survived so many attempts, many not recorded, let God keep her safe still…

Somebody else had arrived, was panting breathlessly, saying something to Tovey. "Sir, the Queen's people have been warned," he said slowly and clearly, "P…please drink this, sir, we must purge you."

He drank whatever it was and found to his annoyance it was salted water, spat it out. The young clerks still sitting on him and holding his shoulders were turning themselves into the singing saints and the whole church was billowing. He gulped more seawater, damn it, the storm was terrible, he was sinking through the floor and…ach…Jesu…

Suddenly the wisps of church had blown away and he was lying on something soft, saints holding his arms and legs whenever he tried to shake them off. Was he in heaven? Well, he couldn't hear harps though the singing of that Spanish air was starting to annoy him, no visible angels. Maybe? He was looking down on something that looked like a wonderful map made of cloth with green velvet grass and fringed trees and blocks of stone poking through. Perhaps he'd turned into a bird.

Green, came the thought, so not autumn.

"Sir Robert, please drink this, sir, please…"

Christ, he was thirsty. The lip of a wooden cup (they had wooden cups in heaven?) knocked his teeth and he smelled water, downed it in one. Seawater again, ach, salty…

His belly twisted and heaved and his body jackknifed. Sour stuff gushed out of his mouth. He couldn't see properly, everything was flaring and blurred, part of him was on a cloud somewhere high up, the other part felt the rough staves of a bucket and he puked into it helplessly.

"Again, please, sir."

He drank again, hoping for plain water or mild ale, but no, more brine. Ach. He hated being sick, but sick as a dog he was, violently, coughing and sputtering disgusting bitterness. In a distant part of his overheated skull, the wry thought came: At least I don't have the squits as well, that's a small mercy.

"Good, that's better. Sip this please sir, just sip."

He was cautious after the saltwater, but this time it was just well-water with a little brandy. He sipped, then gulped, had to puke again.

"This is good, sir," Tovey's voice said soothingly. "It's washing you out…"

There were voices above him, Tovey answering steadily. Somebody else looked in his face with the candle held near again, he recognised one of the older Gentlemen Pensioners, behind him one of the Queen's ladies in a fur-trimmed dressing gown, red-haired, didn't know which one, might be a cousin, tried to blink at the goddamned candle still blazing like the sun in his sight.

"You're right, Mr. Tovey," said the lady-in-waiting. "His pupils are fixed wide open, it must be belladonna."

"The Queen?" He had to know. What if his aunt had had her usual nightcap of spiced wine?

"She's well, Sir Robert, she hasn't had any of this at all. She knows what's happened and we are searching Rycote now for the poisoner. Please sir, lie down."

"I've brought my pallet for you, sir, please lie on it until we can move you." Tovey's voice.

Really he preferred the stones which were cooler, but his stomach cramped and twisted humiliatingly again and Tovey's blurred angular face was wobbling and stretching, drawn upon the finely woven veils around him.

Looking down from his straw-smelling cloud was fun. He laughed at the sight of men on horseback, riding hell-for-leather across country along the line of the old Giant's Wall. He recognised the man at their head—good God, was that what he looked like in a jack and morion? Not bad, quite frightening in fact, and from the look of his face, he was in a rage about something.

Carey peered with interest over the other edge of the cloud to see more riders, a remarkable number, in fact. It looked like a full-fledged Warden raid, though for some reason all the riders were heading eastward rather than north or south, riding bunched in their surnames. From the quilting on the jacks there were Dodds, Storeys, Bells, a lot of Armstrongs, Grahams…good God, *Grahams*? Following him? What the hell was going on?

And somehow he saw in a flash what it was that had enraged him, which was Elizabeth Widdrington in nothing but a blood-stained shift, locked in a storeroom, with a black eye and a swollen face and dried blood on it.

The bolt of fury that drove through him at that sight knocked him right off his cloud and into the uproar of his body which seemed to be fighting the people trying to strap him to a litter. He could ride, he needed his sword, where the hell was Dodd…? More light blurred into his useless eyes making his enormous head hurt. Had he been struck blind? Dear God, please not?

Heavy weights coloured red and gold twisted his legs from under him and landed on his shoulders and hips, pinning him down. There was murmuring in the background. Someone with a foreign voice was advising caution, the delirium from belladonna or henbane could make a man four times as strong as normal.…

The war drums were beating around him but he could still hear Tovey dropping to his knees and stammering something. What was he saying?

"Y…your M…Majesty?"

The fear in the boy's voice was what suddenly cut through his rage. Despite his agonising headache, his heat, the suddenly more distant rage, the drought, and the unsettling discovery that the world was really made of the finest, most delicate silk, Carey smiled.

"Robin, Robin, can you hear me, my dear?"

Yes, it was the Queen. He knew his aunt's voice, though when he squinted to see her she was a blotchy pink and white moon, framed by sable fur and topped with a thatch of grey-red. Red and gold lumps were next to her, behind her was a dark column with a doctor's cap.

He managed a grunt through a throat too dry to make any other sound and he couldn't think of words. Some of the rage was draining out of him, despite the pounding of his heart. Garbled foreign noises surrounded him. She was talking to

Tovey in Latin and the boy responded, he couldn't understand a word of it, now the doctor was talking it too. Bloody hell, he hated learned people talking about him in Latin.

He felt the Queen's hand on his shoulder which was going numb because of the large Gentleman Pensioner kneeling on it.

"Robin, I have brought my own Doctor Lopez who is an expert in poisons, one of my lord Essex's physicians as well," said the Queen's voice. He frowned. The last thing he wanted was a doctor—he didn't want to die.

"He has purged, Your Majesty," said Lopez' nasal Portuguese voice. "He has drunk some water. I recommend the empiric treatment of this belladonna poisoning, as suspected by Senhor Tovey. I 'ave a decoction of beanpods which has been efficacious in the past…" A click of fingers, somebody trotted off into the night, he heard them, what the hell was a decoction of beanpods?

He tried to shift the weight of the two Gentlemen Pensioners with their knees bruising his shoulders and couldn't. The Gentlemen were not scrawny young clerks to be knocked sideways like ninepins. There was another argument going on above him, this time in English.

"No, he certainly can't stay here. So long as this is no illness, not plague…"

Nobody thought it was plague, especially not Dr. Lopez. That was good to hear. The argument went on while he drifted in and out, sometimes on his cloud, sometimes wishing they'd stop holding him down so he could go and kill the bastard who had hurt Elizabeth Widdrington.

Cool bony fingers touched his forehead.

"Robin, listen. I'm having you moved into the manor house," said the Queen in a voice that brooked no argument. "We'll kick out one of Essex's pack of hangers-on and make room."

She patted his cheek and he heard the rustling of dressing gowns as she left with her two ladies. It wasn't the first time he'd seen his aunt in her dressing gown, after all. Not that he'd seen her this time, since his eyes weren't working at all.

The weights came off his shoulders and hips, but something was tangling his wrists so he couldn't lift his arms. He tried to sit up, was pushed down firmly and a strap came across his chest. Goddamn it to hell, he had to get up, he didn't have time for this nonsense, he needed his broadsword, he had to save Elizabeth. He tried to shout, but couldn't, he wanted to piss but couldn't. He wanted to see but couldn't. He was hot as hell again and the world was turning back to silk veils as he somehow jerked high in the air, blinking at the shadowed stone forest of the church, the branches in their orderly stone patterns and the gargoyles laughing at him. Christ, where was his sword, where was Dodd? He was somehow bobbing along on his back, a stone lintel went past above him and now he was flying through the sky where the stars were and now he was on the other side of the fake painted silk walls of the world.

But this time he was looking at himself climbing a ladder to a wooden platform.

Two men were waiting for him in the cold sunlight, and a priest in a plain surplice, speaking the words "Oh Lord, wash me of my iniquity, cleanse me of my sin...."

His own face was white, lips set in a line, but his eyes were sad. He heard himself speaking in the dawn to the small crowd waiting to see him die, apologising for his wicked rebellion against his most loving cousin, the Queen, thanking her for her gentle mercy to him of the axe, who was unworthy of it. Quite a good speech, really.

He saw himself turn, shuck off a worn green velvet doublet and kneel down to the block in his shirt and hose. He heard himself saying the Our Father in a creditably firm voice, words torn away by the wind, then bending to put his neck on the block and the headsman's axe swinging up, glittering in the sunlight.

The blow knocked him out of his dream again and back into his body where someone was making him drink something filthy-tasting. Meekly he drank it and let his miraculously still-attached head down to the pillow again, heart drumming wildly inside him.

Rebellion? Against the Queen? Good God. And it must have been a foul bill that he confessed to because the vision of himself had had no injuries, no signs of torture at all. How could that have happened?

It's a fever dream, he told himself somewhere deep inside himself where the drought didn't matter so much—both of them were fever dreams. And why had he been so badly dressed for his execution? His doublet had looked ten years old and hard-worn. That could never happen. Rebellion was as ridiculous as the idea that he could become so…well, so shabby.

Which was the last thought he knew as the clouds wrapped him in silk again.…

sunday 17th september 1592, noon

Dodd hauled the horse back on its haunches and cursed. He knew he was going the wrong way again…you wouldn't think that riding northwest to Oxford would be so difficult. It hadn't been while he stuck to the Oxford Road, but last night had worried him and so he'd left the Roman street and followed a signpost that took him along a nice road amongst the plump coppies and fields full of cattle and pigs eating up the stubble before they burnt it, ready for winter barley.

That had been early this morning. After a couple of hours of hard riding, he had spent some time in a copse rubbing chewed bark into the telltale brand on Whitesock's hindquarters to stain it brown. It wouldn't fool anyone who checked properly, but would do for the moment along with the mud he slapped on top. Now it was noon and he was tired. He hadn't got any sleep on Friday night, had ridden hard most of Saturday, not got a full ration of sleep Saturday night, and here it was Sunday and he had no idea where he was. He knew the rutted track was taking him the wrong way, despite the waymarker that had pointed toward Oxford.

He would have struck off across country, but this land was separated out into little fields with newfangled tight-woven hedges and forbye; he didn't want to leave so clear a trail as a broken hedge and a crossed field. The lanes between them headed in half a dozen different directions at once and it was all strange country to him—he didn't know the lay of the land. He knew the right way to go, of course, even though the sky had clouded over, but the lanes wouldn't let him and most of the fields had been deeply ploughed or were still stubbled.

He was starting to feel very thirsty and both horses were tired and sulky from being ridden without a saddle. Now the track was heading downhill into a boggy little wood. He went with it in the hope that he could find a stream in it, slipped from Whitesock's back, and led him as well.

The wood closed around them. There were signs that there had been people living there, once long ago and some more recently, too. In one place there was an old fire and the marks of horses tethered to trees. In another he could see clear signs of wagons from only a few days ago. Perhaps there was some kind of manor house or village nearby.

Later Dodd wondered why he hadn't been more careful and decided that as well as being tired, the rotten Southern air had made him as soft and soppy as the Southerners and he deserved what happened.

The track came at the stream from around a small mound and stones made a rough ford. The trees were thick overhead so he couldn't see the sky and the horses pulled forward to the water so Dodd let them put their heads down to drink.

He was just looking at the deeper part in the bend behind him and wondering if there were any fish in it that he could tickle for his supper when something large and heavy landed on his shoulders and thudded on the back of his head.

Bright lights exploded and he went over like a toppled tree. He glimpsed an ugly scarred face with a broken nose under a morion helmet and a flash of bright orange-and-white rags, felt a hand across his mouth so he bit down hard and head-butted backwards at whoever was on his shoulders.

Next thing, two more heavy weights landed on him and his arms were wrestled up behind while his face went into the mud.

Kicking and fighting as viciously as he could, he struggled to breathe, once even managing to rear up with the red rage all around him. Eventually another blow to his head took the world away into a deeper darkness than he'd ever known, although a part of him remained amused to note that he was still fighting as boots thudded into his ribs.

sunday 17th september 1592, morning

The light was hurting Robert Carey's eyes even through his eyelids and two people were shouting at each other right next to him, hurting his sore head with the noise.

"…you ordered *my son* to investigate the Robsart matter…?"

"Who else could I ask, Harry? Walsingham is dead and none of the others…"

"My son! You put my son in danger of poisoning…?"

"I had to do it!" roared the Queen, "I have to find out…"

"You did not have to find out anything, Eliza, for God's sake, you've let it lie thirty years, you could let it lie another thirty. Why the hell didn't you?"

"I could NOT let it lie, you old fool, look what they sent me!"

Silence. What? What did they send you? Who sent it? Carey fluttered his lids, only to find his eyes worse than ever, blurred and blazing with light that hurt him. He shut them again, tried to stretch his ears.

There was a long moment of silence and his father's heavy breathing, then the sound of creaking joints and popping knees as Lord Hunsdon knelt to the Queen.

"I'm sorry, Eliza."

"Why?"

"For shouting at you."

"You understand now? Why I couldn't let it lie?"

A heavy sigh. "Yes."

There was movement, rustle of skirts. "What else could I do?" His aunt's voice had lost its full-throated roar suddenly and the blurred shape was merging with the darker shape, his father kneeling to her. "I was horrified when I found it. What if it all came out now? And then I heard your boy Robin had turned up at Court and it seemed…it seemed as if God had sent him specially to help me."

More creaking as Carey's father stood again.

"I'm so sorry he was poisoned, Harry. I never thought they would try such a thing, it never…Oh, Harry!"

The two figures merged into one. His father had his arms around the Queen and she was…good Lord, she must be crying into his chest, from the snuffling sounds.

Carey was too weak and dry even to moan. Ask her for my fee and my warrant as Deputy Warden, he thought as forcibly as he could. Go on, Father! Fee! Warrant! Ask!

Baron Hunsdon was rumbling again. "There now, Eliza, there now. It's all right. I have the Gentlemen of the Guard checking all the supplies and some of my other men are asking Norris' servants and kitchen staff what happened. Mr. Byrd and Mrs. de Paris are making reports right now."

"Be gentle…"

"Don't worry, I'm certain both Byrd and Thomasina are loyal, but they must be asked, you know. Somehow enough belladonna got into the flagon of spiced wine that Robin drank from to half-kill him and his henchman."

What? Young Hughie had been poisoned, too? That was interesting.

The Queen sniffed and blew her nose. "You're sure it wasn't the servingman? He's a Scot, after all."

"I very much doubt it. It was pure luck he didn't die after drinking about half the contents of that flagon. Everybody thought he was just very drunk. Luckily he puked some of it up and after he collapsed, the other servingmen thought from his fever that it might be plague so they left him where he lay under the hedge. Once Tovey raised the alarm, of course, he was the first one we went looking for and we found him with the flagon beside him. It was very lucky that we did."

"And you're sure it was poison?"

"Certain, Your Majesty. We fed the flagon's contents to a piglet which ran wild, then collapsed and died less than an hour later. Dr. Lopez says an infallible sign of belladonna poisoning is that the pupils of the eyes become fixed wide open and that light dazzles and hurts the victim. Hughie Tyndale is suffering from that, as well as Robin."

So that was what was wrong with his goddamned eyes.

"The fever and the delirium are also typical."

"Harry, your son…" The Queen was sniffling again which was very unlike her.

"What?"

"Your son insisted that the Earl of Essex be told before he would take anything to bring up the poison. He knew what had happened, but he was more worried about me drinking the spiced wine."

There was a pause.

"Quite right," came his father's voice after a loud harrumph. "No more than I'd expect."

"Oh, Harry…" The Queen's voice had a smile in it. "I have a Court full of men who claim they would die for me, but so few of them who really would."

There was another loud harrumph from his father, who seemed to have something stuck in his throat—a confounded nuisance, as far as Carey was concerned, as he needed his father to talk for him. Come on, Father. Ask her! Fee! Warrant! More money! shouted Carey in his mind, to no effect at all.

Through the watery flicker of his eyelids, he made out two blurred shapes embracing again. Very touching, you prize idiot, thought Carey in despair, why the hell won't you get me some more money and a proper warrant, you old buffoon? Or a customs farm or a patent? How about a monopoly on the import of sugar? That would be nice.

"Eliza, may I beg a favour?" His father's voice sounded tired.

Thank God, Carey thought. Come on, Father, you know how to do it.

"Of course."

"Please, Eliza, for God's sake, will you make sure the boy's mother doesn't get to hear of this?"

Arrgh, thought Carey. Then after a moment's thought—well, yes, all right. Sensible.

Now there was something better than a smile in the Queen's voice, more like a giggle.

"I'll do my best, Harry, but you know that Annie has her ways of finding things out, just as I do. Nobody else need know since neither Robin nor his man actually died, thank God, so no inquest is needed and the Board of Green Cloth doesn't need to sit, or not officially. The poison was only in that particular flagon, not in the rest of the spiced wine."

There was the sound of a woman's skirts on the rush mats again.

"In fact, I think the attempt was upon your son, not me." Hunsdon said nothing. "And even so, brother," continued the Queen awkwardly, "as soon as he's well enough again, you understand that I want Robin to carry on with investigating the Robsart matter."

Another pause and his father sighed. Now! thought Carey. A piece of land. A nice monopoly on the sale of…oh…I don't know…brandy…Come on!

"Will you let me tell him what…?"

"No. He has to work under the same conditions."

"For God's sake…"

"Under the same conditions."

"He's working blind. Literally now, as well as metaphorically."

"I have a reason for what I do, Harry."

"Excellent. What is it?"

"I want your son to have an open mind, not to make assumptions about anything."

"That could be dangerous, you know. Not just to his life, but to you. He might find out by himself or work it out but come to the wrong conclusion. Very clever boy, you know, in spite of the way he treated his tutors, probably the brightest of the litter."

By now Carey had gone beyond thinking in words. His head was too full of pain and frustration at his father's incredible dunderheadedness in not setting his penniless younger son up for life. That was mixed with some pleasure at his father at least acknowledging him as the brightest of his brothers—which he knew already, of course, but it was good to hear it from his father's mouth. Even if he did keep calling him "boy" when Carey was over thirty-two years old and had fought and killed.

Suddenly the Queen laughed her amazingly magical laugh.

"Brightest of the litter?" she chided playfully. "Are you saying he's a sleuthdog for tracking criminals?"

"Why not?"

"What does that make Annie?"

Hunsdon laughed too. "Nothing wrong with bitches. Some of my best trackers have been bitches."

"And you, Harry?"

"Your Majesty's old guard dog, always at your heel."

Creaking of joints meant Hunsdon had genuflected again. Well done, Father, very courtly, Carey thought in despair, where's my goddamned exclusive patent for the sale of silk ribbons, eh?

"Send Thomasina to me as soon as you can," said the Queen's voice.

"Ah yes, before I forget…one of the matters we're investigating is the very fine gold and ruby necklace Robin had in his doublet pocket. His friend the Earl of Cumberland said it was a necklace he had given the Italian woman Signora Bonnetti."

Somehow the Queen could make even a silence dangerously loud. "Interesting," she said at last.

"Signora Bonnetti, however, had left the dancing tent with the Earl's party by then and my lord of Essex says that she was playing cards with him while they discussed her husband's management of the sweet wine farm for him. Two of my own men who were there say this is true."

"So the necklace was a fee for the introduction?"

"I think so."

"Nothing wrong with that and quite a reasonable amount considering the value of the sweet wine farm. I remember Thomasina mentioned it to me earlier. Do you think the Italians are spies, too?"

"Probably. They were at the Scottish Court this summer."

"Ah."

Carey's lids fluttered again and he croaked, trying to explain that he didn't think it was Emilia who had poisoned him, despite it being with belladonna, but that she definitely was a spy.

At last they paid attention to him. He caught the Queen's smell of rosewater and peppermint comfits to sweeten her breath. She was leaning over him with a smooth ivory cup of water with brandy in it. Behind her loomed the wide shape of his father in black Lucca velvet and gold brocade as usual.

He'd better drink whatever the Queen was giving him. With enormous difficulty he lifted his head and gulped to soothe his leathery throat. Something bumped his teeth and he just managed to avoid choking on a large dark bitter-tasting stone, rattling around in the bottom of the cup.

"There," said the Queen, letting his head rest on the pillow again, "how are you, my dear?"

"Better," he managed to say. And he did indeed feel better, though for some reason there was a sharp uncomfortable pain at the base of his belly. The window shutters were closed so the room was not so full of painful light as it had been.

The Queen stroked his cheek. "Your fever's gone," she said. "We'll talk later, Robin."

The blur of black and white topped with red swished out of the room. Carey's father came closer to the bed.

"Well done, son," he said, gripping Carey's bruised shoulder, "She won't forget this. It's a good thing you'd stripped off your clothes and dropped your knife belt in the fever. You were in such a rage, laying about you and roaring about saving Elizabeth, it took every single clerk in the church to hold you down. But at least nobody's dead. Now let's hope we can keep it away from my esteemed lady wife, your mother, eh?"

"Yes, Father," said Carey with difficulty. It had just occurred to him what the pain in his groin was. He urgently, desperately, needed a piss. Christ, he needed it right now!

"Father," he croaked, "Ah…pot…please?"

"Eh?" Hunsdon was deep in thought.

"A chamber pot?"

"Oh...ah...I'll send for a servant...."

"Now!"

Carey was sweating, so perhaps Hunsdon could see the urgency because he bent, looked under the bed and, thank God and all His holy angels, brought out what Carey needed, which was miraculously empty. It took a moment to let go but the relief almost brought tears to his eyes.

As Lord Hunsdon put the pot very carefully down on the rush mat next to the bed, Carey smiled. Amazing the way your body ambushed you and the joy in even the basest things when it hadn't been working for a while. He realised his father had gone to the door and he was afraid of being left alone, the first time he had felt like that since...must be the Armada year, when he was ill before.

"Father?"

Baron Hunsdon loomed over him again. "I've sent for your new clerk," he said. "We've checked Mr. Tovey. I think it was a good idea hiring the boy—he's got sense."

"Hughie?"

"Not out of the woods yet—he's in Lord Norris' servant quarters here. He must have drunk more spiced wine than you did. Dr. Lopez says whether he lives or dies depends entirely upon his humoral complexion and there's little he can do save prescribe his sovereign decoction of beanpods. The man so nearly died last night, we don't suspect him of the poisoning, though we haven't been able to find out much about him as he's Scotch. We've not made any progress on who actually did it, but the two prime suspects seem to be out of it."

"How...long...?"

"Have you been asleep? Well, it's Sunday, you missed Divine Service in the church where you were fighting the poor clerks last night, missed a damned prosy sermon, and you're missing Sunday dinner to be followed by a very fine allegorical masque. It's Sunday afternoon."

Carey groped for the water cup and his father caught his hand just before he knocked it over, put it into his fingers and poured more water for him. Carey tried to fish out the stone he'd nearly swallowed.

"Leave that, it's a bezoar stone against poisoning," said his father, "Dr. Lopez recommended it. The Queen's lent you her unicorn's horn cup as well."

"Nearly swallowed…"

"I don't think you should eat it, I think it's actually a goat's gallstone. I'll drop it in the flagon."

Carey couldn't make out anything in the blur, not the cup, not the flagon, not his father apart from as a large shape. The world was a dazzle that made his eyes hurt again so he shut them tight and frowned unhappily.

"Mr. Tovey thinks your eyes will recover by tomorrow," rumbled his father. "Dr. Lopez thinks it might take a couple of days."

The full cup was in his fingers again so he drank the brandy-and-water mix. Now that he'd dealt with his immediate physical problems, he felt better. Slowly his mouth was getting less dry but he still had to keep his eyes shut.

"Father, would you close the bed curtains? Light hurts my eyes."

"Can't see a damned thing in here, but very well." The curtains swept across making the bed stuffy but the pain in his eyes reduced.

"That necklace…fee for introducing Emilia Bonnetti to Essex."

"Want me to warn him about her?"

Carey hesitated. Perhaps that hadn't been a favour to his lord, after all? Would Essex understand how useful a spy so close to him could be? Or would he blame Carey? He couldn't decide. "I don't know," he admitted.

"We'll keep an eye on her. Young Cecil knows about her, too," said his father. "What happened with the bad guns you sold her in Dumfries?"

"I'm not sure but I think my lord of Cumberland got the Bonnettis out of Ireland just in time, unfortunately."

"Would she bear you a grudge?"

He thought about it. After all, she was Italian. "Probably, but once I made the introduction, she was in Essex's party and nowhere near Hughie. And I don't see why she would jeopardise managing the sweet wine farm by poisoning me. If it wasn't Hughie either, I can't think who else it could have been. Most of my enemies are in and around Carlisle now."

"And the rest of them are creditors who want you alive," growled his father. Carey said nothing because this was manifestly unfair even if it was true. "We haven't had any luck with witnesses. They were all too drunk or busy dancing. Ridiculous bunch of popinjays."

For some reason that reminded him of the incident at the duck pond. He told the story to his father, annoyed that he couldn't see Hunsdon's face for the reaction.

It was a mistake because Hunsdon sat down on the bed and took him through the story twice more. Carey's throat was dry again and he was suddenly exhausted.

"A crossbow argues against Signora Bonnetti because of the difficulty for a woman of drawing and carrying it. You say it was a deer-bolt?" Carey nodded once. "So it must have been a full size crossbow. Hmm. I'll set a guard on your door, Robin, and I don't want you going out without at least three men with you."

Carey shrugged. "God looks after me always."

"God likes us to look after ourselves as well, so He doesn't have to do all the work. Be careful in the Queen's matter, Robin."

"What is it that she doesn't want you to tell me? What was the message she got with the music?"

He thought his father was smiling at his boldness. Well, it was worth a try. He got no answer though. His head was pounding again and he felt too tired to do anything else. Hunsdon patted his hand, lying on the coverlet. Carey felt the roughness of sword callouses there which could only mean his sixty-year-old father was still employing a swordmaster to play veneys with him regularly.

"I'll work on her, but she's a Tudor and she knows the value of information. She wants you to come at the Robsart killing with a fresh mind, since nobody else has got anywhere with it."

"But Father, what if..."

"Ah, Mr. Tovey, thank you for coming."

"M...my lord, how is he?"

"Very much better," Carey said, "thanks to you knowing what was happening." Could that mean Tovey was...No. Surely not. Without the clerk's prompt action, he would probably be dead by now. "But I still can't see a bloody thing at the moment," he added resentfully. "And do you know what happened to my Court suit, I left it hanging on a couple of saints in the church...?"

"Yes, sir, I got Mr. Coleman to help me bring it up before Divine Service this morning. It's hanging on the wall here."

Well thank God for that at least, as the Court suit was probably worth more than the church building itself.

"My lord, Dr. Lopez wants a sample of Sir Robert's water..."

There were careful movements around the pot, someone was filling a flask. The pot was then removed and emptied, no doubt by one of his father's men. He didn't really care. He was falling asleep where he lay propped on pillows in the darkness of the bed curtains. He yawned and struggled to remember something else that was very important. Oh, yes...

"Father, where's Sergeant Dodd? Should be here by now."

His father was moving, preparing to leave. "I've been looking out for him," came the rumble. "No sign of him yet. I'll send him straight up when he arrives. Sleep well, Robin. I'll have a man at your door."

Blackness welcomed him with strange dreams that broke apart and fought each other. One was of Elizabeth Widdrington holding him tight and him kissing her the way he had longed to since the Armada year. One was of a prison cell.

sunday 17th september 1592, late afternoon

He woke up to a darker chamber, restless, his stomach aching
and his head hurting again, so he sat up on the bed among the
pillows and tried to think.

The important things were the inquest report and witness
statements. Had Thomasina herself realised just how damning
they were? The men of the jury had clearly been stout honest
gentlemen because despite extreme pressure from powerful
people, they had reported some things that made a nonsense of
their obedient verdict of accidental death. Everyone knew that
Amy Robsart had died of a broken neck. What everyone knew
was wrong.

A little while later someone knocked. It was John Tovey,
coming in carrying candles which hurt Carey's eyes. He got the
fire going again.

"Mr. Tovey, I want you to go to whichever kitchen is serving
the Queen and ask them for food for me and when you come
back, bring your penner and paper. Make sure the food is taken
from a common pot, no small meat pies or penny loaves, for
instance."

"Will you want me to taste the meal, sir?"

The lad caught on quickly; that was good. "Yes please, Mr.
Tovey, if you would. When you come back."

"Yes, sir."

Was Tovey the poisoner or in league with him or her? Very
unlikely since all he'd had to do when Carey called him the night
before was set up a cry of "Plague" and leave him until he was
dead. Certainly the poisoner or his or her accomplice wouldn't
instantly identify what was wrong and get him to purge. Besides,
Carey had picked him out personally, almost at random.

By the time Tovey got back with more food from the Queen's
kitchen, set up in one of the manor's parlours, Carey was hungry
and bored. He'd tried reading his papers but he couldn't make
anything out, in fact he couldn't even look out of the windows
for the dazzle. Goddamn it. Although come to think of it, that

was a very promising metaphor to use on the Queen some-time—being dazzled blind by Cynthia, the Moon Goddess and so on and so forth.

Tovey ate most of the bread, cheese, butter, and sausage plus a good half of the large wedge of game pie he'd brought. Once he started eating, Carey found his stomach and gullet were still sore from being sick and so he mostly just drank the ale.

"Mr. Tovey, where did you learn to spot belladonna poisoning?"

"Ah…my mother was a wise woman, sir. She taught me some things. When she died, I went to my father. He sent me to a good Oxford apothecary to prentice to him and learn my letters better than he could teach me."

"And then?"

"My master taught me Latin as well as many other things and when he found I was an apt pupil he sent me to the grammar school. I was able for all things to do with letters so I went to study at Balliol, sir, as a servitor. He died of plague a little after I took my degree, alas. God keep him. He was a good and kindly master—we often spoke about the mysteries of alchemy and the different qualities of matter. I found it hard to get work in Oxford where there are so many clerks, so I went back to my father and that's why I came to clerk for the Queen's secretaries, in hopes of finding a place."

"Good thing for me you did. Now then, those papers I asked you to translate. You understood the significance of them?"

Silence. Carey couldn't even see the boy's face, much less read it. His voice came as a whisper. "Yes, sir."

"Explain it to me."

"I have friends at Gloucester College where she was buried. Everyone knows Lady Dudley fell down the stairs at Cumnor Place and broke her neck and everyone says she was murdered, but I didn't…I couldn't understand why the inquest found for accidental death."

"Somebody very important told them to," Carey said.

"Well yes, sir, but why then did they say she had neither stain nor bruise on her?"

"Go on."

"She fell down the stairs and hit her head with two dints, one-half an inch, the other a couple of inches deep so her skull must have been broken. How come she didn't bleed?"

"And?"

"And what, sir?"

Carey was surprised he hadn't spotted the other ridiculous thing. "According to witnesses, her headdress was untouched and on her head."

A pause. "Oh."

"Yes, oh. No bruises—possibly that could be because when she actually fell down the stairs she was already dead, though I doubt it. You can bruise for a while after death. No stains—maybe, just perhaps, her skin wasn't broken even though her skull was and so she didn't bleed. But her headdress untouched? With a two-inch dent in her head? I don't think so."

Silence. Carey continued, "They reported it truly even though they had been told what their verdict should be, because they were under oath. I assume that whoever was pressuring them didn't bother to read the whole report because if they had, I expect they would have sent it back to be rewritten."

"Yes, sir. That's what surprised me."

Carey didn't add what had already occurred to him about that, which was that the Queen had clearly not read it. The boy was frightened enough already.

"I don't need to tell you that everything in this matter must be kept most secret and not spoken of to anyone."

"No, sir. I wouldn't dream…"

"There is one circumstance when you must speak of it and that's if I die suddenly for any reason at all without having finished my inquiries. If that happens you must immediately leave the Court, and lie low for a while. Take any papers with you and make sure you give them to…to…" Damn it, to whom?

Who couldn't be suspected in the Amy Robsart killing? "…to my father or the steward at Somerset House. Understand?"

"Yes sir. Who is your father exactly, sir?"

"The Queen's Lord Chamberlain, Baron Hunsdon."

A very loud gulp and then Carey thought he saw a smile. Or heard it rather, in the ambitious boy's suddenly eager voice. "Really?"

"Yes, really. So please make notes." There was a rustle and the soft click of a pen being dipped. "And of course be very careful of poison for both of us. Is there a man on the door now?"

"Um." Tovey went and looked. "It's Mr. Henshawe," he said.

A good man, Carey remembered him. He shook his head with his eyes still closed and frowned. "That was one of the mysteries of the thing," he said to Tovey, his restless mind drifting back to the puzzle the Queen had set him. "Why wasn't Amy Robsart poisoned instead of being pushed down stairs? Certainly she was careful about what and how she ate, but even so…it wouldn't have been so very hard to do by an expert. The Papists insist that it was her husband, the Earl of Leicester, who killed her. But if it was him, why the devil didn't he poison her with belladonna or white arsenic or something? Yes, of course, there would have been rumours but the thing would have been uncertain enough that he would still have had a chance of marrying the Queen."

No answer from Tovey who was probably too shocked.

"After all, killing his wife was a tremendous risk—why would he do it in such a way that would immediately look like murder and draw down suspicion on his head? Dudley was never the cleverest of men but he wasn't crazy and he wasn't stupid."

"Did you know him, sir?"

"Oh yes, of course, he used to shout at me when I was a young idiot of a page in the sixties and seventies. Nobody ever spoke about his first wife but only fools of Papist priests ever thought it had been him that killed her."

"They say it was him at Gloucester College, sir."

"No doubt, being a notorious bunch of Papists there. How much recent history do you know, Mr. Tovey? I mean after the end of Holinshed's Chronicles, about the Queen's father King Henry and his various…er…marriages?"

"Very little, sir. Only that the Queen is his daughter by Queen Ann Boleyn and that her older sister, Bloody Mary, was by the Spanish Infanta, Katherine of Aragon."

"Well, the Queen lost her own mother, Ann Boleyn, my great-aunt, to the axe on trumped up charges of infidelity. The next of Henry's Queens died of a childbed fever, the Queen after that he divorced for ugliness, the Queen after that was executed for infidelity on a bill that probably was foul, and the one after that survived him but then died of childbed fever after marrying later." Tovey said nothing. "It's common gossip at Court that the Queen never wed to get an heir because she's in horror of marriage, because she believes that it's tantamount to a sentence of death for the woman. That's why she tries to protect her maids of honour from the marriage bed. She certainly loved Robert Dudley when she came to the throne and she might have been able to bring herself to marry for his sake, but after he had killed his first wife? Just the suspicion of it was enough to set her against it. He knew that and he wasn't stupid or reckless. If he had decided to kill Amy Robsart, the thing would have been done a lot better and would never have been known as murder, so he could in fact marry the Queen afterward and become King."

"Y…yes, sir. Um…s…sir, isn't talking about the Queen like this treasonous?"

"Yes, it is." Carey said, "if she finds out."

Silence. "Yes, sir."

Carey hoped that Tovey wouldn't take the bait held out to him in case he was somebody's spy, but you never knew. And you might as well add a bit of egg to the pudding.

"Of course, it's plain Amy was in fact killed no matter what the inquest says. And there are plenty of other suspects."

Tovey moved restlessly. "Sir," he said awkwardly, "I…I'm only a c…clerk and you haven't known me long. Should you be… er…opening your mind to me like this?"

Carey beamed at the area of blur where he was. "Probably not," he agreed, "if you're working for someone else apart from me."

"No, sir, of course not."

"Mr. Tovey," Carey admonished, "if you aren't yet, you will be when word gets round you're my clerk now. The people who are likely to offer you money to pass information to them are Sir Thomas Heneage, the Earl of Essex, my father, Sir Robert Cecil—any number of people here and more once we get back to Carlisle."

"I'll tell them 'no,' sir."

"No you won't." He could actually hear the click of Tovey's jaw as he shut his mouth after a shocked pause. Bless him, he was as a newborn lamb to the greedy wolves of the Court. Better educate him quickly.

"What you do is you tell me about it. Whoever it is, whatever they offer, you take it and then you tell me. Especially if it's Sir Robert Cecil. Don't be too quick, play innocent and shocked— they'll expect it. Let them pressure you, especially that bastard Heneage, but then give in. Whoever it is, whatever they ask, no matter how much money you're offered, you swear you'll tell no one, especially not me, and you'll work for them only, and then we'll decide together what I want them to know. I won't charge you commission on your bribes, so long as you tell me about each one."

Another pause and then Tovey chuckled softly. "Was that why my father was so happy not to pay a fee for the place as your clerk?"

"Absolutely. Don't let him drink all your bribes. And learn to lie."

Tovey dipped his pen in a businesslike way. "Shall I put my lord of Leicester at the top of your list of suspects?"

"Why not? Make five columns, head them *Nomine, quomodo, quando ubique, quare, cui bono.*"

"Name, how, where, and when, why, whose benefit?"

Carey was quite proud of himself for remembering all that Latin.

"Yes, Walsingham's system. He taught it to me when I was serving him in Scotland, along with many other things. He always said that practically any tangle could be solved by asking *Cui bono*, who benefits? So, Dudley first. His best method was poison, despite Lord Burghley having a man placed in Amy's kitchen. Where and when was any where and any time since she was his wife. The why is obvious but the benefit—he could not benefit from the way the murder was actually done."

The pen was slipping smoothly across the paper. "Unless it was a double bluff?"

"I doubt it. He hardly bluffed at primero. I don't think he would bluff with the chance of becoming King."

"You said there were other suspects?"

"Sir William Cecil, my lord Treasurer Burghley now."

The pen stopped moving. "Sir?" The fear in the boy's voice now did credit to Burghley.

"Write it down, Mr. Tovey." Carey had an idea of what he would do with the paper later, despite the risk. "In fact put in any of the old guard, the Privy Council of the early years, the men who danced around the young Queen. By blocking out the favourite, the killing of Amy Robsart benefited anyone who hoped to marry the Queen—therefore the Spanish, all of her suitors foreign or English. Hatton, possibly even Heneage. He had the Queen's eye once, I believe, for a couple of months." He laughed at the thought. "Burghley is top of the list because he was desperate to stop her marrying Dudley as they hated each other then and he would have lost his place the instant King Robert was crowned."

He paused to let Tovey catch up. "And then there's the most obvious suspect of all," he said softly, "the Queen herself."

That stopped him. "I'm not writing that, sir," said Tovey.

"Put her down as 1500," Carey agreed, harking back to the code name for the Queen that Walsingham had used. Of course the Queen probably knew it, but it kept the thing decorous. The fact that Tovey wrote it down without arguing further showed he had a brain and could use it.

Because the fact was that the Queen was by far the most likely suspect. Not as she was now, a wise and politic prince, but as she had been in Carey's father's stories of the early days of her Court, when Carey himself had been a baby in swaddling bands in his wet nurse's arms. When the Queen had been a wild laughing young woman with red hair, a flaming temper, and the power to draw men like moths to a flame. That she was ruthless enough to kill her lover's wife could not be doubted. But was she foolish enough, impetuous enough? Had she done that?

He shook his head. If she had, why ask him to investigate? Why not, as his father had advised, leave it lie another thirty years until she was safely dead and nobody cared anymore?

Since the Queen was a woman, she might have any number of reasons, but from the information that Byrd had given him, Carey rather thought that someone else knew for sure who had done it and had sent her a message demanding money along with some kind of token proving he did. Which made things look very bad for the Queen, indeed. Had she really done as her far stupider cousin, Mary Queen of Scots, had done? As her father had done? Had she murdered to clear her path to marriage?

He shook his head, which was aching again. If it really had been the Queen who killed Amy Robsart, how had she done it and kept it secret so long? She was constantly surrounded by her women and had been even when she was running wild with Robert Dudley. The Papists were always claiming that some bastard or other was hers, even one of his father's own byblows had been taken up in France as the Queen's baseborn son, but nobody who knew anything about the Court ever believed a word of it. And if she had done it, surely she would have done a better job, just as Dudley would have? There would have been somebody available to swing for the murder, surely? Carey could think of half a dozen ways the Queen could have quietly abolished Dudley's first wife, not one of which involved pushing the woman down a few stairs. That was why, if he even thought about it, he had assumed what most people now at Court did, that Dudley's first wife had been unlucky or unwell and the thing truly was an accident. Until he read the inquest papers.

If she was being blackmailed about it, she might well ask him to investigate—but surely then she would have given him the message with the Spanish air on it and the token, whatever that was, and told him to quietly find and kill the blackmailer. Surely?

He was feeling tired again, surprisingly so. Sitting in shadows with only one candle lit for Tovey and his eyes shut was making him sleepy. He realised he had been silent a long while.

"Is that all, sir?" Tovey asked hopefully.

"Yes, thank you. I think I'll go back to sleep now though it's far too early. It's infernally boring not being able to see but that might help my bloody eyes recover."

"It might, sir. M…may I advise you to cover them when daylight comes? Your eyes pain you because they have no defence against the sunlight and too much light might actually damage them and blind you permanently."

"Jesu." That put fear in the pit of his stomach. "Is Mr. Henshawe on guard at the door?"

Tovey checked. "Yes, sir. And I've brought my pallet and I'll sleep here tonight."

"Good. Has Sergeant Dodd arrived?"

"No, sir, when I fetched the food, your father's under-steward said my lord was sending riders out along the London road to see if he'd fallen off his horse, as he must have left London early on Saturday. "

Carey frowned. That didn't sound at all plausible; Dodd had practically been born on a horse. But perhaps he was in some kind of trouble. You never knew: after all, who would have thought Carey might end up being poisoned in the Queen's Court? Dodd's absence was worrying—surely he wouldn't have decided to simply head north and bypass Oxford altogether? Even if he'd walked from London to Oxford, he should have been here by now.

◇◇◇

Somebody knocked on the door. Carey was instantly awake, feeling for a dagger under his pillow where there wasn't one, blinking in the darkness of the brocade bed curtains with a pattern of fleur de lis. He heard Tovey's voice murmuring.

"Mrs. de Paris to see Sir Robert," said one of Thomasina's women.

"Let her in, Mr. Tovey," called Carey with resignation, groping at the end of the bed for his dressing gown and finding none. What was the time? He wasn't sure because when he peered through the curtains the room seemed brighter than it should have been with just one blurry watch-candle in it. He heard people talking. "Damnit, Mistress Thomasina, wait a minute, I'm only in my shirt…"

Tovey handed him a fur dressing gown of his father's, marten and velvet, which Carey pulled around his shoulders, opened one of the bed curtains and sat with his legs crossed.

The door was opened a little by Mr. Henshawe, and Carey could make out the small colourful blur of Thomasina still in her tumbling clothes.

"Sir, would you like me to make notes?"

"No," said Thomasina's high-pitched childlike voice. "Please leave us."

Tovey stood where he was. Carey heard him swallow. "Er…?" he said. Carey was liking the scrawny clerk more and more. "It's all right, Mr. Tovey," he said. "Mrs. de Paris is an old friend."

Tovey bowed awkwardly and went out into the passage to stand with Thomasina's women.

Carey felt Thomasina jump up on the bed like a man mounting a horse and then she sat with her legs folded under her, looking like a small lump of forest of tawny and green brocade in the general blur. He smiled in her direction.

"Next time your spiced wine tastes bitter, Sir Robert, may I suggest you throw it away?"

Her voice was withering.

"At the time," he admitted, "it never occurred to me that anyone would try and poison me, but from now on I'll bear it in mind."

"Good."

"Why are you here, Mistress? It's late. And I think you weren't even born when Amy Robsart died…"

"No, I remember the accession bonfires and getting drunk on spiced ale with my older brother," she said. "Perhaps I was about two or three at the time as it's one of my first memories."

Good Lord, she was older than he was. Astonishing.

"Of course, I wasn't then in Her Majesty's service nor even imagining such a thing. I'm here, Sir Robert, to find out if the Queen can help you in your quest."

"She can come and break the matter fully with me, tell me about the message that upset her, so I know where I am."

Silence. "She won't. Not yet."

Damn it, he hated it when people wouldn't tell you what you needed to know. But there it was, neither his father nor Thomasina would disobey the Queen just to make his life easier. So he shrugged.

"Is there anything else I can do?"

"While I'm stuck in this room and not able to see, I might as well keep busy. I want to interview all of Her Majesty's Privy Councillors that served her then and are alive now."

"Oh?" Carey couldn't make out her face but he didn't need to. He could imagine the expression on the midget's face. "Who do you want to start with?"

In for a penny, in for a pound, Carey thought. Let's see if my loving aunt, against all her normal habits, actually means what she says.

"My Lord Treasurer Burghley," he said simply.

Well at least Thomasina didn't laugh at the idea of the Queen's penniless and frankly quite lowly cousin and nephew interviewing the person who in fact administered the realm for her and also ran the Queen's finances, who was the chief man in the realm whatever the Earl of Essex thought, and had been since the Queen's accession.

"When?"

"If he's here at Rycote, now. Tonight. If not, as soon as he can come."

Instead of a grim laugh, a flat refusal, or a placatory platitude, Thomasina said simply, "Very well, Sir Robert, I shall arrange it. He's here, so don't go back to sleep."

Well, he hadn't expected that. She hopped off the bed like a sizeable cat and trotted to the door.

Jesu, thought Carey, what have I asked for? I didn't expect to be given it!

Burghley arrived only twenty minutes later. Carey had wrapped himself in his father's dressing gown, feeling every limb as heavy as if he had just chased a raiding party across the Bewcastle Waste for two days. He was still sitting on the bed because the bed curtains gave him some protection from the light. He had also fastened a silk scarf across his eyes. Partly it was to protect them from the extra candles Tovey had lit so he could take notes, partly for dramatic purposes. He was nervous. Carey knew the Lord Treasurer, of course, had oftentimes seen his aunt lose her temper with her faithful servant and throw things at him. Walsingham had told him a few interesting tidbits but had respected the man greatly, despite his pragmatism and their many disagreements over how best to deal with Papists.

Burghley limped in, wincing from his gout and the man with him had an odd, quick uneven gait. Ah yes, Burghley must have brought his second son whose body was clenched and hunched from the rickets he had suffered in his youth, despite the careful supervision of three or four doctors.

"My Lord Treasurer, S...Sir Robert Cecil," announced Tovey in awed tones. Carey stood for them, bowed, then felt behind him for the bed and sat again quickly, drawing his legs up. He had actually nearly overbalanced, his brain felt battered and bruised, and his mouth was dry again.

"My Lord Treasurer, Sir Robert, I am very grateful to you and honoured at your coming here. I apologise, my lord, that my temporary disability has prevented me from coming to you as would be more appropriate," he said formally.

"Yes, yes, Sir Robert. Her Majesty asked me to speak to you about these matters but alas, I doubt very much that I can help you," said Burghley's voice. It was a deep voice and paradoxically able to make very dull subjects verge on interesting. Even Scottish politics became comprehensible when Burghley explained them, a remarkable and essential talent. Carey remembered the Lord Treasurer once explaining to him many years ago why it was that his debts kept mounting up. Probably his father had asked him to. Carey vaguely remembered that the lecture was about what four shillings in the pound interest could do given time. Burghley seemed to think that because he was interested in the clever Greek ways of planning cannon fire and siege towers and had read that manuscript Italian book about card play, he could understand accounting. He probably could, he just... wasn't interested. Burghley had given up eventually.

Tovey brought up the one chair with arms and a cushion for Lord Burghley. Sir Robert Cecil quietly took a chair without arms that had been foraged specially from one of the manor's storerooms. The room was too small for any more furniture with the big bed in it, the clothes chest, and Tovey's pallet folded on top of it. Tovey was using the window sill as a desk.

"I have asked my clerk, Mr. Tovey, to keep a note," Carey said and heard the creak of the starched linen ruff when Burghley nodded.

"Good. Good practice. My son will do the same for me."

Carey wondered if the two records would look anything like each other. The chair creaked on its own note as Burghley settled himself in it.

"May I offer you wine, my lord?" Carey asked, then smiled, "though I may say I've been a little put off wine myself."

It was annoying that he couldn't see Burghley's expression, that pouchy wary face with the knowing little smile.

"Alas, Sir Robert," Burghley said, "Dr. Lopez has warned me off wine of any sort and I am sentenced to drink mild ale and nothing else apart from a foul and superstitious potion made of crocus-bulbs as penalty for my gout."

Carey made a sympathetic noise. "How is your gout, my lord?"

"Bad," was Burghley's short answer. "Very painful. Get to the point, sir, Her Majesty will be waiting to cross-examine me after this meeting."

Carey paused. He wanted straight answers and wasn't about to start a verbal fencing match with the finest exponent in the kingdom.

"The point, my lord, is *cui bono*," he said, plunging straight in. "Who benefits? There are those who would say that you were the one man who benefitted most from Amy Dudley's murder."

Both Sir Robert Cecil and Tovey sucked in their breaths with audible gasps. Carey sat with his legs folded, his father's marten and tawny dressing gown round his shoulders and the scarf over his eyes and felt...good God, he was enjoying himself dicing with death again. His hearing seemed to be getting better as well—the cannonfire and shooting muskets and dags in France and on the Borders had blunted his hearing, taken away his ability to hear bat squeaks and noticeably dulled soft music for him. Perhaps with his eyes not working properly he was paying more attention to what he could hear. He had known the moment Tovey's pen and Sir Robert Cecil's pen had stopped their soft movements across paper.

"Explain yourself," said Burghley with cold fury in his voice.

"My lord, with all due respect..." Carey began, knowing very well what the lawyer's phrase meant, as did Burghley. "I am sure I am not the first person to point that out. From what I know of the first few years of Her Majesty's blessed reign, she was very far from being the wise sovereign lady that she now is. She was, God save her, a flibbertigibbet, a flirt, and very disinclined to any business of ruling at all. She ran riot with Robert Dudley and other men of her Court in the first few years. It was a matter of desperate import to you and all her wiser councillors that she marry as quickly as possible so that she would have a man to direct and guide her and calm her unstable woman's humours."

A pause. Tovey cleared his throat. "Sir, d...did you want m...me to..."

"Record all of it, Mr. Tovey," Carey ordered firmly. "I will repeat it to Her Majesty's face and take the consequences."

There was more creaking of chin against linen ruff. Someone, probably Burghley, was shaking his head.

"There was no shortage of good mates for her," Carey went on, quoting his father. "Philip II of Spain offered for her and could not be rejected outright, several German and Swedish princes offered who were unexceptional except that the Queen didn't like them. Even a carefully chosen English nobleman might have been a possibility. Unfortunately the Queen had fallen head-over-heels in love with her horsemaster, Robert Dudley, the son and grandson of traitors, much hated by the older noble families and a man of very little common sense. He was the worst possible lover she could have chosen but she would not listen to reason." The silence in the little chamber was oppressive.

"He was also utterly opposed to you, my lord, and your careful diplomacy, had no understanding of the financial situation which was in a desperate state, and was moreover an intemperate man who loved war, although he himself was disastrously untalented as a general.

"You, my Lord Treasurer, were in terror that the Queen would persuade Dudley to leave his wife and scandalously marry her, making himself king. This you saw as likely to drop the realm straight into civil war as the nobility picked their own candidates for the Queen's husband and called out their tenants. In point of fact, the Northern Earls did revolt a few years later with the Howards at their head. And the Earl of Leicester hated you, my lord, and so with him once crowned, you would have lost your place and the realm gone to rack and ruin even if civil war was somehow avoided." Somebody was breathing hard and Carey knew it wasn't him, though his heart was pounding. God, this was fun—should he be enjoying himself so much?

"So, my lord, logic clearly shows that you were the one man who gained most by Amy Dudley's death in the manner by which it occurred...."

"Don't be ridiculous, Sir Robert," snapped Burghley. "Amy Dudley's death cleared Leicester's way to the throne. However she died, the fact that she was dead made him a widower with no impediment to marriage. When I heard what had happened I was in the worst despair I have ever been in my life because I was sure they would marry immediately and that all would fall out exactly as you have suggested. In fact I started selling land and books so I could move to the Netherlands again if necessary. Amy Dudley was my best bulwark against Leicester's kingship. I had men placed in her household to guard her, one in the kitchen against poison, one as her under-steward, and I was paying a fortune to one of her women, I forget the name, to keep me informed. I had all the letters to and from Cumnor Place opened and read, I took every precaution to keep Leicester's wife safe and alive, and the bloody man somehow managed to kill her anyway!" Burghley was shouting by the end. Carey thought from the sound that he was leaning forward, quite possibly prodding the air with a finger as he often did.

"So, who did kill her?"

"Her husband, Sir Robert Dudley, the Earl of Leicester, the obvious suspect, the man who wanted to be king." Burghley was still shouting and Carey wondered if his face was going purple.

"With respect, no, my lord," said Carey calmly. "It's my belief that the Queen would not, could not marry a man who had killed his wife, no matter how, no matter why."

"Of course she would. She was on heat for him, it was a disgraceful sight."

"So why didn't she, my lord?"

"What?"

"You say Leicester must have killed his wife so he could marry the Queen. Once he had done it, why didn't they marry?"

"God knows, perhaps God managed to drive a particle of common sense into the Queen's head, because God knows none of the rest of her council could." Carey was momentarily entranced at the implied idea of Almighty God sitting on the Privy Council presided over by Burghley. "Or perhaps she realised that the scandal would destroy her. It was then only seventy-six years since the Queen's grandfather ended the civil wars between York and Lancaster by taking the throne. There had been a decade of trouble, religious turns and twists, Queen Mary burning hundreds of good Protestant men and women, the Exchequer exhausted, the currency debased, the…"

"So, my lord, you say that you did not kill Amy Dudley in such a manner that the Earl would be blamed and thus the Queen would refuse to marry him?"

A fist came down on the arm of the chair. "No! That would have been madness! To take such a risk, take away the one thing putting a brake on Leicester's cursed ambition? Never! Thank God, the Queen realised that a man who would kill one wife might also kill another wife, just as her father had, and that pulled her back from the disastrous marriage, much to Leicester's disappointment."

"But you could have done it?" Carey pursued, knowing he was dancing on the lip of a volcano.

"I had and still have the power…the men…to do such things," said Burghley's voice, heavy with menace. "As a general rule, I do not use it. As a general rule."

Carey smiled back at the threat. "You're sure it was Leicester, not realising that the Queen would react the way she did."

There was the faint rustle of lifted shoulders. "I said so at the time and have said so since. It was that bloody man she fell in love with, clearing away the main impediment, despite all I could do to protect her." The chair creaked. Carey wondered for the first time if Burghley might have been a little in love with the Queen all those years ago as well.

The Queen's first Councillor must have read his mind.

"Of course I loved her, Sir Robert," he rumbled into his ruff. "We all did. She was a marvel, a joy, a gift from God. She was enraging and magical, every room she entered was suddenly full of sunshine and lightning, a slender pale creature with a war-beacon of hair and the temper of a king and that laugh…God, yes, Sir Robert, I loved your aunt from the time I first saw her in her brother's reign. I always knew I could never have her as my own. Yes, I hated Dudley because he made her happy and made her laugh and I could not—although I could indeed make her safer. And that was all I wanted. All I still want. All I have ever asked of God is that she should outlive me."

Carey found that he was wordless. He had never expected cautious dull old Burghley to have such passion hidden in him, much less speak of it.

"The Earl of Leicester killed Amy Robsart, his unfortunate wife, married before he realised he had a chance of a kingdom, while Princess Elizabeth still had two lives between her and the throne and a question over her legitimacy. He killed the woman because he was a stupid but ambitious man and he did it to clear his path to the throne."

Burghley was creaking to his feet, making it clear that the interview was over. From the sound, Carey thought the still-silent Sir Robert Cecil was helping him. He tried again.

"My lord, that doesn't work. *Cui bono*, remember? How could Leicester have gained from killing Amy that way?"

Burghley paused. "I told you, I had men looking after her. He had no other way...."

"Had there been any attempts at poisoning her? Any mysterious fevers?"

"She was ill, certainly, she had something wrong with one of her breasts that pained her, but not enough to kill her."

"But had there been previous attempts to..."

"No."

"None?"

"No." Burghley did seem to pause. "I would never have taken the risk of killing Amy Dudley," he said again, but more thoughtfully this time. For a moment Carey wondered if something new had occurred to him after all this time. But then the door slammed.

However his chamber wasn't empty. Somebody else was close to the bed and it wasn't Tovey because the smell was different and the movement even more awkward than Tovey's.

"Mr. Secretary Cecil," Carey said politely to Burghley's hunchback second son whom he had nearly forgotten because the man had said not a word. "What do you think of this?"

Cecil's voice was higher and a little breathless because of his back. "I think it's a very interesting problem, Sir Robert, but I believe what my father says. Killing Amy Dudley to lay the murder at Leicester's door in the hope that it would put the Queen off Leicester…no. Far too great a gamble for him, Sir Robert, and my father never ever bets on anything but a certainty."

Carey had to admit he had no understanding of this way of thinking. Surely a gamble was the finest thing in the world, the breath of life and excitement even if it did go wrong? As he had to admit, it often did for him. But that made all the sweeter the times when it actually worked.

"While Leicester was married, he couldn't have the Queen. As soon as he was free, my father was sure the Queen and he would marry. That they didn't is a mercy he has always attributed to the direct intervention of the Almighty. And that's the beginning and end of it," Cecil added. "Meantime, I understand that your remarkable Sergeant Dodd has not yet arrived, which is causing you some concern."

"Yes? Do you have any news of him?" Carey was a little surprised. In the cockpit of the Court, he was in the opposing faction to the Cecils, that of the Earl of Essex. Why was Sir Robert Cecil, secretary to the Privy Council, offering him useful information?

"I do." Cecil sounded amused. "Sergeant Dodd rode out of the wreckage of one of Heneage's secret London houses with one of Heneage's post-horses under him and another as remount. That was on Saturday morning."

Carey couldn't help it. He shouted with laughter. "Good God, what happened? He didn't raid Heneage's…He did?"

"Yes, Sir Robert, it seems he did, in alliance with the King of London and your extraordinary lady mother and her Cornish… ah…followers."

Carey was too stunned to speak. Surely to God she hadn't set Dodd on to conduct a private reprisal raid on Heneage in the middle of London? To teach him a lesson on not plotting against her husband and sons? Had she?

"The official story is a little different. It seems that the rabble Heneage was employing there had kidnapped several people, including your young lawyer, and there was a riot during which Dodd, your mother's…people, and a few upright men loaned by the King of London freed the prisoners and accidentally set the house on fire."

That was definitely Dodd. He had a worrying weakness for accidentally setting things on fire.

"Fortunately not much damage was done, only a couple of deaths and peace was restored. Luckily. Oh, and another of Heneage's houses blew up the same night."

Carey shook his head in wonder. She had! Did his father know?

"Very fortunately, your lady mother had let me know that the riot was likely and so I was able to be present and help broker peace and so the matter is now, as far as I am concerned, closed."

"Mr. Recorder Fleetwood?"

"He concurs."

This was fascinating. Was it possible that his mother had managed to form an alliance with Burghley's promising second son? His father was always neutral in Court factions and he, of course, was the Earl of Essex's man who was also Heneage's notional lord, unfortunately. His mother had deliberately reached out to involve Burghley's politic son in Dodd's revenge against Heneage, it seemed. And it looked as if she had got away with it.

However it was very worrying now that Dodd hadn't made it to Oxford. With a post-horse and remount, Dodd should have arrived on the Saturday evening, around the time Carey was puking his guts up to get rid of the poison, or early on Sunday morning. So long as he hadn't been stupid or ignorant enough to stay the night at one of the regular post-inns along the Oxford road, of course…Ah.

"I don't suppose…" Carey began cautiously. "You didn't notice any post-inns on fire as you came from London yourself?"

Cecil paused before he answered. "Curiously enough, there was one we passed this morning that was still smoking and had half its roof burnt off, but fortunately no one died." Carey said nothing. "We didn't inquire about it. I'll send a man down to talk to the innkeeper."

"Thank you Mr. Secretary. For…er…everything."

"Please don't mention it. I was delighted to make a better acquaintance of my Lady Hunsdon and Sergeant Dodd."

Again the door banged, more quietly this time, and Carey frowned, absentmindedly pulled the annoying scarf off his eyes, only to find his eyes still pained by the candles Tovey was using. "Mr. Tovey," he said, "did you note down what Mr. Secretary Cecil said?"

Tovey's voice was struggling to sound unmoved. "Yes, sir."

"Please burn that page." He waited until the crackle of paper and the smell of smoke reached him and Tovey pounded the ashes in the fireplace where a fire had been laid but not lit.

What was the time? Somewhere near midnight? Damn, damn, damn it. Where the hell was Dodd? What had happened to him? The man always seemed to be made of boiled leather and very sharp steel but he was only human.

Carey pushed the covers back and got out of bed, intending to get dressed and roust out some men to canter down along the Oxford road and find out what had happened at that post-inn.

Then he fell over the chair Burghley had sat in, blundered into the chest by the wall, and stubbed his toes painfully. While he was still cursing that, there was another knock at the door. Tovey moved to open it a little and there was a murmur of argument. Tovey turned his head, his voice even more nervous than usual.

"It's Mr. Vice Chamberlain Heneage to see you, sir."

sunday 17th september 1592, night

Carey was standing on one leg, holding his toes. Jesu! Heneage! Come to make a complaint, no doubt, damn damn.

He hopped to the bed with the dressing gown flapping, knocking over the little table by the bed as he went and climbed in gratefully.

"I'm resting, Mr. Tovey," he hissed. "Tell him to go away."

More conversation. "Sir, Mr. Vice Chamberlain says that Her Majesty has sent him and he must speak with you."

Heart thumping with annoyance and tension, Carey sat up again, wrapped the dressing gown tighter round him. His knuckles had recovered from breaking Heneage's nose at the beginning of September, but still...Had the man come to demand satisfaction? Was that why Cecil had told him the bare bones of what Dodd and Lady Hunsdon had been up to while he had been riding for Oxford and snoring in the post-inn on the way? It sounded as if Dodd had introduced some of the Borderers' ways of settling disputes to London, and as an officer of the Queen's law, he could not possibly approve of it. Officially.

"Mr. Tovey," he said loudly, "I am at a disadvantage here. Please make notes and if Mr. Heneage does not behave himself as a gentleman should, would you be so good as to tell Mr. Henshawe to remove him and then fetch my father?"

Heneage came through the door with the predictable clerk at his back. Carey couldn't make him out either.

"I think you are hardly in a position to lecture me on the behaviour of a gentleman, Sir Robert," he sneered nasally.

"Quite true, Mr. Vice," Carey said. "I find the presence of the man who tried to use my older brother against my father and then beat up my henchman does annoy me enough to make me forget my manners. What do you want?"

Heneage plumped himself down in the chair that Carey had just tripped over.

"You wished to speak to me, Sir Robert," he said sourly. "Her Majesty told me to come and so here I am."

"I don't believe I did. You weren't a Privy Councillor in 1560 were you?"

"I was far too young. I didn't even come to Court until 1563."

"Why are you here then?"

"Mrs. de Paris insisted as well."

"Why?"

A pause. Heneage's voice when he spoke again was full of compressed fury. "I know very well that you set your man Dodd to burn my Southwark house in complete defiance of Her Majesty's peace and…"

Carey managed a laugh, carefully measured for maximum insult. "I certainly did not, Mr. Vice. I'm afraid I wouldn't have the balls. If, which is not admitted, Sergeant Dodd had anything to do with quelling the riot at your house caused by your negligent employment of deserted ex-soldiers and other riffraff, I'm sure he did it in order to preserve the Queen's peace, not break it."

"Make him drop his lawsuit."

Carey laughed again. "Mr. Vice, you wildly overestimate my control over Sergeant Dodd. If he chooses to drop the lawsuit, he will and if not, then not. My interference would certainly not convince him to stop and may well provoke him to continue. I think you discovered what a stubborn independent man he is for yourself, didn't you?"

"The thumbscrews would have worked eventually," said Heneage.

Carey paused because he was too furious to speak for a moment, though he kept the smile on his face. It might have become a little fixed.

"I doubt it, sir. Mr. Tovey, see Mr. Vice out…"

"I'm not going until I've told you what I need to."

"Then perhaps you could come to the point? Hmm?"

Carey's fists were bunched in the sheets and if he hadn't been blind he might well have punched the bastard again. It was taking him an immense amount of effort not to jump out of bed and try anyway. Speaking in a voice lower than a shout was actually making his throat hurt.

"I wasn't at Court in 1560 but I…know someone. Someone the Queen set on to investigate the Robsart death before you, when she was in Oxford last time."

It had been in 1566. Who had that been? Carey wondered at the back of his anger.

"So, give me Dodd and I'll tell you about him."

Christ almighty, Carey realised distantly, is he just trying to provoke me or is he serious?

"Dodd is riding a stolen horse with the Queen's brand on him and no warrant. He shouldn't be hard to find. Tell me where you've told him to hide out and I'll do the rest."

Carey's jaw was hurting from the way his teeth were clenched. Dear God, it was hard to sit still.

"Goodbye, Mr. Heneage," he managed to say at last. "I know you're accustomed to cheapening over men's lives. I am not."

"He found out a lot, this man," Heneage pursued. "He's very good at it. He found out something he's never told."

"What?"

The sound of a shrug. "Give me Dodd and I'll give you him."

If he says that again, I surely will hit him, Carey thought through the roaring noise of his temper in his ears. Also I don't know where Dodd is. He took the scarf off his eyes and squinted at the shadowed blur before him.

"Go, Mr. Heneage. Go now. Mr. Tovey?"

Tovey had already gone to the door and was speaking to someone standing outside. A large shape appeared in the candle dazzle, a smear of black-and-yellow Hunsdon livery.

"My lord Hunsdon left orders that his son wis no' to be annoyed," said the Berwick tones of Ross, Hunsdon's sword-master who must have replaced Mr. Henshawe for the nightwatch. "On account of it being a danger to his health and the health of the annoyers forbye. I hope your worship will see the sense in it."

Heneage stood, walking out with his clerk. At the door, typically, he turned again to sneer.

"Why do you make your life so difficult, Sir Robert? My informer has made a good thing of what he found all those years ago."

"It would be pointless trying to explain my reasons to you, Mr. Vice," said Carey, "since I would first need to explain to you the meaning of the words honour, loyalty, and friendship. Good night to you, sir."

Ross gestured the man out and at last he went.

Carey leaned back on the pillows, feeling frighteningly weak and shaky, Fury was exhausting when you had to sit still and not hit anybody. He actually felt dizzy.

"Sergeant Ross, please don't let anybody else in until tomorrow."

"Can't do that, sir, Mrs. de Paris is here to speak to you and she's brought supper from the Queen's own table. I can't keep her out."

"I'm not hungry."

"That's why I'm here," came Thomasina's squeaky but extremely firm voice. "The Queen sent me to be sure you eat all of it. She knows what you're like."

"What I really need is a large tot of brandy..." Carey hinted.

"Not at all," said Thomasina. "Dr. Lopez was very clear about it. Nothing but mild ale for you to ease the strain upon your sanguine and choleric humours..."

"Christ!" roared Carey, "If I could just see..."

"...which are clearly still disordered. And it's just as well you can't see, ain't it?" said Thomasina as she climbed onto the chair. "Otherwise I'd be calling the cleaners to sweep away Heneage's teeth and balls, eh? What a fool that man is."

A tray was placed on the bed next to him by her woman and good smells came from it to distract him. He recognised a mess of rhubarb and prunes which were clearly on prescription from Lopez who must have the usual doctor's faith in purging. He groped up a napkin and tied it round his neck to save his father's dressing gown as he ate.

"Who the hell was the bastard talking about?" he asked with his mouth full of pottage and bread. "Do you know, mistress?"

"No, but I'm sure the Queen does and I'll ask her the minute you finish your dinner."

"Did you get a record of that meeting, Mr. Tovey?"

"Y...yes, sir."

"Good. Make a copy of it for my father. Make a copy of the meeting with Lord Burghley as well."

"Yes, sir."

"I'm impressed at your ability to keep my Lord Treasurer from his bed, Mrs. de Paris," Carey admitted. "When can I speak with the Queen?"

"When she chooses."

Instead of protesting, Carey attacked a couple of very good braised quail in wine with his fingers and teeth. "Why the devil is she being so coy?"

No answer from Thomasina. And the quail had been stuffed with prunes as well. Jesu, he'd have the squits soon. He felt carefully amongst the dazzle and found a penny loaf to mop up the sauce. It was enraging, having to fumble around for food and he snarled at Thomasina when she offered to feed him. He found the salat of autumn herbs was too messy to eat and he didn't like herbs much anyway, couldn't understand why the Queen seemed to be so addicted to them, ignored the goddamned rhubarb. Tovey brought a bowl and ewer over to him and he washed grease off his fingers and face. Please God he never got blinded permanently or ever again.

"I don't know how much more I can do before I'm better. I want to go and visit Cumnor Place," he said to Thomasina. "But I don't see the point if I can't see. Most of the people I want to talk to are dead or otherwise unavailable."

The chief of those he wanted to talk to was, of course, the late Earl of Leicester. Despite what he had said to Burghley, Leicester was the second most likely suspect still.

"When's the Court removing to Oxford at last?"

"We're going privately to Woodstock palace tomorrow so that the Queen can rest for a few days and deal with business before she makes her full public entrance on Friday."

"The word was that the Queen was in Oxford a month ago—why has it taken so long?"

"Yes, we were due in August, but they had some cases of suspected plague and we took a detour while the town was checked.

That's why we've doubled back on ourselves from Rycote to Woodstock again. There haven't been any more cases in Oxford."

"Where is Cumnor Place, by the way?" Carey asked casually as he absentmindedly picked up the horn spoon and started eating Dr. Lopez' medical dish. At least they had put sugar and spice in it.

"It's about ten miles from here, due south," said Thomasina.

"And from Oxford?"

"About three miles, southwest. But the Queen would prefer you to wait until you're fully recovered."

"Of course." He drank more ale and then yawned. Thomasina clapped her little hands together briskly and a woman came and took the tray. He yawned again, rubbed his face.

"Sleep well, Sir Robert," said Thomasina. "I'll bring you more Privy Councillors to question in the morning."

"Thank you, mistress," said Carey, suppressing another yawn.

Once the door had shut behind her, he beckoned Tovey over to the bed and whispered to him very quietly. "Would you do me a favour, Mr. Tovey? Would you take this ring to the Earl of Cumberland? I lost it to him yesterday at a very peculiar game of chess and only just remembered." It was his ruby ring with his initials carved in it that the Queen had given him for daring to take the news of Mary Queen of Scots' execution into Scotland. He almost never hocked it. Tovey wouldn't know its meaning but Cumberland did and would almost certainly be game for what he purposed. Be damned to his blindness, horses have eyes, after all.

Bless him, Cumberland was there quickly, swaggering in wearing a particularly loud combination of red and tawny, no doubt for the masque Carey had missed.

"What's this I hear about you having been struck blind for general venery, Sir Robert?"

"Somebody put belladonna in my spiced wine last night. Was it you, my lord?"

"Damn, I never thought of that. Good idea, though. What were you playing at? You introduced my luscious Emilia to m'lord of Essex and next minute she's gone off with him and you're puking and raving all over the church. Completely wrecked my plans."

"And mine. I'm sorry to tell you, my lord, that my eyes should get better soon enough but at the moment I can't see properly which is a confounded nuisance as I have a lot to do."

"And what do you want me to do?" Cumberland sat on the side of the bed and gave Carey back his ring. "Break you out again?"

"Yes, my lord," said Carey and explained his plan.

The Earl put his head back and laughed. "By God, Carey, I'll say this, you're reliably entertaining. Two hours before dawn do you?"

"Yes, my lord. Thank you."

"The Queen will know by sun-up."

"She can hardly complain when I'm simply obeying her own orders."

"She most certainly can, as you know as well as I do. Never mind. I'll see you tomorrow." Cumberland laughed again as he walked out past Sergeant Ross. Carey beckoned the swordmaster over.

"Where's my father?"

"He went to Oxford as soon as he was sure you would recover, sir. He left about midday."

Carey told Ross what he planned and why. "I don't intend to try evading you if you want to stop me," he told the man. "But I hope you won't."

"Your father ordered me to see you wisnae annoyed, sir," Ross pronounced. "Seems I'd be annoying you if I tried to stop you."

"Exactly, Sergeant."

"So I'll come with ye, sir."

In the worrying absence of Sergeant Dodd, that was quite a comforting thought. Carey turned over and lay down in the welcome darkness of the curtained bed, only to have to get up again as Dr. Lopez's prescriptions did their work. Finally he got to sleep, and was grateful not to remember any dreams.

monday 18th september 1592, morning

Somebody had left the door open and he was freezing cold, shivering. The blankets had crumbled to useless papery things and some evil bastard had clamped a black helmet over the whole of his head so it was hard to breathe or see because whoever had done it was hitting the helmet over and over with a hammer.

Dodd tried to turn over and punch him and somebody poked a gun in his ribs. His fingers felt for his knife and found nothing but goosebumped skin and some painful bruises, plus his knuckles hurt.

"Och," he muttered and tried to open his eyes. They were clamped shut which froze his arse even more with fright. Was he blind? Blindfolded?

The banging on his head was getting worse now. Shaking, he put his hand up to his eyes and found crusting all over them and crusting around his nose which he thought might be broken. The bit at the end of his nose was bent. Damn it, somebody had broken his nose. Again.

Before he could think too much about it, he gripped his fingers on the bent part and twisted it back to where it belonged.

Bright white pain flared through the middle of his face and then faded down through red and violet to a dull brown. His nose was bleeding again but not too badly and he could breathe a bit better.

From the feel of them, his lips were busted and a front tooth was loose but not lost. Whoever had kicked him had done it more than once but not aimed well.

The wind was blowing a gale and he was freezing cold. With straining hard work he could turn over and curl up a bit in the rustling leaves and sticks and stones and bright spikes of bramble and twigs.

His mouth was shockingly dry. And he was naked. Bare as a peeled twig. That was why he was so cold. The bastards hadn't even left him a shirt to keep him decent.

Dodd lay still in the little dip full of leaves that his body had apparently crawled into by itself at some time during the night. Something of what had happened was coming back to him. He had been watering Whitesock and the mare at the stream and somebody had managed to creep up behind him and hit him… or more likely, drop on him from a tree. Ay, that was likely since his horses hadn't noticed anything. Stupid bloody soft Southron horses, no Northern hobby would have let anyone ambush him like that.

He thought he'd done his best, fighting in the fog of being hit on the head to start with, mainly by instinct. The front of his head was sore as well as the back so perhaps he'd managed to headbutt someone. He hoped so.

Lying in the darkness of his sealed eyelids in the little stand of coppiced hazels from the smell, Dodd felt the black ball of rage in him that never really went away. It was in the pit of his stomach, swelling. It worried part of him even though the heat of it was giving him strength.

Somebody—several somebodies—had dared to rob him and beat him like a dog. They had taken everything. Carey's loaned suit, his boots, his shirt, his sword that he was fond of, his knife that he'd had since he was a boy and lost several times in mad card games or bets on horse races, but always won back, his hat, his nice new horses reived from Heneage himself…Christ, they'd even taken his underbreeks. And they must have spent quite some time kicking him once he was on the ground too, the bastards, though they'd made the mistake of failing to slit his throat while they had the chance and for that they would pay. All of them would pay. Firstly in money and fire, and then in blood as they died screaming and, if he was feeling merciful, he might not wipe out their entire families unto their babes and seventh cousins. Possibly. If they died painfully enough.

Rage was making his breath come short and he still couldn't get his blood-caked eyes open and find out if he really was blind. Though from the racket the bastard birds were making over his head, he knew it was probably dawn.

Cursing to himself he worked his tongue and snorted to get some spit up, then rubbed and peeled away some of the blood on his eyelashes. His head was full of metal from the blood smell. His whole body hurt, but he didn't think he'd broken any bones—maybe there was a rib busted from the way it hurt to breathe.

Obscurely he blamed the Deputy Warden. It had to be his fault for bringing him south from Carlisle and into foreign parts where they were barbarians and committed long-winded complicated suicide by beating him up and robbing him. Goddamn the bastards. And the Deputy and…

He actually heard the sticky sound as his eyelids parted and he could see past them into the world.

A lovely golden sunrise was stirring up the birds who were shouting at each other with no need at all, it being September. He hated them.

Slowly and carefully, Dodd sat up in the leaf litter and moss. He scraped his head on one of the hazel branches above and was chittered at by a squirrel with a nut in its mouth. Dodd reached for it to strangle it and stop the noise but it "Kikikikkked" at him and escaped with a flirt of its russet tail.

While he waited trembling for all the various parts of him to stop banging and throbbing, he looked at the twigs above. There were cobnuts aplenty and more had fallen. He picked them out of the moss and broke them with his backteeth, ate a few. As the birds calmed down, he heard the sound of the stream nearby, which stood to reason since he couldn't have crawled very far.

His other eye wouldn't open properly because it was swollen. So he squinted his good eye and looked at his hands where the knuckles were raw and a cut in the web of skin between thumb and forefinger of his left hand so he had probably wrestled someone for a sword or dagger.

His knees and elbows were grazed, probably from crawling into the clump he'd been lying in through the damp cold night. Christ, he was cold. He pulled his knees up and wrapped his arms round them and shivered. He hadn't been this low since…Well, ever. He'd had uglier awakenings but never one more humiliating and lonely. Him! Henry Dodd, Land-Sergeant of Gilsland, husband of Janet, Will the Tod's red-headed Armstrong firecracker of a daughter, properly stolen from her father's tower one wild night and her laughing behind him on the galloping horse and her arms tight around his waist and her hands distracting him, ay, that was a warm thing to think of...Of course, lately he had been playing the part of a respectable gentleman in fine wool loaned him by the Courtier, but he was also the rightful winner of the feud between himself and Vice Chamberlain Thomas Heneage which counted for something. Him! Beaten up, stripped and left naked in a ditch to die of cold. They'd got his money too. Forged and true, they'd got the lot.

Jesus God, he was angry. His hands were shaking with it as well as the cold.

And he was affeared as well. What if the bastards came back to finish the job they had so foolishly left undone? What if they were working for Heneage? He didn't know who they were, mind, but if they came back...

He didn't know he was showing his teeth in a snarl. He wasnae deid yet and until he was, they were as good as dead themselves. Once he knew who they were.

All he could remember from the fog and rage of the fight was a flash of dirty orange and white. That was all. Not much to go on.

The sun was fully up now and starting to warm him a little but he sat and listened a little longer. Nothing at all except what you'd expect in a hazel wood turning over to autumn. A little rustling sounded like a blackbird; there were other brown birds still arguing in the further branches and from the sharp smell now attacking his slightly cleared nose, he'd used a fox run to get into the bushes.

Grunting with effort and his left hand cupped to keep his bruised tackle from brambles, Dodd eeled and crawled along the small stinking corridor through the dense brush until he shoved out into the morning sunlight by the banks of the stream.

The mud around it was well stirred up. Further away he could hear deer, nearby the animals had fled the man in their midst. Well he wasn't in a fit state to catch one for breakfast, so they could save their effort.

The brambles that had prickled him were heavy with berries so Dodd ate all he could reach of them and the riper cobnuts. Then he slipped and slid down the bank to the stream snickering at him over the stones of the little ford.

He looked about for tracks and signs very carefully. Yes, as he'd thought, there was a yew tree over the stream with a wide branch that hung over where he'd been watering his horse. Nobody there now, though the bark was scraped. He'd been unforgivably careless. The mud of the bank was rucked up, broken branches all around, a gash in the trunk of a willow tree where the horse had kicked. You could see there had been a fight.

Him against how many? Two? Three? Hard to tell with the way all the signs were over each other. He picked his way about the place on his tiptoes, squinting. There was a drier spot where the nettles were flattened and a few threads of grey wool caught on them. So that was where they must have laid him down while he was unconscious and stripped off his clothes. He could see where the heels of his boots had made dents in the soft mud and been dragged off by the bootprints of the man that did it. There was a scrap of good linen from his shirt there on a bramble.

Another scrap of thread, this time of a faded but once virulent orange. Tawny they called it at Court. So he hadn't dreamed the orange and white clownlike clothes. Dodd felt the thread with his fingers—it was silky, so he kept it by wrapping it round his little finger like a ring. It might make a fishing line anyway.

It was easy to see which way the robbers had gone—at right angles to the stream, following a faint path but heading uphill, single file. Three, maybe four of them, and one very big and heavy, with big feet so it wasn't just something he was carrying. And unless Dodd had forgotten all he knew about tracking, that was the one who had reived his boots.

He found the deepest part of the stream, took a deep breath and waded in, stood there shivering with his toes clenching around the weed-covered stones while minnows investigated his heels. Then he carefully washed himself all over in the icy water, swearing and shivering at it until all the dirt and gravel was out of his various grazes and the blood from the blow to his head was out of his hair and beard and his eyes could open properly again, even the swollen one. His nose was still singing to him and his black eye had that stupid puffy stiff feeling. He drank deep of the water despite the way it made his teeth ache.

Just as he finished turning the water rust-coloured he noticed that the water coming toward him was swirling with little white clouds.

"Och," he said quietly to himself.

He climbed out of the stream, careful of thorns in the leaf litter. Still shivering he squeezed his hair and shook himself all over like a dog, jogged on the spot and waved his arms. Jesu, he was cold, it was a sharp morning and had been a sharper night. He was hungry, too, despite the ball of rage in his stomach. He needed a fire by nightfall and since the bastards had taken his tinderbox along with everything else, that meant he had to find whoever was living upstream.

For a few seconds he stood looking at the blades of sunlight stabbing through the turning leaves and thought wistfully of the faeries magicking his own tower into reach and him going there and Janet putting salve on his grazes and bandaging his head for him and giving him another shirt and wrapping him warm by the fire in blankets of her own weaving. And him then calling out his surname and her surname and anyone else who owed him a favour and taking a fiery bloody revenge on anyone he could find in orange-and-white velvet.

monday 18th september 1592, before dawn

Carey and Cumberland were old hands at slipping away illicitly from the Queen's Court. When he arrived at the door of the small bedchamber, Cumberland found Carey was already awake and irritably instructing Tovey on the art of helping him dress. They hadn't lit any candles although the sky was overcast so the night was very dark. Carey however seemed to be able to see without difficulty.

Cumberland led the way out of the manor house and they picked their way over servants and page boys sleeping in all the corridors while their Courtier masters shared beds and had to dice for pallets in the bedrooms. The courtyard was filled with tents and tethered horses, four of them being led out by Kielder, the most discreet of Cumberland's grooms. Carey picked the second best mount out of deference to the Earl and unthinkingly jumped to the saddle.

"I thought you said you were blind?" accused Cumberland as Carey adjusted his stirrups.

"Only in daytime, my lord," Carey said, highly pleased. "I can see like an owl now."

They walked the horses out through the gate, past the Yeoman of the Guard whom Cumberland had bribed, found the south-ward road and put their heels in.

After getting lost among the maze of lanes only twice, they found Cumnor Place was tidily kept but quite empty-looking in the grey dawnlight. There were no grooms hurrying about to feed horses, nor kitchen staff nor bakers, nor smoke from the chimneys. Hunsdon's excellent swordmaster, Nathaniel Ross, knocked on the least ivy-choked door. An elderly man slowly opened another door to one side of the house and came shuffling out to blink at them.

Carey was already squinting and shading his eyes though the sun wasn't up yet. Cumberland spoke to the man.

"Well," he answered dubiously, "You don't look like them sturdy beggars. What do you want?"

"Goodman," Carey put in, "my name is Sir Robert Carey and the Queen has charged me with investigating a matter that happened here many years ago..." He handed down his warrant upside down and the old man didn't turn it.

"Ah yes, the death of Lady Dudley. I wasn't here then, sirs."

"May we look around the house where it happened?"

"I'll have to ask my mistress, Mrs. Odingsells."

"Is that the Mrs. Odingsells who attended Lady Dudley back then?"

"Yes, sir, nearing a hundred years now."

"Are her wits…Is she able to talk to me?"

"Dunno, sir, I can but ask her. Sir Anthony Forster pays me and my wife to take care of her, sir, she won't leave. Says she likes it here and…well, I'll ask her."

"Thank you, Mr.…?"

"Forster, sir, I'm a cousin of Sir Anthony's."

The kitchen door banged open and a clucking mass of chickens and ducks came out and spread themselves to peck at the overgrown cobbles of the yard, followed by a plump woman in an apron and cap.

Cumberland and his groom had already dismounted and Kielder took the horses and tethered them to a ring in the corner. When Carey dismounted as well, Cumberland saw that he was letting his horse lead him and he tripped on a pothole. The old woman following the fowl stopped still and stared with her mouth open, then started curtseying anxiously.

"S'all right, Mrs. Forster," said the old man, "They're from the Court, not the monastery. I'll just go ask the mistress." He set off to a different door, still holding the warrant. While they waited, Carey cursed under his breath and wrapped a silk scarf around his eyes again.

Forster came back without the warrant. "Mistress says she in't ready to receive you yet, sirs, but you can look to your heart's content." His voice was deeply disapproving. "Here's the keys cos it's all locked up."

Carey clearly couldn't see where the old man holding out the keys, so Cumberland came forward and scooped them up, offered Carey his arm to be led. Carey swore again and shook his head, but took it.

"Remind me never to go blind again, my lord," he muttered through his teeth, ramming his hat down on his head to shade his eyes. It was very clear to Cumberland that his friend should have stayed in bed and given himself time to recover.

"I know what you're doing, Carey," he said quietly. "But why the hell are you doing it?"

"The Queen told me to, my lord."

"Ah." Cumberland started to whistle a very rude ballad about the Mother Superior of Clerkenwell Convent, that famous London bawdy house.

They walked across the courtyard, Carey tripping on a couple of chickens who were fighting each other over a slug, and Cumberland found the door that the old man had pointed to.

"According to all official accounts, this is where Amy Dudley fell down the back stairs from the long gallery, broke her neck and died." Carey explained.

The door was swollen with damp and needed a firm shove from Cumberland's shoulder. Inside the stairwell the only light came from a large boarded trefoil window. Once in semi-darkness again, Carey took the scarf off and blinked around, looked up the famous staircase.

The steps went up along the wall from the small square hall, turned sharp left at a small landing, up again and right to a doorway. The stairwell had been built onto the end of the long gallery, probably for convenience so that family members could come straight out into the courtyard. The door they had come through was large and the stairs were in a line with it so they went forward, stepping carefully on the slippery stones spattered with white. There was a clatter of wings. Cumberland looked up and felt a chill down his neck as he saw little leather gloves hanging from the roof beams and a few bony heaps on the floor. The air was chokingly musty.

"Ugh," he couldn't help saying. "Bloody bats."

Carey shrugged and went forward.

Had anybody been in here since they took Amy's body out and locked the door? Cumberland wondered. "I expect it's haunted too," he added, trying to make light of it. "Stands to reason she'd walk."

Carey said nothing to that either. Probably nobody had been here since the 8th September 1560. They must have locked the door and left it. Carey put his foot on the stairs, stamped a couple of times in case the wood was rotten, and went up to the turn. He stopped, blinked, peered to his right and started fumbling with the keys.

Cumberland had shaken himself like a dog and went up the stairs to find Carey opening another small door from halfway up which seemed the start of a small corridor. It was dark, lit only by what light came through the door behind them.

Carey went through the little door, having to stoop, and followed the narrow passage which led to another door. That one wasn't locked, only latched, but it hadn't been opened for a long time and creaked. Mainly because he didn't want to be on his own with a possible angry female ghost, Cumberland followed.

Carey was looking out into the dimness. They were high up in the high-beamed great hall of Cumnor Place, clearly also unused for decades, standing on the narrow musicians gallery. The small door they had come from must have been for the musicians' use, so they could come in from the back stairs and not bother the family or the rest of the household. Treading extremely carefully and looking out for holes, he stepped onto the gallery, creaked to the rail, and looked over. Cumberland, followed, teeth bared.

Below, benches and trestle tables for feeding a large household were stacked against the panelling and spattered with white, the high walls festooned with old swallows' nests and the carved beams of the roof well-inhabited with creatures that rustled and moved. The lantern window gave only small light due to ivy but some slats of wood were broken and a couple of pigeons fluttered out in a panic. Cumberland had a sensation of eyes watching him and hoped devoutly it was only rats.

"A desolation and an habitation of owls," Carey quoted conversationally to the Earl who nodded without commenting in case his voice shook. They went back to the door they had come through and along the short corridor that connected with the stairs leading up to the long gallery.

Once back on landing at the turn of the stairs, Carey looked about him carefully. Cumberland took his tinderbox out, but Carey touched his arm.

"No need, my lord, I can see better without it."

"Damn it's dark in here," said the Earl. "Are you sure?"

"Quite sure."

"What if she…er…"

"If Amy Robsart's ghost turns up, I'll be delighted, my lord. I'll be able to ask her directly who killed her and save myself some trouble."

Cumberland knew his short laugh wasn't very convincing. He was starting to sweat as Carey stood still and looked about. Why wasn't he getting on with it, whatever it was?

Suddenly Carey moved. He went up the steps and touched something on the wall at a little lower than his chest height.

"Look at this, George," he said in a soft voice full of suppressed excitement.

Cumberland was doing his best not to think of the rustling bats above and the probable rats below. He didn't mind rats, didn't like bats.…What if the rustling wasn't bats? What if it was…? What was that? Carey's sudden movement had made his heart thud, and he followed his friend, felt the small round hole Carey had somehow seen.

Well, that certainly was interesting. They both knew—from the way the edges of the hole were punched inward but the wood not broken—exactly what it was.

Carey was looking about for the bolt, but found nothing. He put his finger in the hole, followed its flight down the stairs to the turn where they had been standing, with the door to the minstrels' gallery behind them.

Carey's eyes narrowed and he stepped backwards through the small door again, looked up, blinked and smiled.

"Would you give me a boost, my lord?"

Sighing, Cumberland went through the door, couldn't see anything at all up above the wall which Carey seemed to find of interest. He went on one knee and let Carey use his thigh as a step, which was less painful than using his cupped hands for the boost.

Nobody had bothered to finish plastering the musicians' corridor. Above where the wall ended on the inside was the darkness of the roofspace and beams above. Carey had caught one of the supporting beams there and was pulling himself up into the space, knocking down choking dust and mummified owl pellets in a rain on Cumberland.

There was a triumphant "Hah!" Either Carey had taken leave of his senses or he had found something. There was a clatter, a grunt from Carey, scraping, and then the madman dropped back to the floorboards with something large in his hand.

That something was a crossbow. It was probably brother, or more likely grandfather, to the crossbow that had been fired at the two of them at the duckpond the day before, a large hunting bow, no need for a windlass to wind it up if you had the strength to bend it, but very lethal.

"What the…"

"This was hidden behind one of the roofbeams, hooked on a nail."

Carey was triumphant, holding the rusted thing, covered in nameless white and black stuff, insects and spiders bailing out as fast as they could. He waved it, set it to his shoulder, and took aim at the hole in the wall that Cumberland could no longer see. Cumberland's gorge suddenly rose because he had looked at the other end of the bow. It was dented, some small threads caught in the splintered wood there.

Carey saw it too and his eyes narrowed as he looked carefully at the place where the steel of the bow crossed the wood of the stock. To Cumberland's horror he pulled off a couple of the caught threads, put them carefully in a leather purse he kept in his doublet sleeve pocket.

"Hmm." he said.

"Jesu," was all Cumberland could say.

"According to the inquest report, before she broke her neck, Amy was already dead from two large dents in her head, one two inches deep, the other one an inch deep." They both looked at the crossbow. "See here? He fired at her, missed, then when she tried to run past him and out the door, he hit her on the back of the head with the crossbow hard enough to kill her. The stock itself made the two-inch dent, the metal bow the one-inch dent."

"Jesu."

In the pause, Cumberland thought that now if ever would be the moment for Amy's ghost to show herself. But she didn't. All the movement came from Carey who leaned the crossbow, stock down, against the wall and went up the second set of steps, turned right at the top of the second set of steps where there was a much larger carved door.

Another search through the keys eventually found the one that opened it and they looked into a very fine long gallery running above the wing of the manor house that adjoined the hall. That, too, had shuttered windows but it seemed in better condition, though it was dusty and smelled pungently of mice and rats. Thank God there were no bats. Somehow it didn't...feel haunted.

Carey was frowning. "So. Somebody shot at her with the crossbow, she tried to get out the door at the bottom of the stairs, which meant she had to run past him, and that's when he hit her with the crossbow."

Cumberland nodded. It made sense of a gruesome kind.

Carey stepped out into the long gallery where Amy Dudley had walked on rainy days and probably practised dancing. He paced all the way to the end, where there was another locked door, blinking rapidly when he passed a window that let daylight squeeze through the shutters. The portraits and hangings that must have been there once had long since been taken away. Only the things built in were still there, like the window seats and the carved linenfold panels on the walls.

Carey moved purposefully back to the long gallery door onto the back stairs. They stood looking down into the entrance hall.

"Right, George. I'm Amy..."

"And very pretty you are, too..."

"Thanks, my lord," said Carey drily. "You are the assassin."

"Grr."

"So you stand inside the musicians' door until you hear the sound of my steps."

Cumberland did as he was asked with great theatricality. Carey came down the stairs slowly, stopped on the landing. Cumberland stepped out from the musicians' door, aimed an imaginary crossbow because he didn't feel like picking up the one that probably killed Amy Dudley.

"Kerchunk!" he said, firing an invisible bolt at Carey.

"By some fortune, you miss at point-blank range and I see you. Then I run *down* the stairs past you…"

Carey came down the stairs past Cumberland who mimed hitting him on the head with the imaginary crossbow.

"And down she goes and breaks her neck in the bargain," finished Carey looking annoyed. "It's wrong. It can't be right."

"Makes sense to me."

"But why would she run past the doorway where a man was standing who had just tried to kill her? She could have turned and run up to the long gallery again, screaming blue murder and escaped through the door at the other end."

"Tried to fight him?"

"Don't be ridiculous, my lord, she's a woman."

"My wife would."

"Your lady wife is made of stronger stuff."

"Your lady mother would, too."

Carey sighed. "All right. I don't know where the dents on her head were, back or front. They might have been on the… No, the inquest report would have said so, said they were on her face, not her head. She must have run past him…no." Carey shook his head irritably.

"What's the problem? You've found the murder weapon. Amy Robsart was killed by someone who tried to shoot her with a crossbow bolt and then used the crossbow to bludgeon her when he missed. You should be pleased. You've solved a thirty-year-old mystery."

"No, I haven't, I've made it worse."

"How?"

"For God's sake, my lord, why didn't she run back into the long gallery?"

"Panicked?"

"When you panic, you run away from the danger, not straight past it!"

"Not necessarily," said Cumberland who believed he had never panicked in his life.

"You do!" Carey went back to the small door and looked at it again, seemingly found nothing that pleased him. He went back up to the long gallery door, opened the door, looked through it, locked it again, came down the stairs, counting them, checked the bolt hole in the panelling, went past Cumberland and clattered on down the stairs to the bottom. Through the open door to the courtyard, they could see Forster waiting for them.

monday 18th september 1592, morning

Dodd decided to take a closer look at the clear trail left by the robbers before it rained or something. He knew he was conspicuous in his unpeeled state and also completely unarmed, but he needed to move to keep warm and he might as well do that by finding out more about his enemies.

He found the narrow path again with the footprints and some hoofprints from Whitesock, a tail hair on a branch. The path turned, went two ways. Upstream there was a dog turd, downstream the footpads' feet, and Whitesock's hooves continued in a different direction, heading south.

Dodd went carefully and quietly along the path by the stream. His feet told him that the path had once been a better-made road because it had smooth blocks of stone in places, some robbed out, some covered in weeds. It wasn't as deep down as the Giants' Road up on the borders, though. He bent to look at the stones more carefully. One was freshly chipped by a shod horse's hoof.

He carried on up the path, his feet already prickling and sore from the stones and twigs. Once the soles of his feet had been like leather, when he was a wild boy, but he still knew how to go quietly.

He smelled them first. There were men somewhere up ahead, smoking.

His nose tingled. He recognised that smell. The bastards had stolen his pipe and expensive henbane of Peru, mixed with that magical Moroccan incense that made the world soft-edged and his rage far away. He scowled. Jesu, what he would give for a pipe and some smoke to drink.

He slipped among the stands of bracken and gone-over shepherd's purse and mallow. There had been buildings here once, the path had a tumbled masonry wall beside it and a great multi-trunked yew tree growing from it.

It was a while since he'd needed to do it, being senior enough now that he could send Bessie's boy or Bangtail up a tree for him, but you never forgot how. He circled the tree to be sure there weren't any crows in it, found a place to start. He hoisted himself up onto a branch and then climbed slowly to the crown of the tree, and then out along a branch where he lay down and got his breath with the sun dappling on his bare back.

They were sloppy. Imagine leaving a tree that gave an over-view of their tower? It wasn't a tower of course; they didn't have those in the soft South. Below he could see crooked flat stones and lumps of stone sticking out of the earth at angles. Ahead was another well-robbed wall. Beyond that was…

Once it must have been a small monastery, a hive of indus-try, no doubt, full of monks. The roof was gone and the walls showed the old blackening of fire and the green flourish of plants breaking it apart. Perhaps the monks had rebelled against King Henry's men and so been burned out. That had happened in other places.

By squinting and leaning over, Dodd could just make out the two men standing on a bend in the path. It wasn't so hard. Every so often puffs of smoke could go up from them and he could hear quiet talk.

Past them, further on, where the monastery gatehouse must have been, there were signs of thatch having been added to some of the building which was roughly planked along one side.

Dodd nodded to himself. They had a bolthole, that was why they were so bold. Who was their headman? He'd give a lot to know that and his surname. For a moment he thought about carrying on round the place and working out where the weak spots were.

He was more tempted to stay in the tree and wait for nightfall and then go in quietly and slit some throats. It was a very attractive thought, but in the end that would be stupid. He might well slit a few throats but at some stage someone would wake up or catch him and it stood to reason there were a lot more of them and then they wouldn't make the same mistake again.

Sighing, he climbed very carefully down the tree, sliding a little on the flaky bark, then retraced the path upstream. He stopped at the ford to drink as much as he could. He wasn't hungry anymore, the ball of rage in his gut was food enough really, as it had been in the past.

Then while he was drinking, he heard the rattle of dog paws trotting down the path toward him, smelled the dog himself too who was panting and snortling on a trail, and he heard a high voice speaking to the dog.

He stood still and thought for a second. He already knew there were people upstream who had goats or maybe even a milch cow. Why would they come down the path with dogs?

There was one obvious answer. Would he run or would he meet them? That was obvious too. He looked about for a soft place and when he'd found somewhere behind a bush without too many thistles and brambles, he lay down there, curled up and shut his eyes.

monday 18th september 1592, morning

Once out in the early morning sunlight, Carey shaded his eyes and cursed, then irritably wrapped his scarf round them again, rammed his hat back on his head.

"Mrs. Odingsells will see you now, sir," said the man, "Though she's not very happy, I'll tell you. It's a good thing you're not a black-haired man, is all I can say."

"I am," said Cumberland.

"You're too young, sir, both of you are, Mrs. Odingsells was very particular about it."

They followed Forster in through the door to the opposite wing where the great doors to the hall were and then up a larger set of stairs that led on to a corridor in the inhabited part of the house.

They went into a chamber with a very large curtained bed, with the curtains pulled back and the shutters half open. The smell of old lady in the room was not too bad, Cumberland thought, quite similar to the Queen's under all the rosewater, although the chamberpot was clearly unemptied.

Propped up on the linen pillows was a bony form in a knitted jacket and embroidered cap. Her hair was white, her eyes yellowed and milky with cataracts, and her beak the most powerful part of her face which had mostly fallen away back to the skull. Carey's warrant lay on the bed, now right way up.

"So Her Majesty is trying again, is she?" she demanded in a stronger voice than Cumberland expected.

"Er…yes, mistress," said Carey, sweeping off his hat in a bow, removing the scarf.

"Sit down, sit down, both of you boys. What's your name?"

"Sir Robert Carey, mistress," he explained, "seventh son of my lord Baron Hunsdon, Chamberlain to…"

The old woman had sucked in a breath.

"Henry Carey?"

"Yes, mistress."

"Why isn't he here then, eh?"

"I'm not sure, Mistress Odingsells, I think he's supervising the Queen's move to Oxford on progress."

"I didn't like the man she sent last time she was there, whats-isname? Slimy villain for all his fancy gown."

Carey had sat on the chair by the bed, Cumberland modestly took the clothes chest by the door, the better to escape if necessary.

"Kept shouting at me and hectoring and then offering money. Stupid man. Must have been a very good liar to get the job. So. What do you want, my lad? *I* didn't see who did it, you know. I was playing cards, God forgive me."

"Do you know the man's name? The one who questioned you before?"

The wrinkled lips pinched together, then smacked apart.

"No, and I'll have forgotten yours by tomorrow. Ugly tall man, black hair and eyebrows, one of Lord Shrewsbury's crew, I think. The Queen was at Oxford."

"Well, can you tell me the story of Lady Dudley's last few days?"

"I can," said the old lady and shut her lips.

Carey smiled. "Please will you, mistress?"

"Perhaps. Why should I?"

"I have a warrant from Her Majesty."

The old lady lifted the warrant and squinted at it from the side of one eye. "Queen's seal, give aid and so on. Yes. So what? Might be a forgery." Carey said nothing. "And why would she want it all dug up again after thirty years?"

"I don't know, mistress," said Carey with surprising humility. "She won't tell me. She won't tell me anything, which is extremely annoying."

The old lips stretched in a smile.

"It's a puzzle isn't it? And the man most folk say was the murderer died four years ago."

"Do you mean my lord of Leicester?"

"Of course," said Mrs. Odingsells, "Who else? Not Sir Richard Verney nor Bald Butler as the Papist book said, they weren't anywhere near. And yet it wasn't right."

Cumberland was suppressing the urge to shout "Stop talking riddles!" Mind you, it would be interesting to hear about the thing that changed the Queen's life forever from someone who was there. Not as interesting as a sea battle, but still interesting.

"Mistress, please, would you tell me the tale, starting with about a week before, around the 1st September 1560?"

The old lady shut her eyes. "I suppose I'll get no peace until I do."

"I'm afraid not, mistress."

The eyes snapped open. "Well the last thing I want is peace. So there!"

"Yes," said Carey quietly, "It's very dull being blind, isn't it? A…an accident happened to my eyes on Saturday and I own I have never been so utterly undone with tedium as since then."

She laughed a little. "What's wrong with 'em? French pox?"

"Someone put belladonna into my wine."

"Tut. You see, that was why I always thought it couldn't have been my lord of Leicester. Yes, Sir William Cecil had a man placed in the kitchens, but it would have been easy enough to get round him and do the deed."

"I think so too," Carey said.

"Hmm. Good. Why didn't you die?"

"I was very lucky, mistress. Or perhaps I should say that God must have watched over me?"

That's right, thought Cumberland, give it a bit of Godly piety, that should unlock the old oyster.

"Hah! Such arrogance. So why didn't He watch over poor Amy?"

"I don't know, mistress. I'm not privy to His counsels. Perhaps God never meant Her Majesty to marry, as she says now."

There was a cynical look on Mrs. Odingsell's face. "So why didn't He find a way that didn't mean killing poor Amy?"

"In fact, you might say, in order to stop the Queen marrying Leicester, God only had to keep Amy alive."

Mrs. Odingsells slowly shook her head, looking pleased with herself.

"Not necessarily."

"What do you mean?" Carey's voice had gone down to a murmur.

"Something was afoot. Something…I didn't know. A messenger arrived from my lord Leicester and put Amy all in a tizzy.

She ordered a new gown from her tailor and then when a new message came before it was ready, she sent me into Oxford to have her best velvet gown refashioned, to put gold brocade on the neck. She wouldn't let me read any of the letters. She burnt them. Then she wrote three herself, though her penmanship was poor. I thought Leicester was planning to visit her but…"

"Did he?"

Again the slow shaking of her head. "He hadn't seen her for months. A year maybe. *He* didn't visit her."

Cumberland missed the inflection but Carey didn't.

"Who did visit her?"

There was a very long silence while Cumberland said nothing and rather thought Carey was actually holding his breath.

"According to the inquest papers, she wanted the house empty for the day," Carey prompted finally. "She sent everyone else to the fair at Abingdon, but you refused to go and she was angry about it."

"I knew poor Amy was terribly worried about something. It was very important. But she never killed herself, she wouldn't do that, no matter what wicked men say. Never never. Amy was a good Christian woman, she spent hours on her knees praying for the wisdom to judge rightly."

Another long pause.

"She did love her husband, you see," creaked the old voice sadly, "In spite of everything. She loved him. She knew he didn't love her, never really had, and she knew he was completely enchanted by the Queen but…she still loved him."

Carey was tense as he sat, poised. Cumberland had to admire his patience and wondered where he'd got it.

"As for going to the fair…" The old creaky voice was far back in the past. "The youngsters were all for it, I wasn't. I liked peace and quiet then. Go to Our Lady Fair at Abingdon on that Sunday…No! I don't think so. Only the ungodly would go to a fair on a Sunday. There was to be a football match as well and why should I watch something so boring and unseemly?"

To Cumberland's surprise, Carey didn't explain to her what fun football was—but then no woman could possibly understand such things. Even his wife thought football was a waste of time.

"I refused to go and we had an argument about it. Mrs. Owens was going to stay with her but Mrs. Owens was deaf as a post and not too firm in her wits. Amy screamed at me that I would spoil everything, but I held fast and then finally she told me…She was meeting two courtiers. She would not say why but the meeting was vitally important. So I offered to help her dress for it and at last she said I could stay so long as I never moved from the parlour, on my honour." There was a long creaking sigh. "And I never did, till it was too late."

"Do you know who were…"

"The two courtiers? One was your father, Henry Carey, the other one of the Queen's women. I didn't know them, of course."

"Did you see them?"

Mrs. Odingsells nodded. "Through the window of the parlour, through the glass so I couldn't make out the faces. I saw Amy curtsey low to them, call the man my lord Hunsdon. He helped the lady-in-waiting down from her horse and they went up to the Long Gallery to speak.

"I played cards with Mrs. Owens, trying not to listen. I didn't leave the parlour as I had promised."

"What did you hear?"

A heavy frown and her lips puckered, a movement deeply carved into her mouth and chin.

"I heard nothing, they must have been talking quietly. Then doors opening and then a sound…a crack. A cry. Feet. Something like a cook splitting a cabbage. Then a woman's voice crying, screaming "No! Oh no!" Scraping, thudding. A man's shout. Running feet. Then a long pause and I looked at Mrs. Owens who hadn't heard a thing and said, "What was that?" and she shrugged and bet me a shilling that the next card would be low.

"Then I heard nothing more and as there were no more cries and I was annoyed at losing four shillings to Mrs. Owens who was not a good player, I didn't do anything until I heard the hooves galloping away."

"What did you see of the lady-in-waiting?"

"She was wearing forest green with a brown velvet gard along the kirtle hem, I think. Quite a plain hunting dress. She had a headtire and a linen cap on her head and under it black hair as far as I could tell. She had…she was very pale.

"And you didn't know her?"

"Neither of them, they were blurred by the glass. I only knew your father because of Amy greeting him by name."

Carey rubbed his temples. "Mrs. Odingsells," he said very softly, "did you ever find out who the lady-in-waiting was?"

Another long pause. "I guessed eventually. After the inquest."

"And?"

"I will die before I tell you or anybody. That's what I said to the evil black-haired bastard that came and tried to bully me in 1566 and I say it to you. So now."

Carey took breath to speak, to argue with her.

"I'm an old woman," shouted Mrs. Odingsells, partly sitting up in bed. "I'm old but I know you, Mr. Topcliffe, I've lived too long but anything you try with me will kill me anyway so you can do as you like and be damned to you!"

There was spittle on her lips. Carey stayed where he was.

"Mistress, I'm not Richard Topcliffe."

"Get out and be damned…! You're not?"

"No, mistress. Sir Robert Carey."

"Oh."

"What did Topcliffe do?"

"He was here before, the last time the Queen was at Oxford, when I was still young and could still see. He came and questioned me and he asked the same questions as you, but when I wouldn't answer, he shouted and roared and threatened. Nothing came of his threats however, and he didn't get what he came for. Oh no."

Carey was leaning forward, his elbows on his knees, squinting at Mrs. Odingsells who had her hands clasped to her breast. As far as Cumberland could make out in the dimness, Carey was pale.

"What were the courtiers discussing with Lady Dudley?"

The bony old shoulders lifted and dropped. "They didn't tell me."

Carey's eyes narrowed. "But you know?"

Mrs. Odingsells said nothing. Cumberland listened to her breathing as Carey let the silence stretch, but Mrs. Odingsells was too old to be worried by it and simply glared back at him.

At last Carey tilted his head in acknowledgement. "Is there anything else, anything at all you can tell me of that day?"

"It was a nightmare after we found her, I couldn't believe she was…There were people all over the place, coming and going, messengers to the Court, to Sir Anthony, to my lord of Leicester. The undertaker came from Oxford with his best hearse to pick up Amy and most of the village was there gawking and getting in the way, trampling about in the gardens and orchard and stealing apples and quinces. Dreadful. They buried her in one of the colleges of Oxford and the inquest spent a year debating what had happened. Pah!"

"That's a very long time for an inquest?"

"Well the foreman of the jury was one of the Queen's own men so you couldn't expect them to come up with anything other than they did, but the rest of the jury was decent solid men from this county. And then…" She paused and looked as if she was about to add something else but whatever it was, she shook her head again and shut her eyes.

"I'm tired now, Mr. Top…Carey, please leave."

"Yes ma'am," said Carey with surprising meekness, stood up and went to the door. Cumberland followed him. "Thank you for speaking to me. If there is anything more you want to say…"

"Yes. Tell your father that I would like something tidied up. I cannot control what will happen to my possessions when I die, which will be soon, please God. Be sure you tell him to come here himself as I will speak to none other, not even you. Good-bye."

As Carey made a Court bow to the old lady, Cumberland could make out the milky eyes, wide open, staring hard at him, assessing.

Once back in the corridor and the bedchamber door shut, Carey went along the corridor to the carved door at the end, opened it. There was the long gallery, seen from the other end, their own footsteps in the dust. Carey shut it again, felt his way back with his eyes squeezed shut in the light from the small windows along the courtyard side.

Then he stood, staring down the great stairs for what seemed an hour. Cumberland had no idea what was going on in his friend's head except it seemed to be making him absentminded.

"Do you know who was the lady-in-waiting with your father?" he asked, more to break the silence than anything else. Carey started slightly and squinted at him.

"I'm not sure."

"But you suspect...?"

"There's a family story. My father's sister, my Aunt Katherine, was one of the Queen's senior ladies-in-waiting, and there was a story about a green hunting kirtle of hers being somehow damaged a month or two after I was born."

"You think it was your aunt?"

Carey paused. "Yes, I do. But not my Aunt Katherine."

For a moment Cumberland couldn't work out the inference and when he did he sucked in his breath as if he'd been punched in the stomach. Only not with surprise because, after all, there had to be something like that going on.

Carey's father, Henry's by-blow and the Queen's half-brother, had brought Elizabeth Tudor to Cumnor Place, disguised in her half-sister's plain hunting kirtle, probably wearing a black wig. The Queen had been at Cumnor Place on the morning of the 8th September 1560, the day her rival Amy Robsart had been killed.

Carey found he was gripping the banisters with his left hand, the fingers of his other pressed hard into his temples to try and ease the headache. Something inside him was fighting to be heard. After a moment he breathed deeply and relaxed because this still wasn't the answer.

How could the Queen possibly benefit if her lover's wife was killed by a crossbow bolt, especially if she was actually present?

The Queen was the sharpest, most intelligent woman he had ever met, apart from Elizabeth Widdrington. Would she set an assassin with a crossbow to kill Amy Robsart and actually be there to watch? The idea was ridiculous.

He shook his head again and groped his way slowly down the stairs, followed by a silent Cumberland. As they went into the courtyard and he tied the scarf on again, pulled the brim of his hat down against the sunlight, he said quietly,

"I don't need to tell you to keep quiet about this, my lord."

"Christ, no!" said Cumberland with feeling, offering Carey his arm again. "I've forgotten already. You deal with it. I'd rather take on three Dutch sea-beggar fighting ships in a rowing boat."

"Thank you, my lord."

"Please don't mention it again." Cumberland said firmly and beckoned for Kielder to bring up the horses. Carey called Ross over and the swordmaster went over to the stairwell where Amy had died, came back with a heavy sack.

"Where are we going now?" Carey asked as he felt for his horse's girth to tighten it.

"I've had men at Oxford setting up an encampment in a field north of the city wall, just past that alehouse with the good cider. It's handy for the Schools and Balliol, there's a stream and it's not too marshy. We'll stay there."

"Why not in one of the colleges?"

"Don't be wood. Unless you fancy going three in a bed with strangers…"

"No, my lord," said Carey, climbing into the saddle with much more effort than usual. He was suddenly infernally tired, was thinking longingly of going to bed, alone, and staying there. "I've done that."

Cumberland laughed.

It was only three miles to the outskirts of Oxford but by then Carey's head was having nails pounded into it by invisible carpenters. The bedlam of Oxford's streets didn't help. The High Street, Cornmarket, and Broad Street were filled with scaffolding, stages, fences, and the noise of hammering and shouting made

Carey feel physically sick again. He set his teeth, drove his horse on and let the animal follow Cumberland's lead. At some stage the Earl must have quietly put a leading rein on the animal, which was humiliating, but otherwise Carey didn't know how he could have stayed with the party. At last they turned aside through a gate and Cumberland shouted for grooms. Carey slid from the saddle, forced his knees straight and stood holding onto the horse's reins, the world dissolving into a bedazzlement of light and noise that he could make no sense of. The horse dipped his head and nudged him, nickered with concern.

"Are you all right, Carey?" It was the Earl's voice.

"Yes. No." He had to admit it. "I need to rest."

More bellowing by Cumberland, who seemed to think there was a gale blowing, and a man with a comforting Glasdale accent arrived to lead Carey to a tent behind the main ruckus, and to a pallet laid on a bed of sweet rushes. The man helped Carey with his doublet and boots, helped him to drink more mild ale and gave him a magnificent bear fur rug which he pulled over his head to keep out the light.

Despite the frightening exhaustion of his body and the pounding in his head, Carey's mind was whirling. Could the Queen have got to Cumnor Place that day? If she had been hunting at Windsor Castle, she most certainly could. In her late fifties she could still ride like the wind for hours and leave her courtiers behind in the hunt. Windsor to Cumnor was only thirty miles and with a remount she could have done the distance in a few hours. But why? For what conceivable reason could she have disguised herself in Aunt Katherine's hunting kirtle and ridden out with his father to see her lover's wife?

Not to kill the woman. That didn't make sense. Thirty years ago, the Queen had been much younger, of course, so probably more impatient, more ruthless, less cautious…but…

Unlike Mary Queen of Scots, she had a brain. He couldn't believe she had plotted to kill Amy. Although Henry VIII had committed judicial murder of inconvenient women at least twice in his marrying career, Carey couldn't believe it of the Queen.

Not for morality's sake, but for expediency. What a king could get away with, a queen couldn't, as the Queen of Scots had proven.

He needed more evidence, and to talk to more people. Could Thomasina fetch him Topcliffe? Would Topcliffe tell him the truth if she did?

And he simply must do something about finding Dodd, who must either have headed straight for the Border with his loot or got into serious trouble. If ever he needed to be up and about, now was the time and his bloody eyes and head and body weren't cooperating.

And who had poisoned him? Emilia? Surely not. Hughie? Unlikely. Someone unknown? Why? Emilia perhaps? He knew his father would have taken care of the lad and intended to find him as soon as he could, ask a few questions. He would be sure to warn the Earl of Essex, though there was no chance Emilia would try to poison the Earl. However it would be embarrassing for everyone if other bidders for the management of the farm of sweet wines suddenly started dropping dead.

Carey awoke once into daylight, heart pounding. Sunlight was shining through the canvas of the tent, he could see the shadow of a man sitting by the flap and another on the other side to stop anyone coming in that side. Although the painful light made him shut his eyes immediately, he smiled, quite comforted. George Clifford had a simple view of most things and a mysterious assassin was one of them. You put men in the way.

Something had woken him. Something loud in his mind, but there was no sign from the two men on guard that there had been a real noise of a blade slicing through a neck....And his heart was beating like a drum, his shirt drenched, cold shivers down his legs.

Christ! It was the half-remembered fever dream from Saturday night. Or no, it was another installment of it. He had been shaving himself carefully in a small mirror in...Yes, definitely a stone cell, though quite well lit. His hand was steady, but looking into the mirror he had seen an older man, hair retreating a little up his temples, streaks of grey in the chestnut, a pouchiness to his face that he had seen in men who drank too much too often.

His shirt collar was frayed and had been badly darned. He was facing the axe, he knew it, was sad about it but not angry. He had made many stupid mistakes and had unforgivably let himself be talked into rebelling against his royal cousin and aunt. He could not quarrel with the sentence, only hoped the headsman would be good at his job. If only Elizabeth Widdrington...The face in the mirror stopped pulling the razor over the sides of his face and just stood staring. If only he had married Elizabeth Widdrington.

Then it was as before, the shock his watching self felt at the worn green velvet doublet, the glitter and swing of the axe, the sound that had woken him...

He was sitting up now, all the hairs on his body prickling upright. Was that why he rebelled? Because he didn't marry Elizabeth Widdrington? Why hadn't he? It was the one thing he wanted most in the world, he was quite clear he would trade anything at all save his honour for her. Had she turned him down? Had she died?

Was this a prophecy from God? Had he been sent a warning? What was he supposed to do with it?

Slowly the strange feelings down his legs and in his heart calmed and faded, leaving him exhausted again. He didn't like sleeping during the day but he didn't want to get up. What was he supposed to do? What did God want?

He knelt on his pallet with his eyes tight shut against the light. As he couldn't think what to say to God, he just recited the Lord's Prayer and hoped the bit about leading him not into temptation would do the job, whatever it was.

Of course, it was clear that the Queen would consider accusing her of being the actual killer of Amy Dudley as treason plain and simple. Would she have him executed? Perhaps not, although the Tower was a distinct possibility. But he didn't think that of her because it didn't make sense, even if the Queen actually was at Cumnor Place when it happened.

He growled softly to himself with frustration, lay down again and instantly fell asleep.

Then somebody prodded him awake and he blinked into the dazzle at a small person in a small but stunning cherry red-and-gold wheel farthingale with a tiny black doublet bodice and a raised cambric ruff behind her head like a saint's halo.

"Well, Sir Robert," came Thomasina's voice, "What have you been up to?"

"Ah um…" moaned Carey, wishing his head would stop pounding. He shut his eyes against Thomasina's outfit. "I'll tell you, Mrs. Thomasina, on condition you stop any other bastard waking me up and let me sleep."

"Certainly," she said.

And so he told her the whole story of what he had found at Cumnor Place and what Mrs. Odingsells had told him, including her wish to see his father. He didn't say anything about what he thought of the matter. Thomasina sat perfectly still while he spoke and then nodded once. She settled back on her cushion with her legs crossed and he heard the click of ivories as she started playing dice with herself. No doubt it was her full set of crooked dice, highman, lowman, bristleman, quite hypnotic. His eyes fell closed again and he slept.

monday 18th september 1592, morning

Dodd waited, forcing himself to breathe slowly in the prickling leaves and stones. There was a crunch of wooden clogs, but quite light, perhaps not a man…The dog was snortling about and came right over to Dodd. He stayed still where he lay, let the animal sniff him all over, heart beating.

A wet nose thrust into his face and started licking his face, chin to forehead, slobbering his beard hairs the wrong way.

"Ach, awa' wi' ye!" he complained and shoved the dog off. The dog put his paws on Dodd's shoulders and panted in his face, so Dodd stayed where he was and reached out to pat the dog's hairy flank. "Ay, what d'ye want?"

"Goodman," said a girl's voice on the other side of the bushes, "Are you all right?"

"Eh…nay, lass, Ah've got nae clothes nor gear and yer hound's droonin' me…"

Silence. Then: "Are you a foreigner?"

Dodd sighed deeply and said it again more Southern, which hurt his lips and face.

"Oh. Are you very much hurt?"

Considering the battering he'd taken, he'd been very lucky with only a possible busted rib and nose. But…

"Ay, Ah think ma leg is broken."

"Oh no, I'm so sorry. The robbers must have jumped you at the ford, didn't they?"

"Ay," Dodd said, thinking fast, "Ah'm no' a pretty sight for a lass. Ha' ye any breeks wi' ye?"

After more tiring translation, a bag was thrown over the bushes and in it Dodd found a rough hemp shirt and woollen breeches. He pulled them on at once, hoping the other man's lice wouldn't be too ferocious.

The dog had lain down beside him, watching with his nose between his paws and his eyebrows working as Dodd looked about for a belt. There was none, nor shoes nor clogs neither. He sighed, having a shrewd idea what was going on.

"I'm decent now," he called and the girl peered around the bushes.

She was a grubby little creature, about seven or eight years old and her greasy brown hair hanging out under a smeared biggin cap. Impossible to say if she would ever be pretty.

"Oh, Goodman," she said with a polite curtsey, "I'm ever so sorry about the robbers, they're terrible wicked men. My granny says, would you like to come and stay at our house until you're recovered?"

"Ah have nae money," Dodd explained. "I could likely get some in Oxford town but the robbers took a' I had on me."

It was a real nuisance having to repeat everything he said more Southern. His right leg was the one more bruised from the kicking so that was the one he decided would be broken.

"It's all right," said the child with a smile that seemed hard work for her. It certainly never reached her eyes. "My granny says it's our duty to help poor travellers attacked by the robbers."

"Ay," said Dodd, careful to keep his suspicion off his face and not ask why they didn't try a bit of warning then. And also how it came about that she had clothes for him. "Would ye… ken…d'ye know the name of the reivers…the robbers' headman…their captain?"

"No, Goodman," said the child in a pious way which told Dodd that she did. "They're wicked men."

Dodd made a great palaver of getting up, screwing up his face and groaning loudly in a way he never would if his leg actually had been broken. Then he leaned heavily on the child's shoulder as he hopped along the path with the dog padding quietly ahead of them.

After only a mile or so uphill they came to a tiny little bothy with low walls and a roof of turves and branches, not even respectable thatch like the remains of the monastery. An old lady in blue homespun was sitting on a stone by the door knitting and she looked up and smiled toothlessly as Dodd came hopping along with her granddaughter.

He made the motion of taking off his cap to her but of course he wasn't even wearing a statute cap which made him feel as if he was still naked.

"Missus," he said respectfully, "yer grandaughter says I can come and recover ma strength with ye, which I'm grateful for, but I'll tell ye now I havenae money with me for the…bastards took the lot includin' ma breeks."

"They do that so you won't chase them," said the old woman. "Can you work, Goodman?"

Dodd made a helpless expression. "A little, missus, but I think I've broke me leg."

That got only an unsympathetic grunt from her and the child left Dodd to wobble on one leg and went to whisper fiercely in the carlin's ear. Another grunt and a chomping of jaws. Before he fell over or had to put his leg down and give the game away,

Dodd grabbed the bush he was standing next to. He had felt unaccountably dizzy for a moment there which was odd. Still maybe not surprising, considering the battering. He had already sworn a mighty internal oath that he would never ever come to the soft safe South again, where people beat you up but didn't bother to kill you.

The old woman's eyes were narrowed in their crumpled beds and her jaws worked again. "Who's yer master?"

Dodd had thought hard about this inevitable question. What would be the best thing to say?

"Missus, I dinna ken…know ye and I'm grateful for the duds ye've lent me, but until we're better friends I'd be happier in my mind not to gi' ye my master's name, seeing he's a courtier."

The old eyes were narrowing and the child's as well. You could see they were related.

"Is he rich?"

"Not him, his family," said Dodd truthfully, "but Ah dinna ken if they'd ransome me…"

That was a dangerous thing to say because there were people on the Border who would just slit your throat if they thought you weren't worth anything. On the other hand, it was worth it to see the reactions—disappointment, guilt, then…

"We wouldn't ask for ransome, Goodman, we're not robbers and you're not our prisoner," said the old woman, working hard to look pious. "We only want to help you."

"I'm sorry, missus," Dodd said, with as charming a smile as he could get his bruised face to stretch to. "I meant a reward, payment for yer trouble…"

The carlin smiled and nodded, the child continued her very hard stare.

Ay, thought Dodd with some satisfaction, I know ye, missus, and how you're placed and what you're up to.

In fact, there was no chance whatever that a little cottage with a garden and…yes…from the smell, goats…could have survived next to a troop of broken men like the bastards who had temporarily bested him, without they paid blackrent of some kind. They were the carrion crows to the wolf pack of the broken men. What did he want the wolves to know? That was the question.

monday 18th september 1592, noon

Captain Leigh was playing dice with the old Spaniard in the still watertight monastery parlour, when little Kat Layman came trotting in ahead of John Arden who was drunk again. Her grim little face was less tight than usual which meant she had good news. She curtseyed nicely to him and waited to be spoken to, manners he had taught her with the back of his hand.

She took the cup of watered wine he always offered and sipped it, no expression.

It was stupid really, but Edward Leigh found the child unnerving sometimes. She was so unchildlike.

"Now then Kat," Leigh asked, rubbing the large bruise on his chin where their most recent target had punched him, "What have you found out?"

"His name is Colin Elliot, he's a Northerner which I knew anyway because you can't hardly make out what he do say." Leigh nodded encouragingly. "He was taking a message to his master which is a courtier and one of the Earl of Essex's men."

Leigh stopped breathing and looked over at Jeronimo, sitting still with the dice cup still poised between his long fingers. His cadaverous hawk of a face was intent. Was it possible the Spaniard had been right?

"Where was he headed?"

"Oxford, of course, he says if the Queen ain't there yet, she will be and his master is at Court to get money and a warrant out of her because he hasn't any, no tower nor land, he's just a bloody courtier with a smooth tongue."

Leigh nodded carefully. The Court was at Oxford and so was the Earl, only ten miles away. Holed up in this old monastery for the last few weeks, it had been hard to get news. But perhaps at last, at last they could move.

Kat was still speaking. "…and he hurt his leg or it got hurt when you was kicking him, he says it's broken, so he can't work much…He says 'canna,' you know, and he's good with his hands and with stock so he says he'll help as much as he can until he's well and his master's father will give a reward for him if my granny will send me off to Oxford to tell him."

"He's a good fighter," slurred John Arden whose black eye was flowering well, "took five of us to take him down. Could we get him to join us?"

Leigh shook his head. He didn't want another fighter, he wanted someone who had connections with the Earl of Essex. And that, thank God, despite all his doubts, he seemingly had at last. Now how could he parlay the Northerner into what he really wanted much more than a simple reward or ransome?

"*Katarina, cariña,*" said Jeronimo, "who is the father of this courtier the man serves?"

"He told me not to tell the robbers but it's my Lord Hunsdon, the Queen's Chamberlain."

Leigh blinked in awe at Jeronimo. "You were right," he said. "His master is Captain Carey."

Jeronimo nodded, took a deep breath, then winced and rubbed his stomach where it was swollen.

"We've got him this time," he said in French so the child wouldn't understand. "You can ask him for an audience with the Earl."

The Earl of Essex owed him a large amount of back pay, owed all of them, and Leigh intended to get it. If necessary he would have marched his remaining men down Oxford High Street in their once-fancy tangerine-and-white livery and demanded his rightful pay from the man he had trusted while that man was in the act of licking the old Queen's arse for her. In fact that had been his original plan.

"All right, Kat," he said to her, handing over a bag of bread and apples from the remains of the monastery orchard. "I'll likely come and take a look at him myself, so don't be alarmed."

Kat's face looked cunning. "Will you be fierce?"

"Roaarrr!" Leigh shouted, showing his teeth as he used to at his little brothers and sisters. This unnatural child didn't even flinch. "I'll be fierce, Kat, so make sure you tremble and run away."

She nodded disdainfully, hefted the bag, looked in it and scowled.

"I want paying. I want money, not just food."

"Kat," said Leigh, pulling her nose to nose with him by her kirtle, though not roughly, "I told you, we're only here because we fought and died for the Earl in France for eighteen months and got not a penny of the shilling a day he promised us, not one penny, though he spent plenty on pennants and livery and feasting."

She glared straight back at him. "I want a shilling like you promised. You got all the money from that Northerner, give me some."

"What if you're lying? What if he's lying?" Leigh was still nose-to-nose with the child.

"Can't help it if he's lying but I'm not," retorted the child, "and he said he'd lost the suit his master gave him to look more respectable than his homespun and he wished he hadn't looked so rich and there'll be the devil to pay for that too and there was money in it too, plenty of money."

Nick Gorman was wearing the man's suit now because it fit him best and it was certainly a gentleman's suit. Smithson had his hat, being in most need of one. The money was Leigh's now, naturally, as captain.

He let go of the fistful of rough kirtle he'd been gripping. Kat straightened herself and her apron with a brow of thunder.

"Give me my shilling," she said shrilly. "You'll just drink it and I need it for my dowry."

"Don't make me angry, Kat."

"*I'm* angry! I bring you things you didn't know that are important like he's a Northerner and who his master is and everything and you won't even give me a shilling like you said!"

"We could burn you and your old hag of a grandam out of your hovel!" Leigh shouted, outraged at being defied by a little girl. "I could send Harry Hunks down to you, do you want that?"

The ferocity of the child's glare actually stopped him.

"Don't be like that, sweeting," he said after a moment in the kindest voice he could muster. "Of course, we won't burn you out, you just made me cross." Nothing. Stony brown eyes stared steadily back at him. He gave her a comfit of sugarpaste taken from a rich packtrain a week before. She held it in her fingers and didn't even taste it, curtseyed silently and went out of the monastery parlour where Arden was waiting for her.

Jeronimo was shaking his head. "You should have paid her," he said in the French he found more comfortable. "She's right, she needs a dowry. It was only a shilling."

Leigh shrugged, he was the captain, not the Spaniard. "I need it more than she does. How am I going to afford the ribbons we need otherwise?"

Jeronimo said nothing, only winced and drank more of the brandy after adding laudanum that he kept in a small bottle in his doublet pocket. He only had one arm, his right had been taken off above the elbow with the sleeve neatly folded and sewn up. Perhaps the arm that had been broken by a musket ball and cut off many years ago still pained him as sometimes happened. His doublet had once been a very rich silk brocade and had worn well, but his shirt and falling band were as frayed and grubby as everyone's was. Perhaps he was ill: his dark skin had a greyish tinge that Leigh didn't like, though he had no fever.

They finished the brandy and Leigh decided that he, John Arden, and Harry Hunks, the biggest man they had who was nursing bruised ballocks from the Northerner's final headbutt, would go and chat to this Colin Elliot they had caught. Jeronimo he left in charge of the rest of the men, despite the fact that he was Spanish, because after you had fought together for a while, things like that didn't matter anymore and the Spaniard was owed money by the Earl of Essex too. And the Spaniard had certainly been a captain in the past and knew how to do it, which was more than Leigh felt he did, even now.

So with the cold autumn sun already westering, they sauntered down the overgrown cobbled path to the cottage. Leigh knew that they could follow the path northwards for a couple of miles and find the village of Cumnor with its haunted almost empty manor house, then three miles north of that would take them to the city of Oxford. The Spaniard had found the place for them and it couldn't be bettered.

The dog set up a-baying at Harry Hunks, whose real name was Percival but had been given the name of a famous London fighting bear because of his size and ferocity. Harry Hunks growled back at the dog and showed his teeth, at which the animal whined and hid behind the cottage.

The old woman came out still toothlessly chewing some of the bread her granddaughter had brought. Kat however was nowhere to be seen.

"Where is he?" shouted Leigh at the old woman, for general effect. "I know you've got him hidden, where is he?"

"Backyard sir," she quavered. "He's mending the chicken coop."

Stupid old bat, why had she given him a job that involved a weapon? They tramped round the tiny cottage, Harry Hunks deliberately squashing some of the winter cabbages already planted, out into the little yard where the chickens pecked and the muckheap teetered.

The Northerner's face and swollen nose was colouring nicely and he held his right leg awkwardly out to one side, tied with long hazel poles to keep it straight. He was weaving withies in and out to darn a gap in the side of the chicken coop. He stopped to look at them, didn't stand but did duck his head. Leigh couldn't see a hammer in his hands but assumed he'd have a knife to cut the withies.

The Northerner watched them from under his brows, his plain long face sullen. He was sizing them up, Leigh felt, including Harry Hunks, no doubt noting their Essex livery of tangerine and white despite its raggedness.

"Colin Elliot?" Leigh said as firmly as he could.

"Ay," he said. "May I help ye, sirs?"

That was civil enough for a Northerner, perhaps someone had been teaching him manners. Leigh had fought with a few Northerners.

"Good day, Goodman," said Leigh, doing his best to charm. "I hear from little Kat Layman that some wicked robbers attacked you at the ford. I came to see if there was anything we could do?"

Just for a second the man's eyes flickered and then his face became even more mournful.

"Ay," he said. "And they took ma maister's suit that he lent me, these duds arenae mine, sir, ma wife's capable o' much better. And ma boots forbye."

He looked disgustedly at his bare toes. His feet certainly were wide. Harry Hunks had been delighted with his share of the pickings and was wearing the boots now. A little too late, Leigh wondered if Elliot had noticed this.

"So who's your master?"

"Sir Robert Carey, sir."

Leigh nodded. It was wonderful news if true, but was it true?

"Yes," he said, "I think I met your master in France when he was a captain. One of the Earl of Essex's men? A very able captain, I think."

The Northerner finished the end of the withy, put down the coop and sat back. "Ay," he said, "I heard he wis knighted when he was in France wi' the Earl."

Lucky bastard, Leigh thought, who had once hoped to be knighted as well. "King of Navarre took quite a shine to him too, offered him a place, I believe."

The Northerner shrugged. Fair enough, it was unlikely Carey would share anything of that sort with his henchmen.

"Tell me, my memory's not too good I'm afraid, your master's a dark man, isn't he? Black hair?"

Contempt crossed the Northerner's face briefly. "Nay, sir, he's got dark red hair which he calls chestnut and blue eyes. And he's allus dressed verra fine though he canna pay his tailor."

Leigh had to smile. That was Carey all right. "He had one entire packpony for just his shirts, I remember, until the Earl of Cumberland got them off him for a night attack."

The Northerner's mouth turned down at the ends. "Ay, sir. It's shocking."

"So clearly I must help you get a message to Captain…er… Sir Robert Carey. Where do you think he'll be?"

"At Court wi' the Queen, wherever she is. Oxford, I heard."

"And the message you were carrying?"

"Dinna ken, sir, it was a letter. The robbers got it nae doot along o' ma purse and ma silver and ma sword," said the Northerner bitterly.

Thank God nobody was actually wearing the man's sword, Leigh thought, though it was a good solid weapon, clean, oiled, and would have been sharp if it hadn't been using for something like gathering firewood. He wondered what had happened to that letter.

"Do you know what was in the letter?" he asked and the Northerner shrugged, looking highly offended.

"Cannae read, sir. Ah can make me mark and puzzle oot ma name but nae more, sir. I can fight, though. Ay, I could fight." He looked gloomy and rubbed his broken leg.

Leigh clapped the dejected man on the back.

"Mr. Elliot," he said encouragingly, "I'm sure your leg will get better soon enough. And I'm sure that as soon as we find Sir Robert and explain things to him he'll…er…he'll see you properly equipped again."

"Ay, he might beat me though."

"Oh I don't think so, goodman, not his style at all." Leigh had never seen Carey flog a man for anything less than unauthorised looting or rape. Generally the sheer volume of noise he could produce when he was angry did the job just as well. "I'll send someone to Oxford to find Sir Robert," he went on, "We'll soon sort you out."

"Ah doot he'll mind ye," he moaned. "He's a courtier."

"Well true," said Leigh. "but my experience of Carey as a captain is that he did his best to keep his men alive and paid, even if he occasionally came up with mad plans to achieve that."

At which point the Northerner gave a brief bark of laughter before turning sullen again, which was what convinced Leigh that he had actually struck gold at last.

"Is there anything else?"

"Ay, sir, I had a good post horse under me and a remount when the...eh...the broken men took me, and the nags might be runnin' loose. I wouldnae want the broken men tae have the benefit of them. There's a gelding with a white sock and a chestnut mare."

That was interesting: they'd found the mare not far from the ford, but the other horse must have bolted further, perhaps heading for home. He'd send a couple of the boys out to track and find the animal; they needed horses desperately.

As he walked back to the monastery, he thought hard. Why the devil hadn't his men found that letter? Admittedly, it had been a scramble at the ford and at one point the blasted man had almost got away—he fought better half-stunned than most men fully fit. However once they'd got him down they had stripped and searched him thoroughly, finding no papers, which was a surprise. Jeronimo had said he was connected with Essex which was why they had switched the waymarker stones so they could ambush him.

He called the men together. There were twenty-five of them left from the fifty men he had taken with him to France. It had been a long hard road back from France after the Earl betrayed them. The ruined monastery had been by far the best billet they'd had since Arles. They were in some of the Earl of Oxford's neglected hunting forest and in the autumn there was a good amount of forage, including hazelnuts, mushrooms and berries, plus the game of course. But they only had two horses left of the twenty fine beasts that had gone to France.

Leigh sighed as he looked at his troop, all of them bony and bearded, grubby and ragged, very different from the strong brave young men who had followed him from their villages. Four of them, including Jeronimo, were strangers he'd picked up in France. A couple of them had persistent coughs that wouldn't go away, several of the boniest also had squits that wouldn't stop. All of them had a harder look in their eye than he liked to see. He sighed again. He had changed too. An older man looked back at him when he trimmed his beard and he knew he was going bald on top. War hadn't been anything like that glorious adventure the Earl of Essex had so eloquently convinced him to expect.

"Gentlemen," he said quietly, "is any of you hiding a letter that the Northerner was carrying? A letter to Captain Carey? Some of you may remember him from France?"

Nobody said anything.

"You know I need to see anything of the kind." Silence. Nobody was blushing, some of them were looking suspiciously at each other.

Leigh felt the stirring of the angry unhappiness that had settled around his gut sometime during the first months in France, felt it twist around his entrails. Just in time, Nick Gorman who had got the Northerner's suit to replace his remnants of Essex's livery, he stepped forward.

"There was this in the doublet pocket, sir," he said, holding out a stained bit of paper. "I didn't know it was important."

Leigh took the paper, glanced at it but it was all numbers. A cipher of some kind.

"Jeronimo, can you break codes?"

The Spaniard shrugged, stepped out of his place ahead of the line and took the paper. "I don't know, Señor," he said, squinting at it, "Perhaps in Espanish, but...I can try."

"Thank you." For a moment Leigh stared worried at Jeronimo. "It turns out you were right about the Northerner. Do you know anything about Captain Carey yourself?"

"The son of Henry Carey, milord Hunsdon?"

"Yes." The Spaniard smiled radiantly at him, quite shocking in his normally tense face and said something that sounded like *Gracias a Dios*.

"Why? Do you know him too?"

"No Señor, I know of hees family. From when I play lute for the Queen."

A likely story. Leigh had instantly dismissed Jeronimo's colourful past as the usual nonsense old soldiers spouted. He thought about the problem. Whom should he send to Oxford with the all-important letter? He could go himself and also try and buy the ribbons they needed, but that meant leaving the men without a leader and that always meant trouble. He could send John Arden but with Arden there was a good chance that he might pop into an alehouse for half a quart and not come out again until all their money was spent. On the other hand, Arden was probably the best second-in-command he had, though he was standing there with his hip cocked, one hand on his sword and a bleary expression on his puffy once-handsome face. He was certainly better than Leigh at planning a fight, should probably have been the captain, but didn't want the office. He preferred to get drunk every afternoon rather than worry about supplies and getting the men paid. Although it beat Leigh completely where he was getting his drink from.

Leigh sighed again. He couldn't rely on any of the others and besides it would be better for Carey to be contacted by someone he knew, so it had to be him. He would leave Arden in charge along with Jeronimo and hope for the best.

"Nick," he said, "I'm afraid we'll have to swap clothes so I look more respectable and nobody realises what we are. You can have the suit again when I come back. And in the meantime I want you, Tarrant, and Clockface to go and find the Northerner's remount, a good gelding with a white sock. As it came from the South it's probably heading back in that direction, trying to find its home and we don't want that, do we?"

Gorman nodded philosophically and then remembered and tipped his hat. "Yes, sir."

Meantime Leigh had to make sure the Northerner didn't take it into his head to make for Oxford on his own, barefoot as he was. He would have to be locked in at night, possibly chained, only they didn't have any such things, of course. He'd just have to send Harry Hunks down to the carlin again and tell her to keep the man in the pit at night.

monday 18th september 1592

Kat was munching stolidly through one of the crusts from the bread she brought back from the soldiers while Dodd did the same more cautiously because some of his teeth still felt loose. She had just finished counting up on her fingers.

"There's twenty-one of 'em," she said, scowling with the effort. "Then there's Captain Leigh and John Arden and Jeronimo and Harry Hunks."

Even Dodd had heard of Harry Hunks. "A bear?" he asked.

"What?"

He explained about the famous London fighting bear of the Eighties that could still be found engraved on horn cups and plates and in stories told on ballad sheets, though he'd died nearly ten years ago. Barnabus had told him all about the star of the bearbaiting.

Kat scowled even more. "I hate him," she said. "He's like a bear but he's bad. He's horrible. John Arden is nice and gives Granny nice things he finds in the monastery and she gives him her apple aquavitae. Captain Leigh is stupid and stingy and mean and I hate him too."

"Jeronimo?"

"He's a furriner," Kat said dismissively, "a Spaniard who's dark and skinny and hisses through his teeth sometimes."

"Ay," said Dodd.

"So there's too many of 'em. What can *you* do?"

Dodd contemplated telling her, but decided not to in case she changed her mind again and went back to the soldiers.

Kat had come to him as he awkwardly dug a trench from a sitting position, using a small wooden trowel, for the old grandam to plant more winter cabbages in. Kat was still carrying her bag with the bread in it and her cheeks were flushed with fury and her eyes steely slits.

"If I tell you about the men at the old monastery, will you promise to kill them?" she had demanded. "Especially Captain Leigh?"

Well that was easy enough. "Ah cannae promise I'll do it," Dodd told her, "but I promise I'll try."

She paused, thinking about it.

"Yes well," she said after a moment, "you don't have to do all of them, just Captain Leigh."

"Ay."

"He promised me a shilling for what I could find out and didn't pay me last time and he didn't pay me this time so he owes me two shillings for my dowry and I hate him."

You've a cousin in Carlisle, Dodd thought, highly amused and wishing the Courtier was there to manage the conversation with an angry little maid. She cocked her head on one side.

"So I'll tell you everything the captain told me not to tell anyone and then you can decide how to kill him."

Dodd had listened carefully while the child spilled out her fierce heart to him. It seemed the tale of the broken men was a disgraceful one of noble promises unkept, but common enough. You hardly ever got paid for soldiering, bar what you could steal or kill for, everyone knew that. It seemed that the unfortunate Captain Leigh still hadn't worked it out.

"What happened to the last messenger they caught?"

"Oh, he was all right. They just knocked him out and took his stuff and then when he was a bit better, Captain Leigh came along and said they'd got his duds and message back from the robbers and off he went again, on foot of course, as they had his horse. They got some wagons a while ago too and they were pleased with that and the men guarding it didn't fancy a fight and ran off back to London."

"So Leigh will use me to get hisself an audience with the Earl of Essex?"

"I suppose so. He thinks he can talk his lord into paying him."

Dodd laughed once at this and then clamped down again. It was a serious matter. The men of Leigh's troop had put a brave on him but they hadn't killed him when it would have been easy to do it. At first he had taken this as an insult like Heneage's, that they thought him some nithing that need not be feared for vengeance. But perhaps it hadn't occurred to them that he might be a man of parts, even if he was in a foreign county. On the other hand, he intended to get his gear back, particularly his sword, his knife, and his boots. His hip felt very strange without the weight of a weapon on it and his feet were already cold and sore.

Who would go to put the bite on Carey? He hadn't seen the Spaniard, but had seen the drunken walk of John Arden and the large shaggy man with a slight limp that had looked coldly at him. Probably Leigh would go himself as he already knew Carey from France. Hmm. That would be good.

"Whit happened to the monks in the monastery when the King's men came?" Dodd asked.

Kat shrugged. "My grandam said they were just a few stupid old men and boys by then and they tried to fight so they all got killed and they burnt some of the monastery. So it's haunted, of course."

"Ay, do the soldiers ken that?"

"Grandam told Captain Leigh when he came but he laughed at her and said he didn't think so. But it *is* haunted."

"Ay." Dodd rubbed his bottom lip with his thumb. The glimmerings of an idea was coming to him. For complexity and madness it was one nearly worthy of Carey himself, perhaps being near the Courtier was causing him to catch courtierlike ways of thinking. Still.

"Grandam told the boy Nick Gorman when he came to get cheese from us, she warned him about the ghosts of the burnt monks and he didn't laugh. Captain Leigh came and told her off, he said no good Protestant believed in superstition like that and Papists couldn't hurt Godly men like them anyway."

Dodd tutted. He'd never heard of a ghost that cared about such things.

"Kat," he said, "I want ye to go back to Captain Leigh and act verra nice tae him. Can ye do that?" She frowned, opened her mouth to say something. "Not to be friends again but to find things out from him. I want ye to find oot who he's sending tae my master and what he's doing next. And get me some paper."

"Can you write then?"

"Ay, but dinna let on."

It was a useful test. If she came back with paper as he hoped, then he'd know he might trust her which was important for the most complicated part of his plan. If she came back alongside Leigh demanding to know why he'd lied about his ability to read, then he might be in for another leathering but he'd know what he needed to about Kat. Her face had suddenly fallen.

"But what about your leg? How can you kill Captain Leigh with that?"

"Whit about it?"

She looked at the splint and then stopped. He put his finger on his lips and winked and got from her the first real smile he'd ever seen on her face.

Then she dusted crumbs from her greasy kirtle and jumped to her feet and trotted determinedly away with her wooden clogs clacking on the cobblestones of the path.

The old woman came out later and watched him at his digging with her hands on her hips.

"Will ye have that ready by this evening, Goodman?" she demanded.

"Ay," he said, "the dog's helping."

The dog had done some digging and found a greenish bone which he was gnawing on quite happily. Suddenly he lifted his head and sniffed the air, then whined nervously, pawed the bone back into the earth and skulked round to hide behind Dodd.

The carlin went out to the front of the cottage and Dodd could hear the big bearlike man called Harry Hunks tramping to the front door in Dodd's own boots. The sound of talking came to him. Quick as he could, he hopped over to listen by the path and caught Harry Hunks' last sentence.

"...and make sure he sleeps, we don't want him getting out."

"The pit will hold him, Harry, he's broken his leg."

"Make sure he don't get out or I'll burn your cottage."

"Captain Leigh wouldn't like that."

"Then I'll kill your dog."

Nothing more, so Dodd hopped back and sat down by his trench just in time. Harry Hunks loured round the side of the cottage and pointed at him.

"You!" he shouted. "You stay put or I'll break your other leg."

Dodd did his best to look cowed, touched his capless head and quavered "Yes, sir!" at the big lout. Harry Hunks turned about and stamped away, damaging Dodd's good boots by kicking a hole in the hurdles of the goat pen as he went.

Dodd's belly gave a great growl and grumble then which wasn't surprising since he hadn't eaten all day. He went over and shoved back the inquiring goat's head that instantly came through the gap.

"Missus," he called, "ye'll need tae move yer goats."

The grandam came out the back of the cottage, saw the damage and shook her head. Then she hobbled over and put a halter round the billy kid's neck. There was a nanny kid as well that she haltered and the two others were nannies with still-heavy udders.

The grandam dragged the two half-grown kids back toward the cottage, both protesting at being separated from their mothers. The nannies pushed through the gate to follow.

"You can herd the nannies, if you're minded to, Goodman," shouted the carlin.

"Ay missus," said Dodd, who caught the nannies by a horn each and looked them in the long-pupilled eyes. One said "Neh!" in a testy way, so she was the one he led ahead of the others and they came quietly enough. It was as well to respect rank among goats as well as men.

Kat had joined them by the time the goats were in their tumbledown shed beside the cottage and Dodd had already mended the hurdle. She was looking smug and she whispered at him,

"Can you milk goats?"

The question irritated him. Of course he could milk goats, he could milk anything with teats and had once milked a sow for a bet and nearly got his nose bitten off. "Ay," he said.

"Can Mr. Elliot help me with the milking, Grandam?" asked Kat artlessly and the old woman nodded. The day was cooling and Dodd wondered where the pit was where he'd sleep that night. He hadn't expected that there would be room for all three of them in the bothy with its yard-high walls, quite apart from the propriety of it.

The child brought a stool and two good big earthenware bowls to the shed, sat down and started on the younger nanny's udder, pulling at the teats roughly and impatiently. Dodd squatted by the older one, rubbed her flanks, butted his head a couple of times where a kid would nuzzle and made a quiet goat noise. Then he licked his fingers and wibbled the teats, rubbed the spit on. As soon as the first few drops had oozed out, he started the rhythmic work with his hands which he hadn't done since he went to Carlisle. It took him right back to his boyhood when he'd had four goats to milk every morning and evening. The goat let down her milk almost at once and he soon filled the bowl with warm milk to the brim. Then because his stomach was griping him something terrible and he wasn't convinced the carlin would waste any supper on him, he ducked his head and milked a stream of warm creamy milk straight into his mouth.

He stopped when he saw that Kat was staring at him.

"Whit?" he asked, wiping milk off his beard.

"How did you fill it up so quickly?" the child asked, still wrenching away at the other goat's udder in a way that made Dodd feel sore in the teats he didn't have. Had nobody ever taught her?

"Tell ye what," he said, "let me finish her off and ye can tell me what Captain Leigh is planning."

She gave him the stool and he squatted down again, butted the nanny's pungent flank and let her poor udder rest a little. The bowl was hardly half full and only with the thin first milk, none of the cream. He patted and rubbed her neck and waited.

"So why aren't you getting on with it?" demanded the angry child.

His mother had taught him to milk goats this way, God rest her, and so he told the angry child what she had told him.

"Because ye'll get more milk by kindness than ye will any ither way. They won't give ye the milk if ye hurt 'em or mek 'em sore."

Kat's eyes narrowed suspiciously. "What do you mean?" she demanded, "They've got food. Nobody's beating them."

He teased the teats a little with his wetted fingers.

"Ay, Kat, listen, the milk's for their kid. Ye've got to fool 'em you're their kid, then they let out all their milk not just the thin stuff." He did it again. "So what's Captain Leigh planning?"

She was still scowling. "I tore some clean paper out of a book in the parlour when Captain Leigh went to look at your other horse that they found, the one with the white sock and I got it from John Arden that him and Jeronimo are in charge along of Harry Hunks when Leigh goes off to Oxford in the morning to find your master and the Earl of Essex too. The Queen's not there yet."

Dodd raised his eyebrows. Carey had been talking about the Queen being at Oxford for a month but then she was a woman. He held out his hand for the paper and took it—nice thick creamy stuff it was, with a pretty border of flowers. Some monkish thing, no doubt. He'd forgotten to ask her to find ink, but some charcoal was a better proposition, less complicated than a pen.

"You heard about Grandam keeping you in the old monk's cellar until Captain Leigh comes back."

"Ay."

"He's going to buy *ribbons*!" she spat, her face twisted in fury, "with *my* money!"

That was when the younger nanny decided to let down her milk and the drops came, so he took the teats and started milking two steady streams into the bowl.

"How far is it tae Oxford from here?"

"I don't know."

"How long does it take ye to walk to market there then?"

"Maybe two hours?"

"How d'ye ken…know?"

"Well when we go to market with the cheeses we start before sun up and when we get there the gates are open and the market's started."

Maybe six or seven miles then. He could run that in an hour and a bit, given a reasonable path and not too many hills. However he didn't like to think of what that would do to his poor soft feet. He wasn't about to do it if he had a better plan, which he did. And besides, he wasn't crawling back to Carey in rags and bare feet and no sword. Not him.

"How will yer grandam be sure I'll let her put me in the cellar?"

Kat smiled patronisingly. "She'll put wild lettuce juice and valerian and poppy pod juice in your pottage tonight."

"Ay?" He sighed. "Where's the cellar then?"

The bowl was full and milk still coming so he took that straight into his mouth as well. It was deliciously creamy. Kat stared at him "Could you do that for me?"

She was a skinny little mite with a hungry face—why hadn't he thought of that before? She looked like his littlest brother, the one he'd often taken down into the pastures to steal milk for after the Elliots killed his father and took all their herds. So he beckoned her nearer and pointed the goat's teat at her open mouth and the jet choked her a little but she got quite a lot down. She smiled at him.

"Grandam says it's all got to go to cheese to sell in Oxford for the rent money to the Earl of Oxford, and the bastard soldiers are likely to do even more damage before they go so she'll likely need more money for that and to pay them off too."

"Ay," said Dodd, "broken men are hard on everyone. Ye've got a good couple of bowls there now if we dinna spill it."

On his insistence they wiped down the goats with wisps of hay and fed and watered them, they had salt licks from their palms as well. All goats were mad for salt. Then he got Kat to show him where the monks' cellar was.

It was in the pile of stones that said this had been a part of the monastery and the cellar was actually a stone-lined pit that they might have used for grain or even tanning. It was deep enough that he wouldn't be able to climb out of it without a ladder or something similar, though there were gaps between some of the stones to put your toes in. You had to hope there was some kind of roof to put over it and that it wouldn't rain in the night or you'd be floating by morning. There was dried bracken at the bottom on the least muddy bit. Dodd had seen worse prisons.

"Does she put a hurdle across?"

Kat waved at a hurdle of withies, next to the ladder. The important point was whether the grandam would chain him to anything but he couldn't see any chain or ring down in the pit itself so he devoutly hoped she wouldn't.

"You can't get out, my dog will stop you," Kat told him. She turned her back on him to give the dog a hug and play with his ears so Dodd took the chance of dropping a few things into the pit that might come in useful later.

Then they went and collected the bowls, took them into the cottage where the carlin nodded approval at the amount and set them on a stone shelf at the back that was probably looted from a church as it was marble.

"You're a good stockman, then," Kat's grandam said.

"Ay, missus," he said to her politely, touching his nonexistent cap, "Ah am."

"Come in and have supper," she said which caused his stomach to make an almighty comment that got all of them laughing.

It wasn't so bad a place to live, dry and snug and it had a tiled pavement with rushes over it. The roof wasn't high enough for him to stand upright but it was high enough for the little old woman. A modern chimney of stolen bricks was in the corner for the fire and a pot hanging over it, so the place wasn't nearly as smoky as the turf bothies he had spent his teens in. There was hardly even enough smoke to make you cough.

Dodd squatted next to the fire where the carlin had a stone bench and Kat had her milking stool, took the wooden bowl of pottage and the wooden spoon. He took a few spoonfuls which was hard on him since it was good stuff with some bacon in it, even, beans, lentils, even carrots. He had a bit of old bread as well, so he made the most of it.

The dog was prowling about the yard to keep the foxes off the chickens. When the carlin went to tap some of her own wine from a barrel at the back of the cottage, he put his head quickly out the top half of the door and dumped most of his pottage on the ground, whistled softly through his teeth.

He had to squat down again quickly and happy snortlings told him the dog was slurping up the drugged pottage.

She came bustling back with a horn cup of her elderflower wine so he took that and it was excellent, such a pity she'd put laudanum in it too.

"Ah've a need for the jakes," he said yawning deliberately.

"Dungheap's behind the cottage."

He knew where that was, so he caught Kat's eye as he went to the door, cocked his head.

She was a cunning little piece. She waited until he finished, then came out with his wine cup.

"She's put more sleeping potion in it," she hissed at him. "She didn't see you finish the pottage."

Dodd tipped out the wine and refilled it with water from the water butt. He'd been busy while he'd squatted at the furthest end of the dungheap.

He showed Kat the charcoal writing on the nice paper.

"Ye know the way to the market in Oxford, ay?" he said to Kat who nodded intently. "D'ye know the man that rules the market, one of the Mayor's men, mebbe?"

"You have to pay him even if you don't sell nothing," she sniffed.

"Early tomorrow morning, I want ye to walk tae Oxford, fast as ye can. Go to the market clerk or whoever it is, curtsey, call him sir, say ye've bin sent by a...a man at arms in service to Sir Robert Carey, son of Lord Hunsdon, and give him that paper. Tell him where ye live and a' that and warn him of the broken men. But be sure and gi' that bit o' paper tae somebody of worship, official, mind? Naebody that disnae wear a gown."

She nodded slowly. "Why?"

"Ye asked me tae kill Captain Leigh for ye?" he reminded her. She nodded, eyes narrowing with suspicion. "How'd ye like to watch him hang for coining and maybe horsetheft, eh?"

Her eyes went round and her mouth opened in delight. "Really? Truly?"

"Ay. This letter is laying information agin him. I happen tae know that a lot of the money that he's gonnae be spending on ribbons is false coin. That's a hanging offence, is uttering false coin. And he'll be riding a reived horse forbye."

She blinked in puzzlement and then nodded firmly. "I'll do it. I know the way really well and once when Grandam was ill I ran to the 'pothecary in the Cornmarket and got laudanum for her." Dodd didn't tell her the final refinement to a plan that he was quite modestly proud of. Suddenly she laughed. "Did you really steal the white-socked gelding?"

"Ay," he said heavily. "It wis a mistake."

monday 18th september 1592, afternoon

For the first time since Saturday, Carey woke feeling more like himself. The day had greyed over and so the light wasn't so bad for his eyes, besides he fancied that they were improving a little. He was also hungry.

John Tovey appeared when he stuck his head out of the tent to see who was about and came to help him on with his doublet.

"Any idea where my henchman is, Mr. Tovey?" he asked the boy who seemed to be as bad at tying points as he was good at penmanship.

"Um…sorry, sir," said Tovey, fumbling about at the back of Carey's doublet, "Who?"

"Hughie Tyndale? He was poisoned at the same time."

"Ah. My lord Earl said your f…father had taken him into the rest of his household when they moved into Trinity College."

"Excellent. Go find me some food and then we'll take a walk round the corner and talk to him."

Tovey came back with a couple of pies and bread and ale which Carey demolished at speed. He then strapped on his sword and poinard, crammed his hat as low on his head as he could and stepped outside the tent, past Henshawe sitting wittling something and the Earl at his peculiar chess play and various rehearsals for a masque going on.

The traffic would be far too bad to bother with a horse, so Carey simply walked out of the makeshift gate between the bright flags onto the muddy rutted path that joined Broad Street which went alongside the old Oxford city wall and was at least cobbled for the horse market there. The alehouse on the corner with the lane that went down to New College was crammed with menservants shouting at each other. The schools and the Bodleian library loomed opposite.

Even in the annoying dazzle Carey could see the men in his father's livery at the door of Trinity College, tucked between a field and a small bookshop. He went straight over, made a few enquiries and ten minutes later was unbolting the chamber door where Hughie was still recovering.

The window was shuttered and although Hughie didn't rate a proper fourposter bed, somebody had rigged up a curtain of old-fashioned tapestry with pointy hatted women and moth-holes.

Hughie looked pale and frightened, which was an odd sight in a young man as large and well-shouldered as he was, with his black hair and square shuttered face and his beard starting to come in strongly.

When he'd blinked at Carey, he tried to get up but Carey stopped him with a raised hand.

"Hughie, don't trouble yourself, I came to see how you were doing."

"It wisnae me, sir," growled Hughie in Scotch. "Ah tellt 'em, Ah didnae spike yer drink…"

No doubt his father had made sure the lad was well-questioned, but Carey had better methods. He pulled up the stool and sat himself down, blinking and rubbing his eyes.

"I've only just been well enough to get up," he said affably. "How are your eyes doing?"

"Mebbe I've bin struck blind," muttered Hughie dolefully, "I cannae mek out…"

"No, that's what belladonna does to you, it seems, fixes your pupils open so you can't see in daylight. Dreadful stuff. It's lucky I didn't drink as much of that flagon as you did. You should start being able to see properly again tomorrow."

"Ay?"

"Oh yes. Now I'm completely certain it wasn't you who put the belladonna in my booze, but you must have seen who did it because…"

"But I canna remember, sir, I'm so sorry."

That might be true. Carey couldn't think how he'd got to the church and couldn't remember much of what happened there either, apart from the puking which he would have preferred to forget.

"Well we'll start with your last clear memory and see what more you can remember? Do try, there's a good fellow, you're my only chance at tracking down whoever did it."

"Ay," Hughie looked very gloomy, his jaw was set. "I wantae ken that masen."

"All right. Do you recall me sending you off for spiced wine?"

It was like pulling teeth. Hughie remembered the girls dancing the country dance. He remembered seeing Carey speak to the pretty Italian woman and he remembered heading for the spiced wine bowl and pushing through the other servingmen. He couldn't remember any more.

"Did you see who was serving?"

He shook his head, there were too many people around the table, he couldn't get through.

"So how did you get your flagon filled?"

He'd passed it forward to the table and got it back filled with spiced wine…

"Ach," he said, scowling, "that's when it happened."

Carey nodded. "They wouldn't take the risk of poisoning the whole bowl, it had to be very specific. So when whoever it was saw you with the flagon, he knew you were my man, he blocks your path to the spiced wine and he helpfully gets it filled then adds the belladonna. The idea, I think, was that you would be blamed for it."

"Ay?"

"Well of course. It's only because you illicitly drank enough to half-kill yourself that my father doesn't have you banged up in the Oxford jailhouse right now."

There was a long thoughtful pause while Hughie digested this.

"Ah hadnae thocht o'that, sir."

"No? Well, think about it now. You bring me wine which is poisoned, ideally I die and it's only thanks to God that I didn't, and then as my henchman who brought the wine, you would be the first and probably last suspect."

"But I didna…"

Carey leaned forward, blinking at the young man's sullen face and wishing he could see more clearly. "Hughie, I'm sure you didn't but if I was dead and you unpoisoned, you would be in very big trouble no matter how innocent you were. I can't guarantee that my father wouldn't have you put to the question to find out what had happened; he's a decent man and doesn't like that kind of foreign rubbish, but he would be very upset if he had my corpse to bury. To put it mildly."

More silence. "Ay, sir," said Hughie heavily. There was some kind of rage smouldering in him somewhere. Carey hoped Hughie would put the rage to good use, by finding the poisoner, for instance.

Carey stood and clapped a hand on the young man's shoulder. "I'll talk to my father, make sure he releases you to me once you're better. Think about it. Oh and Hughie…"

"Ay, sir?"

"I'm a very tolerant man, you know. I served at Court for ten years before I decided it would be more fun to do some fighting on the Borders. I know how Courts work and I know how the King of Scotland's Court works as well because I was there with Walsingham years ago and I've been back a few times since.

The only thing I don't forgive in a man of mine is lying to me. Understand?"

More silence.

"If you're taking money from someone to keep an eye on me and report back, I don't mind at all—so long as you tell me about it."

Nothing. Carey nodded and crammed his hat further down over his eyes. "See if you remember anything more, drink plenty of mild ale and if you feel up it you can be back at work for me tomorrow. God knows, Mr. Tovey my new clerk doesn't know one end of a doublet from another."

Not a glimmer of a smile, the saturnine young face was clearly masking a brain that was thinking furiously.

Quite pleased with himself, Carey went out and found Tovey sitting on a window ledge peering out the window into the quad. His face was wistful.

"Happy memories, Mr. Tovey?"

"Yes, sir. Though I was at Balliol not Trinity and working my keep, I loved it here." The shy smile among the spots was like that of a man remembering an old love. "All the books, it was just…It was heaven here. So many books to read."

Carey nodded politely. While he liked reading and enjoyed romances like the *Roman de la Rose* or adventure stories like Mallory's *Morte d'Arthur,* he usually got restless after an hour or so. He wasn't a clerk.

"Let's go find one of my brothers," he said. Tovey hopped down and trotted after him obediently.

Luckily the one he found was George who was unenviably in charge of organising the Hunsdon household. The household was enormous even on progress and spilled out of the main college quad and into the gardens behind. George was Hunsdon's heir, in his forties and very harassed by the lack of provisions.

"What?" he snapped irritably when Carey asked him the question for the fourth time. "You want to know whether your man Dodd's turned up and also about Aunt Katherine's riding habit thirty years ago? For God's sake, Robin, why?"

"For a good and sufficient reason," Carey said. His hat was helping the dazzle but he was getting another headache and his guts were in a sad state, no doubt thanks to Dr. Lopez' prescriptions. And he was now seriously worried about Dodd—none of his father's men had any idea whether he had been found yet. It was as if he had been stolen away by the faery folk. And Carey did not personally want to think about a faery that could do that to Dodd.

Carey passed a hand down the leg of the horse that seemed skittish, while his elder brother gloomily checked the hay stores which had clearly been got at by rats and possibly humans.

"I don't know what the devil happened to her skirt," said George pettishly. "And as for Dodd, my bloody wagons left London ten days ago with food supplies and they haven't arrived yet either. Maybe the sergeant ran off with them."

Not impossible with Dodd, but unlikely, Carey thought. The skittish gelding next to him blew out its lips and hopped a bit. Running his hand down again, Carey found the hot sore place on the knee which he suspected would need a bran poultice. He pointed this out to George who wasn't pleased to hear about it as he was also short of horses. In Carey's experience nobody, in any situation, ever had enough horses.

"Come on, George," he insisted, "I'll leave you alone if you tell me. You must remember more than I do and I remember quite a fuss years later. Aunt Katherine's riding habit?"

"God, I don't know," snorted George, sounding very like a lame horse himself, "I'm not so bloody interested in fine clothes as you, I don't..."

"I don't wear kirtles, George," Carey said coldly, wishing his brother wasn't so pompous. "I'm asking for a reason. Do I have to show you my warrant?"

"Oh. That. Well..." George sighed and stared at the ground. "Far as I can remember she was at Court early in the Queen's reign. Lettice hadn't come to Court yet. I was a page still, and yes, her riding habit went mysteriously missing. And then one of her tiring women was complaining that it was ruined but then the Queen was very kind and gave Aunt Katherine a dress length—a whole twelve yards—of fine green Lincoln wool, and arranged for her own tailor to make a new habit for her."

"Anything else? How was the kirtle ruined?"

"Got splashed with blood or something. And the headtire had been lost as well. Aunt Katherine probably fell off her horse and didn't want to admit it, she was never a very good rider."

Yes! Carey stood stock still, staring into space. "I don't remember Aunt Katherine ever liking the hunt," he said carefully. "What style was the headtire?"

George shrugged. "She was very old-fashioned, usually wore French hoods that went out with Bloody Mary, I don't know."

Carey's heart was pounding and the hair up on the back of his neck, it was like what you felt when you saw a chorus of Kings in your hand and a fat pot on the table.

George was still droning on. "Sorry, brother?"

"I said, Robin, if you'd care to listen for a change, that Aunt Kat was very upset about it and so was Father and he told us not to mention it at all."

"Right." That fitted too. Carey decided he had to find his father and talk to him. "Where is Father?"

"He's out with some men, trying to find out what happened to the pack train—and your Sergeant Dodd as well. He was saying if you hadn't been so infernally careless and got yourself poisoned, you could have been very useful. He wants to know when you think you'll be fit to ride?"

Leaving out the detail of where he had gone that morning, Carey shrugged. "Maybe tomorrow if my eyes are better. I'm quite busy too, you know. In addition to the warrant matter, I'm also trying to find out who poisoned me. Thank you, George."

He walked carefully out of the Hunsdon camp, still trailed by Tovey, with the sunlight peering under a sheet of dirty linen cloud to dazzle him again and make his head hurt. He would have to find out from Cumberland who was serving the spiced wine on Saturday and then talk to the man to see if he could remember any of the people crowding round the table. Meantime his head was buzzing because he had thought of a possible reason for the Queen to be at Cumnor Place on the 8th September 1560. It was far-fetched but it made better sense than the notion that she would personally murder Amy, that was sure. He might have to go back to Cumnor Place and press Mrs. Odingsells for whatever it was she had kept. And his Aunt's missing headtire made sense of something else.

Unfortunately the new explanation once again made a prime suspect of Lord Burghley.

monday 18th september 1592, night

Back with the Earl of Cumberland's encampment, he found the man who served the spiced wine who was understandably extremely nervous. It took some time to calm him enough to get any sense out of him at all. He said he was certain there had been no woman at all amongst the servingmen wanting spiced wine for their masters, which took out Emilia's direct intervention. As for which of them had passed forward Hughie's flagon—the man had no idea at all, blinked helplessly at the flagon Carey showed him and said he'd filled hundreds that looked just like it, he was sorry, sir, but…Carey sighed, gave him thruppence for his time and promised him another ninepence if he could remember anything else.

Carey would bet a lot of money that whichever man it had been, he'd left Rycote on Saturday night, but so had plenty of other people. Or had he? There were so many servingmen, henchmen, and general hangers on at Court, even on progress, the poisoner could easily have stayed with the Court if he kept his nerve.

He was restless and out of sorts. He couldn't even enjoy playing cards with Cumberland when he could hardly make out the pips. Darkness fell which eased him somewhat. And so Carey sat and drank mild ale in the little alehouse on the corner of the Hollywell Street, staring into space, trying to filter out the noise of a lute being played by an idiot and some extremely bad singing.

The hammering and sawing died down and the workmen started filling up the alehouse, spending their wages. Flocks of students moved restlessly along the street in their black gowns, arguing and drinking and, occasionally, fighting.

Somebody else got hold of the lute, somebody who could actually play the damned thing because he started by tuning it. No alehouse lute was ever in tune. When the man began playing, Carey sat up and put his mug on the table.

It was the Spanish air he had sung at Rycote. The tune didn't have the same arrangement that Byrd had given it, but it was still the same wistful melody. And the man playing the lute was the man who had disappeared from Byrd's music consort on the Saturday night after hearing Carey sing.

Carey's neck felt cold. Had he put the poison in Carey's booze? Why would he do that? He'd annoyed Mr. Byrd by leaving the musicians' consort—that didn't say he'd left the whole party.

The man finished playing that air and then played two other tunes more. Despite applause and calls for more from the workmen, he put the lute down and walked out of the alehouse without even passing a hat round.

Goddamn it, he needed a man at his back, he wished he hadn't sent the yawning Tovey off to his bed. At least Tovey could have run to Trinity College and rousted out Sergeant Ross and a few Northerners to arrest the man.

No help for it, he couldn't afford to lose the man so Carey put his half-finished ale down and followed. At least now that the streets were fully dark apart from occasional public-spirited lanterns on college gates, his eyes worked very well. He could see as clearly as if it were a moonlit night and not as overcast as it was.

The man walked purposefully along the road to New College, went into the tiny boozing ken next to it, picked up the violin there and played that. Once again the Spanish air rang out, followed by two more tunes and the man left once more.

Carey pulled his hat down, wished he'd bothered with a cloak and pretended to be staggering drunk as he followed the man on down the lane that eventually wound up passing by

Magdalen deerpark where he turned right and came back along the High Street.

There were a lot of inns and alehouses on the High Street and the man went into each one, played the Spanish air and a couple more tunes, then left without passing a hat round or accepting any of the beer offered to keep him in the place.

He stayed and ate the ordinary at the London Inn on the southwards road from Carfax, then off he went again, having maybe one quart of mild per five boozing kens and playing the Spanish air at each of them. And there certainly were an amazing number of inns and alehouses in Oxford. Studying must be thirsty work.

Just as Carey was loitering in a doorway on the corner of St. Giles after a foray to the Eagle & Child where the alewife had scowled at both of them, he saw a looming pair of shoulders and a statute cap pulled down low on Hughie's saturnine young face.

"Ay, sir," said Hughie, when Carey caught up with him, "I came to find ye because I minded me of something. The hand of the man that gave me the flagon back…it was…Ah…ye ken, his fingernails wis long and he had rough ends tae his fingers."

Carey paused, his heart lifting. Hughie was screwing up his eyes and frowning and Carey knew that the very little light from the torches on the college gates was still bothering him.

"Hughie, well done!" he said, clapping the man's shoulder, "That's wonderful because I think I may be following the villain. Come with me."

They went into the White Horse where the musician was just setting down the house lap harp and being applauded. There was a flicker over his face which could have been fear. As far as Carey could tell he had a square handsome old face, grey beard and hair, a solid-looking, dependable man, not at all what you might expect a musician to look like. He didn't even have a drunkard's red nose. Perhaps he and Hughie could lay hands on the man?

Then he heard a quiet cough behind him, turned and found Sir Robert Cecil sitting in a corner booth. Cecil lifted his quart to Carey.

"Sir Robert," said Burghley's second son, "I'm glad to see you up and about again."

"Thank you, Mr. Secretary," said Carey warily.

"May I get you anything?"

In the corner of his eye, he could see the greybeard musician moving toward the back of the alehouse. Under his breath he said to Hughie, "Is that him?" Hughie made the indeterminate Scotch sound "Iphm" which probably meant he wasn't sure. "Go after him, keep him in sight," Carey hissed. "Do it quietly."

"Ay sir," said Hughie with a shy smile, and went over to the bar.

Cecil had already beckoned the potboy. Carey certainly couldn't ignore a Privy Counsellor in favour of an old musician, so why not? He had run out of money again, having come out with only a shilling in his purse. "Thank you, sir, I'll have brandywine."

At Cecil's gesture, he sat down in the booth facing the youngest member of the Privy Council. Meanwhile Hughie had carried his jack of ale straight over to the musician, tapped him on the shoulder and asked him in a harsh slurred voice how you set about playing a harp, it was something he'd always wanted to do. The greybeard paused and then warily let Hughie sit next to him and started showing him how to tune the instrument.

"Ye have to do that, eh?" said Hughie, after a big gulp of ale. "Why?"

"No sign of Sergeant Dodd yet?" Cecil asked while the musician stared at the lad and clearly struggled to find words to explain something so obvious. Carey shook his head.

"My father's gone south again to try and find him."

Cecil smiled. "I wanted to tell you that I found a distraught innkeeper at the post inn that had its roof burnt off on Saturday night. He had been suspicious of Dodd because he was, of course, riding one of the Queen's horses but didn't present his warrant to get half-price booze."

"Ah."

"By his account, he locked Dodd into his room, and put one of his men on guard, planning to alert the authorities in Oxford."

Carey winced slightly. "Yes, indeed. The mysterious fire started in the wall between Dodd's and the next chamber. However when I had my pursuivant find and question the merchant in that room, a Mr. Thomas Jenks, he insisted that Dodd was clearly a man of worship and no horsethief, had very kindly helped him carry out his strongbox when his two pages had run away, helped his young groom in the stable to get the beasts out, refused any reward and behaved very gentlemanlike all round. Mr. Jenks last saw Dodd make an impressive flying leap onto the back of his horse and chase a bolted nag out of the inn gates."

Carey laughed outright. Sir Robert Cecil smiled. "And then, I'm afraid, the trail goes cold again. Nobody between the London inn and Oxford has seen hide nor hair of him—they would have noticed him because he would have been riding without a saddle, of course."

Hughie and the musician were getting along famously. Hughie had the harp on his lap and was clumsily twanging the strings. He started a song, some Scotch caterwaul about corbies which was Scotch for crows and no crow could have made a less musical noise than Hughie when he sang. Even Cecil winced at it and glanced at the barman, while the musician closed his eyes in pain. Something niggled Carey about Hughie then. What was it?

Hughie was looking soulful. "Oahh," he said, "I've allus wanted to be a musician. I love tae sing. What would lessons cost?"

The potboy sniggered while the musician stoutly explained that a shilling an hour was the minimum possible amount.

Sir Robert Cecil was speaking again. "I even had my people check further south and on the Great North Road in case he decided to go home without visiting you in Oxford but again, no traces."

Carey lifted his silver cup to Cecil. "I'm indebted to you, Mr. Secretary," he said formally, wondering why Cecil was being so pleasant to him and what he wanted in exchange. "Thank you for taking such trouble over it."

"Not at all," Cecil was genial, "I feel a sense of responsibility for Sergeant Dodd's troubles. I realise now I should have warned him not to...er...reive any of Heneage's horses that had the Queen's brand on them, but I'm afraid it never crossed my mind."

Carey nodded. "Why should it, Sir Robert? Only someone who had to deal with Borderers regularly would know what they're like with good horseflesh." Should he mention to Cecil the musician he had been following, who so liked the Spanish air? No. Perhaps not. After all, Cecil's father had suddenly become a major suspect in Amy Dudley's murder again. And goddamn it, both Hughie and the musician had gone. They must have left the place by the back door to the jakes while Carey's attention was on Cecil.

"Her Majesty is in a terrible temper. If she were not the Queen, I would go so far as to call it a foul mood." Cecil paused. The pause was a polite opening for Carey to tell Cecil what he had been up to.

Carey continued to say nothing. It wasn't easy to do in the face of Cecil's tilted face, his grotesquely curved back disguised by the clever cut of his doublet and gown. Cecil shifted on the bench and winced slightly.

"I understand you brought something back from Cumnor Place today," said Cecil. Of course Cecil had spies everywhere, just as his father did. It was part of the game of Court politics.

"Quite so, Mr. Secretary," Carey said evenly, "I did. I believe it was the murder weapon. A crossbow."

Cecil raised his eyebrows as if this was new to him. "Did you find Lady Dudley's damaged headtire?" Of course he would have read all the paperwork by now and seen what Carey had seen.

"No, Mr. Secretary, I didn't."

Cecil nodded. He hadn't expected Carey to find it, he was making a point. There was a long silence again. "I may be able to help you in your quest," Cecil said slowly, "I am not without... resources of my own."

Carey thought very carefully about this. There was more to it than simple information exchanged for assistance. Carey was the Earl of Essex's man and of all the great men at Court, it was well known that Essex and Sir Robert Cecil hated each other. At least, Essex despised Cecil whom he occasionally teased about his hunchback. Cecil, it was obvious to everyone except Essex, virulently hated the Earl.

On the other hand, Cecil was as loyal to the Queen as his father and did, indeed, have resources of his own. Although it was Essex who had hurried to take over Walsingham's intelligence networks when Sir Francis died in 1590, Cecil was where the pursuivants and intelligencers went when they got tired of dealing with Heneage. He was even more close-mouthed than his father so it was impossible to know how much information he had access to, but Carey's guess was that he would be a lot better at the work than Essex was, who tended to boast. And Cecil had been behind the subtle coney-catching lay of the Cornish lands, Carey was certain of it.

Yet when Lady Hunsdon had taken that colossal risk to pay back Heneage for covertly attacking her husband through her son, she had deliberately involved Cecil in the business. And Mr. Secretary Cecil had cooperated.

Cecil would want to protect his father, might even be acting on his father's orders. And what if Essex found out? Nonetheless, some gut instinct was telling him to talk to Cecil.

"She wasn't shot?" Cecil wasn't really asking a question.

"Of course not. She was struck hard on the head with the end of the crossbow and broke her neck as she fell down the stairs."

Cecil nodded. "The Earl of Leicester?"

Carey shook his head. "I really doubt it, sir. Why would he set on a man to shoot his wife with a crossbow—so clumsy, so risky—when a little belladonna could have sufficed as it nearly did for me?"

"No, I've never thought it was him either. So. Interesting. I will leave it in your capable hands, Sir Robert. Do not hesitate to call on me if you need any...er...advice or assistance."

"Thank you, Mr. Secretary," Carey said with a polite tilt of his head. "I will."

Cecil smiled, a sweet and charming smile that lit up his saturnine face. "Have you ever considered a place on the Privy Council?"

Carey shuddered. "Good God, no, sir! I had rather go back to France and fight for the King of Navarre."

"Why not?"

"Too many meetings, too much paperwork. And I hate paperwork."

Cecil laughed. "It is an acquired taste, I admit. I only acquired it perforce but now I find it quite entrancing."

"It would be good to have such an influential position," Carey admitted. "And I'm honoured you think I might be suitable, Mr. Secretary, but I'm afraid that the Queen knows me far too well and would never appoint me."

Cecil tilted his head and raised his cup in toast. "To your continued freedom from paperwork then, Sir Robert."

Carey touched cups with him. "And to your expert navigation of it, Mr. Secretary."

monday 18th september 1592, night

Hughie and the old musician walked down the lane at the rear of the White Horse, the musician going ahead to lead the way to his lodgings where he had brandy and a variety of instruments for Hughie to try.

Hughie was in a quandary. His first impulse was simply to get out his stolen harpstring and throttle the man in vengeance for daring to try and poison Hughie's prey without Hughie's permission—and nearly poisoning Hughie into the bargain. Why, why had he done it? The itch to know was as urgent as the itch to kill. The jeering voice inside was with him on this one—shouting at him to hurt the old man, make him suffer, find out if anyone else had been set on to kill Carey.

Despite Carey's gift for making enemies on the Border and at the Scottish Court, Hughie didn't think there was any real competition for the £30 in gold he expected to reap once Carey was dead and buried.

Perhaps he'd even have a lesson with the old fool. His interest in learning to sing and play an instrument was genuine. When you saw the mewling idiots who could impress the girls with their warbling and strumming, music couldn't be so very hard to learn. It was just noise that went up and down to a beat, wasn't it?

Now the musician had turned down a very narrow wynd, Hughie paused at the corner, loosened his knife. It occurred to him the musician must have marked him to give him the poisoned flagon in the first place and so...

He swayed back as the cosh came at him from a shadowed doorway on the other side of the wynd where the musician had been waiting.

Hughie laughed for sheer delight—knocked the cosh away with a sweep of his arm, then dived straight forward with his large left hand splayed, caught the man's throat and shoved him back against the wall. A knee in the man's groin finished the matter.

"Ay," Hughie said, "we do have business, but ye canna beat me in a fight."

The musician was hunched over creaking for breath. A light punch in the kidneys put him on his face and Hughie knelt on his back, forced his left arm out on the ground and pinned the wrist, then started sawing at the man's thumb with his knife blade, which was shocking blunt, he'd have to sharpen it.

"No! No!" screamed the man, "Please!"

Hughie stopped sawing. There was only a cut. "Why did ye try tae poison me?"

"Not you," gasped the man, "your master, Hunsdon's boy."

"Ay?"

"He knew Heron Nimmo's song, I thought... But he's a spy, he'll ruin it all."

"Ay?" said Hughie, "All what?"

There was a pause. Hughie shrugged and started sawing at the man's thumb again.

The jabbering took a while to get through because Hughie was intent on the pretty way the dark blood came out, but at last he stopped and listened. And then he let the weeping old man sit up and even wrap a handkerchief round his thumb and spoil the nice look of it.

"Och, shut yer greeting," Hughie said, tossing his knife up and catching it. He found a likely looking cobble stone and started sharpening the blade—how had he let it get so bad? "Start at the beginning. Say it slow."

The musician took a long shuddering breath and did as he was told. Hughie listened carefully. It was an astonishing tale, stretching back into the past well before Hughie's own birth during the troubles that ended the mermaid Queen of Scots' wicked Papistical reign.

At the end of it, Hughie laughed. "Och so all ye want is tae kill the English Queen? Is that all?"

The musician goggled at him. Hughie shrugged. "I'm a Scot," he said, "what do I care fer yer witch Queen, eh?"

The musician stammered something about treason. "'Tis nae such thing for me," Hughie explained, "if she goes, in comes the King o' Scots and that'll be a fine thing for me." Especially if he could take the credit for it. Though King James, who was notoriously against bloodshed, might take a poor view of the man who did the deed, however much it might profit him.

"A'right, a'right," he said to calm the old man's begging. Seemingly it all had to do with a great friend he hadn't seen for years, who made the song, or some such. Hughie couldn't be bothered to work it all out. "Ah'm no worried about yer killing the Queen, but ye willna take another shot at Sir Robert Carey, d'ye follow me? Eh?"

The musician nodded, eyes like a hanged man's, beard full of turnip peelings, doublet smeared with shit, his hand cradled.

"I swear it," he said. "Nothing more against Carey."

For a moment Hughie was tempted to tell the old fool what he himself was about, but why? Knowledge was gold. There was no need to give it away free.

They shook on it. "Off ye go then," Hughie said, dismissing him with a gesture. "Dinna cross me again."

Once the musician had stumbled off down the alley, Hughie brushed himself down and set off in the opposite direction, back to Broad Street.

He found the White Horse inn again, but no sign of Carey who must have gone back to his bed. It was a very tempting thought, he was unusually tired.

The candles and the fire in the grate bothered Hughie's sore eyes and he wasn't feeling very well, so he was turning to leave when a shadowy twisted figure in one of the booths beckoned him over.

The gentleman Carey had spoken to respectfully wasn't ill-looking under his tall hat and his doublet was a smart black brocade, well cut and padded to hide his hunchback, clearly London tailoring and very skillful. The cloak was tidily folded beside him.

"Are you Hughie Tyndale?" asked the man.

"Ay, sir," he said, a little nervous.

"Your master Sir Robert Carey has gone back to the Earl of Cumberland's camp. How did it go with your music lesson?"

"Och," said Hughie with a genial smile. "It wisnae very good and then I want tae another ale house and tripped on the way out, muddied maself something terrible."

The man's face was sharp as an Edinburgh merchant. "Set ye doon," he said in passable Scots, "Ah've a mind tae speak wi' ye. What's yer right name?"

Hughie said nothing and shrugged though his heart was beating hard. The man smiled shyly.

"I've an idea yer right name is Hughie Elliot, youngest brother to Wee Colin. Is that right?"

It was the password he'd been given by the man who said he was working for the Earl of Bothwell.

"Ay sir," he said. So this was the man who was supposed to be his contact in England. A rich hunchback. Well, so be it.

"What were you to do for me?" asked the man.

"Nobbut send ye tidings of Carey's doings in the West March," Hughie told him and the rich hunchback nodded gravely. "And then after a year and a day, when I've killt him, let ye know so ye can warn the goldsmith to give me ma gold."

The shadow of something that might have been amusement crossed the hunchback's face.

"Indeed? Can you cipher, Hughie?"

"I can read and write, if that's yer meaning, sir?"

The rich hunchback brought out paper and some pieces of graphite and showed him what ciphering meant. It was a way of putting signs or numbers instead of letters in a system which meant you could still read it. Hughie was impressed at the cleverness of it.

"How do I send ye messages, sir? In the dispatch bag to Berwick?"

"Certainly not," said the hunchback. "Do you know Carlisle at all? No? Well there's a man there called Thomas the Merchant Hetherington that will do anything at all for money. Go to him when you get to Carlisle and show him this token."

It was a blood jasper, carved with the image of a snake. A nice piece.

"That's the Serpent Wisdom. He'll know then that he's to take your letters and send them south with his own letters to London. They'll reach me."

"Ay, sir."

"Oh and Hughie, please hold off on killing Carey, would you? Remember your pension stops when he dies."

"Ma pension?"

"Certainly. I'll instruct Thomas the Merchant to pay a shilling to you for every letter I receive."

"Och." It would take a great many letters to equal the £30 in gold he was owed for Carey's head. Six hundred in fact. But still…It was money in the hand not the bush, as it were.

"Ay, sir," said Hughie, carefully tipping his cap to the hunchback. "Thank ye, sir."

"I'll look forward to your reports with interest," said the hunchback.

"Ehm…Who should they be addressed to?"

"Mr. Philpotts at the Belle Sauvage inn, Ludgate Hill."

"Ay? What shall I do till I get yer money, sir?"

"See if Carey will pay you," said Mr. Philpotts lightly. "You'd better go now, he wants you to help him with his doublet."

As Hughie turned the corner and saw the chequered Cumberland flags he thought to himself, "I'll kill him when I choose, not when ye say so, Mr. Hunchback Philpotts." It was exciting to be earning money for letters though. He'd come a long way since the bastard Dodds burnt out his whole family when he was but a wean, a long, long way.

tuesday 19th september 1592, 2 a.m.

Captain Leigh struggled awake in the black night before dawn, heart thumping, his sword already grabbed from its usual place by the side of his bed. He stood there, listening for a moment.

A horrific shriek rang out that was neither an owl nor any creature being eaten by a fox. Then there was a thunder of running feet and shouting then horses…

He already had his hose on and he pulled his buff jerkin over the top of his shirt, drew the sword and ran outside into the burned monastery's cloister. A large shape galloped past him and nearly knocked him over. Another shape cannoned into him in the dark and tried to punch him. The smell of booze told him who it was.

"Goddamn it, I'm the captain!" he shouted at John Arden who sheepishly let him up. A man in a shirt ran past screaming blue murder, another couple of men were scrambling up onto a lookout place like milkmaids chased by a mouse.

The horse in the cloister reared and kicked, another galloped past neighing with panic. Leigh grabbed for its mane and it tried to bite him. Both nags galloped out the gate into the forest.

In the murk, more men appeared groggily, some with their buff jerkins on, most without their boots. One was hopping on one leg with a nasty gash in his toe.

Finally someone got the lantern alight again which only helped a little as the night was so dark.

"It…it's ghosts, sir. Burnt monks."

"*Al infierno con esos capullos*," hissed somebody behind him. Leigh spun to see Jeronimo stamping across the flagstones with a loaded crossbow clamped under his shortened arm, a torch in the other, his buffcoat and boots on and his morion on his head. At that moment Leigh knew the man was not lying about having been a *terceiro* of the third Imperial Spanish legion as he boasted.

They checked the carrels below the monks' dorter which was in use as their stable. Three of the horses had bolted, leaving only the Northerner's Whitesock still there, pulling at his tether. Leigh went to him and managed to calm the animal down, gave him some hay to eat. The doors had been broken outwards.

Eventually under Leigh's bellowing and Jeronimo's withering scorn, the men gathered together, sheepish and cold. Harry Hunks was there, blinking, looking witless and still in his shirt.

"God's teeth!" shouted Leigh in disgust, "Christ save us if we ever do find ourselves attacked in the night. None of you will. The only man among you that wouldn't be dead right now is Don Jeronimo."

Jeronimo flourished a bow. The men didn't like being compared unfavourably to a foreigner and one of them muttered rebelliously.

"Speak up, Smithson," Leigh snapped.

"It was ghosts, sir, I heard 'em singing."

"I saw one, it was white, sir, and it moaned."

A gabble of frightened stories broke out. Allegedly the burned monks had been singing the Papist hymn for the dead.

"For God's sake, it was probably just another one of you idiots, blundering about screaming in the dark."

"All the watchlights went out, sir, all at the same time. And then there was Papist singing. It's the burned monks, sir."

Leigh rolled his eyes. Nothing annoyed him more than superstitious nonsense about ghosts. He should have seen ghosts by now if they existed and he hadn't. So they didn't. It was clean contrary to good religion in any case—the dead slept until judgement when most of them would be damned. It didn't matter whether you buried them or not, they slept. How many piles of bodies from battles or camp fevers had he supervised being burned or buried? If ghosts walked, there should be troops of them following him and following the men he led, ghosts of innocent people they had killed or burned. He shivered for a second. Of course, he would be among the damned.

"Look," he said, trying to get them to think, "The old monks are dead and gone fifty years ago at least."

Somebody muttered. "Don't matter to ghosts."

"I saw it, sir, it was white and moaning, sir."

"I expect that was Mr. Arden, hungover, trying to stop you killing each other in your fright." Arden smiled a little.

Leigh was thinking hard. He sent some men out to catch the bolted horses again, beckoned Smithson over and they walked quickly down to the old witch's cottage in the ruins of the monastery gatehouse. If that bloody northerner wasn't in the monk's pit, he'd flog the bastard.

The dog was snoozing in the yard, lifted an ear and one eyelid at the sound of their feet, gave a short lazy "Woof!" and went back to sleep.

They found the turfed wickerwork roof over the mouth of the pit and peered in.

The man was asleep there, curled up in a rough old blanket and snoring. The light from their lantern woke him and he lifted his head and put up his hand against the dazzle.

"Ay, whit d'ye want?" he snarled. "Can Ah no' get ma sleep?"

"Was it you causing trouble?" Leigh demanded.

The Northerner propped himself on his elbow and scratched his brown hair vigorously.

"Ay," he sneered, "Ah've wings to fly and Ah flew over ye and shat upon ye for entertainment."

Leigh let the hurdle drop again. They went back to the old monastery and tried to clear up and sort out the mess. Leigh decided he had to run some proper exercises for his men. They'd got soft sitting around here. In France they would never have let a couple of bolted horses and a few shrieks from an owl spook them so badly.

But nobody was dead. That was what finally convinced Leigh he was only dealing with superstition and stupidity. If the Northerner had done it, surely he'd have slit a few throats, it stood to reason?

It was past sunrise before he was in the Northerner's respectable suit which was tight at the waist, the Northerner's fat purse full of gold angels in the crotch and some counted out into the front pocket. Whitesock was in perfectly good health despite the night, though the saddle from one of the other horses didn't fit him properly. The other three were no doubt out in the forest eating yew and whatever else they could find that would poison them. The men would have to find them, he didn't want to delay any longer.

The Oxford road was only a mile away, near Cumnor Place. As he prepared to leave he beckoned John Arden to his stirrup. Jeronimo was sitting slumped on a stone bench, his crossbow discharged now, his face grey and unreadable.

"Listen, John," he hissed at his old friend, "stay sober, stay in charge, make sure nothing else happens. If that Northerner gives trouble, knock him out but don't kill him. This is our one chance for our pay, you understand?"

Arden was clearly already drunk. He blinked owlishly up at Leigh.

"I know that, Captain," he slurred, "I won't get drunk."

Leigh shook his head and put his heels in.

tuesday 19th september 1592, morning

Dodd had gone to sleep again after the excitement of the early morning and he only woke when the old woman heaved the hurdle off the top of the pit and threw pebbles on him.

"Whit?" he asked, annoyed.

"Where's my granddaughter?" she demanded shrilly, "What have you done with her?"

"Eh?" he blinked as stupidly as he could, "What could I do wi' her, missus, I've bin in this pit all night? D'ye see her here?"

The carlin set her toothless jaw. "Then what was all that shouting? Did that frighten her?"

"Mebbe, missus." Even if she hadn't known all about it, Dodd would have bet that it wouldn't frighten young Kat. "I dinna ken."

"Well you can stay there today, I don't trust you."

Dodd shrugged, spotted his feet and pulled them cautiously under the rough blanket he'd been very grateful for last night. "Suits me, missus," he said and she stamped away. He could hear the goats protesting as she milked them and led them out to feed, muttering all the while.

Then he lay back with his head on his arms, blinked at the sheep's wool clouds caught on the cold blue sky and smiled quietly to himself. It had been fun last night. Getting out of the pit had not been easy, but he had once raided gulls nests on the cliffs by the sea when they were starving and had learnt how to climb with his toes and wedge billets of wood between gaps in the stone. The poles of his splint had come in useful, tied together at the ends, to push the hurdle-roof off the top of the pit. Little Kat had been waiting for him in the blackness and cold before dawn, snuggled next to the snoring dog and he had taken her on his shoulders and had her tell him the way to the main Oxford road so he'd know it later. Once she was off, trotting up the road determinedly in her clogs in a way that reassured him, he'd turned back to the old monastery and set about seeing to it that Leigh didn't beat her to Oxford city.

In the days when his feet had leathery soles and he was smaller and lighter, he could move like a shadow. He was no longer a boy but he could still put his feet down softly and he did that, slipping through the clearer parts of the undergrowth in his loose woollen breeks, the shirt and the blanket under his arm, mud smeared in stripes and splotches over his face and chest.

There were only two guards set, chatting in the darkness by their watchlight at the bend in the road, smoking his tobacco. Getting past them had been almost insultingly easy. And then he had free rein over the sleeping men in the monastery. After he had taken a knife out of the boy's scabbard, hanging by his bed in the dorter, he carefully trimmed the wicks on the watch candles so they'd go out a few minutes later. He broke the tethers of the horses that weren't Whitesock by scorching the rope first with a watchlight and then he broke the bolts open by levering with one of the halberds. And then he'd cracked the nags over the backside with the pole of the halberd and let out a good Tyneside yell. His throat still hurt from it. He had the shirt over his head and the blanket round his shoulders and he'd spent a happy few minutes running through the shadowy dorter shrieking about the burned monk, singing the one piece of plainchant he knew which was some nonsense his mother used to sing to get them to sleep. "Dee is eery, dee is iller, solve it sigh clum in far viller!" he'd intoned, finishing by howling and then shouting "Alarm!" and "Ghosts!" for good measure. Once the darkness was full of frightened men in their shirts running about and punching each other, he'd pulled the shirt down properly and tied the blanket round his waist under it and done a bit of running and punching himself.

As a final flourish he'd run directly across the cloister screaming and out the gate while the dimwitted Captain stood there blinking with his sword in one hand and the lantern in the other. The old Spaniard came out then with his crossbow on his shoulder and Dodd picked up speed into the darkness.

Then came the hard part. As he ran he stripped his shirt off again and picked up a branch to drag behind him and pounded through the woods as fast as he could back to the old carlin's pit, doing his best not to shout when he bruised his foot on a stone or trampled through brambles.

At the edge of the pit he'd used the blanket to wipe the mud off his sweating body and face, dropped it and the shirt into the pit, let himself down on the wedged billets of wood and the stone he'd propped against the wall, pulled them out and used the two poles from his splint to manoeuvre the hurdle back over the top of the pit, leaving it dark. And then he'd groped about, found the shirt and blanket, pulled the shirt over him, dropped onto the bracken and wrapped the blanket round him, panting hard as he heard Leigh's boots approaching.

He hadn't had time to put the splints back on his leg for effect but he hoped they wouldn't notice. It seemed they hadn't and they'd been fooled by his imitation of the noises Carey normally made at night. He'd stay meekly in the pit now and hope like hell young Kat would get to Oxford in time. He'd done all he could, mind, he couldn't think of anything else he could do for the moment.

After some more thought he sat up again and looked at his feet. They were a sad sight, bruised, muddy, still bleeding in a couple of places. He pulled the thorns out with his fingernails and as he didn't have any water to wash them with, he carefully pissed on them which stung but at least left them cleaner. Then he strapped the splints on again. After that there was no sound from the old woman so he might as well go back to sleep as there was no chance she would feed him.

Yet she did. She woke him with more thrown pebbles and then let down a pail with bread, cheese, and a quart of ale which Dodd assumed would be full of valerian and wild lettuce. He was thirsty from all the running around and needed his rest, so he drank half of it. And had to admit that the old woman's green goat cheese was excellent, maybe better than Janet's.

Ay, Janet. He'd have some tales to tell her of the south. She'd laugh her spots off, his freckled leopard of a wife and then he'd see to her, ay, he'd see to her well and perhaps he'd plant a child in her this time.

He was dozing in the middle of a particularly pleasant day-dream of something unusual he could do with fine goat's cheese if his wife would only cooperate, when the branch he'd dragged behind him to hide his tracks came over the edge of the pit and landed in front of him.

He'd hidden the stolen knife by driving it into the earth between two stones and so he stood and moved closer to it.

A man in a morion was standing near the dressed stones at the edge of the pit, idly pointing a loaded and cocked crossbow down at him one handed. His other sleeve was folded up short.

"Señor Elliot," said the Spanish accented voice.

"Ay," Dodd said after a moment. The man had him cold, nothing he could do about it, so he sat down on the pile of bracken and crossed his legs.

"Last night," said the Spaniard, hissing in through his teeth like a man hiding that he was wounded, "it was very *divertido*, eh? An excellent *camisado* attack."

Dodd shrugged. "It wasnae me, whatever it was," he said, more for form's sake than anything else, as he didn't expect this one to believe him. "What's a camisado attack?"

The bony hawk face smiled briefly. "A night attack. We call it camisado because the attackers have shirts over his armours so they look equal as the sleepers."

"Ay?" said Dodd, interested. You wouldn't call a night attack that in the Borders, of course, because everyone would be wearing jacks, whether they'd been asleep or no. These Southerners were pitiful, really.

"The thing is strange," said the Spaniard, "No deaths. None killed. Why not, Señor Elliot?"

Dodd shrugged again

"I watched with admiration," said the Spaniard, "one man against twenty-five idiots, what a chaos!"

Dodd said nothing, didn't see the point.

"My name, Señor Elliot, is Don Jeronimo de la Quadra de Jimena."

He said it as if it should mean something to Dodd, as if he was stating his surname, but of course Dodd didn't know anything about Spanish surnames.

"You are Don Roberto Carey his man, yes?"

Did don mean sir in foreign? "Ay," said Dodd.

"He send you find me?"

Dodd almost said no, but then he thought it might be more interesting if he lied. So he did that. "Ay sir," he said, "but he didna tell me why. I was tae bring ye to him."

The man frowned so Dodd sighed and said it again more Southern. He knew Carey would back him, whatever this was about. The grizzled soldier nodded slowly. Then he took out the bolt and released the crossbow string, squatted down at the edge of the pit. Dodd watched with interest as he filled his clay pipe one-handed with Dodd's expensive medicinal tobacco and started smoking.

"I like this herb," said the Spaniard, "very good. Did Don Roberto tell you anything?"

"Why would he?"

"No. What do you intend tonight?"

Dodd had never heard such a cheeky question in his life. What did the foreigner think he'd say?

"Sleep," he said coldly, "as I did last night." He was watching the Spaniard from below so the shape of the face was different, but then as Jeronimo turned his face away and winced for some reason, he suddenly knew him. It was the man who had stared at him at the Oxford road inn. He almost said something about it but then he decided it could wait. If Jeronimo was the one responsible for all the pain and aggravation he'd suffered since Saturday night, Dodd didn't want him alerted to his doom. And when Dodd caught a whiff of the smoke from his pipe, he could have killed him just for the tobacco.

"Señor, let us tell a little tale. Shall we say that some...yes, some *diablito* creeps into the burned monastery and cause chaos, what is his purpose?" Dodd shrugged. "You could have slit some throats, taken back your sword. But no. So what was your purpose?"

"I didna do it," Dodd told him. "I was asleep."

Jeronimo sighed. "Señor," he said, "I know you are a man of virtue, I know you are more than you say. Perhaps I talk to Captain Leigh of what I see and you not play your game again. Perhaps I hamstring you."

Dodd had to hide a flinch. Cut the cords at the backs of his legs so he couldn't walk? Christ, please, no. But Jeronimo could do it, if he had enough men on his side. Dodd had no doubt that he would be willing to do it.

"Or you cure my childish curiosity," said the Spaniard with another hiss of pain, adding more of Dodd's tobacco to his pipe and puffing. No more of the smoke was coming into the pit, it was all going upwards, damn it.

The maddest part of his plan came back to him. Maybe? Dodd stood up. "Whit d'ye think to the Captain, Don Jeronimo?" he asked.

The Spaniard shrugged. "He is adequate though not very bright. He is *flojo*. Lazy. I come to England with him for protection, company. There must be a captain and I do not want it. I was many things, Señor, a musician, an assassin, a soldier, a Courtier, a captain, a hero, a cripple, many many things. I have no desire for being a captain again. I have other business here. And I will die soon."

"How d'ye know?"

Jeronimo sighed, put down his pipe on a stone and pulled up one of his canion breeches to show his thigh. His leg was covered with ugly black spots and sores. Dodd felt sick. Was it plague? No. Couldn't be. He'd be lying down, not walking around waving a crossbow.

"It is a canker. I asked a physician in France, a good one, though a Jew. He had seen such things. It was first one mole, it bled, it itched. Then it grew, it had children. Some become sores. Now I have pain and stones in my *estomago*, now I have a thing like a rock in my liver and I bleed sometime like a woman."

"Och," said Dodd, because he couldn't help it. His legs felt wobbly. He hated sickness, hated it. Men with swords you could fight. What could you do against black spots or a rock in your belly? Bleed like a woman? From his arse? Och God.

Jeronimo smiled slightly. "So, all men die and I will die soon. I hoped once it would be bravely, in battle. It makes no matter. But I have a business in England now. When I was young and clever and very stupid, I try to please my natural father with a great deed—but it went badly. Later I lose my arm and my music, I think this pays for it, but when I make confession to a priest last Easter, he say no. I must make it right."

Jeronimo shrugged and grimaced. "I should go to a more easy priest. But he was right so I set off to do it, and here I am."

"Ay," said Dodd, cautiously, wondering what was coming next.

"Don Roberto is son of el conde Hunsdon, no?"

"Ay."

"Hunsdon is a bastard and so I am too. He is bastard of the King, me...Less important. I must see his sister, the Queen," said the Spaniard, "That is all."

Dodd's jaw dropped. "See the Queen?" he repeated.

"Si, Señor, Her Majesty the Queen Isabella of England."

"Why?"

"My business, Señor. Can your master manage such a thing?"

"Ay, he could," Dodd said instantly, seeing no call to disappoint the old madman. "But why should he? Men pay hundreds of pounds for a chance just tae talk to the Queen." Jeronimo nodded.

"It is sure," he said. "She will wish to see me. All I need is the man to...ah...to connect."

"But..." Madman, assassin? Why else would a foreigner want to speak directly to the Queen? Dodd set his jaw. "Why?"

Jeronimo tutted. "Only give me your word of honour you will speak to your lord, Señor Elliot."

Dodd folded his arms and looked up narrow-eyed at the man. "And?"

"I will let you go, free you."

"No," he said.

"Why no?"

"Ah dinna ken who ye are nor why ye might wantae see the Queen, but I can guess since you're Spanish. So ye can go to hell."

"I will not harm her, not a hair of her head."

"No."

"I swear it on my soul."

"No."

"Why so much trouble, so much chaos and no killings, Señor Elliot? How can we agree?"

Don't threaten my hamstrings, Dodd thought, don't put me at risk of hanging, drawing and quartering. Instead he showed his teeth. "Let's call vada and I'll see your prime," he said, a phrase he had picked up from Carey. "Help me and I'll think about it."

"I will bring the ladder."

"Och," Dodd shook his head at the man's ignorance. Still he was nobbut a foreigner, he couldn't help it. "Nay, I'll want more than that."

"Indeed? What, Señor?"

Dodd told him, leaving out some important details in case this was all some elaborate ploy of Leigh's to interrogate him. Jeronimo started to laugh which got a sour look from the old woman as she came past with her small flock of goats. Then the Spaniard took his hat off to Dodd and walked away, leaving Dodd with nothing to do but worry that he'd been coney-catched himself and that Leigh would come back from Oxford and slice his hamstrings so his legs would be like a broken puppet's, unable to stand. And Christ, bleeding like a woman from a rock in your belly. It made his skin shiver just thinking about things like that.

tuesday 19th september 1592, morning

Somebody was shaking Carey awake. It was Ross. Carey sat up, feeling groggy which was a very strange experience because normally he was awake before dawn and out of bed immediately. Was this how Dodd felt every morning? Poor man. The night had been full of complicated incomprehensible dreams about Elizabeth Widdrington.

"You've a lady visitor, Sir Robert," said Ross, looking amused. "Best get up and look tidy."

Carey rubbed his face, wondered who it was. Couldn't be the Queen, she was at Woodstock palace by now, resting, and she'd roust him out to visit her, not the other way round. Couldn't be his mother, please God, she should be on the high seas on her way back to Cornwall. Couldn't be Emilia as she had been such a hit with the Earl of Essex. God, he was stupid this morning. If only there was some potion you could drink which would wake you up.

"Who is it?"

"M'Lady Blount, sir."

"Who?"

"The ex-Dowager Lady Leicester."

Jesus Christ, Lettice Knollys as was, his cousin. The woman who had snaffled the Earl of Leicester from the Queen. It came back to him slowly that Thomas Blount, one of her son's hangers-on, had scandalously become her third husband.

"What? What's she doing here? She's not supposed to come to Court, the Queen can't stand her."

Ross managed not to smile. "Well sir, the Court's not arrived yet officially and nor has the Queen so she's here to see her son, I expect."

"Oorgh. What time is it?"

"Half past eight o'the clock, sir. My lord Earl of Cumberland said not to wake you."

"That late?"

Carey swung his legs to the floor as the camp bed creaked its straps under him. How on earth had he slept so long? Normally he was awake the minute dawn came, no matter what time he went to bed. Was he hungover?

Hmm. Perhaps still a bit poisoned. But at least his eyes weren't as bad as they had been. The light coming through the tent walls wasn't actually hurting him. He rubbed his face again, felt bristles around his goatee.

"Do you know how to shave a man, Mr. Ross?"

"Not really, sir. I'll send for some hot water and a razor."

"Please apologise to Lady Blount and explain that I'm not in a fit state to see her yet but I'll be as quick as I can. Get her sweet wine and some wafers and sweetmeats if you can find any."

Twenty minutes later, wearing a fresh shirt belonging to the Earl of Cumberland (who owed him at least five from the abortive *camisado* attack in France a year before), beard trimmed, cheeks shaved, hair combed, hat pulled down low against the grey daylight, clean falling band and his forest green hunting doublet unbuttoned at the top in the fashionable melancholy style, Carey breezed into the marquee where Lady Blount was sitting, magnificent on a cushioned stool which was entirely drowned by her large wheel farthingale.

"My lady cousin," he said making a full Court bow with a flourish of his hat, "how delightful to see you here!"

She was the daughter of his aunt, Katherine Knollys, she of the lost riding habit, and the mother of the Earl of Essex by her first husband Walter Devereux. She had earned the Queen's undying hatred because, after her husband, the first Earl of Essex died conveniently in an Irish bog of a flux, she had firmly set her cap at and succeeded in stealing the Queen's only real love, to wit, one Robert Dudley, Earl of Leicester. She had been a beautiful woman in her youth, flame-haired, white skin, blue eyes, but had got quite stout recently. She made no concessions to this and creaked in a low cut pointed bodice plunging into her vast farthingale in eye-watering yellow brocade and emerald-green velvet. Her feathered hat was tilted on her white cap and her famous red curls peeked out under it, quite possibly helped by alchemical magic. Her face was well made-up so she looked like a child's poppet with her white skin and red cheeks, and her hands were heavy with rings. She no longer looked so similar to the Queen as she had in her youth because the Queen was still slender and she was not.

"Well Robin, what have you been doing to yourself?" she cooed maliciously. "Are you hungover again? You really shouldn't drink so much...."

Carey smiled with equal sweetness, "No, Coz, somebody put belladonna in my drink on Saturday night," he said. "Was it you?"

She ignored this. "What is it my lord son tells me about my gold-bearing Cornish lands?"

Carey sighed. Somebody had to have bought them—clearly he was right and the Earl had been buying them on behalf of his mother.

"If my lord Earl of Essex was repeating what I told him," he said slowly and clearly so as not to overtax her very womanly brain, "the lands were a lay set by a coney-catching Papist called Father Jackson and are about as worthless as land can be."

"Of course they're not, Robin, I have seen the assays. You really mustn't try and lower the price on them, I expect dear Henry wants to snap some up cheap the way…"

I don't really have the time or the inclination for this, Carey thought, how can I get rid of the old bag?

"Perhaps you would like to discuss this with my mother," Carey said, "She's the one who spotted what was going on. She's at sea now, I think, but I'm sure my father would…"

Carey knew perfectly well that his mother and Lettice hated each other. Lady Blount tightened her mouth which was wrinkled exactly like an old purse.

"I'm asking you, Robin."

Don't call me Robin, Carey thought and smiled again because he'd been on the verge of commiserating with her about the failure of her speculation. His father had suffered a few: You can't speculate in property without occasionally making a costly mistake.

"Lady Blount, if my mother says the lands are worthless, they're worthless. And they're in Cornwall where I doubt you're willing to go to find out."

"Why not? Where is Cornwall anyway?"

"About four hundred miles west and south of here."

"Really? Are you sure?"

"Er…yes, cousin." He decided not to try and explain the details because it would probably melt whatever passed for a brain under her fake red curls. "And I'm very sorry, but I'm not completely recovered from the poisoning and…"

He wasn't being entirely truthful. He felt tired but now he was more awake and in the dimness of the pavilion, his eyes were behaving themselves at least.

"Well that wasn't why I came." Lettice was staring sideways at him now. "I heard from my son that you were looking into the…er…the death of my late second husband's first wife."

Carey paused. Surprisingly, the Earl must have kept his promise. "Yes, my lady cousin, I am. Very reluctantly but the Queen ordered it."

"Reluctantly?"

"The thing happened thirty-two years ago, the year I was born in fact." To his unkind satisfaction he saw Lettice flinch slightly. "That's how long poor Amy Dudley has been dead and buried. I know Her Majesty set someone on to look into it in 1566, but he got nowhere...

"Topcliffe certainly did get somewhere," Lady Blount contradicted him. "He just never said what he found, only I think he's been blackmailing the Queen about it very cleverly."

"Oh?" Now that was very interesting. Was that why Topcliffe was mysteriously untouchable, no matter what he did? "Do you know what he found out?"

Lettice shrugged her powdered white shoulders and then looked cunning. "Maybe you should ask what he found, not what he found out. Just knowing something wouldn't be enough, would it?"

Carey perched himself on a table and wished for wine, his throat was infernally dry again. "Sergeant Ross," he called, "could you find me a boy to fetch us some wine...some more wine? Not spiced, please. And some breakfast for me."

After last Saturday night, Carey doubted he would ever again be able to stomach spiced wine; just the thought of it made his gorge rise.

Lady Blount had clearly finished the first plate of sweetmeats and looked disappointed when the boy trotted in with a plate of bread and cheese alongside a jack of good rough red wine, then brightened when he produced another silver plate of wafers and comfits. Carey didn't like sweetmeats and they pained one of his back teeth every time the Queen made him eat one. He soon felt full so he let Lettice munch on the other half of the penny loaf and only took a bit of cheese himself. However the wine was Italian and better than usual so he drank that.

"Do you know what thing Topcliffe found, Lady Blount?"

"No, of course not." The kohl crusted eyelashes batted at him. "And I would tell you if I did, Robin, because nobody likes Richard Topcliffe despite the way he gets lands off the Papists."

Carey suppressed a sigh. "So was it Topcliffe you wanted to talk to me about, my lady?"

She made a face. "Ugh no, he's a horrible man. My son wanted me to tell you something my lord Leicester said to me once when he was drunk."

She paused significantly. What would she want for the information?

"Yes?"

"Of course, you know this is secret. This is very, very secret. I've never told anybody this, not even my darling Robin until now."

"Yes?"

"So you won't tell Her Majesty who told you?"

"I can't promise that, my lady. If she asks me the question direct, I will tell her of course."

The pouchy rosebud lips tightened. Then she shook herself. "Well, I don't see why I shouldn't tell you, the scandalous old cat. Especially if she's digging it all up again."

"Hm?"

"My lord husband…" said Lettice drawing the words out slowly and Carey worked to keep the impatience off his face because it would only encourage her, "…my lord of Leicester said once after dinner that it was damned unfair, the whole thing had nearly been arranged, Amy would divorce him, and if he ever found out who murdered her before she could set him free, he would kill the man with his own hands, for taking his Eliza from him. There."

She sat back and looked pleased with herself.

"A divorce?" Carey breathed. It was obvious, but he had only just started to wonder about it.

"Yes," said Lettice. "Good King Henry did it twice of course, so much less upsetting than finding someone guilty of adultery and beheading them. It was before Bess of Hardwick divorced her husband and it would take an Act of Parliament but still…What couldn't happen was my lord of Leicester doing the divorcing or the scandal would be too much and Convocation would block it. The Queen didn't want any trouble like that, she was so hot for him. So the plan was for Amy to ask for an annulment on grounds of non-consummation." Lettice nibbled a third wafer like a greedy squirrel and winked. It was a frightening sight.

Carey's lips were parted at this brand new angle on the story. "But…" he began.

"Convocation would have granted it—they'd been plumped specially. Parliament would have granted it if Amy petitioned because they were desperate for Her Majesty to marry and get an heir even though they hated the Earl. She was getting old, after all, she was 27 in 1560. Amy would be given a nice pension and some property and be free to marry again while she could still have children and my lord of Leicester would become King."

Now that made a lot of sense. A lot more sense than the notion of the Queen being so insane as to murder her lover's wife.

"So perhaps Burghley did the…"

"Fooey," said Lettice unexpectedly, "I don't think Burghley did anything because he didn't know. Nobody knew. Just the Queen, Amy, and Robert Dudley. Nobody else at all. They made sure the musicians played loudly when they were planning it and they didn't speak in English and sometimes they wrote to each other but then they burnt the letters. It was a secret. Amy was still at Cumnor Place but she sent letters saying that she was willing to talk about bringing a petition for divorce. She was just dickering for more money and a nicer manor house and more land. She wouldn't come to Court; she didn't like it, said she didn't want to be bullied out of her money."

Lettice pursed her lips again and leaned forward confidingly. "She was a dreadful girl, dull, twitter-headed, greedy, obstinate. I never liked her and I certainly didn't know anything about all this at the time. And she was so pious. Robert laughed about how worried she was about having to swear in court that they hadn't consummated their marriage because they had, she just never quickened, no matter what she did, she was barren. But she was terrified about hell and damnation for swearing it falsely. That drove the Queen mad."

Carey kept to himself his immediate thought that the Queen, whose indecisiveness drove every one of her servants crazy with impatience, had well-deserved to face the thing herself.

"And then…the stupid girl fell down the stairs or somebody pushed her and the whole thing fell apart. Poor Dudley was the one everybody thought did it so he couldn't even marry the Queen though he was free." Carey nodded and Lettice smiled smugly. "Of course, it was lucky for me because then I could marry him, not the Queen." A shadow passed over her face. "I wish she would let me come back to Court now he's dead. It's not fair of her, is it?"

Carey shook his head sympathetically.

"I so love to see all the new fashions and hear the new music. My son tells me the news of course and I advise him and his wife. Poor Frances. She's so brainy for a pretty girl. It's terrible for her really. She's pregnant again, you know?"

Lettice finished the last wafer and sat back as far as she could in the gaudy cage of her dress.

"Hmm. What did my Lady Essex think about the Cornish lands?"

"Oh, she has no idea. She wouldn't let poor Robin so much as ride down to look at them, said her father taught her that anything that looked too good to be true probably wasn't true, the boring old creep. So he missed out on them."

Carey nodded again, thinking better of Lady Essex. He, too, had learned that maxim from Walsingham.

"She'll be sorry when the gold starts to flow," said Lettice brightly, nodding her head so her feather bobbed. "I'll tell my lord son I've told you about the Queen's divorce and he can tell you anything else he learned from his stepfather. You know, my lord of Leicester was a wonderful father, he taught Robin to hunt and ride—even after his own poor little boy died, he was kind to his stepson. I remember once when…"

Carey smiled and nodded at a very fond tale about the young Earl of Essex's first pony. He had forgotten how boring Lettice

Knollys could be but he now had to get rid of her urgently because Dr. Lopez's potions were summoning him.

"My lady cousin," he said with as much unctuous sincerity as he could ladle into his voice, "I am so grateful to you for coming all this way and telling me this extremely important secret. I am truly amazed at it."

Not really, more amazed he hadn't thought of it before. Lady Blount looked pink-cheeked and happy and creaked obediently to her feet as Carey offered his hand to help her up.

"Please don't tell anyone at all what you've told me," he warned.

"Oh don't worry, Robin, not even my lord Treasurer Burghley, though he's such an old friend and he was asking me the other day. You know he was the one who introduced me to my lord of Leicester after my lord realised the Queen would never really marry him?"

Which put Burghley squarely back in the dock for the murder of Amy Robsart, despite all his protestations. If Amy had agreed to petition for divorce that would ultimately make Dudley king and Burghley would have been out of a job the same week. Desperate men do desperate things. In 1560, the then-Sir William Cecil had not yet made his fortune from the Treasury and the Court of Wards. It was all very clear. The Queen wouldn't like it coming out at all though and what about Mr. Secretary Cecil? Speaking of which, why on earth had she set all this in motion anyway? Why hadn't his father warned him?

Carey bowed Lettice, Lady Blount out of Cumberland's pavilion, blinked longingly at the men playing veneys in the central area of the camp while Sergeant Ross ran the sword class with his usual combination of wit and bullying. Unfortunately he had an urgent and probably unpleasant appointment with the jakes.

tuesday 19th september 1592

Some time later, Carey ambled into town again to see if he could spot the musician he had been following the previous night. His eyes did seem to be getting better—he had to squint and things were a bit blurry but at least he didn't have to tie a scarf across them. He was in search of a good tailor in case he could find a better doublet for ordinary wear than his green one and perhaps one of the short embroidered capes that were all the rage and possibly one of the new high-crowned hats...Passing Carfax he heard a great deal of shouting as a short puffy man was arrested for coining and horse-theft. The man's face was purple; he kept shouting that he was Captain Leigh on urgent business. His henchman, a big louring thug, suddenly broke free of the two lads holding him, knocked down a third and took to his heels down the London road. A few people gave chase but didn't try too hard on account of his size and ugliness. Carey didn't fancy it himself. Meanwhile, the horsethief had been cold-cocked on general principles and hauled off to the Oxford lockup.

The first tailor he found on the High Street, was showing some very good samples of fine wool and Flemish silk brocades in his window, so he wandered in and asked questions. Alas, the prices were even more inflated than in London and the man explained smugly that he couldn't be expected to produce anything in time for the Queen's Entry on Friday as all his journeymen were working flat out already. And there were only two other tailors in Oxford town.

Carey picked up one of the little wax dolls showing the latest French fashions in women's kirtles, looked deeper into the shop which was full of men sitting cross-legged stitching at speed. "Who is the oldest man here?" he asked idly.

The harassed man in thick spectacles frowned. "I am."

"When did you do your prentice piece?"

"In 1562. I cry you pardon, sir," he added with the sharp voice of someone who spends his days sitting down, worrying. "I have fully worked my time as an apprentice and journeyman and I am simply not able to fill any more orders at all at any price...

Carey smiled. "I was just wondering if I could ask you a question or two, Mr. Frole."

It was a pity, he would have liked to order a couple of alterations to his Court suit to make it a little more in fashion, but never mind. Hughie could do it when he was better.

"I'm looking for the tailor who made gowns and kirtles for Lady Leicester," he said. "Not Lettice Knollys, but Amy Robsart, his first wife. Did you work for her?"

The man went pale and his eyes flickered. Suddenly he was sweating.

"No sir," said Frole shortly, "I didn't. I have only been in business as Master Tailor these last ten years and…

"Do you know who was her tailor?"

"It was Master William Edney in London." The man shut his mouth like a trap. Carey watched him, wondering how to get him to open up.

"Mr. Frole, I know this is a sensitive matter despite being as old in years as I am myself. Were you prenticed in Oxford?" The master tailor nodded. "I know gossip travels around the 'prentices. Is there anything at all you can tell me about the end of August 1560, anything about Lady Dudley…? I have been asked by the Queen herself to make enquiries."

The man was looking narrow-eyed and suspicious. Carey sighed. "I believe she set another man, by name Richard Topcliffe, to find something out about it only six years after Lady Dudley's death, while Her Majesty was on progress in Oxford the last time. But the man has an ill-reputation and I'm certain he…"

"He had a warrant," said Frole. "Do you?"

Carey took it out of his doublet pocket, his heartbeat quickening.

"Did Topcliffe offer money which he didn't pay or did he grab people and beat them up until they told him what he wanted to hear?"

"Both," said Frole, thin-lipped, and held out his hand. Carey handed over the warrant which Frole read quickly and gave back.

"We told him all we knew which was that Lady Dudley was in a hurry to have a new gown although she already had plenty of the best quality. She had ordered a new one from London but it hadn't come. This was the first week of Spetember and she sent her best bodice, kirtle, and gown into Oxford by her woman Mrs. Odingsells to have the collar changed to stand up and have gold lace put on it, very costly. We did the work while she waited, for Lady Dudley intended to wear it in a few days."

"Who did the work?" Carey asked, "you?"

Frole shook his head. "One of the journeymen, she was too important a customer to risk an apprentice's work. He died of plague in '66. Mrs. Odingsells paid for it in gold at once. Just as well, really."

"How about her headdress? Did that need altering?"

Frole shook his head. "Her headtires all came from London as she didn't like the shop here. I believe they were very old-fashioned, from the boy-King's reign. I never met Lady Dudley, you know, she was always at Cumnor Place, waiting for her husband."

"Did Topcliffe let slip anything interesting?"

Frole gave a cautious look. "He was an evil man, broke my best friend's fingers so he couldn't continue in the trade. He went off to Cumnor Place after he spoke to us and I heard him boasting in an alehouse that night that he had found something that would make him a great man at Court—he was the Earl of Shrewsbury's man then—and comfortable for the rest of his life. He said other things that I can't repeat about the Queen, terrible obscene things. But at least he had lost interest in us prentices and took himself off back to London the next day, following the Court."

Carey nodded. Terrible obscene things—Topcliffe was notorious for the way he spoke of the Queen and yet nothing was ever done about him. Generally the Queen rightly had a short way with anyone who was offensive about her in way that often made them shorter by a head or another important limb. So what gave Topcliffe his extraordinary immunity? Blackmail, surely. But with what?

"Mr. Frole," he said to the unhappy looking tailor, "I am very grateful to you. If you have any further memories or ideas, please tell me—you can find me with the Earl of Cumberland while the Queen is here or by means of the Lord Chamberlain if I am gone north again. He will make it worth your while."

Frole bowed Carey out of the shop who stood in the street and havered between heading off down the London road to look for Dodd and continuing his sweep of Oxford. He even had five pounds from the Earl of Cumberland won on a bet as he left. George Clifford had been loudly offering to take Carey on as a permanent general purpose gleeman and fool if he got tired of soldiering in the starveling and dangerous Debateable land. George had explained how Carey would only have to wear a cap and bells on Saturdays and would have his very own kennel with the dogs…Carey had thrown a pennyloaf at the Earl on this point and challenged him to a veney which he had narrowly won.

Did he want to spend it on overpriced ale and beer? Well, yes, he did and he could kill two birds with one stone if he went round the multitude of Oxford taverns. So that was settled. He would do that and then he'd take a horse and ride down the road, see if he could spot where Dodd had gone. Or find his body, which was starting to look more and more likely.

tuesday 19th september 1592

It took a lot of work to wait in that pit without doing anything. Dodd drank the rest of the drugged ale and dozed, filling his head with lurid pictures of the welcome his wife would give him when he got back to Gilsland and what he would do and…Well, it passed the time, didn't it? He had heard little Kat coming in, her clogs slow and tired and her stout lie that she had climbed a tree to avoid a pig in the forest when she was looking for more cobnuts and then got stuck in the tree. Her Grandam shouted at her and sent her to card wool in the cottage with no dinner, which made Dodd feel sorry for the little maid. His guts were churning with nerves about what he would do that night. After all, a mere night raid, a bit of fun running about shrieking and spooking horses, that was easy. His plan for this night was a lot more ticklish.

Still. He couldn't go back to Carey without at least his sword and his boots. So there was no help for it and if everything went well he'd be bringing a lot more than just his sword and his boots. He might be able to make something of a show. He dozed off again, smiling to himself.

There was a clatter at the lip of the pit and Dodd jumped to his feet. Jeronimo was there, letting down the ladder, smiling enigmatically in the dusk. "Captain Leigh and his bullyboy have not come back from Oxford as they said they would, John Arden is drunk, and the men are afraid they have been tricked again. I spoke with your *pequenita* when I carry her the last mile, she was much tired, she said she had been questioned but then went away. She says it is sure Captain Leigh was taken because she heard him shouting."

Dodd allowed himself a grim smile as he stepped onto the cobbles of the yard. For all the odds against it, that part had worked, at least.

"Where's the old woman?"

"I said her stay in her cottage with the child. She has the dog beside her and barred the door."

"Ay." She'd come to no harm from him, but who knew what might happen? "She fears Harry Hunks might try again to seduce her granddaughter."

"Good God," said Dodd, disgusted, "She's nobbut a child."

Jeronimo shrugged. "They have no man for protect them."

Dodd had the stolen knife in a belt he had woven himself from the bracken fibres. He bent and scraped up mud, swiped it over himself. "Who's got ma sword?"

"Garron has it, he won it at dice."

"Tch," said Dodd. "Big, small?"

"Young," said Jeronimo with a wolfish smile, "and frightened."

With Jeronimo and his loaded crossbow at his back, Dodd quietly climbed the tumbledown monastery wall and padded forward to where the lad who had his sword was supposed to be on guard. He was leaning against a tree, dozing.

Jeronimo said something that sounded rude in foreign. Dodd paced quietly to the tree, put his arm softly round the lad's neck from behind and squeezed. There was only a brief struggle before he went heavy against Dodd's arm.

Dodd let him down gently, turned him, put his knee into the back and used the lad's scarf to tie his hands and feet together like a deer carcass. Then he unstrapped his sword belt from the lad, put it back on at a notch tighter than normal and drew his weapon. That was when he found that the stupid child hadn't cleaned it or oiled it or even sharpened it since he got it. So he used the boy's lank greasy hair to oil the blade again which woke him up with a squawk and a smooth cobble to sharpen it as best he could. Dodd had already taken the boy's boots off and chucked them into the undergrowth since they were far too small for him, and so he stuffed the boy's mouth with one of his own tattered socks.

"Ah've let ye live since ye're nobbut a lad," Dodd told him conversationally. "Ithers may no' be sae lucky, dinna push it."

From the wild eyes the boy hadn't understood a word of this but Dodd didn't have time to strain his larynx talking Southron. The lad should be able to work his way free by which time it would all be over, please God.

Dodd straightened, with his sword warm and comfortable in its rightful place on his hip, and headed for the monastery parlour where there was a fire in the hearth and a powerful smell of booze.

There was the second in command, John Arden, slumped in a chair with an empty horn beaker in his hand and a barrel of brandy before him.

It went against Dodd's grain to slit a man's throat sleeping, which forebye would be messy. Instead he removed the man's sword and poinard, put the long narrow poinard blade to the thick neck and grabbed a sticky doublet-front to shake him awake. He was reminded of Robert Greene a few weeks ago, for it took some doing.

"Arah, wuffle," said the man at last, focussing blearily on the long shine of his own dagger at his throat.

"Ay," said Dodd sympathetically, "Ye've a choice. Ye could allus surrender and gi'me yer word. Or not."

There was a pause while the man's drink-sozzled brain fought to understand. Then his body gave slightly.

"Quarter," said the man. "I surrender. My name's John Arden."

"Good man," said Dodd with the friendliest face he could manage. "Pit yer hands behind ye."

They tied Arden to his seat and Dodd took the sword and knife. He liked the poinard which was clearly of good Italian make, so he slid it on the back of his own belt, where Carey wore his. He would have nothing to do with a nasty long pig-sticker of a rapier so Jeronimo took the sword.

They walked into the monastery's cloister with its central yard and Dodd went up the stairs to the dorter. These lads weren't used to setting any kind of proper guard. They were drinking and dicing. Those that were still asleep, he tied up. Those that were awake he asked politely if they would prefer to surrender or die on his sword. Most of them were sensible. One arrogant young man thought he ought to fight for honour's sake and died honourably with Dodd's sword down through the centre of his skull while he was still struggling to pull his unoiled blade out of its scabbard.

The others stared wide-eyed as Dodd wrenched his sword out of the bone and grease with his foot and cleaned it again. Jeronimo crossed himself awkwardly and muttered something Latin over the young man as his heels drummed., Of course, all Spaniards were Papists, they couldn't help it, but he didn't see the point in praying for someone you'd just sent to Hell. It felt as it always did when he killed someone: hard labour and a sense of satisfaction that it was the other man and not Dodd that was dead.

"Ay," he said, "anybody else?"

They all shook their heads. "Come down to the yard and I'll talk to ye," he said, turned on his heel and walked back down the worn stairs with the painted pictures on the walls. His back prickled. He was showing he had no fear of them, though of course he did. That was the moment when they might have rushed him if they'd been Borderers. Which they clearly weren't, but still, you never knew. That was the thing about fighting. You never knew.

He methodically went from the lookout place to the rickety watch tower, taking more surrenders. Finally he stood in the yard with his sword still in his hand. He faced eighteen frightened young men with only Jeronimo to back him, smoking his goddamned tobacco again, face shadowed and intent and the crossbow dead steady in his good hand. Only two of them had their buff coats on and had lit torches.

"Yer previous captain is in jail in Oxford," Dodd told them. "His lieutenant is tied up and has surrendered. Now then, I have a proposition…"

"What about that God-rotted Spanish traitor?" demanded a hollow-eyed man with a cough and flushed cheeks.

"He's my ally," said Dodd coldly, "and the ainly decent soldier among the pack of ye dozy idle catamites. Ye can be polite tae him or fight me."

"Or fight me," said Jeronimo, with a lazy smile. "*Pendejos.* Assholes."

"I have a business proposition for ye," Dodd continued. "Here I am, I've taken the lot of ye and it would ha' bin easier to cut all yer throats and save myself a lot of bother. It's only thanks to my kindness ye've still got gullets to gobble wi'. So. Now. I'm making myself yer captain. Is there anybody here wants tae tell me no? And make it stick?"

Behind him, Jeronimo made a noise between a snort and a laugh.

"I mean it. I'll fight any man of ye that wants the captainship instead o' me. Come on." There was a moment of balance while Dodd waited, consciously breathing out and relaxing. He didn't think a man of them had the ballocks to try it, but you never knew.

At the corner of his eye, he saw movement, saw something before he knew what it was, something raised to strike from the other side and so he slipped out of the way, ducked, brought his sword round almost gently and cut the man's head part off. There was no thought in the movement at all.

The others sighed as John Arden collapsed to his knees, dropping the veney stick in his fist, blood pumping in a fountain from his neck and a look of surprise on his face. Dodd watched him as he crumpled over into the black pool of his life. That was a nice stroke, probably one of his best. You rarely got the neck so neatly that you cut through because it was a small target and there was so much meat and bone in the way, you usually got the shoulder or the jaw by mistake.

"Ay," he said, "anybody else?"

They huddled together like the scared boys most of them were.

"What about our pay from the Earl of Essex?" shouted one of the youngest. "That's why Captain Leigh went to Oxford."

"Och God, is that what it was?" Dodd said, scratching his ear which was sticky. "Was that why Leigh was sae hot for the Deputy Warden?"

"He was going to get us into the Queen's procession and then petition the Earl in front of all the people and Her Majesty herself!"

For a moment Dodd was honestly flummoxed. "Did ye truly think it would work? That ye could just walk into a procession like that?"

"He was going to buy us white-and-orange ribbons so we could fit in," said another lad.

"And then we got you and he was going to talk to Captain Carey about us."

Dodd shook his head sadly. "Ye never had any chance of getting any of your pay nae matter what," he said explained, "for the reason Essex has nae ready cash to pay ye and even if he did, he's got no reason to do it."

"But he promised us," wailed the youngest boy.

"Listen," said Dodd, patiently, "the Earl of Essex is a lord and he disnae give a rat's shit for any of ye. Ask him if ye like. Jesus, as yer new Captain, *I'll* ask him, but trust me, ye willna get what's owing. You went to fight and if ye didna keep any plunder, then ye'll take home nae more than stories."

He looked about at the young dismayed faces and felt pity for them. "But," he shouted, "if ye follow me as yer Captain, I can get ye home if ye're so minded or it might be if ye dinna care to go home wi' nothing, I could find ye places as fighters at Carlisle, where I'm from. I willna promise it, but if ye can back a horse and heft a pike, there might be a place for ye in Carlisle. I willna promise it, but if ye come, ye'll get a share of the Deputy Warden's fees and ye'll have a place in the mostly dry and food ye can mostly eat. What d'ye say?"

Another babel of voices broke out while Dodd waited for them to settle it amongst themselves, ready to fight if they decided to rush him together. If they did that, he could only give himself a medium chance so he stayed ready with his sword still out. He cleaned it again before John Arden's blood dried.

What was Carey's main problem? Not money as he thought, because money could always be stolen. No. It was that he did not have enough men that would fight only for him. And here Dodd had a solution if Carey was clever enough to take it. And if not, well, he might take the men over to Gilsland anyway and put his wife in charge of them. They had been easy meat for a night raid but they must be good for something or at least might shape up with some shouting and kicking.

And the raiding season was fast coming, already here. God only knew what outrages had happened in the Debateable Land or what the Grahams or the Scottish Armstrongs had been up to, or, God sakes, the Maxwells and the Johnstones, no doubt at each others' throats again and lesser surnames taking the scraps.

This was something Dodd had been thinking hard about. He had seen what it was like in the South, where there were no pele towers but there were orchards and fat cows and sheep and sure, there were broken men and troubles, but still mainly people who could live their lives without being raided. It made them soft, true. But a sudden decision had come upon him that afternoon while he thought of Janet and the child he fully intended to plant in her the minute he got her on her own in their tower. He wanted his sons and daughters to grow up where the cows were fat and there were orchards, not raiding and killing the way he'd had to all his life.

And how could you do that? Well, among other things, clearly you needed soldiers, men who were not related to anybody they were fighting. Men who would do what they were told and not hold back in a fight because they were swapping blows with their brother-in-law. Men who had no feuds. That was hard to achieve on the Borders from the way all the surnames went at the marrying and breeding and killing there. But here, right here, he had the start of a solution. So.

Dodd had already taken the swords he could find. The lad Nick Smithson was leaving the huddle of young men, coming toward him with an eating knife laid across his two palms. Dodd waited, said nothing but shook his head when Smithson made to bend the knee to him. The lad genuflected anyway and Dodd let him.

"Sir," said Smithson, "Mr. Elliot, we would like to ask you to be our Captain."

He offered Dodd the knife and Dodd put his sword in his left hand and took the knife with his right as dignified as he could.

"Ay," he said. "Now. My right name's not Colin Elliott, that's the name of my blood enemy in Tynedale. My true name is Sergeant Henry Dodd, headman of Gilsland and I'll be your Captain under my own lord, Sir Robert Carey. Understand?"

He had all of them line up and swear allegiance to him, the old way, kneeling, their hands in his while he looked at their faces. Some looked a little shifty but most seemed relieved. It was hard to decide things for yourself, but harder still to know in your heart that the man who was leading you couldn't or wouldn't do the job properly. He knew what that felt like. So they had been easy meat for him and had now got themselves a captain who could do the job.

"Get yerselves ready to move out," Dodd said. "We'll leave tomorrow morning at dawn. We'll take everything with us. I want all of ye to take turns on watch."

The only thing that still annoyed him was that he hadn't found his boots yet. Ah yes, Harry Hunks had been wearing them, of course, and he must have gone to Oxford with Leigh so his boots were probably being damaged kicking against the door of the Oxford lock-up.

Leaving Jeronimo in charge to set watches and start the business of packing up, Dodd sheathed his sword and limped down the path back to the old woman's bothy in the hope he could lay hands on some scraps of cloth or leather to wrap round his feet which were feeling even more sore and cold now the excitement was over.

He felt much better. Certainly when he first woke up in the forest, he'd been determined to kill all of them but it was better that he'd only had to kill three of them and now had eighteen men sworn to follow him. He had his sword on his hip again, the comforting weight of it across his shoulder and he had a nice new poinard as long as the courtier's blade, which he'd envied. Carey would teach him how to use it properly, that useful-looking two-handed sword and dagger work. He'd wake up the old woman and tell her and Kat to be ready to move as well.

He paused. There was a commotion coming from the goats' shed and something was wrong with the entrance to the cottage, there was...

He smelled the fresh blood before he saw it and felt rather than saw the battle axe coming down on him.

His body flung itself sideways and rolled, followed hard by a huge bear-like shape and another chop from the axe. Christ, that was Harry Hunks, taller even than Carey or his dad, broad and big as Richie Graham of Brackenhill and twenty years younger. Dodd rolled again and struggled up in a nest of nettles, panting.

Harry Hunks was named after a bear and was as big as a bear, but he fought like a serious man. No roaring, he was quiet as he came after Dodd again, battle axe in one hand, short sword in the other, teeth gleaming in a fighting grin, eyes catching little flashes of light in the dark of his eye sockets.

Dodd's sword was in his right hand, the poinard in his left, he backed up, not at all liking what he saw. The big man wasn't moving heavily, he was light on his feet, almost bouncing like a child's pig bladder. And that axe…most Borderers only used an axe if they couldn't afford a proper sword or billhook, it was a much harder weapon to get the mastery of and you needed to be big and strong.

Harry Hunks came after him again, Dodd dodged as the axe came whistling down past his chest, just missing his shoulder, you couldn't block that with a sword. He turned, sliced sideways but Harry Hunks wasn't there any more.

The goats were creating a bedlam of noise, there was a bit of starlight, occasional moonlight. Dodd's mouth drew down angrily. It was his own fault. The night had been too easy, he should have realised that and no doubt Leigh had somehow got out and was even now re-establishing who was in charge of his troop of men, knocking heads together. So Dodd didn't have long to kill this bear of a man and get away. And it had to be done because it looked like the bastard had killed someone whether the carlin or the child he wasn't sure but he could smell the fresh blood on the man's axehead…

Again, it was his body saved him, not quite ready for Hell yet. He dropped to his knees as the axe came whistling from nowhere exactly for his neck. He rolled again as one of his own boots tried to kick him in the face.

Goddamn it, Harry Hunks had his boots.

Dodd's eyes narrowed and he finally stopped thinking. He came in and out a couple of times, feinting to see where Harry Hunks' weaknesses were but he didn't have any. Each time Dodd's sword bit nothing but air as Harry Hunks moved just enough out of the way and while Dodd was off balance with the missed blow, he nearly lost an arm and then his nose. You didn't get wounded by a battle axe, you got dead, there were no first bloods, no second chances.

Harry Hunks came after him again and he tripped, stubbed his foot on a stone and nearly had his crotch split while he went over his shoulder and up again behind a tree.

The tree took the full force of the battle axe again, the axe stuck for a second but when he tried to slice the man's arm as he tried to free the axe, Dodd nearly ended spitted on a short sword.

Jesu, said the little cold voice at the back of his head, this one's bigger and faster and stronger than you and he's better. He's going to kill you.

He dodged again behind another tree and ran, turned tail and ran like hell for the clearing by the old stone shed and the ruins of the monastery gatehouse.

tuesday 19th september 1592, noon

Carey was just deciding that it had been a mistake to try quartering the alehouses of Oxford for any clues to Topcliffe or Dodd, mainly because there were so many of them and he couldn't find the musician again. His head was pounding from the grey daylight in his eyes and his stomach turned at even the smell of wine. Nonetheless it was past time to get a horse and remount and go down the London road in search of his man.

As he turned his back on the High Street with its forests of scaffolding and hurrying men with ladders and hammering and sawing, a page in Cumberland's livery came running after him. "Message, sir!" shouted the boy. "Message for Sir Robert Carey!"

The lad gave him a folded letter with the Vice Chamberlain's seal. Carey opened it, skimmed the Italic.

"Sir Robert, I have just arrested your man Dodd on a charge of horsetheft and forgery. Please reply by this messenger, with your terms." It was signed by Heneage.

For a second, fury scorched through him as he stood with his hand on his swordhilt. The boy read his face and stepped back nervously.

"Is there a reply, sir?" asked the lad. Carey stared at him for a moment. Heneage must have just caught Dodd and come straight over to Cumberland's camp to gloat because otherwise, why would he send one of Cumberland's pages?

"Yes, please tell him I will meet him at Carfax to discuss terms with him when I have consulted my father. An hour from now."

The boy bowed and ran off, heading up the Cornmarket. Carey took a circuitous route but headed out of town for the Oxford lock-up, jingling what was left of Cumberland's five pounds in his purse.

A little to his surprise, it wasn't a trap. The guard was as bribable as usual and unlocked the little cell with great ceremony. Carey's eyes still weren't working properly and sunlight was coming in at the barred window so at first he only thought that the suit he'd lent Dodd had taken some damage and there must have been a fight, which made sense.

"Come on," shouted the guard, "Get up to your master, Dodd, don't sit about."

The man didn't turn his bare head, which was balding. "My name," he said with dignity, "is Captain Leigh, I am a gentleman and I've never heard of anybody called Dodd. I demand that you set me free immediately."

Carey nearly exploded with laughter. By God it was hard to keep a straight face. Then he thought to lean in and ask,

"Then how did you come by that suit?"

Leigh lifted a shoulder. "I won it from a man called Colin Elliot."

Carey grinned and nodded to the man to lock up again. Then he went to visit the Jailer and made him richer by five shillings.

"No, sir," he said, "By information laid. A small girl brought this letter from a Mr. Colin Elliot, informing the Sheriff's man that this is Dodd, a notable horsethief and forger, wanted by Vice Chamberlain Heneage. We checked his horse and found it had the Queen's brand though a bit coloured over to hide it and there was no proper warrant. His purse had several forged angels in it so the information was correct. Unfortunately his henchman got away, but we have informed Mr. Vice."

Carey took the smeared bit of parchment decorated with blue flowers. The charcoal scrawl was Dodd's horrible penmanship and Colin Elliot was his usual *nom de guerre*. Reading the script, Carey almost cheered at the elegance of its contents.

"Where's the little girl?"

"She got away, ran south. Said she lived to the south of Cumnor Place."

So at least until yesterday, Dodd had been alive and scheming to get someone else arrested for horsetheft in place of him. They must have been within a couple of miles of each other when he and Cumberland were poking about at Cumnor. Meanwhile he could rejoice at the splendid way Dodd had dealt with the problem of the horse he had stolen from Heneage's stable.

"I'd like to talk to my man," Carey said to the Jailer.

"You can't bail him," he said at once, "Mr. Heneage's man was very particular about it."

"No, that's all right, I'll have a word with his honour later. I just want to talk to him."

Another shilling got him back inside the cell with a quart of beer to share. Leigh seemed grateful for it and very willing to talk especially once he focussed and recognised Carey from France.

Half an hour later, he had the full sorry tale and Leigh's desperate petition that he ask the Earl of Essex for their pay. He insisted that the man he knew as Elliot was being held in a pit—not chained, of course, not at all and the pit was not at all uncomfortable, quite dry in fact—but had a bad leg. Some mysterious trouble with the horses had broken out in the night and Leigh had been delayed in setting out with only the stolen horse to mount…His lieutenant would be fully capable of keeping the prisoner safe and all Sir Robert needed to do to free him was promise to get their pay. They were owed a lot of it, a full year's service in France and not a penny from the King of Navarre either.

Carey had been financially crippled himself by soldiering for the Earl of Essex but had at least gotten a knighthood out of it and was in any case used to debt. He nodded sympathetically, promised to try and sort out the mistaken identity with the

Vice Chamberlain but had not given his word on the matter of pay. He couldn't. He knew perfectly well that the Earl of Essex wasn't going to pay anyone.

Meantime it sounded as if Dodd was healthy enough and would stay put for a while. It was a relief that he wasn't a corpse with a broken neck in a ditch somewhere. Carey thought about enlightening Heneage and then decided not to—why make trouble? Presumably once Heneage bothered to go and visit the man he would know Dodd had given him the slip again and Leigh would have to be released as the bill was spoiled. Carey smiled as he set off for Trinity College and then frowned because he had decided it was time to talk frankly with his father.

He was distracted by the sound of singing from the church halfway up Cornmarket and went in to hear it. These weren't the chapelmen, but a choir of boys, anxiously practising a very complicated piece in Latin with five parts. They were good but they hadn't quite got it yet. He stood at the back of the church, holding his hat, far away from the candles so as not to be troubled by them, thinking.

The signs all pointed in one direction. Well perhaps two. Carey realised that was why he had a headache. He would rather think that Burghley had done the deed, fearing Amy Robsart's divorce from Dudley and Dudley as king—quite rightly. But there was a much better suspect if Amy had balked. Possibly two of them.

He had lost track of the music with his anxious thinking, found that his fingers were holding his hat tightly enough to bend the brim. He wanted to broach the matter privately with the Queen but knew that was both unwise and impossible. He would have to talk to his father; there was no help for it, but he didn't want to because he was actually afraid of what might happen when he did. Was this where his dreams of being in the Tower on a charge of treason had come from? Were they just devilish phantasms or true warnings? How could you tell? Was that why his doublet in the dream had been so worn and faded? Would the Queen execute him for high treason just for asking?

Surely not. But he wasn't sure. He wasn't even sure if he could ask his father. He didn't mind if his father lost his temper and hit him, though he really didn't want to get in a brawl with the old man. And he certainly didn't want to be locked up by him. There was a polite cough beside him and he realised that someone had come in and was standing next to him, a round man in the Queen's livery gown.

"The tenor's good," said Mr. Byrd, "Perhaps I'll poach him for the chapel men. Not as good as you, sir, he don't have your round tone."

Carey tilted his head at the compliment though as always when being told he had a good voice, he didn't feel he could take the credit.

"It's a pity you weren't born of lesser stock, sir," Byrd went on, "we could have made something of you."

"Hmm. I'd have enjoyed that trade, Mr. Byrd, though my instrument playing is atrocious."

"Lack of practice, no doubt."

"I truly did try with the lute…I don't know. Singing seems so natural and playing the lute so complicated. I can tune it and make a perfectly reasonable sound but it's wooden, lumpish. I can hear the fault but I can't mend it." That was true, he had been very disappointed not to be able to master the lute as he wished.

"Hmm. Fighting practice won't improve your playing, veneys coarsen your hands."

"Perhaps."

Byrd smiled. "I remembered something that might help you, sir, so I'm pleased to have found you. You know the musician who ran away on Saturday night?"

"The viol player you hired from the waits?"

"Yes. I finally remembered when I'd seen him before. It was when I was a singer for Mr. Tallis at the Chapel Royal, he used to play for the Queen then. It was in the early part of her reign, but he and his Spanish friend that played the harp and the lute, they ran away from Court, didn't even collect their arrears of pay and we never saw them again."

Carey frowned. "When did they do that?"

Byrd shook his head. "I'm not sure, sir, I think it was very early, perhaps the summer of 1560."

Carey blinked. "His friend was Spanish?" It was common enough then to have Spaniards still at Court, since there had been so many of them during the Queen's sister Mary's reign. "Do you know the names?"

Byrd shook his head. "I can't remember, I'm afraid. I remember his Spanish friend better, a very handsome proud man, like a hawk. He could play any stringed instrument like an angel but his voice was worse than a crow's. He was base-born, his father was a Spanish grandee."

"What was the viol player's name when you hired him?"

"Sam Pauncefoot. That's what he told me last week—he may have changed it."

"To Pauncefoot? Thank you very much, Mr. Byrd. I'm not sure what I can do with this, but it might fit in somewhere."

There was no point waiting any longer, Carey had to go and see his father. He wanted to know what had happened to Emilia's necklace which he needed to sell for ready funds and he urgently wanted to borrow some men to go looking for Dodd, and most importantly, he needed his father to tell him the truth for the first time in thirty-two years.

Outside an immense arch was being covered with canvas and painted. He stood squinting at it sightlessly, his hat pulled down against the watery daylight. Where did a Spanish musician fit in?

He had to talk to his father. He set off, walking fast, trying to make out the pattern forming in his head somewhere just out of reach. And what was the worst that could happen? Well his father might well lose his temper at what Carey was going to put to him. Probably would, in fact. If what he suspected was true, then he wasn't at all sure what he himself would do.

Once on Broad Street he went in at the gate of Trinity College where the usual porter and one of his father's under-stewards were sitting glowering at each other.

For a moment, he hesitated. He had a bit of money. He could hire a horse from Hobson's stables in St Giles, ride to Bristol in probably no more than a day, take ship for the Netherlands and sell his sword there or to the King of Navarre...

He'd wondered about it before; he always did. It was a dream of freedom he had acted on the summer before last, going to France with the Earl of Essex in the tidal wave of enthusiasm that the Earl had somehow generated. He had done well there, learnt that the Court was stifling an important part of him.

So he didn't have to confront his father, he could just go. Dodd was no longer worrying him; he didn't believe a word of the damaged leg, he thought the problem with the horses last night was definitely thanks to Dodd who would clearly cope perfectly well without him. So he could join a crew of Dutch sea-beggars and raid the coast of Northumberland and carry off Elizabeth Widdrington from under the nose of her foul husband and make her a widow in the most satisfying way possible. He could. He knew he could. He was able for it, wanted it, what was standing in his way?

He had his hand on his swordhilt again which was making the porter eye him fishily.

"Your father is here, sir," said Mungey the steward.

What if his father hit him and he lost his own temper like that misunderstanding when he first arrived in London?

Carey smiled sunnily at the college porter and unbuckled his swordbelt, lifted it off and laid the ironmongery on the wooden counter in front of him.

"Look after these, will you?" he said. "Mr. Mungey, where's my father?"

"In the walled garden, sir, he was asking for you." Both of them were blinking nervously at the bundle of Carey's sword, poinard and eating knife before them. Carey felt odd with no

weight on his hip, but much happier. He paced out into the
quadrangle as if marking out a battlefield.

tuesday 19th september 1592, evening

Harry Hunks was coming after him, breathing hard but not
shouting, Dodd's own stolen boots crushing the brambles and
stones that were ruining Dodd's bare soles and toes, too close,
too fast for such a big man, Christ, come on move, ye bastard.

He sprinted the last bit in the open, legs and elbows pumping, mouth open and gasping, and at the last second jumped
over the pit he'd been in. Its ladder was still sticking out, but
he cleared it, landed in a soft muddy bit and rolled again to his
feet, turned and…

Yes! Harry Hunks was teetering on the stone edge of the pit,
heavy for such a leap and he fell in, scrabbling as he went.

Dodd swapped sword and dagger so the poinard was in his
right, went in a crouch to the side of the pit where the ladder
was, stuck his sword in the earth where he could grab it again
if he had to. Harry Hunks came up the ladder, he heard the
creaking and puffing. Just before his head would clear the top
of the pitwall, Dodd reached out, grabbed his hair and stabbed
the man in the eye with the poinard, hard as he could, felt the
soft jelly, the slight resistance of the bony back of the eye socket
and then the give as the blade went into the man's brain and
stuck in the bone of his skull on the other side.

The hilt was wrenched from his fist as Harry Hunks roared
and struck blindly for him, then toppled backwards into the pit,
screaming and clawing at his eye. He landed with a thud and a
clatter and then his back arched and his feet drummed and the
smell of shit told Dodd he was dead.

Dodd sat down next to the pit, gasping for breath and shaking. Christ, that had been close. Christ. All he could do was sit
there and pant until the shaking had gone down a bit.

Then he wiped his wet hands on the ground, looked down
into the pit and wondered if he wanted that poinard back at
all. He'd leave it in Hunks' head until he decided. But he had to

get up and find who Harry Hunks had killed before he arrived. He avoided looking at his feet and forced himself up onto still-trembling legs.

The goats were wildly indignant but unharmed. The old woman lay across the door of her cottage, nearly cut in two by the axe, her cooking knife in her hand unbloodied. Dodd pulled the old body away from the door and called softly through into the darkness, only a few embers of fire still lighting it. Was she still alive?

"Kat?" he said, "Kat, I killed the big yin, are ye there, hinny?"

Nothing at first. For no reason he understood, his belly swooped and clenched itself against his backbone. Was the brave little maid split in two as well?

Then there was a stealthy sniffle. "Kat, I'm coming in, will ye no' stick me? I'm tired and ma feet are sore."

They were burning with pain, bleeding badly from their stickiness, cut to ribbons when he sprinted desperately away from Harry Hunks. He ducked and limped in, leaving prints on the tiles under the rucked up rushes. The sniffle had come from under the marble shelf where the bowls of goatmilk were still sitting to let the cream rise for cheese.

Dodd sat down next to the place, cross-legged, partly to have a feel of how bad his feet were and partly so as not to get stuck by the little maid in her panic.

"Kat," he said conversationally, "how many were they? Ainly Harry Hunks or another man as well?"

No answer.

"I killt Harry Hunks. He's in the pit I was in, but deid, ye follow? D'ye want tae come and look and be sure?"

Her head poked out with its grubby little cap sideways and her face covered in mud. "Is he completely dead?"

"Ay. I put a knife in his eye. Was he alone?"

She nodded grimly, not a tear shed, still shaking. "I think so, he tried to come in for me and Grandam kicked him and he pretended to go away and she made me hide and then...and then..."

"He come back wi' his axe?"

"He chopped her and then he was feeling about for me and I shut my eyes because I heard you whistling as you came back and I prayed to the Lady very hard…"

Good God, had he been *whistling*? The South was having a terrible effect on him and he would never ever come here again.

"So nobody else?"

She shook her head.

"Did ye see Captain Leigh taken?"

A lovely smile broke out across her grim little face. "I did and he went purple and shouted and that was when I just moved away so they wouldn't make me stay with them and talk to Captain Carey and I ran back as quick as I could but I was very tired."

"I've taken over the broken men as Captain, we're packin' up and leavin' for Oxford in the morning. I came to ask you if ye'd care to come wi' us."

She was staring at his poor feet now, making a face. "Tsk," she said, "How will you walk?"

He gave a grim snort of laughter. "I willna, I'll ride. And we'll take the goats and sell 'em."

She nodded. "We can take the cheeses too. What about the curds? Can I give them to Wolfie, he loves the curds and there's no point straining them for…Oh!"

Dodd was slightly ahead of her. He tried to beat her out of the cottage door but his feet were too painful and she slipped past him and out into the darkness and then he heard a scream. He was swearing and wincing and hobbling after her now he wasn't fighting for his life and the fighting rage wasn't carrying him and he found her weeping over the lump of dead fur and meat that was all that was left of the poor dog. She certainly wept more for the dog than for the grandam which showed you something, he supposed.

Since he was up and out he limped over to the pit and found Harry Hunks still lying there on his back with the poinard sticking out of the eye.

The ladder was unbroken so he put it straight and went down carefully, unreasonably scared that the big man would suddenly rear up and attack him again like the Cursed Knight in the ballad. But Harry Hunks was cooling now. Dodd hauled the poinard out and cleaned it by driving it deep into the earth a couple of times, its point was a little bent. That would have to do, he'd sort it properly with an oil rag and a whetstone when he had the time.

Then he set to pulling his boots off the man's feet and managed it finally. He felt about in the man's old doublet and found the little luckcharm Janet gave him and that made him smile. He didn't know what was inside the little leather pouch and he didn't want to know, but he felt quite pleased with it and his wife for playing his enemy false for him. There were a couple of shillings that he took and the buff coat which was too big but would at least make him a bit more decent than the hemp shirt and ragged breeks he had on. Climbing up the ladder again took most of what was left of his strength and then when he tried to put the boots on again he found that his feet were so swollen, it hurt too much.

"If you didn't give me that message then Harry Hunks wouldn't of killed Wolfie and my Grandam," said Kat, standing by the dead dog, hands on hips, narrow-eyed. "Would he?"

Dodd was too tired to deal with this. "Ay, and Harry Hunks is deid, I killed three ither men this night and now I'm master of them all and Leigh will hang for horsetheft and forgery. Whit more d'ye want?"

"I didn't know Wolfie would get killed!" Her voice was going up in pitch and it went right through Dodd's head. He could almost hear his temper snap.

"No, ye didn't. That's because ye don't know what will happen when ye set out for vengeance," he shouted, "ye canna ken until the fight's over which side will win." He was nose to nose with the little maid, full credit to her, she didn't flinch. "People die and ye canna help it, no matter if ye love 'em or no'...*Especially* if ye love 'em! D'ye hear me?"

He stopped, realised he had hold of the front of her kirtle and let go, turned away. Somebody tapped him on the shoulder. "What?" he snarled.

"Thank you for killing Harry Hunks," said Kat with great dignity. "It wasn't your fault about Wolfie and Grandam. It was mine."

"Och no, hinny," he said, and knew she wouldn't believe him, would never ever believe him. "It was Harry Hunks that did it." And me, he thought.

She shook her head, went to the back of the cottage and came back with a bucket of water the old woman must have drawn, ready for the morning. She dipped a pitcher out for their drinking water. Then gratefully he put his feet in and the water went dark.

"Do you think I could marry you?" she asked after a moment, "I'm good at cheese and butter and I've got some bits of monkish gold I found and a shilling to my dowry?"

Dodd managed not to sputter. "Ah…no, Kat, I'm a married man mesen and ye're by far too young for me but I'll see ye wed tae a good man of yer ain if ye like. When yer old enough." She frowned, puzzled so he said it more southron and she went and dug a hole in the floor under the place with the curds and pulled out a leather bag and slung it round her skinny body.

"I'm ready," she said. "You can't bury my grandam the way you are, so we'll set fire to the cottage and that'll do it."

She had good sense. Dodd got his poor feet dry again, hobbled out and pulled the dog's corpse into the cottage to lie next to the old woman. Harry Hunks could be buried by the foxes and the buzzards and ravens. Then they got the coals under the earthenware curfew going again, both lit handfulls of dry reeds they pulled from the thatch and the roof was dry enough and so the fire flowered where they lit it all about and it made him feel better. There was something clean about fire. He knew a couple of prayers from the Reverend Gilpin but he'd never seen the point in them. He told the ghosts of the Grandam and the dog not to let Harry Hunks walk and he warned God not to play the little maid false again.

tuesday 19th september 1592, afternoon

Henry Carey Baron Hunsdon, Lord Chamberlain to Her Majesty Queen Elizabeth, first of that name, was sitting in the college garden, looking at the fallen leaves clotting the grass and worrying. He had his walking stick with him which he generally didn't use in public because he hated to admit that he had arthritis in his knees, as if he were old.

He saw his seventh son before Robin saw him, as his bench was in a shadow between yew trees. The boy…no, even a fond father had to admit that the youngest of his sons was long past full grown, in fact, in his prime, tall, well-built with a breezy swagger that he supposed his sons had picked up from him since they all had it. In fact, of all of them, Robin reminded him of nothing so much as himself when he was a young man, although with the useful addition of his wife's ingenuity. He knew he didn't have that wild streak. He was profoundly grateful that Mary Boleyn had been so much less determined than her sister, that she had been married off to the complaisant William Carey while pregnant with him, the King's bastard. If she had hung onto her virtue the way her younger sister Ann had done, well, he might have been King Henry the IX and had a much worse life, his sons would have been Princes of the Blood Royal and even more trouble than they were anyway. Or more probably they wouldn't even exist because he would have been married off as a child to some thin-blooded crazy barren Hapsburg or Valois Princess, or God-forbid, Mary Queen of Scots herself and then…He shuddered. No Annie Morgan to marry in a whirlwind. Being a King.

Thank God for bastardy, that was all he could say. His half-sister and cousin, Ann Boleyn's volcanic daughter, wove and politicked her way to the throne and was the finest Queen any nation had ever had since…Well, no nation had ever had such a Queen. Some fools might have been resentful at being barred the throne, he was not, he loved his firecracker of a half-sister and would do anything for her. Which was why he was Lord Chamberlain, of course, in charge of her palaces and her security, in charge of protecting her sacred person. It was the uttermost trust she could place in anyone. People called him nothing but a knight of the carpet, but when it mattered he had taken Lord

Dacre's hide in the revolt of the Northern Earls. What did he care if men thought him a fool? It made them less careful of him when they plotted.

And here he was, looking at his youngest son who was now a danger to the Queen. He was digging up the early days of her Court when she had been, frankly, a menace, a cocotte, and a flirt who scandalised the Court and the nation and the foreigners in Europe as well. And Robin was doing his considerable best to stir that dirty puddle on the Queen's own orders.

Insanity. He had urged her to leave it, not to repeat the deadly mistake of 1566, her previous visit to Oxford. So she had used his youngest son as her tool because he had a fine mind and Walsingham had taught him a few things during those months he had spent at the Scottish Court with Walsingham's embassy and then nineteen months in France for polish, also with Walsingham's household. Three months he had taken to learn fluent French, a very diligent student for the first time in his life, and then sixteen months to cut a scandalous swath through the French ladies of the Court that even the French had found noteworthy. Perhaps he too had left a scatter of unknown bastard Hunsdon grandchildren among the French aristocracy, adding English yeast and Tudor blood to Parisian style.

Hunsdon smiled. He hoped so. And the boy had spent an astonishing amount of money as the French grandes dames taught vanity, luxury, and extravagance to an apt pupil. His time in a Parisian debtor's prison had taught him very little about economy, something about power.

And here he came, a little off balance because he wasn't wearing his sword.

Hunsdon frowned. Why? Why had his son disarmed? Had he worked it all out or made a terrible mistake?

He was on his feet, thumbs in his swordbelt, unaware how much his broad frame made him look like his royal sire—although he had never suffered the gluttony born of misery that had swelled King Henry and given him leg-ulcers and turned him into a monster.

Robin came right up to him and genuflected very properly and respectfully on one knee to his father. Hunsdon had to resist the impulse to raise and hug his son who had been so near death from poison only a couple of days before. He was wary. Generally, his son was only that respectful when there was trouble brewing. Or he wanted money.

Robin stood in front of him and hesitated. Their eyes were on a level. It was always a surprise when the baby of the family did that to you.

"Well?" said Hunsdon, guessing one reason why his son might have left his sword behind.

"Was it you, my lord?" Robin's voice was strained and soft in the quiet garden, his face unreadable. "Was it you killed Amy Dudley for the Queen?"

For a moment it was hard for Hunsdon to speak.

"If it was you, father," Robin went on gently, "If it *was* you... I'll take my leave and say no more about it."

This was tricky. The Queen had used a good young hound to find an old trail and he had done very well, far better than she could have expected. But he had to be careful. The Queen had given her orders. On the other hand...

"Do you really think I could have done a such a dishonourable thing?"

"For your sister the Queen? Yes. I would do it for Philadelphia if she needed me to."

Hunsdon couldn't help smiling although it might be misinterpreted. Robin and Philly as the two youngest had always been close and had constantly got into terrible scrapes together. Only the absolute cold truth would do here, that was obvious, although it had to be edited.

"Well, Robin, it's true I would have done it if she asked me, despite the wickedness and dishonour, but the fact of the matter is that she didn't ask me to and I didn't kill Amy Dudley. On my word of honour."

Robin looked no happier, standing tense with his fist where his swordhilt would have been.

"I had hoped you would say you had done the killing, father," came Robin's voice, softened to a breath of sound that the wind in the red and yellow leaves could cover, so he had to strain to hear it.

"Oh? Why?"

"Because otherwise all I can think is that the Queen did it herself."

Hunsdon nearly gasped. It was clear Robin had worked out a great deal of what had happened at Cumnor place in the year of his birth. But he didn't have all of it.

"No," Hunsdon said positively, "I'm not saying she wasn't capable, but no. She didn't."

"Nor ordered another man to do it?"

"No. My word on it, Robin, she didn't."

"But you and she were both at Cumnor Place when Amy Dudley née Robsart died."

It was a statement not a question. Hunsdon's eyes widened as he saw how he had been trapped and he couldn't help a shout of laughter. Damn it, the boy was bright. Carey didn't join with the laugh.

"You were there to discuss the divorce, the Queen's Great Matter," Robin went on remorselessly, using the term Cromwell had used for Henry VIII's long-ago divorce from Katherine of Aragon. "Amy Dudley would petition Parliament and convocation for an annullment of her marriage to the Earl of Leicester, on grounds of non-consummation. Amy was being difficult about it so the Queen decided to convince her in person. And so she dressed up in Aunt Katherine's riding habit, put on a black wig and a married woman's headtire, and rode out from Windsor to Cumnor Place thirty miles away, under cover of hunting. You went with her because really you were the only person who could. A man to protect her, but her half-brother so there could be no suggestion of impropriety. You would agree the deal for freeing Dudley and perhaps make a downpayment in gold. It was a deadly secret for if Burghley had realised what was afoot, he would have put a stop to it immediately by blocking the annullment in Parliament and Convocation, much as the Pope did thirty odd years before. It was ironic, really. Nobody would have given Dudley the divorce, but they might have done it for Amy given enough oil and pressure, because there was no breath of scandal whatever against Amy and she had borne no children in ten years of marriage."

He was good, damn, he was good. Hunsdon watched Carey's face and his heart swelled with pride. Carey had started to pace, squinting a little when the sun poked through the clouds.

"Amy lived so quiet a life, so carefully, she couldn't be treated the way Ann Boleyn was and have charges trumped up against her. She had to sue for her divorce. And the Queen decided to visit her personally to get the agreement."

"Not quite," Hunsdon said softly.

"Amy was in a panic that week, trying to get clothes fine enough to feel confident in. She had one gown ordered from London that didn't come in time, altered another to put gold lace on the collar. That's what told me it was the Queen for sure, that she had to dress fine. You might say it was for her husband, true, but gold lace wouldn't have impressed Leicester. A beautiful French lady once told me that women dress for other women, not men."

Hunsdon said nothing. He was back in the past, when he was young and the finest tournament jouster at the Queen's Court, when the Queen was young. How often had he actually noticed what any woman was wearing?

"So you and the Queen rode to meet her at Cumnor Place, since Amy couldn't or wouldn't ride herself. You took remounts, rode thirty miles across country at top speed. Meanwhile Lady Dudley had bidden all her servants out of the house for the meeting, sent them off to the Abingdon fair though some of them didn't want to go. She was alone apart from a couple of her women playing cards in the parlour."

It had been a wild ride, the Queen egging him on, challenging him, risking her neck for joy, taking hedges and ditches on her fine hunter, named Jupiter, a fire sprite, light in her sidesaddle, laughing as their horses ate the miles with their legs.

"And then…"

Hunsdon put up his palm to stop him. "Robin, you're very nearly right. But…I must ask Her Majesty before I break the matter fully with you? Do you understand? I simply can't…"

Robin had taken out his warrant. "So why did she tell me to dig? Come on, father, this authorises you to break silence."

"This is dangerous ground," Hunsdon rumbled, "Trust me, Robin. It was neither me nor Her Majesty…"

"Then who was it?"

"We don't know."

"You must know. You were there!"

"We tried. I tried when it happened, but I lost him, had to get back to the Queen. Unfortunately, the Queen hired Richard Topcliffe from the Earl of Shrewsbury in '66 when she came to Oxford. He must have found something and I know he turned against her and…"

"He's been a licensed monster ever since."

"He has. He was very clever. Whatever it was he found, he took it to one of the Hamburg merchants at the Steelyard and sent it overseas. If he ever dies unexpectedly or is arrested or word gets out, the box will be sent unopened to the Jesuits at Rheims who will know how to embarrass the Queen with it."

"Burghley? Surely if he'd known a divorce was in the wind, he might have organised the murder to stop…"

Hunsdon shook his head. "I don't think so. It would have been safer to block it in Convocation and Parliament. Cecil was never a gambler, he has only ever bet on a sure thing. If he was going to murder anyone, it would have been Dudley, I think. And not a bad idea at that, if he didn't mind being hanged, drawn, and quartered for it."

"But it only had to be made obvious that Dudley had killed her. Burghley could have seen to a verdict of unlawful killing from the inquest and put Dudley in the Tower no matter what the Queen thought. She wasn't so secure on her throne then; she would have taken notice of her entire Privy Council and her magnates calling out their tenants."

"Would she? I doubt it, Robin. You didn't know her then. She learnt a lot from the troubles of her cousin Mary Queen of Scots."

"The only thing I don't understand is why the Queen took the risk of meeting with her at all."

"Amy Dudley was an appallingly obstinate woman, no doubt how she trapped a Dudley in the first place. She was a God-fearing dull woman who loved her husband deeply and could never understand how Eliza could fascinate men, the magic she had—still has, for God's sake. Amy struggled terribly with her conscience, I think because she would have to testify on oath that the marriage had not been consummated when of course it had been. She was just barren." Hunsdon sighed. He could no longer see the matter as he had as a young man. "She kept changing her mind and asking for more money, more guarantees and she insisted she had to meet the Queen and see her sign the agreement. Nobody would do as a go-between, it had to be the Queen herself. Eliza was furious about it."

"I'm sure."

"They looked extraordinarily alike, you know, red hair, white skin. Amy was like the Queen diluted with milk. I'll ride over and see Her Majesty tomorrow, to talk about the arrangements for Friday and I can ask her…"

"Can I ride with you?"

Hunsdon was surprised. "Robin, won't you be bailing Sergeant Dodd and negotiating with Heneage…" Robin's grin of triumph did his heart good to see as he hadn't been looking forward to dealing with Heneage for the man's release. He bellowed with laughter when he heard what had happened.

"Colin Elliot? He's called himself…?" Hunsdon knew more than he really wanted to about the Border surnames and he knew that there was a vicious bloodfeud between the Dodds and the Elliots which had burst out with spectacular nastiness in the 1570s after the Revolt of the Northern Earls. Wee Colin Elliot was a very dangerous raider and headman about the same age as Robin.

"Yes," said Robin, "Dodd always uses that name as an alias, it means anyone who knows him gives himself away with shock and any crimes he might commit are blamed on Wee Colin by the ignorant."

"Excellent. You can certainly ride with me to Her Majesty tomorrow, Robin, if your eyes are recovered completely."

"They're much better, thank you father, though to be honest I was never blind, only dazzled. I could actually see better in the dark. That's how I found the murder weapon at Cumnor."

"You found the crossbow? Where was it?"

"High up in the space between the passage ceiling and the roof of the hall. The man came through the little door to the minstrel's gallery."

"I know that, damnit, I chased him. How the devil did he have time to hide the crossbow there, I thought he threw it away. We spent a day looking for it with blood hounds a couple of days later."

They stared at each other and came to the answer at the same moment.

Hunsdon felt the blood leave his face. "Oh my God, there were two of them." He actually staggered at the enormity of what he had done all those years ago. Robin was at his shoulder at once, supporting him to the bench again, holding his arm. Hunsdon's legs had suddenly gone to water.

"I left her alone," he croaked, "I chased after the man I saw and I left her alone with a killer…"

"Father," came Robin's distant voice in the roaring, sounding worried, "He didn't kill her, didn't do anything…"

Hunsdon shook his head slowly. Suddenly there was a band around his chest and his left arm was aching. I need to be bled, he thought distantly, I'll see Dr. Lopez when I can.

Robin was anxiously patting his hand and looking around for a servant.

"I have…some physic in my sleeve pocket," Hunsdon wheezed.

Carey felt for it, pulled out the little flask, poured some of it into the cap.

"That's enough," Hunsdon said, took it, pinched his nose and drank it down. While Robin fumbled his flask back, Hunsdon waited for the pounding to subside and the roaring to quiet.

"Father," said Robin tactfully, "You mustn't blame yourself. In the event, she wasn't killed!"

"You're right," Hunsdon said with an effort, "But I was an impulsive fool and I chased the man that had shot at Amy and then clubbed her down with his crossbow while Eliza tried to help Amy. I didn't catch the bastard, even then I wasn't fast enough and all the time the man had a confederate. Well, if I didn't know it before I know it now: Almighty God wanted her for Queen."

"What did the Queen do while she was alone?"

"I'm not sure. She must have been crazy with the shock for she took off your Aunt's headdress that she was wearing and put it on Amy's head—I suppose to make her respectable because Amy's was dented beyond wearing. She supported Amy on her skirt I think, from the way it was dirtied and used it to wipe off the blood that came out of Amy's ears and eyes. I forced her to leave the woman though she was crying with frustration and we rode away. Stupidly, I made her throw away the bundle she had made, into a bush by the old monastery, and that was one of the few times she obeyed me. I wish she hadn't."

"I expect that bundle was what Topcliffe found in 1566."

Hunsdon shook his head. "Perhaps. I went back with bloodhounds, I told you, Robin. We didn't find the crossbow and nor did we find that bundle. They must have tidied them up and taken them away."

The pain was subsiding from his arm and the invisible iron band was loosening. Hunsdon suddenly felt exhausted.

"So why on earth did she suddenly bring it all up again?"

Hunsdon shook his head again, trying to clear it, his brain was no longer working. "I'm sorry, Robin, I have to get to my bed. Would you…er…accompany me?"

"With good heart, Father," Robin said, considerably more filial than normal, must still need money. He gathered up Hunsdon's stick and supported him on his arm back across the garden and with some trouble up the stairs to the Master's lodgings. Hunsdon's manservant came to help him undress and bring him watered brandy. Hunsdon could hear them muttering to each other, that he had had a couple of these attacks before, that Dr. Lopez thought it was a syncope of the heart and had prescribed an empiric dose of foxglove extract to reduce Hunsdon's choleric humours. Of course my choleric humour is unbalanced, he thought, there's my devil of a sister to deal with.

"Don't go to the Queen tomorrow, sir," Robin urged. "You need to rest first. Please?"

"Nothing wrong with me," growled Hunsdon, leaning against his high-piled pillows. "Just need bleeding. I'll see a barber surgeon tomorrow and go in the afternoon."

"But…"

"Damn it, I can still play a veney, I shall be perfectly well tomorrow. I'm just overwrought at the moment, what with the progress, Her Majesty's tantrums, your bloody inconsiderate and careless drinking of poisoned wine and now this…"

Robin grinned exactly like the boy Hunsdon had so often had to shout at for running away to play football with the stable hands and dogboys and occasionally beat for more serious crimes. "There may well have been two of them but God looked after Her Majesty as He always seems to look after me."

"Can't think why, it must be a time-consuming business keeping a bloody fool like you safe…"

Quite surprisingly Robin put his arms around his father's shoulders and hugged him tight. Hunsdon gripped back which eased his heart a little more.

wednesday 20th september 1592, early morning

They had left well before dawn from the old monastery, with two of the three remaining horses drawing two of the three carts still left from the Lord Chamberlain's provision train. A couple of the men had run in the night after refusing to dig graves for the three men of the troop Dodd had killed there. He had sixteen men following him and they walked reasonably well for the ragged starveling creatures that they were. No doubt they had done a lot of walking.

Nobody except Kat had got any sleep—she was curled up in a blanket on one of the carts. The rest of them had spent some time making themselves as tidy as they could and their weapons as clean and sharp as they could under Dodd's tongue-lashing. What had come over him, he wondered? It was only a few months since he had furiously resented Carey's ridiculous whims in the matter of cleanliness and tidiness, but here he was forcing his new followers to clean and sharpen their swords, knives or pikes and their faces as well. He himself spent an hour cleaning and straightening his new poinard and his familiar friendly sword, sharpening them and oiling them.

All three of the carts had a mark he recognised instantly, the mad duck of the Careys, or, as Carey called it, the Swan Rampant. The two remaining carthorses were in bad condition, mainly from neglect and bad feed, so Dodd set two stronger men to each cart to help it along on the rutted track north from the monastery, and four of the ones he thought might make trouble to pull the third cart and really give them something to moan about.

They had reached Oxford city gate after it opened and joined the queue of farmer's wives laden with produce to sell, some nasty covert looks from them as well. Dodd was comfortable on the bare back of the mare he had part-ridden from London, bandages round his feet, Harry Hunks' large buffcoat making him a bit more respectable and his recovered hat on his head. And he had his sword at his side and his own boots in the cart next to Kat.

He didn't dismount to talk to the sheriff's man at the gate, noticing a couple of the Queen's Gentlemen Pensioners of the Guard behind him. He did strain his Adam's apple to talk Southern.

"Ay've the baggage train sent up from London by may lord Baron Hunsdon that wis waylaid by sturdy beggars. These men helped me get it back."

"And you are?"

The goats at the back being led by the youngest man, rightly suspecting something was up, started making a racket and trying to escape. The gateman was eyeing him with distaste.

"And you are?" he repeated.

Dodd drew himself up to his full height and glared down at the man. He knew the black eye and bruising that flowered green and yellow on his face and nose were hardly helping him but why should he care?

"Ma name is…" he started, then caught himself. "Ach…Mr. Colin Elliot, Sir Robert Carey's man."

Now that got a reaction. The gateman turned and shouted at one of the lads quietly collecting weapons from the men wanting to come into the town. The boy touched his forehead and pelted off and Dodd and his party were waved aside into the space by the gatehouse, where another merchant was protesting about paying so much tax.

Dodd sat back and tried not to doze. It was hard work being a captain, that was sure, especially when you had no wife to threaten people with. And his belly was rumbling too—when was the last time he had a decent meal, he wondered. Saturday?

There was a stir and a shout: Carey was riding through the crowds at a trot, followed by four mounted liverymen of his father's, his face full of delight. Dodd was appalled to find that he was glad to see the courtier too, so he scowled and his mouth turned down with the effort of not smiling back.

"By God!" shouted Carey, "Mr. Elliot, I'm very happy to see you at last. That wicked man Dodd is safely locked up in the town jail. Now is that the baggage train my brother so carelessly lost?"

"Ay, sir, I think it is, there's a bit left o'the supplies."

"Do you know who took it?"

Dodd was trying to communicate urgently without words. Carey's eyes passed over the men behind him who were looking self-conscious.

"Nay sir, but these lads helped me…ehm…get the supplies back."

Eyebrows up, a look of perfect comprehension on Carey's face.

"Spendid, splendid! My lord father's in Trinity College and my brother will be very happy to hear that at least some of the train is here. Do you know what happened to the carters bringing it?"

"Ah think they went back tae London, I dinna think they was killed."

"That's a relief. Perhaps they'll turn up again at Somerset House. Now then, gentlemen, I think I recognise some of you from France."

Dodd made a few introductions, ending with the Spaniard who swept off his hat in an accomplished Court bow. "Don Jeronimo de la Quadra de Jimena," he said.

Dodd hadn't often seen Carey do a double take. "Indeed?" he said, responding with a fractionally shallower bow. "The musician?"

Something in Jeronimo's lean weary face settled and hardened. "*Si, Señor,*" he said, "*El músico.*"

"Ehm…" Dodd put in with a clearing of his throat. With great reluctance he slid down from his horse and hobbled into a corner of the yard, beckoning Carey to follow him.

"What happened to your feet, Sergeant?" Carey asked, looking at the rags Dodd had wrapped around them.

"Ah'll tell y the whole of it over a meal, sir, but first I want ye tae arrest Don Jeronimo and keep him safe."

"Why?"

"He's asked for a meeting wi' the Queen…"

"He has?"

"And he says she'll grant it."

Carey's eyes narrowed and he took breath to shout an order. "Take him quietly," Dodd put in, "so the lads arenae upset by it."

Both of them moved toward where Jeronimo was waiting, his back set against the guardhouse wall, eyes hooded.

"He helped me for nae reason but that he wanted tae talk to ye. I think he was the one convinced Captain Leigh to come this way in the first place and I seen him at the inn the night before the bastards took me and robbed me in the forest."

"Of course they're the sturdy beggars who have been making the Oxford road so dangerous."

"Ay, sir, I wis careless and they had me easy an' ma suit and horse and ma boots and sword. They're wanting their pay fra the Earl of Essex and had nae ither way of making a living. I cannae say I wouldna do the like in their place, though I'd do it better, I hope." He vaulted back onto the mare to save his feet again and scowled at them.

Back with the little knot of worried looking men, Carey went over to Jeronimo, leaning on his wall, and made himself extremely affable, speaking French to the man. That was amazing, in Dodd's opinion, how Carey could suddenly switch into speaking foreign, easy as you like. Mind, when you looked at Jeronimo carefully, you could see he was hollow-eyed and often drank his medicine now. Perhaps it was true he had a canker.

They walked their horses together up a street with a roof over it that was high enough so they didn't need to dismount. They were tactfully escorted by Hunsdon's liverymen, to Trinity College whatever that was, tucked away on the other side of a wide street that must be taking the place of a moat for opposite was the patched and pierced old northern wall of the city. Oxford was an interesting place, full of huge archways and pictures made of canvas and behind them were good sturdy houses and a number of places that looked like monasteries with high walls and gatehouses like mansions. Quite defensible, for a wonder. However, now that he'd seen London, Dodd wasn't easily impressed.

As they went past the gate into the courtyard, Carey spoke quietly to the porter and Dodd heard the sound of the gate they had come through being locked and barred. Jeronimo looked up at him. "Do not arrest me when the men can see," he said quietly. "Wait, settle them. I give you and Don Roberto my parole that I will not try escape until I have seen the Queen."

The business was done quickly. The other men were shown into the college hall to eat a late breakfast from the remains left by Hunsdon's servants. Jeronimo waited as four large liverymen appeared and surrounded him.

He deftly unbuckled his swordbelt one-handed and handed it to Dodd who took it grimly.

"I surrender to you, *Señor* Dodd," he said. "I ask only that I may speak to the Queen."

"With all due respect, Don Jeronimo," Carey said, "I don't think she will agree."

"She will, Señor," said Jeronimo, reaching with his only hand into his doublet pocket and taking out something quite small, wrapped in old linen. Carey took it and opened it. Dodd could just glimpse it was a richly embroidered woman's kid glove, badly stained with brown and with one of the fingers cut off. He could also see the breath stop in Carey's throat as he took it.

Carey's eyes were a bright cold blue as he stared straight at Jeronimo for a long silent minute.

Jeronimo inclined his head. "If you give her that, Señor, she will see me. If you do not…" He shrugged elaborately. "I will die soon in any case and then she will never…know something she has wanted to know for many years." He smiled gently, his dark hawk of a face as arrogant as Carey's. "In the end, it will not matter, all will be as God decides."

Carey tucked the little package into his own doublet pocket, holding the Spaniard's gaze for another minute, something unseen in the air between them. Then Carey turned and issued a blizzard of orders.

Kat had woken up while all of this was going on and watched with frank fascination, her pointed chin on her arms on the side of the cart.

"So that's why he helped you, was it?" she asked without surprise. "I did wonder."

Jeronimo went quietly and Dodd made introductions to Carey who smiled and said nothing about yet another waif added to his father's household. The goats were inspected and approved of by the Steward, although the young billy kid was likely to meet his inevitable fate soon.

And the inevitable time came when Dodd had to get down from his horse again. He sternly refused a litter but took a dismounting block and tried not to wince. He still couldn't put his boots on and so he followed a servant to one of the downstairs rooms usually lived in by scholars. When Carey offered him a shoulder, he took it and soon found himself seated on the side of a comfortable half-tester bed, next to a small fire in the hearth, his feet soaking in cool salted water with dried comfrey and allheal in it, which stung like the devil, and drinking a large jack of excellent ale. The chamber gave onto a small parlour that had another chamber leading off it where there was a pile of packs and Carey's Court suit hanging up on the wall. Dodd started to explain to him what had been going on but when he started yawning every other word and losing track, Carey called in the barber surgeon who had been sent to bandage Dodd's feet.

"The story can wait. I'll be riding out with my father immediately," he said, "Get some sleep, Henry and…by God, I'm pleased to see your miserable face again!"

Carey clapped Dodd on the back and went through the parlour to clatter down the stairs. The barber surgeon peeled off the clouts, cleared out a lot of thorns and a sharp stone splinter while Dodd drank more ale and wished the man in hell, then put clean linen socks on him and bowed himself out.

Dodd found a decent linen shirt waiting for him on the bed and was pleased to put it on rather than the filthy hemp shirt and woollen breeches although no doubt the lice would be sorry. He was too tired to be hungry, ignored the platter of pork pie, bread and cheese and finished the contents of the jug of ale. He fell into bed, asleep almost before his head hit the pillow.

His last thought was a question as to what the hell was it Carey had been up to while Dodd had been busy, which had made him look distinctly pale and unhealthy, coupled with a forlorn hope that he might let Dodd sleep for a couple of days at least.

weDnesDay 20th september 1592, late afternoon

Sunset was coming through the small glass window as Dodd woke because someone had just come into his room.

Yes, it was Carey. Dodd knew he hadn't slept nearly long enough, but he didn't see the point of complaining about it. Carey's face was unreadable, closed down into the affable, slightly stupid-looking mask he wore when he played primero for high stakes.

"Ay," sighed Dodd, "what now?"

"Sergeant, I hate to have to tell you this but we absolutely must visit the stews."

"Eh?"

It turned out to be one of the strangest experiences of Dodd's life and it was only a pity he was too tired and hungry to enjoy it properly. He had to get dressed again in a respectable suit of wool that Carey said was borrowed from the Under-steward and apologised for it being well out of fashion as it had been handed on from Carey's father. Dodd didn't care, at least it wasn't as tight and uncomfortable as Carey's previous loan, now being worn by Captain Leigh in jail.

Dodd had leather slippers to put on and low pattens to save them from the disgraceful cobbles and he wobbled painfully across Broad Street and down a tiny alley with the sign of a magpie hanging on an alehouse at the corner. Did none of the scholars here know that horse muck was good for gardens and making gunpowder?

They went into a little house that smelled of woodsmoke and was full of sly-eyed women with very low-cut bodices, but Carey swept straight past them, for a wonder.

The next thing was shocking. They were in a room full of shelves with a tiled floor and Carey proceeded to strip off all his clothes as if he were about to go for a swim, even his shirt. An ancient attendant folded his doublet and hose and handed him a linen cloth which he wrapped around his hips like someone in an old religious picture. Then he put on a new pair of wooden pattens from a row by the wall. Firmly ramming down his multiple suspicions and wondering if he was in fact delirious and hallucinating, Dodd did the same and clopped after Carey along floors that got hotter and hotter until they were in a small room with a brazier in it. Several other men were sitting about on wooden benches—old men, mainly, with grey beards, wrinkled stomachs and twiglike arms, a few spotty youths like peeled willow wands and with a tendency to peer.

The heat from the brazier was fierce and Dodd could feel the sweat popping out all over him.

"We never got round to doing this in London, which is a pity as they're much better there," Carey said conversationally, as if it was the most natural thing in the world to take off his linen cloth, fold it and sit on the edge of the bench on it. He stretched his legs negligently in front of him, peering at one of the white scars. "This will do."

"Ehm…whit the…why…?"

Carey didn't meet his eyes. "Sovereign for bruises and damage generally, helps sweat out poisons and so on and so forth."

Dodd had never heard of a medical treatment that required you to get this hot though he had heard of some alchemists curing the French pox with mercury and sweating.

"Och," he said, as Carey had done so he didn't burn his arse on the planks and tried not to fight the heat as the sweat started dripping off him in rivers. You had to admit it was sort of relaxing.

"We're lucky it's the men's day today," Carey said. "Otherwise we'd have had to pollute the Isis."

The older men and youths left a little later and Carey opened his eyes and smiled lazily at Dodd who was dozing where he sat.

"Now then," he said, "what have you been up to, Sergeant, apart from recruiting a sorry pack of my lord Essex's deserters for the Carlisle castle guard?"

"Ay," Dodd said, sticking his jaw out, "but they are nae related to onybody, are they? And they can shape up or die."

Carey laughed. Dodd told him the story. Carey was a good audience, exclaiming with anger at Dodd being ambushed, laughing at his description of Kat.

"That's the child in the cart?"

"Ay. How is she?"

"Still asleep as far as I know, with the wife of the Trinity College cook looking after her. Last I heard she was insisting she had to stay with you."

Dodd carried on with his tale until he brought it to the death of Harry Hunks and his own decision to leave the ill-starred monastery.

"If ye ask him, d'ye think the Earl of Essex will pay his men at last?"

Carey's expression became unhappy and he looked away.

"Ay, well, their stupid captain's plan was tae get into the procession in their stupid tangerine and white rags and ask him in public why he betrayed them?"

"I gathered something of the sort from the unfortunate Captain Leigh. It would not have been allowed, believe me."

Dodd said nothing although he suspected that with the number of alleyways and passages in Oxford town and some men who weren't too fussy what they did, it might be easier than Carey thought.

"I dinna think they expected more than tae humiliate him and perhaps get the Queen to pay them instead."

Carey made a non-committal grunt.

Dodd sat up, despite the puddle of sweat on the floor under him and the way he was starting to get dizzy with the heat.

"Sir," he said sternly, "they should be paid. They ainly went wi' the Earl because they believed him. The maist of them are not fighting men, or they werenae, they was younger sons of farmers that wanted adventure and found that fighting wisnae as he painted it. And the maist o' them died and not one o' them was paid aught but promises."

"There are plenty of others like them," Carey pointed out with typical aristocratic callousness.

"Ay, sir," said Dodd, clenching his jaw with outrage. "And the more shame to the lairds for it. None o' the Grahams or the Armstrongs or the Kerrs would do the like. Take a man that wis happy at the plough and make a soldier of him and then leave him to die or rot or starve."

"How's it different on the Borders?"

This showed a Courtier's bloody ignorance, in Dodd's opinion.

"I've niver bin aught but a fighter," he told at Carey. "Raised tae it. Ay, ma mother sent me to learn ma letters wi' the Reverend Gilpin but I could back a horse and shoot a bow long before. I killed ma first man when I wis nine, in the Rising of the Northern Earls…"

"So did I," said Carey, softly enough that Dodd nearly didn't hear it.

"Ay?" he said, surprised and a little impressed. "Well, if I was to take some foolish notion in ma heid and gang oot tae the Low Countries or France or the like and sell my sword, it wouldnae be sae great a change for me, I wouldnae be made different, ye ken." He couldn't quite catch the words to pack his anger in, the way it grated on him how the young men who had turned sturdy beggars and robbers had been betrayed, even though they'd beaten him up in the quiet Oxfordshire forest. How he knew they would mostly find it hard—bordering impossible—to return to their villages, even if they got their back pay. "There's a difference, and it's…Och. Ye'd ken if ye kenned."

Carey stood up and mopped himself with the cloth, then tied it round his hips again. "Yes," he said quietly, "It's like hunting dogs. Once you've hunted with a dog, he never can really go back to being nothing but a lapdog. There's always something of the wolf in him afterwards."

It was a good way of putting it. "Ay," said Dodd, standing up himself and wincing, some of his deeper cuts were bleeding into the wooden sandals. "Like a sheepdog if it goes wrong. Once it's tasted sheep, ye must hunt wi' it or kill it, ye canna herd sheep wi' it again. So that's what's been done to the lads, they dinna ken themselves but I doubt if more than one or two of them can go back tae being day labourers or herdsmen or farmers."

"No," said Carey.

"Will ye pay 'em?"

"I can't give them their backpay. If they want to come north, they might be useful and then I'll find a way to pay them."

Dodd knew that was the best he was going to get and he knew he trusted the Courtier more than the high and mighty Earl of Essex.

They went through to the next room which was even hotter and full of clouds of steam from idiots like Carey sprinkling water on the white hot coals in the brazier. Dodd couldn't stand it for more than a few minutes, scraping himself with a blunt bronze blade. He did Carey's back and Carey did his which felt odd but also pleasant, like somebody scratching your back for you after you'd been wearing a jack for a couple of days. Which thought took him on to thinking of his wife and then he had to put his towel back around his hips and think of other things before he embarrassed himself.

"We might have time for a girl," Carey said, deadpan.

"I wis thinking o' me wife," Dodd said with dignity. It was the truth too so Carey's cynical laugh was very annoying. Then they were out in the dusky garden and going into a kind of tent lit by candles. Odd. There was a glint of green water—it covered a big square pond like a fish tank.

And then the next thing was that the bloody Courtier had pushed Dodd into the fish pond with an almighty shove. The cold water made him gasp and he dog-paddled to the surface again filled with vengeance just in time to get a faceful of spray as Carey jumped in next to him. He coughed and spluttered and trod water as Carey splashed past on his back. The wooden pattens were somewhere at the bottom.

"Whit the hell did ye…"

"Didn't want another argument," Carey said, blowing water out of his mouth like a dolphin on a map. Dodd found a place where the water only came to his chest and there were indeed fish in the tank but not too much weed or slime. The fish immediately started nibbling at his feet and legs and he tried to kick them away. "It's the final part of the treatment. You'll feel a lot better for it." The man was looking insufferably smug again.

A suspicion struck Dodd. He suddenly remembered the other purpose of stews, the one that didn't involve women.

"Is this yer way of getting me tae take a *bath*?" he demanded furiously, "*Again*? Not a month after the last one?"

Carey sniggered and so Dodd went after him, ducked him, held him under then decided not to drown the bastard because he was too tired to deal with the consequences. So he let go and climbed out by the mosaicked steps. Carey stood coughing, shaking his head and still bloody laughing, the git.

A little later he was dry, skin glowing, feet in another clean pair of linen socks which had been very helpfully put on by one of the girls who had patted them dry and tutted sympathetically and even put a green salve of allheal on. They were drinking brandy in the stews' parlour while Dodd waded into an excellent dinner of steak and kidney pudding with potherbs and followed by a figgy pudding with custard that filled most of the corners in his belly. However he had maintained a dour offended silence throughout and continued it as they walked back to Trinity, trying not to limp. Carey was not in the least concerned.

"See you in the morning, Sergeant," he said in the upstairs parlour that overlooked the large courtyard that Carey called a quadrangle for some reason. There were a couple of straw pallets and some blankets by the fireplace, so it seemed some servants would be sleeping there. It was nice that Dodd had an actual bedchamber. "We're riding out before dawn."

"Och," said Dodd, wishing he could have a day off too.

At least there was ale and bread and cheese waiting for him in his chamber, and a manservant came in to help him undress, a luxury he still found suspicious but was grateful for as his eyes had started shutting by themselves again. He went to sleep with his skin still feeling very peculiar and his hair damp.

thursday 21st september 1592, dawn

Mrs. Odingsells always woke at dawn, even though the fog that filled most of her world meant she only knew when it was full light. Her window faced east and she left the shutters open so that when the weather was bad enough she could see the threatening colour of dawn a little.

She was always amazed at how tiring it was to lie down all the time. She had a girl come the village most mornings to help her dress and sit in a chair by the window but lately the trembling had got too bad and she couldn't make her legs work. Why the Devil couldn't she die? She prayed most nights to die and welcomed each cough and sniffle in the hope that it might be bearing the gift of a lungfever. She was not afraid of death, had hopes that her faithfulness might count for something with Almighty God, with whom she intended to have words in any case. She was not even very worried by pain.

So why was she still alive, she wondered. She had borne two children to Mr. Odingsells in the 1550s during the boy-king's reign, only to have all three carried off by the English sweat. It was an old horror now, well-scabbed over. With no heart for another husband, she had become a gentlewoman to her distant cousin Amy Robsart when she made her very good match. And then Amy, too, was mysteriously struck down. She had stayed at Cumnor Place afterwards, thanks to the kindness of Sir Anthony Forster, and lived a quiet and prayerful life on her small jointure, running the manor for him, with occasional visits to Oxford and Abingdon, reading mainly scripture and the Church Fathers. She had a long memory and a good one: she remembered the bonfires for the Princess Elizabeth's birth, had in fact got drunk at the feasting and danced with the young man she had liked then, who only got himself killed in France. Yes, she would have words with the Almighty.

She had outlived everyone she loved so what was she doing here? Was it about the Queen's matter, from decades before. In which case…perhaps there was hope that the pleasant young man would have passed on her message to Her Majesty.

She knew he had as soon as she heard the hooves of several horses in the courtyard, heard old Forster with his voice full of fear greeting the man with the rumbling voice. She remembered that voice, remembered it very well and managed to sit up in bed. More than two horses, three or four, she thought, including a pony from the shorter stride.

She pulled on a bedjacket she had knitted herself a decade before, of silk and wool mixed, against scripture, of course, but very practical. With infinite effort she rearranged her pillows so she could stay sitting up, then felt for the sewn silk packet she had kept on a ribbon round her neck all this time, safe. That ill-affected man Topcliffe had tried to find it to take it off her years ago but she had convinced him the papers were burned.

Forster soon knocked on her chamber door and she bade him show her visitors in.

It was the man and the woman again. The same two. She squinted sideways, lining up the tiny patch of her eye that still worked. There was Henry Carey, even more like the King in his age, older and greyer, of course. There was the woman she had never actually seen before but had heard, screaming. She was wearing a black wig again. Forster withdrew.

"Mrs. Odingsells, with your permission, we wish to make use of your hall…" began Hunsdon courteously.

"Well?" That was the woman, the strong contralto voice, accustomed to command.

"Your Majesty," Mrs. Odingsells said steadily, for hadn't she practised in her imagination for this meeting many times? "Please forgive me for not rising, my legs no longer obey me."

The woman stepped forward. "Do you have them?"

Mrs. Odingsells nodded. "Yes. Please use whatever you want of this house—Mr. Forster will help you."

"All this time?" said the Queen in wonder. "Why did you keep it? Why not burn it?"

Her bedroom was not cold, there was a curfew over the fire, to keep the coals hot. Mrs. Odingsells looked sideways at it, not able to see it any more.

"I couldn't. I tried to many times, especially when that evil man Topcliffe tried to take it. But…It was in your handwriting, signed by you, Your Majesty, and by poor Amy. And…I thought you might want it one day." She couldn't see, of course, but she thought the Queen coloured.

"Why? To remind myself of how near I came to losing my kingdom?"

She did understand. Mrs. Odingsells smiled joyfully into the fog where the Queen loomed. "Yes, Your Majesty. Nothing good could have come from poor Amy forswearing herself, breaking her Bible oath. No amount of gold or land or manors could have made that right." She didn't add that the Queen's love for Robert Dudley was the mystery of the age, considering how he had treated Amy who loved him too.

"No." The Queen was agreeing with her. "I think that poor Amy saved my life and my kingdom that day."

It was time. Slowly, with fingers that trembled and fumbled no matter how hard she tried to control them, Mrs. Odingsells lifted the little packet on its ribbon over her head and held it out. The Queen took it, her long slender fingers cold and smooth. The paper crackled as she opened it out. She took a long breath.

"Hmm. Good penmanship," said the Queen after a moment in a self-satisfied tone. Mrs. Odingsells nearly laughed. Amy's handwriting had been poor so the Queen must have been her own clerk that day and done it well. "I thank you heartily, Mrs. Odingsells, both for your discretion and your faithful keeping of this to give to me. Is there anything we can give you or assist you with in token of our thanks?"

"No," said Mrs. Odingsells. "It was my duty to keep it safe and now you have it once again, perhaps the good Lord will call me to Him at last."

There was another long pause, and a sharp movement from Henry Carey. "God speed," said the Queen. "Thank you, Mrs. Odingsells."

The two of them walked out leaving a sense of empty space behind them. Mrs. Odingsells called in Mr. Forster and told him to let them do whatever they wanted within reason.

Once out in the passage the Queen looked down at the single sheet of paper. Written on it, in her own excellent Italic, was her agreement with Amy Dudley née Robsart that Amy would petition Convocation for the annulment of her marriage on grounds of non-consummation and in return receive large estates, a pot of gold, a manor house and a house in London and a pension from the Queen. Both parties had signed it, of course, but… Harry was staring at it, appalled. In all the hurry, thirty-two years ago, they had both clean forgotten the agreement they had come for and now…

"Where's the other one?" he whispered. "There were two copies."

There had to be two copies. One for Amy, one for her. Two copies, both signed by both parties. Mrs. Odingsells had only handed over one.

The Queen shook her head, refolded the paper and put it under her stays, then walked down the stairs swiftly and out into the weedy courtyard. Her lady-in-waiting Mary Radcliffe and Thomasina her Fool had already gone into the old hall to supervise its tidying and sweeping. The horses were tethered in the corner. To be so free of attendants—as always it made her feel light and giddy. She had her brother get out his tinderbox and light the stump of candle in it so she could burn the paper she did have and stamp the ashes into the mud. The other copy… Well, that would have to wait. Perhaps she would set young Robin on to find it one day.

Then she had the final argument with her brother about the meeting she had planned. It didn't matter what he said. She had to receive the old musician who had plotted so carefully to meet her. She must finish what she could of the business at last. Obviously she couldn't do it at Woodstock, so full of courtiers and spies, nor at Oxford. There was a fitness in things and for all

Henry's spluttering about the risks, this matter must be finished where it started.

thursday 21st september 1592, morning

It was full light when Dodd woke up to someone knocking on the door. That was some comfort.

"Whit the hell…?" he growled, confused into thinking he was still in London.

"We leave in about half an hour, Sergeant," came Carey's voice filled with his usual loathsome morning cheerfulness.

Dodd rolled out of bed, used the jordan under it and slowly got himself dressed. There were good thick knitted hose with it to go over the linen socks, so he took a chance and pulled on his boots that someone had already done a good job of mending and polishing. It wasn't what you could call comfortable but it was bearable and he would just have to hope they were riding not walking. He went into the parlour where there was food ready on the table, neither Tovey nor the Scotsman visible. He gulped down more mild ale and fresh bread and cheese.

In the quadrangle were horses and men and Carey efficiently sorting them out. Nobody was wearing buff jerkins or helmets or jacks but they all had their swords and were looking smart. Dodd's own sword was at his hip and he felt much the better for it. To his surprise, Don Jeronimo was also there, on a horse with his only hand loosely attached to the saddle so he could still use the rein, one of his feet was tied to the stirrup. His face was unreadable under his hat but he looked worryingly humorous.

Dodd mounted without touching the stirrups, despite it being so early, then leaned over and unbuckled the stirrup leathers, handed them to a surprised groom. "They'll ainly mek ma feet sore," he told the lad who didn't look like he'd understood.

"So," he asked Carey, "where are we gangen tae, sir?"

"Not far, about four miles from here."

They went through the College gate, walked along the wide road where they must have markets, down a narrow road past another of the odd-looking monkish fortresses, curved along the line of a high wall, over a bridge and then they went to a canter in a body, Don Jeronimo constantly surrounded by Hunsdon's liverymen. Dodd recognised several typical Border faces among them, though their speech was from the East March.

They had to slow down soon. The road into Oxford was choked with people and packtrains coming the other way, so they used the verge, where it wasn't too muddy, and pounded along. It was mostly a broad road, well-built perhaps by the same giants that had built the Faery's Wall that once was the Border line. Dodd recognised the look of the stones and some of the waymarkers carved with square letters in foreign.

They turned aside only a little south of Oxford so it was hardly any time at all before they were clattering into the courtyard of a mansion that had clearly been closed up and not much inhabited for a long time, from the grass growing between the stones and in the gutters. As usual there was no proper tower and it was not defensible but there were four horses tethered in the corner, two beautiful hunters, a palfrey and a little pony.

"Where's this, Sir Robert?" he asked.

"Cumnor Place," Carey told him, "about a mile and a half north of where you were being held. This is where Amy Dudley née Robsart was killed."

Dodd had never heard of the woman so he concluded that it was some dirty business Carey had got himself tangled in. And the south must be getting to him: he hadn't even thought how to steal those very pretty and unattended four horses in the corner.

Jeronimo had slumped in the saddle but when Hunsdon's liveryman untied his foot and reached over to tie his wrist to his belt instead of the saddle, he looked around himself as if recognising the place. Then he swung his leg over the horse's neck and jumped down forwards, only staggering a little as he landed. Dodd dismounted the same way and managed not to yell when his boots hit the ground.

And then they were going into the hall which seemed to have been hastily swept, though the tables were still piled on one another and the benches stacked by the wall.

On the dais sat Carey's father with two, no, three women beside him. One looked like a child but had a face that was somehow not childish. She was sitting cross-legged in tawny velvet at the feet of a black-haired elderly woman in a green woollen kirtle and a gown of velvet, who was sitting a little behind Hunsdon. In front of her and on a better chair was another older woman in richer clothes, with red hair.

Carey made an odd little half-bob, then bowed to his father. Dodd copied him, less elegantly. Jeronimo paced in, surrounded by Hunsdon's men, his face haughtier than ever. His dark eyes travelled along the people in front of him and he let out a half-smile. Then he stepped forward and went gracefully to both his knees and stayed there, ramrod straight.

"I have been asked by the Queen to question you, Señor Jeronimo de la Quadra de Jimena," gravelled Lord Hunsdon, chin on his ruff. "Her ladies-in-waiting here will carry the account back to her."

Jeronimo tilted his head slightly but said nothing.

"Please tell me why you have asked for audience with the Queen and where you got the...item you gave to my son, Sir Robert Carey."

"Milord," said Jeronimo, "the last time we meet here you chased my friend a mile down the road. It is thirty-two years since. Now I am old and dying. I have a canker growing in me and I bleed. I have come to make right what I did that day."

"Go on."

"I am the bastard son of Don Alvaro de la Quadra who was the Spanish ambassador at Her Majesty's Court then. I was a young fool of eighteen, good with the lute, good with the harp, very very good with the crossbow. All stringed instruments were friends then." He smiled as if remembering a long-lost lover. "My father bought for me a place among the Queen's musicians from Mr. Tallis so I could spy on the Queen. I was proud for the work."

Jeronimo smiled. "At that time I truly believe that the Holy Catholic Church was the only refuge of mankind, the only dwelling of God, and that all heretics must die." He shook his head in wonder. "Since then I learn better. But I was a young idiot."

"Indeed."

"*Entonces*, milord, while playing my lute I hear Her Majesty who was then so beautiful and scandalous and in love with her horsemaster, speak with her lover about how to deal with his wife. Perhaps she thought I would not understand Italian. She wanted the woman to divorce him but it must be done with much care in case Sir William Cecil hear of it and make a stop. But the wife was being difficult, stupid.

"Milord Leicester sent me with a letter to his wife ordering her to divorce him and stop delaying. She read it while I waited for an answer and then she began to cry. What could I do? I was a young idiot and not ugly—she was pretty and distressed. I put my arms around her and held her. And so I was lost.

"No, alas, milords, I never took her to my bed but I certainly sinned with her in my mind. She was a virtuous woman. We talked much and she told me she wanted to kill her rival. And…"

There was a concerted gasp from everyone.

"She wanted to kill the Queen? And you told her how it could be done?" Hunsdon barked, leaning forward.

Jeronimo bowed a little and coughed. "Of course." Everyone in the hall shifted position in some way. The black-haired woman with the tiny woman beside her crossed her arms. "I told her to bring the Queen with as few attendants as possible to the manor where she lived very sad and lonely for her husband and that if she can do this, my friend and I will do the rest. And for the first time she smiled at me and said, yes, she could do it. And we kissed." He smiled, his eyes crinkling.

"Did your father know?"

"Of course. I spoke with him immediately. He was still trying to bring about the marriage between the young Queen and his master, King Philip II. He knew that the horsemaster was a fierce heretic and a fighter, desiring war. He believed it is a disaster for Spain if they marry.

"And when I put it to him, he could see how it solved all. I kill the scandalous Queen, the last Tudor. There will be two contenders with a good claim, the Queen of Scotland, a Guise, or His Most Catholic Majesty himself through his marriage to the Queen's ugly older sister. If there is war, it is in England, not in the Hapsburg lands, but there was no reason to think the Queen of Scots will fight for her English throne as she then was still the Queen of France, married to the young King who was unwarlike." Jeronimo shrugged. "I knew it might mean my death but I was young, I no believed I could die. I was in love with the poor Lady Dudley and I thought that when the Queen was dead, I would challenge Leicester to a duel and kill him and so take her for my own. It was very romantical.

"So my friend warned me when the Queen took a good galloper and a remount for a hunt in Windsor Great Park and when you, milord Hunsdon, did the same to go with her. We slipped away from the Court and rode to Cumnor Place. My Amy had arranged it all. We were there first, I wait in the darkness of the musicians' passage with my friend keeping watch. I never see the Queen arrive with you, milord, I was in the dark behind the door. They went into the Long Gallery to meet Amy and discussed the divorce. She agreed, they signed paper, there was gold. It took a long long time. And then, as we had agreed, the second door opened to the back stairs where I was waiting. I had my crossbow wound and ready.

"I hear them come through the door, my eyes accustomed to darkness, I step out and I am dazzled by the light through the window. I see the woman in front with her red hair and the gold on her collar and I shoot at her. Somehow, I miss. She tries to run down the stairs to me, screaming in English but I do not understand so well. I step back, I take my crossbow by the stock and I strike her down the side of her head and she falls like a sack down the stairs and that is when I know who she is." He paused, breathed carefully, his voice husky. "I still can see my beautiful Amy crumpled at the turn of the stair, her neck bent on the wall. You, milord, had put behind you the other woman, the one I had only seen as having black hair, you had drawn your sword and so I turn and stumble back through the gallery where my friend is waiting. But I cannot move for shock, he is a faster runner than I and I climb up into the rafters as milord Hunsdon thunders past me, chasing him."

"Si, Señores, I could have wound my crossbow again and killed the black haired woman too, but why? What was the point? I couldn't think, I believed she was only a lady-in-waiting. I looked at her as she knelt by my Amy's body, crying over her body, trying to stop the blood coming from my Amy's ears and eyes. I climbed up to hide the crossbow among the roofbeams, climbed down again and I saw she was taking off the broken headdress, using it to mop the blood, try to make all clean. I saw her take off her own headdress and place it on Amy's head where there were two terrible dents from my crossbow. Perhaps to hide it.

"And then milord came back and he pulled her to her feet. She had rolled all together in a bundle, the headdress, her gloves dirtied with blood. They argued, he ordered her to ride and called her "Your Majesty" and that, Señores, was when I understood that she was the Queen but wearing a black wig and someone else's kirtle. I stood there, turned to stone as I heard their horses gallop away.

"Later I found the bundle in a bush. I kept one of the gloves, the bloody one, and my friend took the other and the headdress. ER was embroidered on the gloves and they were the finest gloves I had seen. Then when my friend had stopped my weeping and I could think again, we rode back to my father."

Jeronimo's face darkened. "My God, my father was furious. He would not let us in the house, told us to go and lie low and he will do what he can. We hid in the Spanish embassy for a while. Then we went to Oxford where my friend had his family. We lived there a while and then when the Queen came back to Oxford six years later and the place was full of pursuivants and that evil man she hired to hunt us down, I rode to Bristol and took ship for the Low Countries where I learned other things than lute-playing."

"You could simply have told me this, Don Jeronimo," said Hunsdon, "Why do you insist on seeing the Queen?"

Jeronimo was not paying attention to him, looking hard at the women beside him. He narrowed his eyes and then smiled.

"If I could be received into Her Majesty's Presence, if I can have such favour though not deserved," he said quietly staring into space. "I will say this to Her Majesty: I am not now the hot-headed young idiot that I was. Now I am a cold-headed old idiot. I have a canker that came from a mole that broke open and bled. My liver is full of stones, there is a rock in my stomach. Soon I will take to my bed and die in pain and then I will go to Purgatory to answer for all the men and women I have killed in my life. For my *querida* Amy, I have already paid much. It is just.

"I will say this to the Queen: Your Majesty, I ask pardon that I tried to kill you. I am happy that I failed but I am also sorry that because I so stupidly killed your horsemaster's wife, the scandal meant you could not have him. A very strict Jesuit confessor sent me back to England to make amends. And so here I am. I beg your forgiveness with all my heart. You may take me and execute me if you like, you will do me a favour." He paused in the silence. "He was a clever Jesuit, I think.

"This I will say to the Queen for the end: Now I thank God you were incognito so I made such a mistake. And then I will wait for Her Majesty's judgement and mercy."

He bowed his head and there was silence. Hunsdon leaned over to talk to the women beside him and then lifted a hand. "We will consult on it." A nod to his men and Jeronimo was helped to his feet and led out of the hall, walking slowly as if he was in pain. At another nod from Hunsdon, Carey went with them.

"Sergeant Dodd," said Hunsdon after a moment, "I understand from my youngest son that you have dealt in your inimitable way with the troublesome band of sturdy beggars who took my supply train and beat up my men and that you propose that my son take them into his service."

"Ay, sir," said Dodd after a moment to collect his thoughts. "They wis only raiding because they had nae ither choice, being betrayed in France by the Earl of Essex and getting none of their pay."

Hunsdon's eyes were hooded. "We will offer them the chance to go back to their villages near Hereford. If they choose not to, Sir Robert will take half and I'll send the other half to Berwick to my other son who is Marshal there."

Dodd shrugged. It was eight men not sixteen for Carlisle, but he supposed the Captain of Berwick Castle would need unattached men as badly as they did. He was glad Hunsdon saw the advantage there.

The black-haired woman with the tall hat cleared her throat. "Sergeant Dodd, my mistress the Queen asked me to…talk to you about what has been happening."

"Ay, missus," said Dodd warily. "Milady."

The woman beckoned him so he went over, trying not to hobble, and did the best bow he could over her hand. She looked far too old to be any of the women constantly pestering Carey's father and son to bed them so perhaps she did work for the Queen. You could tell she was a powerful character with that beaky nose and the snapping dark eyes and you'd think there would be clashes. The other woman was sitting back, talking to Hunsdon.

She took him through the entire past four months in detail, since Carey had arrived at Carlisle to be Deputy Warden to his brother-in-law, clearly knowing far more about the various happenings on the Border and in London than any lady-in-waiting really ought to. She laughed at some of Dodd's comments which emboldened him so he gave her more stories than he normally would. Her laugh was delightful for all her age and the fact that her teeth were stained.

"Sergeant Dodd," she said eventually, "I take it that you approve of Sir Robert Carey and his various…actions?"

Approve? That was a little strong. "Eh, he's canny but he takes mad plans in his heid," Dodd said cautiously. "He's a bonny fighter but he's allus a Courtier, no' a Borderer and that holds him back." In the corner of his eye, Dodd caught a brief flash of a smile from Lord Hunsdon and wondered why. Conscientiously he added, "Mind, he's no' himself at the moment, he seems... eh...a little unwell."

"Perhaps you could tell him that I have already spoken to Mrs. Odingsells before you arrived. I personally received from her the...document she kept for me all these years, so faithfully."

"Ay missus," said Dodd, with no clue as to what she was talking about. The lady nodded once, seemingly approving, then smiled again.

"He will understand. I have made provision for her as well although she insists she needs nothing. Now then. This matter of Don Jeronimo," continued the lady, narrowing her eyes. "Do you think I should advise Her Majesty to see him?"

"Good God, no!" snapped Dodd. "He says he's sorry for it all but there's a long plan here. He's the one brought the broken men here tae Oxford, he saw me at the inn on the Oxford road, heard me say I wis Carey's man, and then he took me prisoner in the forest, easy as ye like. And then he comes and helps me escape and take over the troop...I dinna think it wis kindness nor to make amends. And why was he at the Oxford inn at all? Eh? What had he been at before? He says he tried to kill the Queen thirty years gone and he got the wrong woman, his ainly love." Dodd's lip twisted in a sneer. "Och, the puir wee manikin, whit a sad tale to be sure." Dodd stabbed the air with his forefinger. "He's a Papist—he admits he tried it on once, you tell the Queen *hang him today!*" Dodd realised he was shouting and toned it down so as not to frighten her. "He said she'd be doing him a favour."

Hunsdon banged with his stick on the floor. "Well spoken, Sergeant!" he boomed.

The lady-in-waiting smiled. "Thank you for your advice, Sergeant Dodd. My lord Hunsdon, I think we are done here."

Hunsdon harrumphed. "Indeed, I shall indict him on a charge of high treason..."

"Och for God's sake," groaned Dodd, goaded beyond endurance by this stupid Southron way of doing things, "He's said hisself the bill's foul, ye have him, string him up now and be done wi' it. Ah'll dae it for ye if ye're too…"

"Sergeant, the laws of the Border and the laws of England are different. We can't simply string a man up here without trying him first…"

"A'right, give me a crossbow and five minutes and…

The lady-in-waiting was almost laughing again. "Sergeant, then we would have to arrest you for murder."

"What? Och, no, see, I took a shot at a deer in the forest and what a pity, I missed and hit…"

"No, Sergeant."

"But he's *foreign.*"

Both Hunsdon and the lady-in-waiting were laughing outright now. Dodd took a deep breath and set his jaw so no more words would escape for them to make fun of. It was obvious they were stupid fools with no idea of how to deal with a dangerous bastard like Don Jeronimo, because of living in the soft south no doubt. So it would be up to him. He knew Jeronimo would understand and so would Carey and if the worst came to the worst he could always join his Armstrong brothers-in-law in the Debateable Land.

Suddenly there was a confused noise outside. Dodd heard Carey's shout and instantly drew his sword, ran as fast as he could hobble out of the hall.

There was a scene of chaos in the courtyard. The horses were plunging about, one of the Borderers had already caught one and mounted, Carey was lying on his back holding his face. Dodd struggled over to him.

"He's awa'?" he asked.

"Oof," said Carey, obviously part-stunned as he climbed back on his feet, shaking his head and feeling his jaw where there was blood coming from his lip, "Bastard!"

"Ay," said Dodd.

"He started to puke, I went to help him and he decked me and ran. Caught one of the horses, got on board and off he went. He's not as sick as he makes out."

"Ay," said Dodd.

The two Borderers were galloping down the path into the forest and Dodd was completely certain that they wouldn't catch Jeronimo.

There was a sound behind him. Hunsdon was in the court-yard, looking furious, behind him were the women.

"We'll ride back to Oxford," he ordered. "Now."

"Och no, we can quarter the forest with enough men…"

"We must first escort the ladies back to Woodstock palace. Then we'll find Don Jeronimo."

Well that was more Southron stupidity, give the women a couple of men to help them and send them off out of the way while everybody else found Jeronimo and accidentally killed him where no bloody lawyers could see. For a wonder, the ladies-in-waiting were not arguing at all, the two women were already at the mounting block, being helped into the side-saddles, one on the handsome hunter, the other on the pretty palfrey, while the tiny person with the unchildlike face was already on her white pony, her face thunderous and what looked like a small throwing knife in her hand.

"Ay but no' by the Oxford road," Dodd said, resigned to losing Jeronimo for the moment.

"Why not, Sergeant?" asked Hunsdon.

"Because Jeronimo can use a crossbow and we dinna ken if he's got one or no' and he knows this forest well for he's been living here for weeks. All he needs is a tall tree and a clear shot and ye're deid, my lord Hunsdon."

"Harrumph."

"Do you know the paths in the forest?" Carey asked. Dodd had to admit he didn't, he hadn't had a chance to learn them. "In that case, ma'am, I think the Oxford road is still the best way. It's reasonably good, the trees are not close to it, we can use the messengers' path to avoid the crowds and we can bunch up close."

The black-haired lady was looking very annoyed as she controlled her big horse, but not particularly frightened. "Very well. But honestly, Robin, I'd thought better of you."

Carey's face was comically downcast. "You're…you're right, ma'am, he made a complete fool of me."

Dodd had found his own horse without the stirrups, sheathed his sword again and jumped to the saddle, then wished for a lance and a good bow. There was something quite wrong with Carey, seeing he was so meek. It was worrying.

Hunsdon's two Berwick men came back looking frustrated and, of course, without Jeronimo. Hunsdon ordered them out in front as scouts, the men bunched up around the women with Hunsdon on one side of them and Carey and Dodd on the other and they took the path that led from Cumnor Place to the Oxford road with Dodd's back itching furiously and his heart thudding. He didn't even have a jack or a helmet and if Jeronimo could find himself a crossbow and some bolts he could do terrible damage from the close woodland around them.

A little to his surprise, they reached the road without anyone shooting at them and from there they went to a canter and then a full gallop with one of Hunsdon's men out front shouting at the people on the road to make way, make way! The red-haired woman was looking uncomfortable and frightened, the child-sized one was narrow-eyed all the way, but the black-haired woman seemed to be enjoying herself and even Dodd had to admit, she rode very well in her fancy side-saddle.

They got back to the bridge in record time, but instead of going into any of the colleges, they rode straight on through the crowded streets, bowed through at once by the gate guards, and trotted right up wide St. Giles to the northward road. From there it was perhaps ten miles to a village Carey called Woodstock. There, overlooking the valley, was a small fancy castle, probably once defensible but quite decayed now. It was surrounded by tents and horses. The ladies-in-waiting immediately disappeared into the castle. Then Hunsdon turned his horses and they took it easier as they rode back down the road to Oxford at last.

Dodd and Carey took their horses to the stabling at the back of Trinity College themselves and walked them round the courtyard a few times to cool them down. It was only mid-morning and no grooms to be seen, of course.

"Whit were ye talking about wi' Jeronimo when he got ye?" Dodd asked casually as he rubbed his horse down with a wisp of hay. Carey was still looking pale as he did the same and kept rubbing his chin where a very well-aimed bruise was darkening the point of it. His lip was puffing too. You had to admit, a Court goatee gave a good target to aim at if you wanted to knock a man down.

"I was talking about music," he said in a puzzled voice. "I said I'd sung the Spanish air he'd sent to the Queen as the signal that she was willing to meet him. I hummed it for him. He said he was hanging around Oxford to hear it, but then he came on you at the inn and decided it would be easier and safer to take you prisoner and use you directly as a lever. He asked me if anyone else had known it and I said no, but then I remembered…goddamn it!" Carey had gone even paler. He was standing like a post staring into space while his horse stamped uneasily. "Goddamn it to Hell and perdition."

"What?"

Carey took a deep breath and shook his head. "I'd forgotten about it. I'd just learnt the tune and was humming it when someone…an old man asked me if I was sent by Heron Nimmo. That's how I heard it. Of course, that was Jeronimo if you pronounce it the Spanish way. But I had no idea what the old man was talking about so I told him, no, the Queen wanted me to sing it specially."

"Ay?"

"About an hour later, someone tried to shoot me with a crossbow. It was pure luck they missed. And that night someone put belladonna in my spiced wine and nearly killed me."

"Ay?" Well, that explained the pallor and slowness. Poison? Jesu, that was a new one even for Carey. "Did ye tell Jeronimo those things?"

"Yes, I asked him if it had been him with the crossbow and the belladonna on Saturday, and why he had been trying to kill me not the Queen, not that I minded, of course. Moments later, he started puking and then when I came to help, he hit me."

"How? His wrist was roped to his belt."

"With his stump—it must have a leather and iron cap over the end from the way it felt."

"Och!" Dodd was reluctantly admiring.

"Then while I was stunned, he part-drew my sword with his teeth and sawed through the rope, then he was gone. Damn it."

"Would ye know that old man again?"

"That whole Saturday evening is very blurred. I don't know. Jeronimo said there were two of them that tried to kill the Queen, his friend and him. The friend who had family in Oxford and gave him shelter. And now I think about it, I wonder if he was the musician from the Oxford waits that played cello for Mr. Byrd when I sang the song again and then disappeared halfway through the Earl of Oxford's ball. Mr. Byrd was very annoyed. I even drank his ration of ale."

They were silent a moment. "I'll tell my father," Carey said. "We'll let the men comb through the forest with dogs, I doubt they'll find Jeronimo. He'll be in Oxford meeting his bloody friend…What was his name? Sam? Punch…no Pauncefoot. Right. We'll get them cried at the Carfax and St Giles." Carey smiled wanly at Dodd. "Even out in the courtyard, I could hear you shouting at the…the lady to hang Jeronimo immediately. That was good advice, but it probably helped make his mind up to escape."

"Ay," said Dodd bitterly, wondering when someone would listen to his good sense soon enough to do something about it.

thursday 21st september 1592, evening

It was a hopeless business, trying to search Oxford for just two men, even if one of them had only one arm. The place was full of strangers, not just courtiers and their attendants and hangers-on, but also scholars and lecturers and readers, all there ahead of the start of Michaelmas term to cheer the Queen, along with any peasants from the surrounding countryside who could bring anything into the market to sell. Oxford roared with people and horses, pigs, goats, sheep, cattle, innumerable chickens and geese, barrels, carts…Dumfries had been more chaotic but there were far more people in Oxford which was a bigger town to start with.

Dodd was fascinated by the idea of the colleges, fortresses where you went to learn things from books. He had never heard of the like, although he vaguely thought that the Reverend Gilpin had studied Divinity somewhere like Oxford. He had a look at Christ Church which was where the Queen was going to stay and thought it well-defensible so long as no one had cannon. However the proposed processional route was a nightmare, lined with painted allegorical scenery, any one of which gave beautiful cover for a man with a crossbow and no shortage of high windows in the houses either.

Halfway through the afternoon it started spitting with rain but then stopped. Dodd was sitting at a table in the White Horse on Broad Street in a private room at the back with Lord Hunsdon, Carey, Lord Hunsdon's steward Mungey, the Captain of the Queen's Gentlemen Pensioners of the Guard and some other men, including Carey's two new servants, the skinny clerk Tovey and the large dark Scot who was as pale and unhealthy-looking as his master. Dodd gave the man an ugly look: he didn't like Scots. The Scot gave him an ugly look right back: no doubt he had his nation's usual irrational hatred of the English. His voice was pure Edinburgh but there was something about him that tickled Dodd's memory.

The Captain of the Queen's Guard was speaking, Dodd forgot his name. He was deputising for Sir Walter Raleigh who was still in the Tower of London for getting a Maid of Honour with child and then marrying her without the Queen's permission.

"Her Majesty will not cancel her entry into Oxford." Nobody looked surprised though Dodd was. He had heard that the Queen was nervous about her safety and very careful of poison. "That's final."

Hunsdon and Carey looked at each other. "Did you bring the Royal coach?" Carey asked.

"Yes we did, although she hasn't used it yet. She hates it, claims it makes her feel seasick," said Hunsdon thoughtfully. Dodd agreed with the Queen, he hated coaches too.

"Well then, I'd persuade her to at least ride in the coach. That makes it much harder to shoot at her and the coach should stop a crossbow bolt."

Hunsdon nodded and his clerk made a note. "She won't like it, but she will do it," he said.

"Would she wear a jack or a breastplate?" Dodd asked. "For when she's out of the coach listening to speeches? The King o' Scotland has a specially padded doublet for entries and the like."

Everyone exchanged looks. "It was hard enough to get her to do it in '88," said Hunsdon, "for Tilbury. There's no reason we can give now and I think she won't do it. It would look mistrustful of the people."

Dodd wondered why a sovereign Queen cared about that. He sighed. "We just have tae find them, then," he said.

As the futile search wore on into the night, Tovey and Tyndale were not much use, Carey was looking more and more glum and said very little. It seemed Tyndale had had a chance to catch Jeronimo's friend the night before but had messed it up. At last it was Dodd who called a halt and they went back to Trinity College. They drank a late night cup of brandy by the fire in Dodd's chamber while Tovey and Tyndale got themselves settled for the night in the parlour.

"Dinna fret yersen," Dodd said awkwardly to the Courtier who was staring at the flames with a remote expression on his face. "Onybody might ha' made that mistake wi' Jeronimo."

"It never occurred to me that he might hit me with his stump."

"Nor to me," Dodd said, though he hoped he would have thought of it. Still, as Jock o' the Peartree had established, the Courtier was soft.

"Come on, Henry, what would you do to find Jeronimo and his friend before they kill the Queen?"

"I wouldna bother searching the town the day," he said after a moment's thought. "I would search her route but yer dad will do it anyway. What I would do is think like Jeronimo. He hasnae kin in Oxford but his friend is one of the waits, so we need to keep a good eye out for them. But yer dad will do that too. So. Where would I put myself to kill the Queen?"

"Somewhere high. No shortage what with all the displays and allegorical arches around, not to mention the buildings."

"What would I use?"

Carey's laugh was humourless. "A crossbow, a dag, Christ, a dagger will do if he can get close. She's only flesh and blood."

Dodd narrowed his eyes and thought. He'd never actually assassinated anyone, in the strict sense, but you couldn't deny, it was an interesting problem. You had to be close, within about ten feet to have any hope at all of hitting the target. Or you needed to know exactly where she would be and lay a trap of some kind. His money was on a trap. Everyone knew her route through Oxford—down the Woodstock Road, St. Giles, Cornmarket, Carfax, and on down to Christ Church.

They talked it over for a while and then went to bed because it was late and they had to be up before dawn. They had come up with a large number of outlandish ideas, including gunpowder, which even worried Dodd. He was shocked to hear Carey praying quietly before he fell asleep.

friday 22nd september 1592, midday

Unlike her cousin who was up before dawn, though at least not too happy, it seemed the Queen did not like mornings. She got up at about seven o'clock and spent the next hour and a half dressing, heard Divine service, and then, on the Lord Chamberlain's insistence, delayed all morning dealing with papers and business with Lord Burghley and his son while Oxford and its environs was searched again.

No sign of Don Jeronimo nor his friend Sam Pauncefoot. After a quick dinner around noon, Carey and Dodd left Tovey and Tyndale with Hunsdon's liverymen and rode north to Woodstock. There they found the Queen, magnificent in a black velvet bodice and black velvet kirtle trimmed with pearls, ribbons, diamonds, rubies, and peacock feathers, a high cambric ruff standing behind her head and her small gold crown pinned to her bright red wig in a cobweb of diamonds, in a very bad mood. There was something familiar about the beaky nose and the shrewd eyes but Dodd couldn't place it, put it down to Carey being related to her.

They were given royal tabards to wear and ordered to ride alongside her coach. Dodd wished for a jack or breastplate, he was only wearing a wool doublet and not even the buffcoat he had taken from Harry Hunks on the specious grounds that it smelled too bad. The bloody tabard was nothing but embroidered silk, of all useless things. At least Carey had managed to find a couple of secrets to put under their hats, iron caps that fitted over your skull and were devilishly uncomfortable but at least gave you a chance if somebody hit you on the head.

The Queen was helped into her coach by Lord Hunsdon who was looking tired himself. She sat there, glowering. The large green and white coach flying the Royal standard like a castle, jerked off along the rutted road, creaking and groaning like any cart though there were leather straps that supposedly made it more comfortable. There were eight stolid carthorses in silk trappings drawing it, with plumes on their heads. Nice beasts too, much the biggest Dodd had seen since Carey's tournament charger was sold to the King of Scots, heavy-boned, powerful and big-footed. They had hairy feet, perhaps there was Flemish blood in them? There were two black geldings, a half-gelding and three mares, originally piebald but dyed black, sixteen to seventeen hands high, their tails docked and plaited up and their coats shining with...

"You're supposed to be looking out for Jeronimo. Pay attention to the crowd and the Queen, not the bloody horses," growled Carey out of the side of his mouth and Dodd coughed and dragged his eyes away from the alluring horseflesh.

His heart was beating hard and slow and his back itched and so did his head under the iron cap. He didn't like any of this though the first mile or so was easy enough, along a road that had been tidied up, the undergrowth cut back from the road properly and some holes filled, lined with peasants from the villages, all cheering for all they were worth and waving tree branches and the occasional banner. About halfway down the louring grey clouds clenched and dumped their rain so the courtiers in the train all covered themselves with cloaks. Neither Carey nor Dodd had brought one so they got wet.

Then they came to a bridge where a large group of men were waiting on foot, some wearing bright red gowns trimmed with marten and behind them more men in black and grey gowns and some in buff coats which Dodd looked at enviously. Their ruffs were sadly bedraggled.

"Vice chancellor of the university, the doctors of the colleges." Carey muttered to him.

The Queen ordered her coach stopped and said she would hear speeches so long as they were short. She stood on the step of it with two of her grooms holding her cloth of estate over her head to keep off the rain. The vice chancellor knelt to her on the stones of the bridge and made a speech in foreign that seemed long to Dodd. He then gave her a bundle of white sticks with more speechifying and the Queen speechified right back in more foreign and gave the sticks back too. Then one of the others knelt to her and spoke even more in foreign and then, thank God, the lot of them arranged themselves ahead of the coach, the rain dripping from their nice gowns going pink from the red dye running, and walked ahead into Oxford.

There was rain dripping off Dodd's nose too and he carefully tipped his hat so the rain collecting in the brim wouldn't spill down his back. At least the weather made a gun unlikely, who could keep a match alight in this? Though if Jeronimo or his friend had a wheel-lock dag…No. Carey's only fired properly one time in four, you wouldn't risk it. Even a crossbow would be chancy if you let the wet get at the string.

Another half mile down the road, you could see a very wide street where another road joined from the north, with another of those odd monkish fortresses of learning, flying a lamb and flag on its banners. More men, this time the mayor with his chain and the aldermen, even Dodd could spot that. They made speeches too, but this time in English and a bit shorter, thank God. They too went into the procession with the mayor and the vice chancellor exactly level at the front and a little bit of shoving behind them between the aldermen and the red-gowned doctors of the colleges.

Now the procession went down past a church and into the lead-roofed street called Cornmarket. The streets were lined with young men in their gowns and odd-looking square caps from the days of the Queen's father. They shouted "Hurrah!" for the Queen and threw the caps up as the Queen went past, which frightened the life out of Dodd for a second who thought they might be throwing stones.

The street's cobbles clattered and groaned under the iron-shod wheels of the royal coach, and Dodd caught a glimpse of the Queen looking very tense under all her red and white paint. She beckoned Carey over. He actually dared to argue and was clearly told to shut his mouth. Carey moved his horse around the coach so he could speak to Dodd, his mouth in a grim line.

"She says she's feeling sick, so she's going to stop the coach at Carfax. And she knows the risk...."

"Ay," he said, "there's a tower there."

"She won't get out of the coach but she'll stop there as long as she can. She thinks it will be quite a while because one of Essex's pets, Henry Cuffe, is the Greek Reader and will be making a speech in Greek to her."

What was it with lords? Why did they like speaking foreign so much?

"Can she no' ride on and have Cuffe come tae her later?"

"She could but she won't. She ordered me to flush the Spaniard out at Carfax for she won't have this nuisance all through her visit to Oxford."

"Och." Dodd saw the young Scot's face behind and below Carey looking as if he was actually enjoying himself. Carey must have told the lad to stick around on foot as backup which Dodd doubted was a good idea.

At that point the rain stopped, blast it, and the sun came out. Typical southron weather, you couldn't even rely on it to rain when you wanted.

Carey was thinking the same. "Now she'll insist on getting out," he said gloomily. "She says she's near to puking with the motion of the coach already."

"Och," You had to say this for the King of Scots, coward as he was. He wouldn't do any such thing. And the result? Nobody had succeeded in killing him yet, despite plenty of good tries and a couple of kidnap attempts.

The crowds were closer now, held back by the Gentlemen of the Guard, the Beadles of the university in their buffcoats who had joined them from the university procession and Hunsdon's liverymen as well. There were townsfolk as well as black-robed scholars, shouting and cheering the Queen and waving their hats.

At least the Cornmarket's lead roof had kept some of the rain off and would stop any attempt from above. It was nicely decorated with allegorical people standing on it to greet the Queen by singing, half naked, painted gold and silver, still streaming with rainwater and shivering. The coach had to stop so the standard could be taken down as the roof of the coach just went under the roof. The corn merchants were lined up on either side in their best, the only dry spectators of the day, cheering the Queen.

The coach came out again onto the square crossroads with the tower and there was more messing about while they put the standard up again. Yet more men were waiting in their doctor's robes and hats, all of them tense. The coach stopped near the tower, which would make a shot from its roof more difficult. Good. Dodd brought his horse round behind the coach, too many people pressing forward to see the Queen. Carey was staring around anxiously, squinting to see if one of the chilly half-naked painted people on the roof of the Cornmarket was armed. The light was suddenly bright and sharp between the banks of grey.

Somebody pulled on Dodd's stirrup and Dodd scowled down at that bloody Scot Carey had hired, Hughie Tyndale.

"Ah've seen him, the greybeard that filled the flask wi' poison, there. He's there!"

"What?" Dodd couldn't work out what the man was talking about. He was pointing at the crowd. There was a bunch of schoolboys in their best with their schoolmasters holding them back with whips, but no greybeard visible. Carey's head craned round, he was squinting. Nothing.

Dodd stared hard at the top of the tower, couldn't see anything there either. A movement caught at the corner of his eye, he couldn't see who had suddenly bent in a bow. Then he heard a kind of scraping rolling sound under the roar of the crowd that bothered him. Tyndale's dark face was there, looking ready to run.

"Under the coach, Sergeant," shouted the lad, sprinting backwards. There was a disturbance going toward the tower.

What was under the coach? From his horse's back, Dodd couldn't see, so he slid sideways to the ground and bent and peered.

Something round and metallic was there, smoke coming out of it…

Dodd's gut clenched hard and his mind slowed down and went cold. Quite calmly he looked at the grenado under the Queen's coach. His horse behind him was stamping. No, it was worse, it was made of metal. It was a petard.

"Git her oot!" he shouted and threw himself down in the mud on all fours, scrambled under the belly of the coach. As he did that he heard creaking, more cheers and then the straps went up a bit. Someone must have helped the Queen down from the coach. From underneath, beyond the deadly iron ball with its burning fuse, Dodd could make out people kneeling and the large velvet folds of the Queen's kirtle.

Damn it, he didn't even have gloves. He grabbed for the petard, it rolled away, he stretched and grabbed again, caught it, brought it toward him, fanned away the choking smoke, saw that the fuse was nearly down to the priming chamber and tried to pull the whole fuse out with his fingers, scorched them, couldn't do it. He grabbed his hat off, pulled the secret from his head and then carefully brought its iron edge down on the smouldering bit of fuse, cut the hot coal away and stubbed it out on the stones. As soon as it was cool, he pulled the fuse out with his teeth. Then he tipped the petard over and let the fine black priming powder scatter on the stones, then the charge smelling of bad eggs, rubbed wet mud on everything.

At that point the world speeded up again, he felt sweat dripping down his face and he heard more foreign windbaggery resounding from one of the kneelers to the Queen. All he could tell about it was that it was a different sort of foreign from the usual with a lot of oy-sounds in it so he supposed that was Greek.

Somebody was pulling on his boots, he eeled out backwards and bounced up ready to punch whoever it was and found Carey facing him. He held up the petard ball and saw Carey go as white as paper. Beside him was Jeronimo for God's sake…Smiling?

"*Bien, mi bravo! Benga, está en el torre!*" said Jeronimo, "*Hombres, vamonos!*"

"But…"

Carey was already shoving through the crowd to the tower, Hunsdon's men let him through, Jeronimo after him and Dodd scrambling behind, still holding the empty petard. Empty of powder but full of metal balls and scraps of iron.

There was a man lying unconscious at the door which was open. Dodd heard Carey's boots, saw Jeronimo's boots and sprinted blind up the narrow spiral staircase because he didn't know if this was another elaborate trick or what was going on. First you put a petard under the Queen's coach which was an excellent target whether the Queen was in it or not and then you…

Well, then of course you sat somewhere high up and shot into the confusion caused by the explosion.

He got to the platform at the top of the Carfax tower. Jeronimo was advancing on an old man standing by the parapet holding a crossbow. The old man had shaved recently from the pale skin round his mouth and one of his thumbs was bandaged.

"*Amigo mio,*" said Jeronimo, panting for breath, "*Sam, no la mates, por Dios!*"

The old man's face crumpled for a moment. "Stop," he whispered, "Let me finish it for you. I've waited so long."

Jeronimo shook his head. His remaining hand was open as he advanced, unarmed. The old man set the crossbow stock to his shoulder, aimed squarely for Jeronimo's chest.

Dodd threw the iron ball under arm. It skittered on the flagstones curving leftwards. Carey swung down with his sword from the other side and in that moment Jeronimo charged, the crossbow twanged, and as the men crashed together, Jeronimo's stump lifted, punched under the old man's jaw and into his throat.

Both of them thudded to the ground, the greybeard choking blood from his broken windpipe and Carey's sword stuck in the bone of his shoulder. Other men were coming up the stairs too late, the Scot at the back, typically. Dodd left Carey to pull out his blade, peered over the parapet, caught Hunsdon's eye and gave him the thumbs-up.

Below them, interminable Greek oratory continued and the Queen stood on the rug-covered cobbles beside her coach, glittering in the sudden sunshine, smiling and nodding attentively at the speech.

The old man was taking a while to die, Carey's blow had only broken his shoulder blade. But he was drowning in the blood from where Jeronimo had punched his throat with his iron-capped stump, turning blue like a hanged man, threshing and straining to breathe. Dodd glanced at him briefly to make sure he wouldn't get up again. Carey had turned Jeronimo on his back and found the bolt sticking out of his chest with water and blood leaking out.

The Spaniard was smiling. "Eh...Lucky," he said, "She is well, the Queen?"

"Yes," said Carey. "We thought you were trying to kill her as well."

"No. Pardon that I struck you yesterday, Señor. When you said...poison...I knew poor Sam was still trying to finish the business after thirty years."

"It was meant for the Queen after he heard your song?"

The blood was bubbling from around the bolt and more was coming out of the Spaniard's mouth, staining his clenched teeth.

"I think so. Last night I tried…to change his mind. But I was too sick to reach him. It took me all my strength to reach Oxford, I had none to find where Sam had gone."

Jeronimo shook his head. "I put the music and a finger of the Queen's glove in her baggage as it passed me on the road to Rycote and asked to speak to her, to confess to her. If she would, she must cause it to be sung. I am so sorry I never heard it sung by you, Señor, because I was busy with Captain Leigh and his men to take your man prisoner after I found him at the inn."

Carey shook his head a little.

"*Pobre Sam*," said Jeronimo, his voice creaking and fading now as the blood filled his lungs. "He loved me and I did not love him. I was cruel to tell him to wait for my music to be played. So long a wait. I think he was taken by the Queen's inquisitor and so lost the headdress and other glove he kept." Carey nodded. "And so this…a petard, a crossbow. He had meant to try at Rycote as well, in my memory, but when he thought you were her spy, he used his poison on you, Señor, instead."

"Perhaps I should be more grateful than I am, Señor."

Jeronimo smiled again. "It has fallen out better than I ever hope," he whispered. "I will not die screaming in bed of my canker, and Sam will be with me in Purgatory. Instead a death of honour. Ask the Queen, if she forgives me, of her mercy, have a Mass said for our souls."

A frown passed over Carey's face. "Well…"

"Yes, superstition, you say. I will know the truth sooner than you, Señor. Only put it to your Queen. Please."

Carey ducked his head. Dodd folded his arms and waited, scowling at Hunsdon's men and the Gentlemen of the Guard now uselessly crowding the top of the tower to keep them back. Soon both Don Jeronimo and his old friend were dead.

◇◇◇

The Queen passed on down to Christ Church, cheered by the scholars and went immediately to the privy chamber to rest and hear reports. A couple of hours later, with their soaked tabards handed over to be dried and brushed down, Carey and Dodd were brought in to see her sitting under her cloth of estate in the professor's parlour she was using as her presence chamber with the Earls of Cumberland, Essex and Oxford attending, along with her ladies-in-waiting, including the red-haired one from Cumnor.

Dodd was in a terrible state of nerves which seemed to amuse Carey. "Now you see why I made you go to the stews the other night?" said the cursed Courtier whose fault it was. "If you were doing this the way you smelled that night, the best you could hope would be that any lapdog she threw at you wouldn't bite you. Though my main worry was that you might then throw it back."

"Och," gasped Dodd, trying to stop his knees knocking. For God's sake, he wasn't this afeared of the King of Scots, was he? Well he might be, if he was going to meet him. But this was a powerful Queen who had been ruling since before he was born and had a short way with people who offended her.

The Gentleman of the Guard led them in and Carey bowed three times with tremendous elegance and then knelt on both knees. Dodd managed one bow, nearly fell over his own boots and landed with a thud on his knees on the rush matting which hurt.

"Well, Sir Robert, I see you have redeemed yourself," came the Queen's voice, very sardonic, somehow familiar…

"Your Majesty is most kind and understanding. If I may mention…"

"You did well with the quest I gave you, but then you fell for an extremely simple trick which could have been very dangerous to me. I will give you both your warrant and your fee, you can be certain of it, and in good time. But not today."

Carey's shoulders sagged a little, though he didn't look surprised.

"Then, ma'am, may I present Sergeant Henry Dodd of Gilsland who dived under Your Majesty's coach this afternoon to grab the petard there and put the fuse out and then helped stop the assassin on Carfax Tower."

"Yes, indeed," said the Queen's voice, sounding very amused. "Sergeant, your advice yesterday was excellent although I could not have followed it, even if my cousin had not let Don Jeronimo escape. And it seems in the event that it was better so."

The face was familiar too. Dodd blinked at the beaky old woman under the red wig and suddenly recognised her. Put a black wig on her and she was the black-haired lady-in-waiting. Now he thought of it, that woman had had ginger eyebrows. Jesu, he had shouted at her only yesterday, wagged his finger at her. Jesu. Oh God. Why the hell hadn't Carey warned him?

His horror was obviously leaking onto his face, because she laughed. Jeronimo must have known who she was despite her black wig. That's why he said what he said, broke his parole. He only gave it until he saw the Queen, after all. God, oh God. What would she do to him for shouting at her like that?

"Come here, Sergeant."

He didn't want to shuffle about on his knees, so he stood up, stepped forward hiding a wince, and knelt again nearer to her, smelling both old lady and rosewater and the incense caught in the velvet of her gown.

"We have persuaded my lord the Earl of Cumberland of your merit and so, Sergeant, we are very happy to present you with this, as a small token of our thanks for your service to us this day."

It was a parchment scroll. Dodd took it and nearly dropped it. The Queen was smiling at him. Something was snuffling at his other hand and he looked down to see a little fat lapdog licking it.

"Felipe likes you," she said. "High praise. I, too, like you Sergeant Henry Dodd and am still in your debt for your actions today. I had considered a pension but Sir Robert thought you would prefer what is in the deed there."

She gave him her hand, covered in white lead paste and powder and heavy with rings, so he kissed the air above it. Then she nodded to him and he realised he was supposed to stand up and back away. He managed it, just about. What had come over him? While he knelt again just in case, and also to take the weight off his feet, the Queen smiled at Carey, too.

"Robin, I know you won't approve, but I have also written to ask the French ambassador to dedicate a special Mass for the repose of the souls of Don Jeronimo de la Quadra de Jimena and Sam Pauncefoot. Mr. Byrd will arrange the music for it."

"Your Majesty…"

"Please be quiet, Robin. You know my opinion on the matter which is that there is one God and Jesus is His Son and the rest is argument over trifles. Now you may go."

Outside on the staircase, Dodd blinked down at the parchment in his hand. Was it a thank you letter? A warrant?

"Aren't you going to open it, Sergeant?" Carey asked, grinning stupidly.

He did. Bloody foreign again. But then he saw the word "Dedo" and then the word Gilsland. What? He looked up at Carey.

"They're the deeds to Gilsland," Carey explained. "You now own it outright, freehold, with the messuage appertaining. She got it off the Earl of Cumberland in exchange for cancelling one of her loans to him."

"The deeds…" There was his name in foreign. Henricus Doddus, Praetor whatever that was. "To me?"

"Yes. Gilsland is now legally yours. You were Cumberland's tenant-at-will, now you are the freeholder of the land and the tower, to you and your heirs in perpetuity unless you sell it."

Dodd's heart was pounding. "Ye mean I dinna owe rent?"

"No. You have the expenses of maintenance of course, but Gilsland is now yours. Blackrent is your own decision."

"Och." He couldn't take it in. What would Janet say? By God, she'd be ecstatic, none of her brothers nor even her father was anything more than a tenant-at-will. Now he could not be evicted legally. Illegally, of course, he could be turned off it if he couldn't defend it, but he was now safe from a landlord's whims and lawyers.

"Of course it won't change much now," Carey was still blathering, "and I hope you'll continue in the castle garrison as

sergeant of the guard as well as of Gilsland. But in due course...
when...er...the King of Scots eventually comes in and not for
a long time, of course, but eventually...you will have a secure
title to your lands. Much better than the Grahams, for instance,
who are in fact simply squatting on the Storey lands. It could
be very important."

Dodd managed to get his mouth to shut and looked back
down at the deeds and then at Carey again. He blinked around
himself at the stairs and a world suddenly changed forever by a
bit of parchment in his hand.

He couldn't yet say thank you to Carey, in case he greeted
like a bairn so he coughed several times and said gruffly, "Ay sir.
Ay. I'll need tae think about it. Ehm...where now?"

Carey grinned with perfect understanding, which was annoying. "Back to Trinity College to pick up my clerk and my manservant and some supplies and horses, gather up the new men."

"Ay, and then?"

"North," Carey was laughing, "north for Carlisle. God knows
what the surnames are up to, it's the full raiding season. We
might make York by nightfall."

Historical Note

Spoiler warning!

All historical novelists rely on proper historians to inspire and guide them. Often one particularly well-written and well-researched book becomes the main reference—if I'm lucky enough to find one. As I've said before, the whole of the Carey series of books was inspired by George Macdonald Fraser's marvellously funny and accurate history of the Borders *The Steel Bonnets*. For the account of Queen Elizabeth's ceremonial entry into Oxford in September 1592, I used the contemporaneous account in Nicholl's Progresses [The Grand Reception and Entertainmen of Queen Elizabeth at Oxford, 1592]—and yes, it was indeed raining.

Amy Robsart, Lady Dudley died on Sunday 8th September 1560. Her suspicious death changed Elizabeth's life story and the history of her reign. For *An Air of Treason*, I used a recent account of the mystery by Chris Skidmore titled *Death and the Virgin: Elizabeth, Dudley and the Mysterious Fate of Amy Robsart*. Chris Skidmore has remarkably tracked down the original coroner's report into her death and prints it in an Appendix—in full, both Latin and an English translation. It makes eye-opening reading because it was clearly not a broken neck that killed Amy Robsart. There is also a throwaway comment in the wildly inaccurate Catholic propaganda libel "Leicester's Commonwealth" where it says "she [Amy] had the chance to fall from a pair of stairs and so to break her neck, but yet without hurting of her hood that stood upon her head." [Skidmore] This intrigued me despite the fact that pretty much everything in "Leicester's Commonwealth" is a fancifully scurrilous attack on the Queen's favourite that would put modern tabloid journalists to shame for venom and lack of interest in veracity. But what if that bit was based on truth?

There are other intriguing tidbits for which there is unimpeachable documentary evidence: Why did Lady Dudley send all her servants out of the house on that day—a very unusual and quite daring thing for a wealthy and respectable woman to do? She had only two women with her who were ordered to stay in the parlour. Why was Amy in such a panic over her clothes, ordering a new outfit from her tailor and then, when it didn't arrive in time, sending another one into Oxford to have gold lace put on the collar? Who was she trying to impress?

I'm not a proper historian, I'm a novelist. I like to look at what the record says—and then speculate wildly about what might really have happened while trying to stay true to the era and the characters of the people I'm writing about. So that's what I did.

I hope you enjoy the result—as painstakingly uncovered by that "concentrated essence of Elizabethan" Sir Robert Carey and his much put-upon Sergeant Dodd.

Glossary

Apothecary – drugstore/druggist

Aqua vitae – brandy

Board of Green Cloth – committee in charge of adminstration and discipline at Court and within three miles of the Queen's person (within the Verge)

Boot, the – instrument of torture popular in Scotland which used wedges and hammers to break the victim's legs

Boozing ken – a small alehouse, often full of thieves etc (Thieves' Cant)

Border reiver – armed robbers on the Anglo-Scottish Border, organised in family groups called surnames who used the Border as a means of escape

Buff jerkin – long sleeveless jacket made of tough leather, originally from buffalo

Carlin – old woman (Scotch)

Carrels – study rooms in a monastery or library

Cloth of estate – a square tent of rich cloth traditionally set up over any seat occupied by a monarch

Cods – testicles, as in codpiece

Coining – forging money

Coney-catch – con-trick (thieves' cant)

Cramoisie – dark purple red, a very popular colour in Elizabethan England.

Culverin – medium sized cannon with a long barrel

Chess – there have been various manifestations of chess over the years; one form of Medieval chess had a queen that could only move one square at a time in any direction. The modern mobile or puissant (powerful) queen was introduced some time around the sixteenth century and may have been a compliment to Elizabeth. When two pieces of equal power were in position to take you could throw dice to decide which piece won

Chorus of Kings – a winning hand at Primero (Aces were low)

Dag – large muzzle-loading pistol, decorated with a heavy ball on the base of the handgrip to balance the weight of the barrel and hit enemies with when you missed

Daybook – diary

Debateable Land – area to the north of Carlisle that was invaded and counterinvaded so often by England and Scotland that in the end it became semi-independent and a den of thieves, as often happens

Dominie – Scotch for a teacher

Dorter – dormitory

Faggots – bundles of firewood, hence also the name of a kind of traditional English meatball made with offal

Falling band – plain white turned down collar, Puritan style

Farthingale – like a crinoline, a petticoat shaped with steel or wooden hoops to make the kirtle stand out in a particular shape; bell-shaped early in the reign, then more or less barrel shaped by the 1590s.

Footpad – mugger

French hood – a style of headtire popular in the 1550s

French pox – syphilis

"Greeted like a bairn" – cried like a baby

Groat – coin worth four pennies

Harbinger – scouts sent out ahead of the Court on progress, specifically to requisition lodgings and food for it

Headtire – woman's stiffened headdress which went over her linen cap, mandatory for married women

Henbane of Peru – an early name for tobacco

Henchman – a male servingman or hanger-on, often providing muscle and armed back-up to a lord, although a young page might be called a henchman as well

Humoral complexion – the personal mix of the humours which dictated your character and which caused disease when unbalanced – Sanguine (Blood), Choleric (Yellow Bile), Melancholic (Black Bile) and Phlegmatic (Phlegm).

Incognito – in disguise

Jack – padded jacket interlined with metal plates

Jakes – outside toilet

Kirtle – skirt over the petticoats

Lay – scam (thieves' cant)

Limner – painter in colours, also meant a miniaturist

Morion – high curved steel helmet, standard in sixteenth century

Muliercula – little woman or midget

Ordinary, the – fixed price meal at an inn

Papist – Catholic

Parole – after surrendering, a gentleman would give his word (parole) that he wouldn't try to escape

Patent – a monopoly on the sale of some luxury granted by the Queen in the later years of her reign as a way of rewarding courtiers without costing herself anything, very unpopular with the ordinary people who had to pay inflated prices as a result

Penny loaf – bread roll. A one pound loaf of bread had its price fixed at 1 d but with the inflation of the late sixteenth century and high wheat prices, the loaf shrank though it still cost a penny

Pinniwinks – Scottish term for thumbscrews, a conveniently portable instrument of torture which broke the victim's fingers

Poinard – long thin duelling dagger with an elaborate hilt, big brother to a stiletto

Polearm – any weapon involving a long stick with something sharp on the end

Punk – whore

Pursuivant – literally chaser, someone who acted for the state in tracking down spies, criminals, and traitors. Often freelance and unscrupulous

Phlegm – mucus or snot, the cold and moist Humour, one of the four Humours of the body and a constant problem for the English who were renownedly Phlegmatic

Red lattices – the shutters of any place selling alcohol would be painted red

Rickets – soft bones caused by vitamin D and calcium deficiency in childhood, common among the Elizabethan upper classes if they allowed their childrens' diet to be supervised by physicians who advised against fresh vegetables (too Cold of Humour) and fish (too lower class).

Screever – professional scribe, later a pavement artist

Sleuth dog – hunting dog specially bred for tracking

St. Paul's Walk – the aisle of old St. Paul's Cathedral where fashionable young men would parade up and down in their finery

Statute cap – blue woollen cap that all common men had to wear so as to support the Wool industry – a statute more honoured in the breach than the observance

Stews – Turkish bathhouses (descending ultimately from Roman baths) that tended also to be brothels

Swan Rampant – this was indeed apparently Hunsdon's badge and looked as described.

Terceiro – elite Spanish soldier

Tiring room – dressing room (from attire)

Upright man – gang leader

Venery – persistent naughty sexual behaviour. Now called sexual addiction, very common.

Veney – exact equivalent of a kata in karate or pattern/tul in taekwondo, this was a set series of sword moves practised with a partner so as to build up strength and agility. To keep the death-rate down, pickaxe handles with hilts (veney-sticks) were used

Wood – woodwild, mad

To receive a free catalog of Poisoned Pen Press titles, please contact us in one of the following ways:

Phone: 1-800-421-3976
Facsimile: 1-480-949-1707
Email: info@poisonedpenpress.com
Website: www.poisonedpenpress.com

Poisoned Pen Press
6962 E. First Ave. Ste 103
Scottsdale, AZ 85251